Angus Wilson was born in England in 1913 of a Scottish father and a South African mother. He spent some of his childhood in South Africa, then went to Westminster School and Oxford. He worked in the British Museum from 1936 and served in Intelligence during the Second World War, at the end of which he returned to the Library of the British Museum, becoming Deputy Superintendent of the Reading Room. The outstanding success of his early writing decided him to resign from the Library in 1955 and become a full-time writer.

In 1963 he became associated with the new University of East Anglia, was appointed Professor in 1966, Emeritus Professor in 1978. He taught part-time during these years at East Anglia, as well as teaching in America and lecturing in many other countries.

His first book, *The Wrong Set*, was a volume of short stories published in 1949 when he was thirty-five; this was followed by a further collection of short stories, *Such Darling Dodos*, in 1950; in 1952 a critical study of *Emile Zola*; also in 1952, his first novel, *Hemlock and After*; 1956, *Anglo-Saxon Attitudes*, a novel and Book Society Choice; a further short story collection, *A Bit off the Map*, 1957; in 1958, *The Middle Age of Mrs Eliot*, which won the James Tait Black Memorial Prize; in 1961, *The Old Men at the Zoo*; in 1964, *Late Call*, which was later made into a four-part serial for BBC Television; 1967, *No Laughing Matter*; 1970, *The World of Charles Dickens*, a critical biographical study which won the *Yorkshire Post* Prize; 1973, a novel, *As If By Magic*; and in 1977, a critical biographical study, *The Strange Ride of Rudyard Kipling*.

For the latter, Angus Wilson travelled extensively through India. He has travelled widely for pleasure whilst not looking after his garden.

Also by Angus Wilson

Novels

Hemlock and After
Anglo-Saxon Attitudes
The Middle Age of Mrs Eliot
Late Call
No Laughing Matter
As If By Magic

Short Stories

The Wrong Set
Such Darling Dodos
A Bit off the Map

Various

Emile Zola: An Introductory Study of His Novels
The Mulberry Bush: A Play
For Whom the Cloche Tolls
The Wild Garden: Speaking of Writing
The World of Charles Dickens
The Strange Ride of Rudyard Kipling

Angus Wilson

The Old Men
at the Zoo

PANTHER
GRANADA PUBLISHING
London Toronto Sydney New York

Published by Granada Publishing Limited
in Panther Books 1979

ISBN 0 586 04902 9

First published in Great Britain by
Martin Secker and Warburg Ltd 1961
Copyright © Angus Wilson 1961

Granada Publishing Limited
Frogmore, St Albans, Herts AL2 2NF
and
3 Upper James Street, London W1R 4BP
866 United Nations Plaza, New York, NY 10017, USA
117 York Street, Sydney, NSW 2000, Australia
100 Skyway Avenue, Rexdale, Ontario, M9W 3A6, Canada
PO Box 84165, Greenside, 2034 Johannesburg, South Africa
CML Centre, Queen & Wyndham, Auckland 1, New Zealand

Made and printed in Great Britain by
Richard Clay (The Chaucer Press) Ltd
Bungay, Suffolk
Set in Monotype Garamond

Granada ®
Granada Publishing ®

The events described here as taking place in 1970–3 are utterly improbable. Our future is possibly brighter, probably much more gloomy. All references to the administration of the London Zoo and to its staff are entirely imaginary.

PRINCIPAL CHARACTERS

Presidents of the Zoological Society	Lord Godmanchester; his wife, Lady Godmanchester. Later, Lord Oresby. Later, Mr Harmer. Then again, Lord Oresby.
A Vice-President	Professor Hales.
Director of the Zoological Gardens	Dr Leacock; his wife, Madge Leacock; their daughter, Harriet Leacock.
Secretary of the Zoological Gardens	Simon Carter, the Narrator; his wife, Martha; their small children, Reggie, Violet.
Staff of the Secretary's Office	Mrs Purrett; Rackham, a messenger.
Curator of Mammals	Sir Robert Falcon; his wife, Jane.
Keepers of Mammals	Strawson (head keeper); Barley; Young Filson.
Curator of Birds	Matthew Price; his sister, Diana Price.
Head Keeper of Birds	Old Filson; his wife.
Curator of the Insect House	Mr Sanderson; his retired housekeepers, Mrs Blessington, Miss Delaney.
Curator of Reptiles	Dr Emile Englander; his wife, Sophie.

7

Prosector and Veterinary Surgeon	Dr Charles Langley-Beard; his family.
Curator of the Aquarium	Dr Harry Jackley.
Research Workers	Dr Pattie Henderson; Dr Newton; Dr Nutting.
Mr Blanchard-White	A Uni-European, interested in Zoo policy.

I

A TALL STORY

I OPENED the large central window of my office room to its full on that fine early May morning. Then I stood for a few moments, breathing in the soft, warm air that was charged with the scent of white lilacs below. The graceful flamingos, shaded from flushed white to a robust tinned salmon, humped and coiled on their long stilts; a Florida pelican picked and nuzzled comically with its orange pouched bill among its drab brownish wing feathers; the herring gulls surprised me, as they did every day, by their size and their viciously hooked beaks. To command one's chosen view of the brute creation was one of the unexpected advantages I had secured by taking on the newly instituted post of Administrative Secretary at the London Zoo three years before. A word with the Director and with Matthew Price, the Curator of Birds, had resulted in a new waders' enclosure opposite my window, replacing a pen for capybaras, creatures interesting perhaps as the largest of the rodents, but, with their ungainly coarse-haired bodies, hardly ornamental for everyday view. Young men with administrative experience and high recommendations from the Treasury were not to be had every day at a nominal salary. The Zoo authorities had been very indulgent to a number of 'milord' whims that were perhaps more in keeping with an aesthetic undergraduate than with an administrator of thirty-five.

English springtime that year had been at its loveliest. Gentle, sweet enough, to banish all bogeys, to bridge all chasms. The lilac scent came heavy with a sudden gust of wind, sensual, almost ruttish. A blackbird sang near by. Blackbirds, gentle, sweet, ruttish. I punctured the rhapsody with a little bathos. Most delicious, springtime suburbia, lush laburnum time enough to satisfy a cockney Keats. But the morning's grace was too complete to be banished by self-mockery. I remained dreamily happy, staring out, registering only vaguely the prettiness of the early Victorian Giraffe House that lay distantly before me, beyond the intervening road.

Nevertheless the conscious checking of my thoughts set my mind free from the enchantment of my senses. I wondered how it came about that I could hear one blackbird's notes when I had become quite deaf to the customary loud orchestra of a whole Zoo after three years. I registered the feeding times only subliminally; even the occasional chorus of panic induced by some low flying jet, a chorus starting perhaps with one high shriek and swelling into a discordant symphony, no longer disturbed me. I hardly noticed such noises more than did the animals the helicopters or hooting water buses that brought staff or visitors from the motor parks of outer London to the Zoological Gardens. But then, the blackbird's was the voice of freedom, not perhaps the great cosmic liberty of Beethoven's thunderous chords, but enough to sound a clarion call to an Administrative Secretary who so often longed to be with his wife rather than at his office desk.

The direction of my thoughts decided me to return to my work. The galley proofs of the forthcoming issue of The Proceedings of the Society lay draped over the desk. Despite the long column of print that ran down the middle of the sheets, they appeared as virginal white as a bride's veil. I thought with satisfaction of getting to work on them with a corrector's pen. The rape would be long and detailed, for zoologists, I had found, seemed to have powers of linguistic expression in inverse ratio to their scientific knowledge. Correcting other people's texts, indeed all ordering of words, always gave me intense pleasure. It was a delightful task for a nice spring day. Not all my work at the Zoo, alas, was so congenial. The Treasury job, however glad I had been when Martha's money released me from it, had called for a good measure of toughness; after it, Regent's Park affairs smelt a little of the parish pump. I had difficulty sometimes in carrying back a sufficiently enthusiastic day's report to satisfy Martha's hopes. Grateful for the absorbing pleasure of proof reading, I turned to Pattie

Henderson's informed but childishly constructed article on 'Nematoda in the digestive tracts of certain Pinnipedia'.

Suddenly the screaming began. I knew that they were human cries, yet the noise was further from what is usually meant by a human scream than many animal or bird calls. As the first deep groans, there must have been eight or nine of them, rose each in turn to a high sound somewhere between a monkey's shriek and a sudden release of air from vast balloons, Pattie Henderson's diagram of a seal's bowels swam on the paper in front of me and my own bowels heaved within in fright and horror. I rushed to the door. By the time I had left my room the noise was drowned in the panic orchestra of roaring lions and baying sea lions, of hyenas' idiot schoolgirl giggles, of wolves, of bears, of howling gibbons and chattering monkeys, of trumpeting stags and the crowing lunatic shrieks of the peacocks near the window. It sounded as though every creature was rushing, as I had done, to leave its cage. In the corridor I collided with both my secretaries. The big one, who liked to mother me, was announcing her views.

'Oh, I knew at once what had happened. It was just the same that time I was walking along Holborn. It took the ambulance a quarter of an hour to get there and this chap went on screaming all the time. You wouldn't believe they'd have the strength.'

At that moment the bell of the Society's private ambulance could be heard clanging above the bestial pandemonium.

'There, what did I tell you?' Mrs Purrett said proudly.

'Well, I never heard anything so horrible in all my life and I hope I never shall again.' The new little pretty secretary seemed as proud of her innocence as the big one of her unpleasant experience.

'I don't think we can help,' I said. 'With the ambulance people there, we should only swell an unnecessary crowd. But find out at once from Exchange, Mrs Purrett, what has happened.'

I followed them into their room. The little dainty touches Mrs Purrett had added of artcraft and home from home seemed more revolting than usual to me as I waited for her explanation of her horrified exclamations into the telephone. At last she laid down the receiver.

'Don't worry, Marian dear,' she said to the little typist, 'it's no one we know very *well*. But we do know him, Mr Carter. And the news is rather bad.'

Clearly she had long practice in breaking bad news; it was as though she was delicately washing our corpses before burying us.

'It's young Mr Filson. Perhaps you don't remember him, Mr Carter. In the Giraffe and Zebra house. The son of old Mr Filson in Parrots. He was in the office a week ago about special leave for some concert he was singing in.'

'Yes, of course I do. Don't be so dramatic, Mrs Purrett.' I hate to see people that I like 'putting on an act'. But it was too late to tease Mrs Purrett out of it.

She moved a bowl of yellow tulips on her desk so that she could look straight into the little typist's eyes. I wondered if she imagined that she could 'hold someone's nerve' by staring at them.

She said gravely, 'He may never come into the office again, Mr Carter. There's been a terrible accident . . .' She was a kind woman, as I knew, but she had already begun to enjoy her story. Before she had really got going, however, Rackham, the ex-serviceman messenger, rushed in banging the door noisily against the wall.

'Got 'im away to 'ospital,' he shouted, then, noticing me, he stopped and drew himself to attention. 'Oh, beg pardon, Sir, I didn't know you was in 'ere.'

'That's all right, Rackham,' I could not avoid irritation, for I guessed that the old man always knew how uncomfortable this N.C.O. to officer stuff made me. 'What's happened to the boy?'

'Oh, they reckon 'e's copped it, Sir. 'E was alive when they moved 'im from the ground. But Walters, that's the First Aid man, 'e's a pal of mine, 'e tells me 'e was dead before they moved off. Mind you, they'll say 'e was dead before they picked 'im up. They 'ave to clear theirselves in law. Multiple injuries to the shoulder, chest and . . .' he took rather conscious notice of the typists' presence, 'and general injuries. Some old chap in the crowd started bellyaching about they shouldn't 'ave moved 'im so soon, but as Walters says to me, it wouldn't 'ave made no difference what they done.' He paused as though expecting applause for having established this point. I turned to Mrs Purrett.

'Ring the hospital. And check exactly what *has* happened, will you?'

Rackham's sharp little foxy face took on an old soldier's sentimental expression.

'They're waiting for Sir Robert's word now whether old Smokey's got to go. If it'd been any of the 'ippos or rhinos, Strawson would 'ave taken action 'isself straightway. There's only one thing to be done when *they* turn nasty. But a giraffe! Its unheard of. Strawson says 'e's never known a case in all 'is years and 'e's been looking after giraffes from before any of you was born. 'E reckons young Filson come on 'im sudden with crepe rubber soles or somethin' of that sort. Then Smokey took fright and Filson 'ad 'ad it. Strawson wants to save old Smokey but 'e reckons 'e'll 'ave to go. Pretty near in tears 'e was. "There's never been a gentler beast than that giraffe, Rackham, that I'll swear." And you could tell 'e meant it. I told 'im shooting Smokey won't bring young Filson back. If I was Sir Robert I'd take it right up to the Director before *I* gave the word for the high jump.'

To avoid losing my temper I said coldly, 'Sir Robert as Curator of Mammals is Deputy Director of the Gardens, Rackham. So I don't think that "right up" is quite the correct phrase.'

I heard the words come out like those of a bad-tempered schoolmaster talking to a boy of ten. Their results were in keeping with their tone; as I walked out of the room I could sense that Rackham was winking at the typists.

Neither the scent of lilacs coming in at the window nor Pattie Henderson's clumsily formed sentences that lay on my desk begging to be put straight, could bridge the chasm when I returned to my room. I stood by my desk feeling furious with the shapeless, purposeless emotions that so meaningless an accident could bring. As so often at conventionally grave moments I was overcome by a general randiness that finally settled to a persistent delicious image of the supple inward curve of Martha's thighs. Living bodies to banish the dead; such comfortable reflexes could no doubt be made respectable by talk about the life force. But even so I could not entirely banish a feeling of shame at being even so remotely associated with such a stupid, cruel death.

Mrs Purrett came in and placed a file of papers before me.

'The draft reports from Dr Beard's people for the Nuffield Foundation,' she said. Then she added very softly, 'The hospital news is bad, I'm afraid, Mr Carter. He was dead by the time the ambulance arrived.'

I said, 'I see. Thank you.'

She obviously expected more thanks for her careful breaking of bad news, for she lingered by me, enveloping me in a sense of unwanted bosoms, of starved affection ready to be hurt.

'Old Rackham upset you with his crude talk, didn't he, Mr Carter? I saw it. I know exactly what you felt. We'd not seen much of the boy in the office here. But he was young and ordinary and nice. And so happy. Engaged to be married to a nice, pretty, ordinary girl. A Butlin's hostess, I remember he told me. It doesn't seem fair of death does it to pick on someone so ordinary? It's the difficulty of making any sense of it. You're not a religious man, are you, Mr Carter?'

To answer, I felt as though I had physically to heave myself up in my seat. Even then I could only muster up enough human warmth to say, 'No.'

'Well, I'm not a clever woman at all, as you know. But I have had a lot of sorrow. Not tragedy, nothing important, everyday sorrow. But that sort of thing gives one conviction. For me and lots of ordinary people there's a measure of certainty. Nothing to do with church going. Well I don't have to tell you that. But the certainty that there is a sense to it all somewhere. After all one and one make two, don't they? Does that help you at all?'

I knew that human charity demanded more than merely foregoing the satisfaction of repeating my negative, yet I could not keep a certain note of sarcasm out of my voice as I said, 'Thank you, Mrs Purrett.'

I realized the full meaning of 'touchiness' as she edged her heavy breasts away from me.

'For goodness' sake! Don't worry about me,' I said, 'we can't do anything about it and that's that. Mr Price'll be taking care of old Filson. And that's the most that can be done.'

She smiled, but I could see that she was still offended. I turned over the leaves of the reports in the folders.

'These things are in a muddle, Mrs Purrett,' I said sharply.

'That's how they came through to us, Mr Carter.'

'Well, I'm sorry they're still in a muddle.' I added savagely, 'Like most things in this place.' I handed her the file. 'Let me have them back after lunch, will you?'

She had not been gone more than a minute or two, before Rackham brought in the morning cup of coffee, slopping it as usual in the saucer.

'I couldn't tell you all of it, Sir, in front of the ladies. But it was a nasty business all right. As I said before, what it seems like young Filson comes up behind Smokey. Strawson reckons the pad of them crepe rubbers was enough to bring back memories of lions to 'im. That's what them giraffes fear most – lions! He wheels his fucking great neck round . . .'

I could tell from the old man's sidelong glances that to his pleasure in telling the story was added the enjoyment of discomforting his listener. Yet to cut him short by an order however jovially given would be interpreted as surrender. Old sadist, I thought, and there's not even a loud bassoon to excuse me.

'Of course,' Rackham was saying, with an added tone of moral righteousness, 'them railings ought never to have been there. Little low spiked railings like that. Strawson says 'e's spoken to Sir Robert about them time and time again. But nothing done. 'E reckons the Director'll 'ear about them this time. Sir Robert or no Sir Robert.'

'Strawson should keep his criticism to himself.'

'Ah! That's right,' Rackham said vaguely.

I could have kicked myself. My strictures would no doubt be reported to Strawson in some general form, when in all likelihood the man had never made the remark. These 'old characters' like Rackham with their 'racy' reported speech were an archaic menace in any decent modern organization.

'Pierced right through 'is shoulder it done, and pinned 'im there. 'E starts screaming! That frightens Smokey more and 'e panics. Gallops off across the yard. Ever seen them giraffes runnin'? Funniest sight you ever seen. Like nothin' else. Back and front by one side then back and front the other. Pacin', they call it. But then you probably know that, Sir.'

'Yes, I do.' I tried to keep up my testy tone but it was no good. Whenever anyone persists successfully in a course that annoys me, instead of getting angry I simply find that I want to laugh. I had now to give all my energies to keeping a straight face before Rackham's calculated impudence.

'Well, they can move all right. First move Smokey made, 'e brought 'is great hoof down on young Filson's chest. Broke a couple of ribs. And the second one – well, it's lucky the ladies are gone – 'e smashed 'is balls to bits. You probably didn't 'ear the awful noise the poor bastard made – up in your room 'ere. Ghastly it was. On account of the pressure on the lung one of these ambulance chaps tells me. More like a hissing of the breath. Only loud. 'Course they soon gave him morphine.' He paused at the word and gave a look that implied long years of medical understanding of analgesics.

I said, 'I think we can all help best, Rackham, by not panicking and by getting on with our ordinary work.'

He glanced at me contemptuously and said obsequiously, 'That's right, Sir. Not that there'll be much work done 'ere today, I can tell you that.' Then, as though reproving me for my morbidity, 'Well, the dead's dead, Sir. And that's about the long and short of it. It's the livin' we've got to think of. Old Filson's only son!'

'Have you seen the old man?'

'No, Sir. Mr Price took 'im straight 'ome in a taxi when the news come through. So as Mrs Filson shouldn't 'ear from anyone else.'

'That's exactly what I imagined. Mr Price has the whole thing under control.'

'Ah,' said Rackham noncommittally, 'I'd better get along, Sir. There may be some news about old Smokey. 'E won't make no noise if they shoot 'im. Got no vocal chords—giraffes. That was the uncanny thing about it, Strawson tells me—the young chap screamin' 'is lungs out and the bloody great animal in a muck panic not makin' a sound.'

'Yes, Rackham. I can imagine it all too easily, thank you.'

I had little hope that my reproof would get through so easily; and it did not.

Rackham said with satisfaction, 'I knew you'd want to 'ear it straightaway, Sir. I said to Strawson, "Mr Carter'll want to 'ear this straightaway." That's why I come along so quick.'

I could think of nothing more repulsive at that moment than the loving old spaniel's look that came into Rackham's amber flecked brown eyes.

'I shall be very busy now dealing with the Director about it all, Rackham. So I shan't require any more instalments of the story.'

The spaniel's eyes changed from 'loving' to 'hurt'. Immediately I found myself grinning boyishly, almost winking at Rackham – the young officer appealing to the old sweat's capacity to take a joke against himself. Rackham responded with an equally boyish grin.

'Well, I'll make myself scarce before I *really* put myself in wrong with you, Sir.' He went out chuckling.

Death, I suppose, always calls for action, however irrelevant. I rang Dr Leacock. But when I heard Miss Chambers's voice announcing rather grandly, 'The Director's in conference with Sir Robert now about this horrible accident. I should prefer to ask him to ring you back,' I felt an immediate revulsion from the official pomposity which I could feel already forming in a heavy blanket of comfortable fog around the wretched dead youth.

'As long as you keep me out of all conferences, you can do just what you like, Miss Chambers,' I said.

As I heard her click of disapproval, I knew that I must either do nothing, or grin and bear the pomposity without the indulgence of levity. I could all too easily imagine the scene in the Director's room. Young Filson's death like everything else at Regent's Park would have been made to serve in the endless struggle between Leacock and Bobby Falcon for their opposing views on the Zoo's future. That I was entirely on the side of the Director in this debate, despite all his phoniness and his slipshod work, didn't seem really to matter in this case. I agreed with Leacock that the Society's worst mistake had been the closing of Whipsnade in some cheeseparing retrenchment; I wanted, as he did, a much larger National Wild Life Park somewhere to replace what we had lost; I did not want Bobby's romantic, childish revived Victorian Zoo. But at this moment I wanted above all to talk only of what could be done to prevent such a tragedy happening again, to bring home the charge to the culpable, yes, to avenge young Filson. Certainly not to hear his death used as a talking point in debate. And yet these old men – Leacock and Falcon – had succeeded all unconsciously in turning some of the most serious of the many war scares of the last year into debates on their pet schemes. Why should the death of an unimportant young keeper escape the same treatment? I went to the window but the long-legged grace of the flamingos seemed grace no longer, only stilted absurdity; and the pelicans' comicality, mere swollen folly. The whole walled, barred and caged Gardens seemed intolerable.

What was my senseless pride in my administrative capacity that had made me come to this place? To put the Zoo's administration in order! When I could have given myself up to long years of watching and studying English wild life far away from all the incompetence and humbug that seemed inseparable from dealing with human beings. And then to have tried to convey that pleasure to a million others on television. 'Tried' – why had I to play the thing down, when I knew so well that my television programmes had been a smashing success? Why did I have to run away from them as an indulgence? Was a solo turn so impossible a luxury? In indulging myself I should after all have been doing what Martha wanted me to do. I felt choked with impatience at my own pigheaded addiction to self-denial. Only the sudden flickering yet sharp memory of a white and black muzzle showing for a moment against the yellowish clayey soil and the knotted elder roots, of a snout upturned to savour the freshness of the July evening air brought me relief from a total, all including claustrophobia. For a few seconds I was back among the lush willowherb and the scent of trodden wild garlic, peering through the oakleaves at entrance D to the sett. Not once in all my many badger watching expeditions, had I found the need for these anthropomorphic adjectives – noble, stately, stupid, comic – that seemed to crowd upon me whenever I considered the animals around me at the Zoo.

I decided to 'invade' the Director's conference before distaste for the diplomacy and, even worse, the high-toned plain speaking ahead of me made me retreat from the business altogether. But a knock on the door was followed almost immediately by the rosy cheeked, gold rimmed spectacled, bland features of Mr Sanderson.

I said firmly, 'I'm just going to see the Director, Sanderson. Can you make it later?'

The little, hollow, oboe like notes that came from Sanderson's large, potbellied body seemed an additional outrage.

'The Director's with Falcon. I was along there just now. They're not letting us small chaps in for the moment.'

I wondered why Sanderson supposed that a watery glint behind his spectacles and a twist of his lips made a condescending remark of that kind any more palatable. Summoning up all the matiness I could, I said,

'Well, I suppose there's no point in being Head if you can't refuse to see the prefects. Since I can't see Leacock, what can I do for you?'

Sanderson looked down to where his toes must have been just visible to him beyond his little potbelly.

He said solemnly, 'What was that chap's name, Carter, who declared that God was dead?'

To check my desire to laugh and to ward off Sanderson's intimacy, I could find only a vigorously facetious note.

'Nietzsche,' I replied, 'but you have to remember that *he* died off his nut.' It did not avail.

'In a way that makes it all the more moving, doesn't it? I wish I had more time for general culture. Things like today's damnable accident make one feel that he was right.'

'Not believing in God, I can't pay much attention to rumours of his death.' This more brutal line of defence proved equally unavailing. Sanderson looked up with a sort of shy reverence.

'I've always wanted to tell you, Carter, how much I admire the deeply felt quality of your agnosticism.'

Then he looked down again as though I, not he, had been embarrassingly emotional. He was a very provoking man indeed.

Now he said, 'The names of young chaps who die in the Zoo's services like this might be inscribed on the war memorial.'

'It's hardly in the country's service. In any case, appalling though the whole thing is, we can't even say for certain that it wasn't the boy's fault.'

Sanderson looked at me with a sweet smile.

'I think we've got to be careful not to run away from our feelings at a time like this, Carter. Of course, you're still comparatively new here. You wouldn't realize what the death of a Filson means. His great grandfather entered the Society's service as a lad of fifteen in 1880. He worked under Bartlett.'

Sanderson was always at his most mawkish when speaking of the Zoo's past and especially about the tough old Superintendent of the Victorian era, of whom he was said to be writing a life.

'I must say even that young reporter seemed to be impressed when I told him that. Tradition has more importance for these young chaps than we're inclined to think. He was very grateful for what I told him. They're fine fellows these journalists really. People blacken them, but theirs is a great trust. And I like to think that they fulfil it.'

I said, 'Ah!' Then I did a quick double-take, and added, 'What reporter?'

'Quite a young chap by his voice. On one of the morning papers, the *Daily Telegraph*, I think. He'd tried to get the Director or Falcon; but, of course, as I told him, they're the men of the hour. Then it seems he knew my name because he'd sent in a specimen of some dictynidae for identification some years ago. He didn't give a very clear description. It sounded like ciniflo similis. Not very interesting; but still it's splendid to think that these chaps keep up their hobbies at all in that rather cynical world.' I picked up the receiver.

'Mr Carter speaking. I want to talk to the Supervisor. Mrs Jamieson? It seems that the newspapers are making inquiries about this accident. It is understood of course that all Press inquiries are to be put straight through to my office. I see. Well, they'll be on the alert *now* won't they?'

To Sanderson I said, 'I'm sorry they should have worried you. It seems that this reporter didn't say who he was. All the same it was not very competent of them.'

'I saw that Mrs Jamieson out the other day pushing an invalid chair. They tell me she looks after a paralysed uncle. That sort of thing's rather fine.'

I made no comment, but I asked, 'It would be a help if you'd give me some outline of your conversation with the Press. Just for the record.'

He said, 'It's a wonderful thing for the Zoo, you know, Carter, to have got in a professional administrator like you.'

Again I made no comment, and, after looking down at the floor for a minute or so, he said, 'They seem to have an idea that there was some negligence. I told the young chap, "that's a damnable thing to suggest at a time like this." He apologized. I must say that after all one hears about the Press, I thought that was rather fine of him. Apparently it was only something they'd been told. About some low spiked railings that ought not to have been there.'

I thought of Rackham, that loyal old servant of the Society, earning his extra ten bob as a newspaper's nark.

I said only, 'They appear to have got on to the story very quickly.'

Sanderson said, 'Yes, this young chap is clearly as keen as mustard about his job. I told him, of course, that there couldn't have been any negligence with Falcon in charge. I had to explain that Falcon was the discoverer of gorilla himalayensis. One forgets that the expedition was as far back as 1963. I don't think this young chap had heard of the Abominable Snowman.'

'It's always as well to be polite but brief with the Press,' I said. A watery but hopeful gleam came into Sanderson's eyes.

'I don't want to flatter you, Carter,' he said, 'but you've no idea what a help it is having a man of affairs like you about here. I'm glad to say that I think I acted just as you suggest. I said there could be no question of negligence. The trouble probably was that poor young Filson hadn't been here long enough to deal with an emergency. I don't know exactly how long he's been on the staff, but only a matter of a month or so. And as I told this young chap you really can't leave full responsibility to anybody who's had less than a year. At any rate where there is any possibility of danger.'

I said, 'Giraffes are notoriously very safe animals.'

'Yes, yes. I said that. He had rather an amusing wit this young chap. I think he must have been a cockney. He said, "Giraffes must be changing their nature then." It's always a good sign when an interview of that sort ends on a little joke.'

I ignored this and told him, 'It's still possible that we may be able to undo any harm. With the Director's agreement I'll get out a general statement for the Press.'

I guessed that this reassurance was what he had come for, but he still had to waste my time with the pretext that he had previously decided upon.

'What I wanted to see you about, Carter,' he said, 'was to ask the name of that clever girl who did the plates for the last guide. Bond who carried out all the illustrating work for my lycosidae book is getting rather old. He's over eighty. A splendid old fellow. He lives at Ongar.'

'Surely it would be rather a fine thing to let him illustrate your new book, wouldn't it?' I said. 'It would make him feel wanted. It must be a little lonely out at Ongar.'

For the first time Sanderson showed some anger. His cheeks became rosier and his oboe voice trembled a little.

He said, 'This new book of mine's a very important thing, Carter. The whole field of wolf spiders has needed a survey for a long time. It would have interested your predecessor. But then he was an extraordinary chap. Very few professional administrators would have taken the trouble to familiarize themselves with the various expert fields here as he did.'

In the end he forced me to waste a precious quarter of an hour discussing his pretext, when I might have been busy saving his bacon by getting out the report for the Press.

When he left he said, 'Don't forget to recommend me to the Director for the post of Press Officer, will you?'

I should have let him feel then the full seriousness of his interfering incompetence, but I had made him angry once already.

I said, 'Now look. You're not to worry. You shouldn't have been fussed with this in the first place. And you did your best.'

'You're a very nice chap you know, Carter,' he said.

Miss Chambers's voice came to save me from further praise.

'Dr Leacock can see you now, Mr Carter.'

On my way to the Director's office, I looked in on Mrs Purrett.

'Look, I'm sorry for snapping at you like that.'

'Oh, that's quite all right. I know how deeply you feel things, Mr Carter.'

'Don't mark me too highly for sensitivity. It's more that I feel there's been some muddle or incompetence somewhere in this business. And it seems too appalling if it is so.'

Mrs Purrett began to mouth silently at me, to point her fingers towards the little secretary's back.

'Little pitchers,' she said in a loud whisper.

To be put in my place in however motherly a way annoyed me.

'Oh, there's nothing confidential about it,' I said loudly. And then felt even more annoyed, because, of course, there was.

I never looked forward to meetings with the Director and Bobby Falcon together. When Bobby Falcon, as an old friend of Martha's family, had sponsored my appointment at the Zoo, Edwin Leacock, with the natural cynicism of the highminded, had taken it for granted that I had been brought in to swell the opposition to his policy. Bobby, on his side, had presumed that since he and I 'spoke the same language', I should naturally dislike the Director as much as he did. When I later showed Leacock that in their dispute over Zoo policy I agreed with him, he had immediately presumed that I was, as he told me, 'one of those rare people, Carter, who can put their intellectual loyalties before their personal ones'. I was, so to speak, put on my honour to show my disinterest by always opposing Bobby simply because he was an old friend. Bobby, too, had accepted my 'defection' as part of the general collapse of the old order of things, and maintained towards me at meetings a sort of hurt friendliness that was intended to show how little he allowed public matters to affect his private feelings. Neither seemed to realize how tedious I found the whole of their public 'carry-on' – it was exactly the sort of display of 'personality' that I had disliked among my more politically ambitious colleagues at the Treasury; and I had naïvely expected that I should not meet it among more dedicated scientific men.

Strangely, I did not meet it that morning. The shock perhaps had brought them together. I cannot say that the thought that young Filson might have died in order to bang a little sense into the heads of Edwin Leacock and Robert Falcon made his death any more palatable to me; it only served to increase my dislike for their unusual touchy, prima donna-ish relationship.

As he waved me to a seat, Leacock's *bonhomie* and grin had a nervous flavour, it is true; but then, in his apparently most confident moods – and these were all but permanent – he seemed forever to be looking over his shoulder at what might be creeping up behind him. He liked best to meet his fellow men full on, face to face even, for he had a habit of drawing very close to one, knees to knees. That morning emotion caused him to go further. He got up from his seat and closed my hand in the soft, padded but tough grip of his own.

'Look, Carter,' he said, 'I am very glad you've come. You're an old friend of Falcon's. You *must* persuade him not to blame himself for this horrible business.'

I did not know whether that could or ought to be my office, but luckily I had to say nothing. Bobby broke in. He was, as so often, twisting a strand of his thick grey curly hair around in his long fingers. Standing in tall silhouette against the sunlit window, he seemed with his ruffled crest more than ever like a secretary bird.

'It's good of you to say so, my dear chap. But I may have to.'

His ravaged handsome Apollo's head with its flushed, sunburnt skin, seemed to snap at the air as he jerked out his words with his savage-seeming stutter. With one leg he jabbed at the ground, as though he were impaling a snake on his claws. The Director, round toucan's eye fixed stolidly ahead, long tapir's nose pointing us ever on, stood full square on his magnanimity.

'No, no, Falcon. If anyone's to blame, it's Beard. If he considered that there was a need for shooting the beast, he should have said so. It's a question of function. He tends to forget that he's Veterinary Adviser as well as Prosector. Of course, it's part of his extraordinary devotion to humanity. Any part of his work, like surgery, that serves human medicine comes first with him. But that isn't the point.'

'I must be fair, Director, and make it clear that Beard did strongly indicate his view that Smokey's tumour was probably inoperable and that he ought to be put down. For the rest the proper care of the mammals in the Society's collection is my concern. And the blame is, therefore, mine.'

Edwin Leacock gave his most matey grin.

'Your friend Falcon's impossible, isn't he, Carter? He will punish himself. Look,' he went on, addressing Bobby in the tone of a helpful scoutmaster in a pep talk on personal problems, 'this is a matter of function. Not of battle order. If we're going to consider *that*, then the whip's got to come down pretty hard on *me*. I'm Director. I knew the giraffe was sick. You had reported it to me. And if you're going to say I'd got a lot of other things to deal with, I should remind you of what our President always says: "The man at the top is never too busy." And to give Godmanchester his due he never is. I suppose it's a great part of the secret of his political success.'

I said, 'During the last two years he *hasn't* in fact been too busy.'

Edwin Leacock frowned. For a number of reasons, in particular those of prestige, he preferred not to remember that our President was out of political office.

'If all I hear is true that may not be for much longer,' he said.

He knew that I doubted whether he had heard a thing more than any of the rest of us. I said 'Ah!' in a tone parodying his solemnity. As a rule Bobby Falcon relaxed with delight when I mocked the Director's pomposity. That morning he seemed not to hear.

He said savagely, 'You'd much better let me carry the can, Director. I'm like Smokey, an anachronism. I belong to the old order of things.' Edwin Leacock faced this with four square honesty.

'My dear Falcon,' he said, 'don't let's clutter up this perfectly simple discussion of right and wrong in a particular affair with the conflict of our general views about the future of the collections. I don't mind saying that an accident of this kind is in some degree grist to my mill. It would probably never have happened if it hadn't been for those out of date cramped paddocks. I shall, of course, say so.'

'And I shall, of course, fight you. In defence of the exquisite beauty of Decimus Burton's designs.'

As always, when praising Victorian taste, Bobby's usual spluttering changed to an arrogant drawl – the dandy within the famous soldier-explorer. But if his voice was arrogant, there was none of the anger he usually showed when Leacock attacked his beloved Victorian Zoo. The Director's smile at Falcon's taste, too, was not as patronizing as usual; indeed there was a sentimental note in his voice as he said;

'Of course you will. I hope at least that we shall always pay each others' views the compliment of opposing them strongly. But just because we've fought so often and will do so again, I should like you to listen to me this time. It would be absolutely shocking if some imaginary blame were to attach to the reputation of the greatest zoological collector of our time. I mean that, Falcon, I have it in mind,' he added earnestly, 'quite as much as any effect this unfortunate business may have on my television address at the end of the month.'

So Leacock's current King Charles's head had popped up. He was shortly to present a television programme on the need for a National Reserve. He surrounded the whole scheme with secrecy, and as a result the rest of us were sceptical of it being more than a piece of self-advertisement. But there was no doubt that in his mind it had become the key to the success of his hopes for the Zoo.

I coughed to avoid laughing; but Bobby Falcon seemed quite content. Blushing, he looked down at the ground like a flirtatious schoolboy.

'You're being much too kind to me, Director, you know.'

Suddenly I could bear their cooing no longer.

I said, 'I'm afraid I can think of nothing except that wretched boy dying a painful and unnecessary death.'

Bobby blushed even more for what no doubt he felt to be a hysterical outburst.

'Unnecessary? If you're suggesting that we're inhuman, Simon, you ought to think that Leacock and I have been up to our necks in the bloody business the whole morning.'

Edwin Leacock was more bland.

'There's a technique for dealing with this sort of ghastly event as with everything else, you know, Carter. I believe one must deliberately lower the emotional temperature. If we're not to lose our heads, that is.'

'We've none of us known the excruciating agony of losing our balls.'

Bobby shouted, 'That's a perfectly filthy thing to say, Simon. Do you mind taking it back?'

The real fury of his voice surprised me. It seemed to surprise Leacock also.

He said, 'I don't think Carter intended any offence. Violent death affects people in very different ways. You must remember that the war can hardly be more than a memory to him.'

Then to demonstrate a more rational form of reproof, he asked rather abruptly, 'Well, Carter, what was it you wanted to see me about?'

I told them the story of Sanderson's indiscretion to the Press. I like mimicking and I can imitate Sanderson particularly well. I suppose that I was anxious to dissipate Bobby's anger. My imitation as I had anticipated put him in a good mood. He filled the room with his deep belly laughter.

'Good God! The bloody cheek of it. Doesn't he know that a giraffe's the most harmless animal living. Just let him wait until one of his black widow spiders gets loose among a party of schoolgirls. I'll have him in the *News of the World* as a sex murderer.'

Imitations and laughter were less to Dr Leacock's taste.

He said, 'I'm glad you told me, Carter. Though I think it's more serious than you quite realize. We all know that Sanderson besides being a first-rate entomologist is unfortunately a complete ass. But this goes a bit too far. Its particularly irresponsible at this time because I explained to him only the other day the very great importance I place upon this television programme of mine.'

Bobby was now relaxed enough to give me an amused look.

I said, 'What I had in mind was the unfortunate effect any adverse publicity might have upon the Ministry of Education grants. The scheme's only been going a year and there's still quite a lot of opposition to it at the Ministry. They have a hearty contempt for incompetence in dealing with the Press. And quite rightly.'

Bobby Falcon said, 'What a civil servant you are, Simon. We haven't changed you. As far as I'm concerned if this beastly business restored us to our private status, it'd be a blessing in disguise.'

The Director was now returned enough to his normal competent, active self to brush Bobby's nostalgia for the past aside with a joke.

'That's sentimental nonsense, Falcon. You simply refuse to remember what things had come to in '68 before Godmanchester got us the Government grant. You used to come in here begging for a loan. "I'm down to my last hippo," you said.'

Then he turned to me. 'This needs dealing with at once, Carter, as you say. I hope I'm not an alarmist man, but if the wrong sort of publicity got into tomorrow's papers, it *could* just mean that the television authorities would cancel the whole programme.'

I felt that his concern was less pettily selfish than his words made it appear, so I clicked my tongue in sympathy.

He said suddenly, 'You know, it's all right. If it had been any paper but the *Telegraph* or *Times*, it might have been impossible to stop it. Not that a lot of the Zoo chaps on the popular dailies aren't most cooperative,' he added hastily. The tightrope he walked between Establishment and servant of the Common Man was one of my favourite aspects of our Director's character.

'I shall be seeing Fitelson of the *Telegraph* at the Athenaeum at lunch. I'll have a word with him then. The best thing I can do is to give him a small piece covering the incident for their Zoo chap, Howard Dudley, to write up. Something that puts it into perspective, and without inhumanity makes reasonably light of the whole thing.'

He sat back in his swivel chair and swung from side to side with such obvious relief that I could not help saying: 'You mean a short paragraph headed "A Tall Story".'

He seemed not to hear. Getting up from his chair, he went to the window. He picked up a hideous mauve watering-can with a long spout and began to water the tulips in the window boxes.

'A present from the twins,' he said. 'They've got it into their heads that Grandad does nothing at the office. So they try to keep him busy.'

I waited for a few moments, but neither of them spoke. Like the Director, Bobby Falcon seemed to have returned to his normal behaviour. His heavy face showed the sort of brooding distaste that he usually evidenced in Leacock's presence.

I said, 'Well that seems to put the Zoo in clear with the *public*.' As neither of them took this up, I added sharply, 'Though we still have the coroner, of course, to deal with.'

Edwin Leacock replenished the little arty watering-can from a large serviceable one.

'Your wife's promised me some Lefebvre tulip bulbs for next year, Falcon. I shall keep her up to it.'

'Oh you must, Leacock. Jane promises the entire garden to at least a dozen people every year. I suppose,' he turned towards me, 'that coroners are sensible enough to know the limits of their knowledge.'

'Oh, yes, of course,' Dr Leacock said. 'They follow what the experts tell them.'

'I see.' I let them have it, 'Then really we can say that all this has worked out very satisfactorily.'

They seemed simply not to take it.

Bobby said, 'Satisfactory? It's been one of the most ghastly days of my life.'

Edwin Leacock was more definite.

'In the very limited official sense in which you're speaking, Carter, yes.' He looked at his watch. 'Look here, I shall have to push you fellows off. I am meeting Mrs Leacock before lunch for some shopping for the twins.'

Bobby gave his automatic glance of amusement at 'Mrs Leacock', but I felt too annoyed to return it.

In the corridor Bobby slapped his hand on the glass case of the large model of Dr Leacock's proposed National Zoological Park.

'Well, today's events have decreased the chances of *this* sort of absurdity. No hippos in their natural lovely setting of the Severn or beavers buggering up the Broads or whatever it is Leacock has in mind to instruct us all with. The public always panics at any gory accident. It's the nature of the beast.'

Every phrase was chosen to annoy me; to upset in turn my respect for education, my egalitarianism, and my genuine support for Leacock's schemes. I said sharply, 'I doubt if Filson's death is going to encourage the preservation of gems of Victorian architecture like the Giraffe House.'

'Oh, no doubt they'll pull it all down. Burton's stuff as well as everything else of dignity. What do you expect under a government that's let everything English go in order to kowtow to the commercialism of France and Germany? Modern Europeanism! Well, I have to be at the Travellers' at one.'

'That's not good enough, Bobby. You know exactly what I'm thinking. Was Filson's accident the result of some muddle?'

As I said it, I thought that I did not really know him well enough to speak so directly. He was Martha's godfather who had helped the young man she had married to change his job. That was all our relationship. Yet if there was an intimate, Christian name tone, it had been his doing; he had clearly wanted to reduce the twenty-five years between us. Now however his large, too brightly blue eyes blazed rather insanely at me.

'I'm perfectly aware of what you've been thinking,' he said, 'but I don't feel any obligation to satisfy your morbid scruples. Nor is it any of your business.'

I was committed now.

I said, 'That's nonsense. If Strawson or someone was negligent and young Filson died as a result, then it's your job or Leacock's to see that it doesn't happen again. *Should* he have been in sole charge of a sick giraffe? After all he had only been here a month.'

'If I may say so, Simon,' his tone now was easier, 'this only shows your complete ignorance. That sort of work is instinctive and the young fellow had the instinct. He was a particular favourite with Smokey. That's why Strawson, who is a first-rate keeper, left him in charge.'

'And a spiked railing for him to fall on.'

'That sort of piffling thing could happen with anyone. The boy should have moved it. In any case Strawson's my head keeper. Any wrong action or failure to act on his part is my responsibility.'

'Oh, come off it, Bobby. Strawson isn't your head Sikh guide, or for that matter your senior N.C.O. at Dunkirk or wherever you won your spurs.' It worked. He laughed.

'I'm sorry,' he said. Then he added, 'Not that I have a monopoly of high mindedness at the moment. You appear to have constituted yourself the conscience of the Zoo.'

He stopped for a moment and stared towards the Monkey House where Yeti, the great orange gorilla he had discovered, crouched forward on its powerful arms and scowled beneath its shiny black forehead at the assembled visitors.

'He draws the crowd all right,' he observed. 'I like to see them in front of the great apes or any of the big cats. Wretched weedy cits and the noble beasts. All right. No more high flown talk. But good God! Simon, you claim to know people. Surely you can understand what I'm feeling. If I'd had that giraffe shot, that boy would be alive now. What does A do about that?'

'I don't understand, Bobby, why you harp on that. If that *is* the only negligence, Beard's to blame, not you. Leacock was right about that. The Veterinary Adviser has a final say in the disposal of animals rendered dangerous by disease of any kind. I don't understand why you insist on taking the blame.'

'Charles Langley-Beard has had a hell of a life. He's the best "Dead Prof" we've ever had. You ask some of the older keepers. The chap's got ulcers with family worries as it is. It would be a disgrace to start bawling him out over a thing like this.'

'Well if he's to blame . . .'

'Look, Simon, I'm too old to travel hard now. That means my serious expeditionary work's over. In any case anything that's any good is being blown sky high these days. Why not go with it?'

The exhibitionistic quality of his defiantly asserted archaism was thrown into highlight as he stood near the exit. His small, curly brimmed bowler hat, his broadly checked tweeds, his umbrella, gloves and vivid chestnut suede shoes seemed such a ridiculous challenge to the open necked shirts and billowing trousers of the ordinary summer visitors around him.

I said sharply, 'You're not going to the guillotine, Bobby.'

Then suddenly as I looked at his lined, sensual soldier-clubman's face, it seemed like that of an old, sick puma that I had watched each morning last winter on my walk to the office, dying out its last days in the uncongenial snow and sleet.

I said, 'I'm much more on your side than you think, Bobby, and that goes for a lot of the younger people.'

In so far as the statement had any meaning at all, I was doubtful of its truth. As a result I was conscious of sounding hesitant. But Bobby obviously mistook the note for sincerity. He smiled.

'Thank you, Simon. But I don't want you to think I'm grousing. I seemed just now to be putting the blame on window dressers like Leacock or on this ghastly government. Who's responsible for letting people like that get there? Me and my kind. We shall get it in the neck and we deserve it.'

This time his jeremiad had no sad overtones. His voice was jaunty as he asked the commissionaire at the exit to get him a cab. The prospect of Götterdämmerung clearly invigorated him. As I walked towards the Staff Restaurant past the melancholy adjutant stork, standing one legged and gloomy in its paddock, I felt that the profit, if any, of our conversation had been Bobby's, not mine, nor that of future young Filsons, nor yet the Zoo's. However the misery in the puma's eye had haunted me all the winter, and now for a moment I had been able to banish it by proxy.

A moment later the Director caught up with me, all redolent with lavender soap to greet his lady wife, as he was apt to call her. He walked beside me with his curious self-assured roll – part jockey, part sailor – neither walks of life that could have played much part in his scheme of things as an ambitious scientist administrator. His walk always suggested to me – it was part of my constant sense of his clownishness – that he was avoiding what my mother would have called 'an accident in his trousers'. Yet neither snobbish nor comic devices could really successfully eliminate the strong liking that I often felt for him. He had the unfair appeal to one's protective instincts of all those who are totally without charm.

He said, 'I've drafted something for the Press. The whole thing shows, of course, how unwise it was of my predecessor to abolish the post of Public Relations Officer. I know there had to be economies, but the last thing to economize on is anything that shows. As it is I can't do anything about restoring the post, because everything's got to be subordinated now to getting a *real* National Park going.' He sucked irritably at his pipe. Then, perhaps charmed for a moment, as I was, by the sun playing on the beds of tulips, he said cheerfully,

'On the whole though, apart from its tragic human aspect, I think today's events may do a great deal of good. I didn't want to harp on it too much in front of Falcon, but an accident of this kind in that cramped old paddock is exactly the thing

we need in order to win over a lot of the Fellows
doubtful about a change of policy. The more we c
dissidents with us the better. There's no harm i
people, ever.' As though to illustrate this, he said   our
support has been one of the most encouraging things for me,
you know, Carter. The younger generation for one thing.
And then Godmanchester thinks highly of you. And you've
got two important strings to your bow. You alone can
challenge this nonsense about the administrative difficulties
of the thing. But almost more important is your field work on
British mammals. It could be a very useful reputation to me
at this time. You've been off those "Wild Life" programmes
for far too long. You're the television chap, not me, you know.
For you it's a form of expression. For me it's only a means to
an end.'

I said, 'We can't say that until after Friday week, can we?
Television stars are born overnight.'

To my delight, he took this in his stride.

'We shall see. You and Mrs Carter will be at Mrs Leacock's
buffet supper that evening, won't you? I shall rely on you for
a sincere opinion of my performance purely from the point of
view of the medium. This chap Maskell who's producing me
seems a good man.'

He left so strong an interrogative note floating in the air,
that I was forced to reply.

'Yes, he's very competent, I believe.'

If I was to be made as important as this, I felt that now
was the moment to insist upon my anxiety. I found it difficult
to speak convincingly to Leacock; his concept of sincerity
was to my ear so patently theatrical that with him I found my
own natural tendency to understatement doubled. However I
tried. My voice sounded to me like a bad movie version of
someone speaking in the confessional.

I said, 'Leacock, I must confess that I'm not happy about
the very possible negligence that may have led to this morning's accident. If there has been any carelessness, it surely must
be brought home to the offender.'

'My dear Carter, Falcon's taken on the blame, although, as I pointed out, it's really not his. I don't think we can ask more of him than that.'

'I don't think we should ask anyone to take blame that isn't theirs.'

'I hope you don't feel that I've been hard on Falcon. That's the last impression I want to give.'

'No, of course not. You misunderstand me. If Beard's to blame, then he should get the rocket. Whoever's responsible . . .'

'I think Langley-Beard's been naughty, if you like. But he's worked off his feet. And he's the best Prosector the Society's had for thirty years or more. Ask any of the older keepers.'

The reiteration of the cliché I had already heard from Bobby Falcon irritated me.

I said, 'I'd prefer the opinion of a first-rate anatomist.'

Leacock stopped and stared into the distance through the antics with which the giant panda on its swing was entertaining the crowd.

'You'll make a great mistake, Carter,' he said, 'if you treat sheer experience lightly in our work here.'

'I've no doubt at all that Beard's excellent. But if he has made so serious a mistake surely something must be said. For the sake of the staff in the future.'

'Langley-Beard hasn't lived in a glass case, I can assure you. He's had a very hard life. He's a brilliant and highly strung man. I should be very sorry if a sound of this rumour got to him before I've had a chance to talk to him myself. People think of him as a specialist, a dedicated man. And so he is. But he's more than that. He's surprised me lately. If anyone might suffer in the early days of a National Park, it's him. Only in the early stages, of course. Eventually, as I've told him, the laboratory work will be on a scale that will make this place look like a school stinks room. But quite frankly I had expected to have some opposition from him. Not at all, he's been most loyal. And I value loyalty very much, Carter, when I need it. Very few people here know him. He's an extraordinarily shy chap. Your wit would probably frighten him.'

As a matter of fact failure to break down Beard's reserve was a very sore point with me. I like to think I make contact with people easily. After all, if a non-specialist can't do that, what can he do? However I'd failed with Beard. But I knew that Leacock had pretty certainly made even less contact with him, so I decided not to admit my failure.

I said, 'As a matter of fact I am one of the few people he talks easily to.'

'Oh! Well, I'd very much appreciate it, if you'd say nothing about *this* to him. I'd like to get it over to him in my own way.' He stopped and, facing me, announced the end of the conversation.

'I value these chats of ours, you know, more than you realize. And probably take a good deal more notice of what you say than you think.'

It wasn't good enough.

I said, 'In that case I should like to say a little more.'

He did not respond to the laugh with which I had hoped to soften the edge of my demand. He looked at his watch.

'You mustn't keep Mrs Leacock waiting,' I said, 'I'll walk with you to your car park.'

Any reminder that he alone on the staff had the privilege of a private licence to drive in London always gratified him.

He said, 'It's a great pleasure to see you so deeply concerned with things that affect the Society. When you first came people said you were aloof. But I always said, "Give him time."'

'I am deeply concerned about the question of Strawson. I can't help thinking that it may well be his incompetence and laziness that were the cause of this accident. At the very least, a serious failure in supervision. As you know, I have no use for the man. Bobby Falcon talks of him as an "institution"; but I think that simply means that he's dug himself into a position where he claims all sorts of rights that the other head keepers – old Filson, for example – never would. He may be "Elephant Joe" to the popular Press, but to me he's a conceited windbag, who if he ever was useful to the place, has long eaten up his fat. I don't think this officer-N.C.O. attitude of Bobby's is good enough. All right, he *is* responsible for Strawson; but in that case he should keep him in order.'

'Look,' said Edwin Leacock, 'aren't we a bit in danger of letting a lot of small issues crowd out the essential point?'

'I can't regard the loss of life as a small issue.'

'No. Of course you can't. But I'll shock you to the extent of saying that there *are* bigger issues. I honestly believe, Carter, that for the first time we have a real chance of creating a National Zoological Park in Great Britain. But the majority of the Fellows are still not convinced. If we could win over Godmanchester for example ... but there's a pretty heavy battery of expert artillery on the other side ... and Falcon's one of their biggest guns. It isn't only that he's a celebrity and a one-time national hero, it must also be said straightaway that he really knows wild life conditions. What is never understood, of course, is that he speaks from a great knowledge of animals at liberty. I'm concerned with limited liberty. But never mind that. He's got great charm and he's very popular. I cannot afford the slightest appearance of vindictiveness against a man like that. I'm considered insensitive enough as it is. And I cannot appear to interfere with the day to day management of the mammal houses. But, in my belief it just wants some incident, some effective showdown, to clinch our argument with the doubters. I don't say this morning's affair is it. Probably not. But properly handled it could strengthen my case enormously. But we *must* stick to the point that antiquated enclosures mean danger to life.'

He waved his hand towards the Decimus Burton raven cage. Its beauty was always to my feeling the one vindication of Bobby's passion for the Victorian Zoo.

'This sort of thing,' he said, 'is a serious danger to both staff and public. We've got to use this giraffe incident so that it brings that home without making it a personal issue.'

The ravens croaked, as well they might at such a naïve lack of scruple.

I said, 'I had always thought of ravens as a Gothic horror rather than as a serious menace to human life.'

I'm afraid my disgust came all too clearly to Leacock through my sarcasm. When he spoke I knew that I had angered him too much to get any satisfaction from him over the issue of Filson's death.

'The trouble with your generation is that you're simply not capable of real seriousness. No, I won't say your generation, I'll say the younger intellectuals. The ordinary man is less prejudiced and has more common sense. If a system or a building or a cage is antiquated and dangerous he will see it. And no amount of talk will blind him to the fact.'

I felt angry now.

'You say that ordinary people are unprejudiced. I think you mean they are more suggestible. Perhaps they are. But I'm pretty sure that once their emotions are touched, their commonsense as you call it will not distinguish between fine shades. An accident like Filson's won't make them say, "Let's have an open Zoo where the animals are free." Far from it. They'll simply say, "Do away with Zoos altogether."'

Edwin Leacock stood quite still in front of a small flowering cherry. Set before an object of such fragile prettiness, his ugliness was quite grotesque. With his long nose and round eyes he was like a proboscis monkey that had wandered – as bears and monkeys seem frequently to do – into the setting of a Japanese print.

'I wonder if you realize how utterly irresponsible that sort of talk is, Carter?' he said. 'I'm trying to do something big. The least I could expect from my colleagues surely is encouragement, not a lot of carping criticism.'

I told myself that the most important thing was to get him to pursue some inquiry about Filson's death. I put on what I always hope is a boyish rueful grin.

I said, 'I'm sorry. It's the way I'm made. The more I'm impressed by anything, the more I feel I must criticize it. It must be infuriating, I know.'

The Director said, 'That's quite all right, Carter. I understand perfectly well. Criticizing their elders is the proper activity of the young. Now, look. Don't bother to come to my car with me. Cut along to lunch. I know what an appetite I used to have at your age after a hard morning's work.'

I looked to see if he was being sarcastic; but it was not so. My boyish grin had been all too successful. From a difficult colleague of thirty-five I had reduced myself to a nice, typical argumentative lad of eighteen.

I faced staff luncheon without any comforting conviction of achievement.

At the staff luncheon table there was seated the Zoo's Prosector, Charles Langley-Beard, and he was eating a vast plate of ravioli that reeked of Parmesan cheese. Shyness and stink! I imagined my arrival home and Martha crying, 'Well, for heaven's sake, what storm's driven you into harbour so early?'; my replying, 'Shyness and stink' and our bursting into laughter, which the bewildered nurse would try to share, making us only giggle the more. The picture made me laugh aloud as I sat down opposite to Langley-Beard.

A pink flush ran through his waxen cheeks and up to the roots of his very sparse hair. He obviously felt himself forced to smile in concord—a glistening somewhere behind his thick-lensed glasses, a faint stretching of his thin lips—then, fearing that he'd done the wrong thing, he gave a dry, little cough.

'I haven't seen Tallis lately,' he said.

Tallis had been at school with me some twenty years before; later he had studied anatomy under the Prosector. We had discovered this link in a long series of halting, excavatory conversations. I had not seen the man for fifteen years; the Prosector, I believe, not for ten. It was unlikely that either of us would ever see him again. I should have had the courage to snap the absurd link, instead I said,

'I believe that when I last heard of him, he'd got an appointment at the University of Sydney.'

'Yes, that's what I heard.'

I then remembered that it was Beard who had told me.

I determined to make an effort to clear away the undergrowth of small talk in which as usual we had become entangled. The Prosector's other colleagues, no doubt, through timidity, had respected his shyness; I had not; it was up to me then to relieve it. But with what? Our Zoological interests were set such poles apart: mine, in so far as they deserved the name, ecological, derived from a life-long hobby of observing British mammals; his so brilliantly yet narrowly physiological and anatomical. More daunting was the extreme yet mysterious misery of his private life that somehow barred every approach to intimacy with a signpost of 'Private. Trespassers will be prosecuted.' Most of his colleagues, knowing the private load of sorrow he carried and not wishing to know too exactly its contents, had placed him apart, conveniently haloed for his self-sacrifice to his family and his devotion to his work. To Sanderson, of course, his unhappiness nobly borne was a source of peculiar satisfaction. Early on in my service at the Zoo he had, so to speak, warned me off holy ground. 'That was very fine of you, Carter,' he had said, 'bringing out our Langley-Beard at tea today. But you'll forgive me if I say that perhaps it would be better not to intrude on his shyness. You couldn't know that, of course, and what you did was very fine. But he's rather set apart, you know, in a life of dedication. To his work, and to his family. Tragedy had set its mark on him before he came here. I don't think it would be blasphemous to call him "a man acquainted with grief". His wife's in Broadmoor. She killed two of the children. He lives for his son, a brilliant young chap but early crippled by polio. And then there are other family sorrows, I believe. It's all taken him out of the ken of ordinary chaps like you and me. I suppose its only his passion for his anatomical work here that's kept him sane. That and the heroism that grief brings out. Great tragedy of that kind, Carter, is a very beautiful thing, you know.'

After the failure of Tallis, I thought a little savagely that if tragedy was so much in his line, what could be a better topic of conversation than Filson's death.

I said, 'The details of this morning's accident hardly bear consideration.'

He remained silent, making little pyramids of the bread he had crumbled in his nervousness. Then to my surprise, he said, 'Let's not consider them then.'

I thought that my overture had worked miraculously: the Prosector had made, however inopportunely, a kind of joke which was certainly none the worse for being a little waspish.

Laughing, I said, 'You have a sharp ear for ghoulishness. I hadn't even realized that my interest was so morbid. But you're right of course. Nobody ever says that details are too horrible or too ghastly without wanting to go into them!'

He said, 'Oh, I suppose the details are much the same as in any violent accident. You forget that I served my time in an emergency ward. No, I only mean that the whole thing is Falcon's affair, not ours.' He blushed, 'I'm so sorry. Of course, it may be yours. I can't tell that. But it's no business of mine.'

I should dearly have loved to retort, but it was difficult to disregard Leacock's emphatic request.

I said simply, 'I think the responsibilities of the various departments here are very clear. It's one of the best aspects of the place from my point of view as an administrator.'

I left it to sink in.

'I suppose you think I'm to blame for not having that animal shot,' he said.

I felt that silence would be a sufficient reply. It was.

'I know perfectly well that my say is the decisive one. I also know that it's not my business to interfere beyond a certain point in the running of another man's department. I told Falcon that the giraffe had an inoperable tumour on the liver and I said it would have to be killed. He asked me if it was in pain or merely discomfort. It sometimes seems to me that people like Falcon don't think. As if a thing like pain can be measured with a slide rule. However since there was no external evidence that the beast was suffering particularly, I had to agree that it might be no more than discomfort. He seized on that opinion to say that it was particularly important that no action should be taken for a fortnight, until Leacock's television show was over. Of course, as you're thinking, I had the power to insist, but it hardly seemed to me sufficient grounds for a major row with one of my colleagues.'

'Unfortunately a young keeper was left to look after the animal and lost his life as a result.'

He looked surprised. 'That really *isn't* anything to do with me, you know. That was Falcon's affair. Of course, you may well feel that you have to criticize him, since it's a matter of use of staff, but . . .'

I asked, 'Isn't it a question of humanity?'

'Humanity would be all right if things were run properly. This young keeper's death is a very good example of that.'

I said, 'All the same you tell me that on this occasion things were *not* run properly and as a result somebody died in a very horrible way.'

He did not answer immediately. He was trying to balance an over-large piece of Cheddar on a small biscuit. He could sense I was watching him and he blushed; but he did not leave off until he had got the whole top-heavy structure into his mouth.

'Lots of people will die messily. That's in the order of things I should have thought. Competence can prevent some of the disasters. The others aren't meant to be prevented; they're meant to be accepted. But, of course, if you don't believe that . . .'

He was intent on noisily stirring sugar into his Nescafé for a few moments, then he looked up and said:

'The last thing I mean to do is to put the blame on to Falcon. As a matter of fact I imagine he was in a very difficult position. Once Leacock's set his mind on things, he can be very hard to move. And Falcon's a romantic, isn't he? If Leacock said that giraffe was essential to his television show, Falcon would feel it was his duty to make the beast available just because he dislikes the whole thing so much.'

I suppose that I looked as much surprised as I did disgusted, because he began to say,

'Look here, if you didn't know that, Carter, I don't want to be drawn into a lot of gossip, Leacock's never been a good zoologist, but his ideas for the display of the collections, appeals to the public and that sort of thing, seem to me a good deal better than most people here recognize . . .'

He stopped and, when I was about to question him further, made a slight negative signal to me with his index finger. A moment later I heard the thick suety voice of Dr Englander behind me. On one thing, at any rate, Langley-Beard and I were in agreement, we would not criticize the Director in the presence of the Curator of Reptiles.

'No giraffe cutlets on the menu?' Dr Englander asked, 'I suppose that means you've hogged poor old Smokey to feed your numerous progeny, eh, Beard? Well, I hope the family cooking pot is a large one.'

The Prosector's hand was trembling so much as he raised his coffee cup that I thought it better to take on his battle myself in order to avoid a scene.

I said, 'I doubt if even with your constitution, Englander, you'd have wanted to eat a diseased giraffe.'

He sat down and ordered roast beef and Yorkshire pudding. He patted the waitress's hand, as he said, 'I like a nice bit of brown outside fat, my dear. See what you can do for me, will you?' Only then did he reply.

'Nothing wrong with the beast was there? Except bad temper.' Langley-Beard was able to answer for himself now.

'It had a tumour on the liver.'

Dr Englander took some time in ordering his wine.

Then he looked at the Prosector thoughtfully.

'You should have had it shot,' he said. 'An animal in pain is always a danger. It might have saved this morning's wretched business. However, I suppose you were too interested in the pathology to put the poor beast out of its misery. All you chaps in the Dead House are the same. You'll have us all there to cut up, but in your own good time.'

There was something about old Englander's comfortable, well padded, insensitive jollying which was so extreme that it made me feel a certain affection for him. However it was not directed at me, but at the Prosector; he clearly found it intolerable. His whole body was shaking and he shot his arm out convulsively. Whatever he intended, he did no more harm than to spill the contents of the bowl of granulated sugar over Dr Englander's expensive, old-fashioned tweed suit and his layers of knitted woollen waistcoats.

Englander got up and brushed himself down.

'Good Lord,' he said, 'your family don't keep you very well house trained, do they? It's lucky for you it was only sugar, Beard. If you'd had to buy me a new suit of the quality of this one, it would have eaten a nasty hole in your monthly budget.'

The Prosector had also got up. Leaning towards me, he said earnestly,

'I hope you realize, Carter, that if I'd supposed for a moment that a P.M. on that giraffe would have revealed anything of the slightest interest to human medicine, I should have insisted on my own way at once, whatever anybody had said.'

To old Emile Englander, he declared, 'Your sense of humour can be very unpleasantly out of place, you know,' and was gone.

Dr Englander finished flicking his suit with a napkin and sat down.

'Jumpy sort of fellow, isn't he?' he remarked. 'Probably not on top of his work.'

'Surely his trouble if anything is being too devoted to his job.'

'It's the same thing, Carter,' Dr Englander said judicially. He added butter liberally to his cabbage. 'He's not paid enough, of course. Nobody here is.'

Since I had played so large a part in securing Government scales of pay for the Society's staff, I was nettled.

'We can't all have your standards.'

'Because I'm a rich man. What's that got to do with it? I'm also an old man. Neither is a credential in itself. But I happen to be a first-rate herpetologist. Granted that, the fact that I'm old and experienced, and that I've had gumption enough to invest my money well makes me a more useful man to the Society than if I was a clever young scientist without a penny to my name. You're like the President and Fellows of this Society, Carter, you believe a lot too much cant. They turned me down for Director because I was too near retiring age and because I had too much money. As a matter of fact if what they wanted was someone to lick their arses, they were quite right. An ambitious chap like Leacock who depends on his salary to bring up a big family is always going to please men like Godmanchester who want to be accepted at their own estimate.'

'I don't think you're quite fair to Leacock. He has some excellent and courageous ideas for the future of the collections.'

'Ideas cost money. Anybody can have ideas, but you've got to get them paid for. If I was in charge here, we'd have cash from every big company that thought they could make use of us. It's the modern world. How do you think they've put through all these new schemes in Hamburg or in Paris?'

'That's an altogether larger question. But I do understand if scientists fear exploitation by industry.'

'Do you? But then you're not a scientist, are you? I'm sorry, but that's all weak man's talk. Of course you may be exploited. But so you may in any walk of life, unless you've got the cunning and the guts to see that you aren't . . . Get me some Stilton, my dear, will you? And none of your pieces on a plate. Bring me the whole cheese . . . You think I'm not concerned with the welfare of the staff, don't you, Carter? Let me tell you that my keepers are the best in the place. I give them market tips that add to their measly wages. And in return, I expect them to work hard and I don't let them forget what's being done in the reptile and snake gardens abroad.'

'I don't think you begin to be fair to the place. Take the Prosector, for example. Without making any show about it, his work is directly geared to all sorts of wider aspects of medicine.'

'Government health service! Look; who are Beard's equivalents abroad? Widmer, I suppose, in Hamburg; and Cuvé in Paris. They get three times the salary and six times the laboratory grant. But then they're subsidized, by chemical firms, pest control producers, and patent medicine companies. If I'd been made Director, Beard would be getting a thumping great subsidy from some of these big pet food people. All right, turn up your nose. He'd have first-rate laboratories and he'd get enough food to nourish his weak nerves.'

'It could be that his weak nerves are entirely the result of domestic troubles.'

Dr Englander at once agreed.

'Yes,' he said, 'I'm sure you're quite right. His wife's in a looney bin. And the chump won't divorce her because of some religious scruple, though apparently he's not an R.C. Then his son's a cripple of some sort. It's not the thing to say, of course, but that kind of thing doesn't happen to first-rate people. But there you are, we can only afford the neurotics here.'

He was about to pour himself out a second glass of burgundy, when he stopped and looked at me – the wrinkled pouches of white skin below his beady eyes made him seem like an attentive old parrot. Then he decided that the wine came first. He savoured it for a moment, then swallowed.

'They've got two good burgundies here,' he said, 'this and the Volnay '57. Of course, that sounded as though I was getting at you. You had some sort of breakdown of health before you came here, didn't you?'

'No *nervous* trouble. I got amoebal dysentery on a collecting expedition with Falcon in Uganda. It's not serious except that it puts all tropical work out of the question.'

'Pity. You've got enough money and you're young enough to afford serious collecting. Anyhow, if you hadn't been ill, we shouldn't have you here. We can only afford first-rate men when they're crocked up. And if they've got enough private means to live on the salary. You can afford to work here, Beard can't, but he hasn't got the initiative to move.'

'It's only because I married a girl with money.'

'Yes, yes, I know. You introduced me to her at that party of Falcon's. Very pretty girl. Now if I'd been Director, I'd have appointed you. Marrying a wealthy girl shows good sense. But marrying a woman who's off her nut is no recommendation for anyone.'

I protested that Langley-Beard might not have known of this at the time of his marriage.

Dr Englander smiled and helped himself to a large hunk of Stilton.

'Oh, that was only my little joke,' he said, 'I'm sorry for the chap.'

Then, seeing that I was about to pay my bill, he added:

'I hope you've got plenty of spare funds to pay damages to this young keeper's family. If a good journalist or a clever lawyer gets hold of them they'll probably get a thumping great award – young man in his prime, wage earner and so on. Shocking negligence. The old story. Who can blame them? The poor devils live on twopence halfpenny. They don't get a son killed every day.'

These lunch-time conversations only made me the more anxious to take action at once; to await the Director's return from his useful Press-handling luncheon and ask him point blank if he was to blame; or to 'have it out' with Bobby, wine-flushed from his luncheon at the Travellers' Club. I knew that either would probably prove a fatal step. Yet my duty was clearly to prevent such an accident occurring again.

But as I thought of the probing, the questioning, the amateur detective work required to make sense of the mysteries and muddles that posturing and incompetence presented me with, I was immediately assailed by the absurdity of the whole thing. The jealousies, ambitions, and paraded loyalties of Leacock and Falcon and Beard and Strawson appeared to me as utterly ridiculous; the whole puzzle of what really happened seemed a ludicrous brouhaha; and myself in the role of unraveller suggested an impossible figure of fun. I could see it only as material which complete with imitations of all the actors, including myself, I might later use to entertain the world at large. Yet Filson's screams had been real. To meet such a dilemma the only course surely was to relax my emotions in proof reading and to return to a decision later.

Of forty-two grey seals dissected by Dr Alison Armstrong of the Edinburgh Zoological Society during 1968, the stomach contents of five alone had proved to be devoid of any trace of nematoda. A footnote told us that Pattie Henderson was grateful to Dr Armstrong for this information as yet unpublished but eventually to appear in an article on 'The diet and longevity of seals commonly inhabiting the waters of the British Isles'. My own contribution to Dr Armstrong's work was, of course, indirect; for 'commonly inhabiting' I substituted 'commonly to be found inhabiting'. It was a soothing exercise, but not for long. Into it broke Pattie's own voice on the telephone as a most unwelcome reminder of the source of human knowledge. 'I say, look here,' her voice was deep and commanding, 'I *had* got a wonderful excuse about subscriptions to learned periodicals made by me as the Society's helminthologist and can I charge them as expenses to my personal account in tax returns? Just the sort of thing to excite a one hundred per cent bureaucrat like you. And God help the girl who tries to excite you in any other way. But I'm not going to give you the pleasure of that little problem. What are excuses between old friends? I simply rang up because of this ghastly business. Nutting and Newton have both heard that the poor chap would never have died if old Falcon hadn't made a balls up. And what's more that Leacock's trying to hush the whole thing up. Are you coming clean or are you playing for the bosses?'

I said, 'I can answer your question straight away, Miss Henderson. I'm afraid that official subscriptions are not chargeable as personal expenditure for income tax purposes.'

'I do think this is pretty bloody of you, Simon. I know you have to play in with the old boys a lot of the time, it's your job. That's what I'm always explaining to the research chaps like Nutting and Newton. But when a ghastly thing like this happens ... It certainly makes one wish that Fred Jackley were here. He'd give the younger crowd a lead and blow these old incompetents sky high.'

'As far as I know the Aquarium has absolutely no connexion with young Filson's death, if that's what you were talking about, Pattie. And if there is any, I'm sure the Director who's deputizing as head of his old department in Jackley's absence, will know what to do.'

'That's a laugh. When Leacock was head of the Aquarium, he did absolutely nothing. Fred Jackley ran the place. But then you're a babe unborn as far as the history of this place is concerned. It simply means that those of us who are determined to make some changes have to count you out as a dead loss.'

Before she could hang up, I said, 'I've been correcting the proofs of your article for the Proceedings, Pattie.'

Immediately her voice took on a note of unaggrieved concern.

'Oh Lord! What's the English like? I thought some passages weren't too bad this time. But I expect you've got out the blue pencil.'

I read her my deletions.

She said, 'Thank you very much. I should have looked a fool if a lot of that stuff had gone in.'

Real humility always bowls me over. I said as I had not intended,

'I'm not absolutely unaware of the other matter, you know. But in fairness to everyone concerned it is essential not to let it spread. Whatever action it may be possible to take, it won't be helped by discussing it over the telephone.'

'There you are, Simon, I knew you wouldn't just be sitting on your backside doing nothing. But what shall I tell Nutting and Newton?'

In Pattie's own idiom, I said, 'Nuts to the one and Newts to the other. Why do they have to go around eavesdropping like two comedians playing spies?'

'That's not fair. If some of the rest of us were a bit less clueless, it wouldn't do any harm.'

As she spoke, there was a knock at the door and, before I had thought, I had said automatically, 'Come in.' Miss Chambers gave me the sort of frosty look which suggested that she knew me to be making a long private call to a criminal associate in Buenos Aires at the Society's expense.

I said into the mouthpiece, 'The Director's secretary is here, Pattie, so I must ring off.'

Pattie's gruff voice sounded ludicrously alarmed.

'Oh, Lord! Has she heard all we've been saying? Well I jolly well hope she takes it all back to him.'

Then deciding that I was pulling her leg, she said in her loudest voice, 'She can tell old Leacock that we've a special tumbril ready for him. And there'll be another for you, Simon, if you play in with the bosses.'

I rang off to prevent further harm.

Miss Chambers showed no more recognition of Pattie's remarks than to say, 'I shouldn't have worried you, Mr Carter, but the Director's kindly given me permission to go off early; and as you seemed likely to be on the telephone for some time, I thought it best to deliver his message personally. He's gone to a rather important meeting, but he *did* want you to know that his efforts with the Press at lunch-time had done the trick.'

I said, 'Thank you. Will you tell him how pleased I am? And say that, as for the other aspects of the affair that I raised this morning, I'm going on with my investigations.'

I couldn't at all see, of course, how I was to carry out this threat. I thought that it would ease my feelings to stroll about among the crowd. If the day's events encouraged anything in me that I disliked, it was my misanthropy. Muddles that resulted in the screams I had heard that morning did not make me wish to be either 'good' or 'easy' with people. And yet a natural liking for people, however much alloyed by ridicule or boredom or sexual desire or physical distaste – seemed central to any meaningful life I could have – else why not the indulgence of the woods and badgers, the mountain forest and the pine martens?

The high, hysterical barking of the sea lions took me to

their pool to watch the crowd watch the keeper throwing fish to feed the beasts. Automatically I registered faces – fat men, thin women, rhomboid children, figures all from a strip cartoon. I tried to give them all lives – a drunken failed mink farmer from Essex, a psychically gifted mother of a North London hairdresser, and so on – but Lavater had so long been dead and I didn't believe any more in physiognomy. In any case who can nowadays play such a social-categorizing parlour game? There are only three classes now – the élite with its boasted open end, the great prosperous mass, and the handicapped or handicap-prone. Age, arrogance, illness or inefficiency at mental arithmetic alone qualify for descent to this last class. Perhaps I should soon have found myself there, if Martha's money . . .

As soon as I realized where this game was leading me I left the crowds at the sea lion pool and made straight for the new Lemur House. A gift of the French nation, during one of our McLeod Government's pan-European phases, it had been intended as a reminder of the greatness of the Union Française – a tribute to Madagascar's loyalty. When, later, relations had worsened again, some question had been mooted through the French Embassy of our paying for it; but, as Dr Englander liked to point out, 'it was far beyond the range of our two-penny halfpenny budget'. It was indeed a miracle of glass beauty, domed, and wired not in cages but as a whole so that from outside the lovely slender creatures could be seen in shadow show, capering and swinging across the roof; while from inside, one looked up to a Douanier Rousseau world of tropical leaves and flowers, ringed tails, great round amber eyes, jet black velvety feet, and long black noses pointed, it seemed, in derision at the absurd human creatures below. Even Falcon conceded it worthy to stand by the Crystal Palace. Our Director used it as an illustration of a necessary step towards free ranging primates. For me it was a mysterious source of solace and of release; for the lemur's antic play was both sensuous and ludicrous; lemurs and gibbons! It would be easy in relation to either, I think, for the sensuous to change to the sensual. They alone have given the simian world the delicate twist that might excite human desire. Why has it not done so more often? Perhaps, in the long run, sheer physical difficulty is the censor that controls our sexual range.

I was puzzling on this that afternoon in the Lemur House, when Matthew Price's voice broke into or rather shattered my abstraction. Curator of Birds, Matthew combined the macaw, the guinea fowl, the peacock and the seagull in his voice. It was a discord that in my years at the Zoo I had come to love.

'How very nice to see you looking so happy, Simon my dear,' he shrieked, alarming the visitors, setting at defiance the lemurs. The nice thing was that he meant it.

'I was wondering why more people haven't been guilty of sinful relations with monkeys,' I said.

Matthew has an old-fashioned aesthete's love of recondite smut. Nevertheless I'd forgotten the scholar in him, which was always most in evidence when sex was in question.

'Oh, I'm not entirely sure they haven't,' he said with great seriousness. 'I expect there was a lot of it with Julia and Messalina and all those Roman ladies, don't you? There's nothing in Juvenal or Suetonius certainly. But I'm not at all sure about the Empress Theodora. I fancy she was rogered by an ape more than once in her circus acts. I've rather forgotten my Procopius, you see. But I'll look it up tonight.'

He gazed up at the lemurs for a second.

'Anyway they're not for *me*,' he said, 'I've got a new lory from Brazil. Now there's a beauty for you. Come and look at it.'

We set off for his beloved Parrot House. Whether his 'lory' would turn out to be a macaw, parrot, parrakeet, or budgerigar. I had no means of knowing. He mocked his own renown as the author of the definitive classification of Psittacidae, and incidentally the scientific pedantry of his colleagues, by the deliberate use of a vague or an out-dated naming of his birds: – 'a lory' – 'a splendid bird of the toucan type, I won't trouble you with its full name' – 'something new to go with our owls and eagles' – or even, on occasion, 'a magnificent addition to our seafowl'.

The bird was a large and very beautiful parrot – golden yellow with a bill of pinkish horn.

'The Queen of Bavaria's Conure,' Matthew announced proudly, '*Aratinga Guarouba*. But you needn't bother about that.

'Completely new to our collections,' he said with pride. His approach to his work was simple – a schoolboy's love of 'completing the series', an aesthete's passion for the decorative qualities of the birds, a scholar's passion for classification. For ecology, anatomy, evolution, demography, indeed for any aspect of zoology that had wider implications he had a great distaste and allowed himself proficiency in them only to the extent that was absolutely essential to his practical purpose.

I said, 'It's a *very* elegant bird, Matthew. What does it feed upon?'

'Oh, grapes and things,' he said vaguely. 'Filson has its diet card. The collecting man drew it up. He was the most ghastly bore. He would tell me all about the bird's nesting habits in Brazil. Well, it isn't going to nest in Brazil. Are you, my love? It's going to live here.'

He paused and produced some nuts from his waistcoat pocket. He pushed his long beaky-nosed face towards the bird. Growing short sight was the only physical sign that he showed of being a contemporary of the other curators. This myopia was not helped by his greying fair hair that flopped over his eyes. As to mental senescence, he was so completely outside contemporary life that it hardly applied. His nose seemed within range of the bird's beak before his fingers had offered the nut; I always feared that he would be badly bitten one of these days, but the mystique which he asserted almost in parody – 'The birds know me, you see' – seemed strangely to hold true.

'Thank God! The ghastly collecting bore came yesterday and not today. Filson's so good with them, you see. And the poor old thing could hardly have been expected to cope today.'

'You must have had an awful day, Matthew.'

'Well, it *has* been rather hell. Still it would have been worse if the old man had seen the accident. He might have died from shock or something. I shall never get anyone so useful again. Luckily a young keeper of the eagles was near that tiresome Giraffe House when it happened and he let me know at once. I whisked old Filson home immediately. I broke the news to him in the taxi and then hung about, you see, while he told Mrs F. Then I sat with them a bit while they talked about the boy. That part was real hell. They were waiting for a summons from the hospital. Actually I knew that he'd died before they'd got him into the ambulance. But it's a good thing to remember with the Filsons of this world that they have to be told about death gradually.'

I went through my egalitarian hoops. 'Don't most of us prefer that?'

Matthew's willowy form swayed slightly – his usual gesture of surprise. 'Well, only children, I suppose. Or people like children – the Filsons and so on. I'm rather fond of my sister Diana, you know, but I should hardly want someone keeping the news of her death from me as though I were still in the nursery.'

The golden parrot, bored with our company or disgusted with our inattention, let out a sudden and cruelly shrill scream that made me jump. Matthew leaned forward to me confidentially, and, as though explaining a point of peculiar scientific difficulty, said,

'That's the noise they make, you see.'

We moved out of this little back room, reserved for new specimens before their exhibition, into the main Parrot House. The combined shrieks of the birds and of two parties of schoolchildren deafened me but seemed only to inspire Matthew to greater feats of crescendo. At intervals he said,

'Oh, for Christ's sake, shut up,' either to the nearest parrot or to the nearest child at random.

Shouting, I asked, 'Did they take the news really badly?'

'My dear Simon, it's hardly the sort of time when I presume to judge people's conduct – especially my head keeper's.'

'I meant were they very upset?'

'Well, I suppose so. They're very ordinary people. Not Arnold Wesker characters. Or whatever that man is called, who wrote about all those brutalized peasants. Mrs F. said a lot of very embarrassing things. But then she does that anyway.'

'You'd met her already?'

'Well, of course. He *is* my head keeper. And then they had this son very late. Mrs F. was only just in time. Naturally he was the great thing of their life. So one must do everything one can for the poor old things.'

'Not every curator would bother so much, Matthew.'

'Well, I don't know about that,' Matthew dismissed the actions of his socially inferior colleagues. 'Anyhow, the main thing now is the funeral. They're R.C.s, so at least there won't be any of that awful cremation with nondenominational prayers and things. Diana and I will go, of course. But there ought to be someone from the Society as a whole. I don't think *quite* the Director, do you? Because after all young Filson was only an assistant to the head keeper. I suppose Bobby Falcon will go since he was the young man's Curator; although, God knows, it can't be said he took much care of him. *You'd* better go, Simon, for the Society. I don't know that normally the Secretary need go to a new keeper's funeral. But old Filson's been here a long time. And the compliment will be to *him*.'

From my first arrival at the Zoo, Matthew had taken over the superintendence of the etiquette of my post.

'I rather liked what I saw of the boy.'

'Did you? Perhaps I didn't see as much as you saw. Anyway he was engaged to a night club hostess.'

'A Butlin's hostess, Matthew.'

'Well, I don't know about that. I don't go to night clubs, you see. He was a ghastly bore about his singing. Old Filson brought him along some years back, before he came to work here. He tried to show off in front of his father by talking terrible balls about the Verdi *Requiem*. So I simply said that of course I adored Verdi but that Gounod was so much better.'

'I was surprised that he should have come here to work at all.'

'Oh, but the Filsons have always worked at the Zoo.'

'But he was rather highly educated for this sort of job.'

'Yes? I don't know about that. They're all rather educated nowadays, aren't they? Anyway Mrs F. was a school-mistress or something. Even this morning when the poor thing was in such a state, she felt she had to talk to me about all this tedious business of war with France and Germany. I didn't like to snub the poor creature at such a time, but it's really hardly her affair. I simply said, "Well, *we* can't do anything about it, can we?"'

I felt it useless to contest this. I said, 'I can't imagine your conversing with a school-mistress anyway, Matthew. She must have something rather special.'

Matthew swayed again in surprise. 'Oh, no. I think she's a ghastly bitch. But what I think is hardly to the point, is it? The only thing that matters now is seeing that the proper wreaths are sent. Mrs F. said something about wanting cheerful flowers. I can't think what she meant. But then I think all flowers are hell.'

'I suppose she meant coloured flowers and not white ones.'

'But you can't have coloured flowers at funerals, can you?'

I said acidly, 'I think a lot of middle-class people do.'

'Oh? How very extraordinary! Well, I suppose the flower people that Diana goes to will know about it. You'd better warn Falcon. He's got rather an odd background, but I should imagine his family had the ordinary white flowers at funerals.'

'Has anyone said anything to you about the accident being due to the negligence of old Strawson, Matthew?'

Matthew looked very grand.

'I really haven't much time to listen to gossip,' he said; 'in any case I should hardly interfere in Bobby Falcon's department, should I?'

'Englander says that some journalist or crooked lawyer will get hold of the Filsons and persuade them to sue the Society for vast sums.'

Matthew stood for a moment, scratching the head feathers

of a blue and yellow macaw. He was oblivious of the crowd that had gathered to watch him.

'Englander's mother was a Belgian Jewess,' he said suddenly.

'I haven't time to listen to anti-semitism, Matthew dear.'

Matthew was very surprised. 'I can't imagine why you should have to do so,' he said. 'Of course,' he went on, 'if there *is* any question of legal action or that sort of thing, I shall introduce old Filson to my lawyers. They'll see that his claim is a suitable one.'

He seemed to tire of the subject, for he led the way to the exit door.

He peered towards the flamingo pool past which were riding children mounted on camels.

'I can't think why they want to have giraffes and camels and all these clumsy mammals anyway,' he said. 'The whole place should be one vast aviary. With orangeries and gazebos. Sanderson could breed insects for the birds,' he conceded, 'and we could retain the llamas to draw the carriages for the public. And perhaps yaks for the winter months.'

He paused for a moment. Then as though a new largeness of vision had come to him,

'There could be gazelles. They're very graceful. Isn't there a Thomson's gazelle? I seem to have heard Falcon talk of some such creature.'

He, too, had his ideal vision, but it strayed too far into fantasy for me to share it.

I said, 'You'll think me sentimental but I can't get the horror of that boy's death out of my mind.'

'I don't *know* about sentimental.' He placed the word in inverted commas as though it was a person or a place of which he was ignorant. 'But after all you were only a child in the war. If you'd been in Crete or at Tobruk, you couldn't possibly get into a state about things like this. Most of one's friends, you see, were either killed or taken prisoner.'

With Matthew the aesthete MC I simply could not deal.

I only said, 'Any injury to the balls horrifies me, I suppose.'

'I suppose so. But who said anything about balls?'

'Rackham told me. The giraffe trod on young Filson's testicles and crushed them.'

Matthew went into hoots of laughter that turned into hiccoughs. Recovering his breath, he screamed,

'Kicked in the balls by a giraffe! Oh God! I can't think why it's so wildly funny, can you? But it is.'

He repeated the phrase and a passing clergyman looked round in horror.

I said, 'Ssh! Matthew. Everyone's listening.'

'Everyone? Oh, you mean that clergyman. He probably hasn't got any. They often haven't.'

Although I was already infected by the hysteria of his laughter, I said, 'An appalling injury like that isn't really funny, Matthew.'

'Nonsense. Of course it is. Even if it had happened, it would be. And in any case it didn't. My eagle man told me exactly what occurred. You know how even the nicest of those people adore the gory details. The wretched man was wounded by some spike. I can't think what they have spikes lying about for. I shouldn't dream of leaving *anything* lying about in my paddocks – not even with those beastly cassowaries. And then the giraffe trampled on his chest and broke his ribs.'

'But Rackham told me.'

'Oh, all those old things like Rackham have minds like sewers.'

He began to roar with laughter again.

'Oh, God! What a bore,' he said, 'I can't possibly tell old Filson, can I? Although he does adore a good dirty joke.'

He began to make his way back to his office above the Parrot House, then he returned for a moment and said very earnestly,

'Oh, by the way, Simon, I shouldn't repeat that to anybody else, if I were you. You see it might get back to the Filsons. And if we can do no more when bloody things like this happen, we can at least see that nothing is made worse.'

He seemed to be rebuking me.

Fortified a little by this meeting I returned to my office, and reducing the submitted statements of work from our six research students to précis, produced our annual progress report for the Nuffield Foundation in less than an hour.

At the North Gate stood Sanderson, holding the evening paper. He said, 'This picture of Princess Anne at the South Pole is so charming. I shall have to save this copy or else Mrs Blessington will be quarrelling with Miss Delaney over theirs. They've both got collections of royal cuttings, but strictly between ourselves dear old Miss Delaney's is the best. And yet she'll never see it.'

I was not in the mood for confidences about Sanderson's two old retired housekeepers; the main thing was that Sanderson had scanned the evening paper and found nothing of his indiscretion to alarm him. For all the Director's successful luncheon, I had not myself felt sure – journalists after all talk to one another.

I said, 'Well so far, so good then.'

Sanderson was evidently bewildered, but he took my words for some generally benevolent sentiment.

He smiled, 'She's doing splendid things for us all in these tours of hers, Princess Anne.'

'I was talking about Filson's death.'

A look of vexation came over Sanderson's face.

'I've decided not to say anything about it to the old ladies, Carter. Mrs Blessington would take it in her stride. She's got extraordinary guts for an eighty-year-old. But it's Miss Delaney I worry for. The blind live in such a world of mystery that we can't be too careful. I only hope there's nothing in the evening paper. The old ladies' copy gets delivered before I'm home, and Mrs B. always reads it aloud to Miss D.'

I think he was afraid lest I should pursue what he had now decided was an 'unpleasant topic', for his eye wandered around the crowd at the gates and settled 'soupily' upon an old mad-man who visited the Zoo each day with Bible texts and bags of unsuitable foods for the animals. The Zoo like all public places had its regular plague of cranks, spongers, beggars, con. men and plain lunatics; it was Sanderson's habit to attach himself to all of them.

Now he said sentimentally, 'Paper Bag Peter! I'm very fond of him, you know, Carter. He's been coming here so many years. I believe things are not easy for him now. He used to live with his old mother but she died . . . I wonder if we could find him some little job about the place. For all his tricks, he's got a strangely childlike quality about him somewhere. He was asking me the other day, and I said you were the man to provide jobs.'

It was also Sanderson's habit to take up absurd philanthropic enterprises and then hand them on to me when they proved difficult.

I turned away. I was too disgusted to say anything to him. I left him to go to his bus stop, and buying copies of all the papers, set off for a seat on Primrose Hill in order to read them before I made my short walk home. Two of the papers, it seemed, had ignored the incident; the other two carried very minor paragraphs about it.

My fears had been groundless, but it was not hard to see why: even Princess Anne, the first royal visitor to Antarctic territories so recently reclaimed from the ice blocks, had been driven from the front page by the newest note sent to our Government from the European Alliance.

The most liberal of our evening papers begged in its editorial that no word like 'threat' should be used to describe this document; judging by its own headlines it preferred the word 'ultimatum'. The other three had less qualms and were unanimous in describing it as a threat. It must be said that if any words have a definable meaning they were right. The European Alliance complained of the increase of smuggling that had followed their embargo on British goods. From now on any smuggler, they declared, who was caught in possession of contraband would be summarily executed. The President of the Board of Trade, while not permitting herself to reveal the nature of our official answer to the note, had spoken of Britain's absolute duty to trade with such uncommitted European countries as Switzerland and Austria. Two of the newspapers saw German arrogance in this new move; the other two divined French intransigence. Our President, Lord Godmanchester's paper declared that our Coalition Government had neither the breadth nor the strength to make the dignified but firm reply that would maintain peace with honour. 'Peace with honour' indeed was its editorial headline and it was clear that the editor felt that he had discovered a new and telling phrase. As this was no time for false modesty, the editorial continued, there could be no hesitation in declaring that in the return of Lord Godmanchester to high office lay our only hope. It added ominously that even then the nation might have woken up too late.

My first reaction, I'm afraid a thoroughly petty one, was a certain annoyance that, however unfortunate the consequences might have been to the status of the Zoo, Sanderson's folly had not pursued him further. This malicious and frivolous reflection was followed by another hardly less so: I was delighted that Leacock would not be able to claim, or at any rate claim with any reason, that his influence had saved the day.

Then the print swam in front of me, the letters diving and blurring and fading only to shape themselves into the one word – War. The stab of terror was sharp. It was also familiar. It carried memories of similar apprehensions right back into my childhood. Yet, just because I had so often seen these stale feeble phrases in print before, I could never be sure that here at last might not be the genuine herald, the true devil's emissary come to warn us of God knew what horror and agony that would precede the annihilation of Martha, of the children, and of me. One day, after all, the real wolf would come to give meaning to all the false cries that had lulled us.

For a few seconds the sharp terror tightened my breathing and constricted my scrotum. But it had happened now so often and so pointlessly that it quickly vanished into the sea of anxious doubts in which like everyone else I had learned to swim my life. It was followed by a more selfless yet no less genuine sorrow for the obliteration of human creation – conventional thoughts of human struggle and human hope and human happiness gave me for a moment a no less conventional choke in my throat. Yet this also was too customary a sadness to last for more than a minute or two. To such quickly effaced emotions had years of war alarms brought so many of us. In the end I could only really feel anxious as to how Martha would take this latest scare. As if, from previous experience I did not know! She would hide her fear for the children bravely from me; we would once again delay and then give way to the familiar debate we had so often held about sending them to their American aunt – would it be right? Would it in any case be to any purpose? Could the holocaust be limited? And so on, and so on. And then at last as I considered how impatient Martha would be with any other news, how little the Zoo authorities or anyone else would have time for investigating the causes of Filson's death, I knew an access of determination to pursue my inquiries, not to let the fear of Armageddon obliterate this smaller wrong. I walked back down the hill to the large late Regency stuccoed house facing the Zoo, with which Martha's money had so pleasantly provided us. Telling myself that to do so would keep Martha's mind off her fears, I went in determined to give an account of *my* day's events.

I did; but not quite in the way I had intended. Perhaps it was because Jane Falcon was there. I got along very well with Jane. Not as she would have wished me to do, although that, despite the fact that she was ten years older than me, might well have been possible had I met her before I married Martha. In fact I was all the more fond of her because I had managed to vault the tricky hurdle of refusing sex and still land on the other side as a favourite.

Anyway there was Jane, large and smart and radiating plenty of good reasonably well-intentioned spiteful fun. Her first remark set me off on a track I had not intended.

'You are wonderful, Simon,' she said in her elaborate high comedy sophisticated drawl. 'You've been at that place three years now and you still don't come home smelling of monkeys or fish or lions' pee. You're awfully lucky, Martha.'

Martha said, 'I wish he *did* smell a bit more of animals, Jane. It would mean that his work was a little nearer to what we'd hoped for. As it is I feel that all this changing of trains might just as well have never taken place. It's not Simon's fault. We're terribly grateful to Bobby for getting him in – but of course, he's the only practical person they've got there and old Leacock uses him. But he went there because he's a born naturalist and I wish he wouldn't *let* them use him as an underpaid civil servant.'

Jane smiled at me. 'I don't believe you're really as taken in by that "little boy lost" act as you pretend, Martha. Simon's my favourite ruthless person. I should love to see someone trying to use him. Anyhow Simon would come home clean from the place if he'd spent all day in the skunk's cage – partly because he's Simon and partly because he's young. All the rest of them are old men, even poor darling Bobby. To give him his due, *he* knows and hates it. But it means they'd probably be beginning to smell wherever they spent their days. That's what I can't understand, Simon, how you can bear to work all the time with old things like Englander or Sanderson. Doesn't it give you a feeling of being surrounded by hardening of the arteries?'

In fact, of course, it was just the sort of flattery I wanted to hear at the end of that day, as Martha's anxieties were those that I wished to forget. But if Jane had to be there preventing me from making love to Martha which was the restorative I had hoped for, then at least I felt a right to her flattering balm to soothe the day's lacerations. Also, quite suddenly, her words placed a pattern upon the day's events that was exactly what I required – ridiculous without detracting from the tragedy or for that matter from the need for redress. I saw the muddle as an old men's muddle, the obstinacy, shiftiness, laziness and weariness of a lot of old men faced with an emergency of violence and suffering. And so I presented it to Martha and Jane.

Filson's death called forth protests of horror. Jane cried, 'No, stop it, Simon. You're just being sadistic. I can perfectly well imagine for myself.' And Martha, American as always when upset, said, 'Oh, no! Isn't that the most awful thing?' But as I really let myself go and gave them Leacock and Sanderson, Beard and Englander all in full mimicry, but hobbling with sciatica, deaf as posts, peering blindly with the vain, failing eyesight of old age, Jane and Martha began to feel relief in laughter until Martha cried,

'No, for Heaven's sake, it's too horrible to laugh at. Something's got to be done about them, Simon.'

Then Jane, fearing the serious direction into which that remark might have led us, said, 'I notice you very carefully avoid giving us Bobby's part in all this. In fact now I come to think of it I've never heard you "do" Bobby. It's slightly insulting to me, you know, this suggestion that I insist on people keeping up appearances about Bobby and me. I know I'm thought to be tremendously brave but surely it isn't quite such an act as all that.'

She looked at Martha as she said it, and it is a tribute to Martha's genuine passion for sincerity that she could not disguise her disgust. To cover up I did give them Bobby, but a little haltingly and feebly because I could see that Martha so much disapproved.

In the end Jane said impatiently, 'Yes. Well let's stop it, shall we? Your Bobby is rather an anti-climax, Simon darling.'

Martha said, 'The awful thing is that Simon makes one think that people really *are* like that. But of course they aren't. They're much nicer and much less funny.'

'You mean they're all bores,' Jane said. 'Well, in that case how nice to be Simon.'

The entry of Jacqueline with Reggie and Violet came most opportunely. It sometimes worried Martha that the children so enjoyed the histrionic ritual of good night, especially if there were visitors present. But it always seemed to me that childhood was the only time in life when showing off was permitted; and so long as their act did not get out of hand and embarrass both themselves and us I encouraged them to put on a bit of a show.

The children, underlining as always their boredom with Jacqueline and their daily round, made a rush for Jane, the visitor.

Jane said, 'The Hippopotamus Family have gone abroad so we shan't be seeing any more of them.'

Violet said, 'I know.'

Jane said, 'You couldn't have done. I've only just invented it.'

The children looked nonplussed, but pleased. They were always delighted when grownups paid them the compliment of puncturing illusions.

Reggie remarked casually, 'We don't care very much anyway, because this evening we're giraffes.'

Martha cried, 'Oh, no!'

The children were immediately alarmed, for they knew that their mother was not friendly to these evening games with visitors. Violet gave her a propitiatory side-glance and Reggie rushed up and hugged her violently. They then turned to Jane and me again.

'If we put our tongues out you can put locust beans on the ends and we'll roll them in.' Feeding Smokey was one of their favourite pursuits.

Jane, glancing at Martha as though to reassure a hysteric, said,

'I don't really care for the sight of two tongues. Anyway it's not very imaginative just both to be giraffes. *You* ought to be something else from Africa, Reggie.'

Annoyed, Reggie blushed and said fiercely, 'What?'

'Oh, I don't know. An aardvark. What a mercy it is I'm the wife of a mammalogist.'

'What is an aardvark?'

'Oh, God! Ask your father. He's probably observed them in their natural haunts.'

Violet said, 'Daddy can't go to Africa because it makes him ill.'

I began rapidly to describe aardvarks.

'They have very long tongues,' I said, 'to collect ants.'

'Oh, God!' Jane cried again, 'more tongues.'

The children put their tongues out at her three or four times.

'Do you hate that?' they asked.

'Yes, I do rather.'

They squealed with delight and did it again.

I said, 'Also they have very long claws to tear the termites' nests to pieces.'

Violet and Reggie immediately began clawing at two cushions. Then Violet bumped her head and began to cry. While Martha was soothing her, Jane said to me,

'Isn't it awful that children can't tell that one doesn't really like them? A little attention and they're all over one. No wonder they're so easy to kidnap. Do you feel as ashamed as I do about being good with them, Simon?'

I felt suddenly very angry.

'You may remain detached from my children because you don't like them. I really don't know or care. But let me tell you that my detachment is simply because I'm frightened by the depth of my affection for them.'

I don't know which was the more horrified by my remark, Jane or I. However it couldn't be unsaid, and I reflected that after the tension of that day I had been bound to burst out against someone; better the unlikely Jane than the likely Martha. I did not try to repair my outburst. I turned to Jacqueline.

'Qu'est-ce que vous voulez boire?' I asked, 'De Dubonnet? Ou même nous avons de la grenadine.'

Later when Jane was leaving I said, 'I was terribly rude, Jane, I'm afraid. But I should have thought you would have known how strongly I feel about my children.'

She answered, 'You are extraordinary, Simon. You will persist in thinking that people can "know" about each other. Especially that *you* know about everybody else. Martha was quite right, my dear, you "get" people awfully well but you get them all wrong.'

Later still that evening Martha looked so wonderful that I became impatient to take her to bed.

She said, 'Please, Simon, I do want to come. But I *must* see the late news. I know it is silly to be so frightened but please be patient with me. After all I haven't said a word about this ghastly news all evening.'

Her restraint in having said nothing the whole evening added such overwhelming tenderness to my desire for her that I had to control a sentimental impulse to cry.

The news, as it turned out, was as familiarly 'comforting' as the earlier news had been 'alarming'. Everybody, it seemed, was saying that they hadn't quite meant what they said. Our Prime Minister, in particular, went out of his way to give a pacific twist to the earlier remarks of the President of the Board of Trade. The whole pattern was so familiar that it aroused no feeling in me at all. Martha, however, was reassured and that was all that mattered. Later still, as, content and relaxed, we were both drowsing off into sleep, Martha murmured,

'You were terribly funny about all those old things this evening, darling. But you *are* going to do something about that boy's death aren't you?'

I said, 'I mean to.'

It was as much as truth would allow me.

2

AN END AND SEVERAL BEGINNINGS

I WOKE the next morning and was almost surprised to find that my resolve was still with me – a resolve strong enough at any rate to determine me to do all I could to strengthen it further. I hated admitting that my most powerful incentive was emotional, but I forced myself to the admission. I decided therefore that in my walk to work I would cross the canal not as usual by the old bridge but by the new Casson bridge. The old bridge led me by the coatis' cage; their charm and their grace gave me the same sort of pleasure as those of the lemurs. I did not need that pleasure that morning. Going by the Casson bridge I should be brought slap up against the paddock where Filson died. I hoped the sight would reinforce my anger.

But before I reached the Giraffe House I came upon the enclosure where the Brazilian tapirs wallowed in their pool like so many primitive horses. It was a recent spacious construction, but even here Bobby Falcon's love of the old Zoo had somehow cluttered it up with planks and chutes and general circus absurdities. A great ladder was perched precariously upon one end of the feeding trough, and across it was stretched an old-fashioned carpet-bag tool container from which protruded hammers and some sharp-looking object. After yesterday's event, it needed no more than this muddle to set me on the warpath. As I turned the corner the grunting of the wild pigs came to me, each species contributing in a different key. There where the peccaries seemed endlessly and pointlessly to jostle one another for the same narrow corner of their ample run, I saw an upturned feeding trough. I doubt if its Victorian cast iron clawed feet could have harmed a mouse, but my anger exploded. And exploded upon Strawson, whose fat, self-satisfied Billy Bunter form waddled towards me at that moment.

'Get these enclosures cleared of this junk instantly, do you understand, Strawson?'

The semi-literate jargon he had built up for himself in his character of Elephant Joe did not appease me at that moment.

'We shall be kept pretty busy, Mr Carter, if we are to give ourselves the job of reforming the porcine nature. You know the old phrase, Sir, "live like pigs".'

'I don't want to hear any more talk, Strawson. These houses are a disgrace. Get on with your job.'

'I was under the impression that Sir Robert was responsible for maintenance . . .'

'After yesterday's accident, Strawson, we're all of us responsible in common decency to see that negligence doesn't become a habit. You might take a look at the tapir's enclosure . . .' He was about to speak but I went straight on. 'Attend to it at once, please. I shall be making a thorough inspection later. And if it assists your touchy pride, I mean an inspection of the whole Gardens, not just of the ungulates under your charge.'

I walked on and left him puffing away like an astonished toad.

When I got to my office I realized that my words with Strawson would mean an almost certain row with Bobby. Nevertheless I was glad that anger had driven me on. At least I had taken measures to prevent further unnecessary accidents. I resolved to make a complete inspection of the Gardens during the luncheon hour. Meanwhile I sketched out a memorandum to send to all curators drawing their attention to the importance of ensuring that all enclosures were free of encumbrances. It was going beyond my office, but at least by generalizing my intrusion I should not seem especially to have selected Bobby's corns to tread on.

I had hardly begun to sort through the morning post with Mrs Purrett when our President Lord Godmanchester came ambling into my office. I knew him well enough now to be aware that on these days when he appeared to pad aimlessly about the Zoo like some fat, lost old bear, he was in fact easing the nervous tension that periodically possessed him since he had been out of office. Leacock, who claimed to understand Godmanchester fully – 'I saw that it was a must to know the man completely as soon as I was Director. And I've made it my job to do so' – said that the President's mooching was never without purpose, always preceded some decisive action. Once or twice, it is true, there were repercussions at Society meetings the following afternoons. But more often than not if any action followed it must have done so outside the Zoo, for we knew nothing of it. However it was part of Edwin Leacock's regard for his own office as Director to invest the President's every move with significance.

This was not an attitude that Godmanchester found any reason to reciprocate. This morning, he said,

'Leacock's got some meeting or other in his room, Carter.'

'I think it's his quarterly meeting with the Fishery Research Bureau.'

'Yes indeed. So he says. I'm surprised he's kept on all that sort of thing now he's left the Aquarium. I'll give you a tip, Carter. Never hold on to what you've left behind. I learned that very early when they moved me from Agriculture to Education. I fancied that I'd really made my mark ... But you don't want to hear all that. Anyway you know it all. You were at the Treasury. Winchester, New College, and the Treasury are the three places where they know everything,' he said to Mrs Purrett, who smiled delightedly at what was evidently a jocular offering from on high.

'I'm just padding around here this morning,' he said, 'making the most of this lovely weather. But there may be an important call for me and as Leacock's made himself incommunicado, I wondered if I could have it put through here when it comes. I shall go and talk to my friend the binturong and perhaps have a word with the kinkajou. But I'd like to know of any call as soon as it comes through. If one of your messengers could spare the time from whatever game of chance he's engaged in and come over to the Small Mammal House, I'd be very obliged to him.'

As he was going out of the room, he asked, 'By the way, what's this business I saw in the paper about a keeper being killed? Got it wrong, haven't they? Giraffes never did any harm that I heard of before.'

I said, 'No, it's true.' And then with a sudden decision I added, 'I'd like very much to talk to you about it, if you have a moment.'

He raised his thick George Robey eyebrows even higher for a second at this suggestion of my by-passing the Director; but, in fact, as I knew from his attentions to me, and indeed to those in more subordinate grades – keepers and so on – he liked nothing better than a Napoleonic going over the heads of his marshals to the common soldier.

He said, 'I *have* a moment and it may be the last that I'll have for some time. I'll confess that my mind's on affairs of rather greater seriousness than those of Regent's Park, but you've heard me say often, too often I'm sure to carry conviction, that I'm never too busy for anything. Let me hear about this if only to show you that the saying isn't just an old man's drivelling.'

That he had so accurately gauged my thoughts gave me more confidence in him.

I said, 'We'll take the rest of the letters later then, Mrs Purrett.'

Godmanchester had difficulty in fitting his vast buttocks into the deep but narrow armchair that I kept for visitors. By the time that his huge, fat, shapeless body had sunk into the cushions, I could see nothing of him except his round, surprised-looking face. Instead of talking to a wise old bear, I found myself addressing a surfacing seal. It was slightly disconcerting.

He said, 'Before you start on what you want to tell me, I'd better say that I may not be able to give a lot of time to Zoo affairs in the next month or two. In fact I hope for everybody's sake that I shan't be able to. It's no secret that the Government's got into a ghastly mess. What is perhaps less appreciated is that they realize it. Pressure of public opinion, or the very little sense that's left to him, may force the P.M. to widen his government. If he does, little though we like each other's guts, he'll be compelled to offer me office. And as you'll see in my papers, that may very well save us from a disastrous war. What it says in my papers is not necessarily true. But in this case it is. Therefore although I have said a very large number of times that I would not accept office from him at the end of a bargepole, I shall.' He paused and blinked at me two or three times. 'I'm telling you this because I don't know what you're going to ask me now. It may entail a request for my assistance which I may promise to give. You will see very readily, however, that in certain events I shall not be able to keep that promise. All right. Go ahead.'

All this 'carry-on' in his slow, emphatic voice which so impressed our Director with Godmanchester's 'greatness', only inspired me with serious doubts. I almost wished that I had not decided to ask his advice; committed to the counsel of the man at the very top, one has no further to go. However, committed I was, and so I told him the full story as I knew it.

Only twice did he interrupt me. Once when I was talking of Sanderson's part, he said, 'Look, is this a funny story you're telling me, Carter, or a serious one? Serious. All right – cut out the imitations, although you do them very well. Anything can be made funny you know, but it isn't the moment for it.'

Again, when I repeated Rackham's remarks, he said, 'You talk a lot with your subordinates.'

'Yes. I find it difficult to accept hierarchies. It was my chief failure at the Treasury.'

He looked doubtful. 'Ah, *I* talk a lot to *my* subordinates. But then I'm old and very eminent. I can afford to indulge myself.'

At the end of my story, he said, 'Yes, I see. And what you want to know is what am I going to do about it?'

'No. Whether *I* should push on with inquiries, try to find out what happened and so prevent it happening again.'

'There are a number of propositions there, aren't there? And they aren't all necessarily in accord with one another.

However, I'm glad you don't want to know what I'm going to do, because the answer to that would be exactly nothing. As to whether you should push on with your inquiries, as you call it – that means in fact pushing Beard or Falcon or even Leacock if you're smart enough, into admitting that they made very bad mistakes. Whether that'll prevent it happening again is a very different question. For myself, following my usual practice, I shall say something that I shouldn't. It wouldn't surprise me in the slightest degree if Leacock or Beard or Falcon or all three of them *have* made serious mistakes. They're probably doing so all the time, only usually there are not dangerous spikes and sick giraffes and inexperienced young keepers about at the same time in the same place. I don't have to tell you that there lies the difference between what is and what is not history. Here we have history. And the senior men aren't perhaps quite up to history. As you say, they're cut off from the world and they're getting a bit set. Old as I am I can say that because one can't get set in politics, events don't allow it. What's less certain is what value it would be to bring that home to them. Or, if you did so, whether any young keeper in the future would be the whit safer than he is now. You can't eliminate carelessness or bad luck simply at the wave of a reforming wand. You'd learn that soon enough if you had real responsibility. As to the old boys, they've had a shock and if that doesn't cure them, I don't know that your denunciations will.'

'It isn't only a question of the future . . .'

'But of justice, is that it? Oh, there's no need to explain what you feel about that. I've felt it myself in my time, although you probably think that I haven't. But justice that brings no practical advantages to anyone and a good deal of disturbance to some people, I can't really recommend. It would be an expensive indulgence. No, I should say you couldn't do better than forget the whole matter.'

'And supposing, that, taking your advice, I still stumble on unfortunate facts in the course of my work.'

Lord Godmanchester wobbled with laughter.

'I've come across a good few disastrous ways in which altruists can act, but stumbling! What you want to know in fact is what *I* should do if you bring any skeleton you're so careless as to *stumble* over before my notice at a Society meeting, that's it, isn't it? Shall I still pretend that I don't see it? The answer to that is – only if nobody else sees it. And that rather depends on the light in which it's displayed, doesn't it?'

I wondered if he was really enjoying his act as much as it seemed. The possibility alone made me impatient with him.

I said, 'I suppose that such tiresome behaviour on my part would definitely be a black mark against me.'

The deep creases in his fat old face seemed all at once to turn downwards. He appeared sad and hurt rather than sly and jovial.

'I'm sorry,' he said, 'that you should think me so poor a judge of character. It has never occurred to me for a moment since I saw you at work here that you were in the slightest degree concerned with career making. I don't say that as praise or blame, of course. Only as an observation. Is that all?' he asked.

'Yes. Thank you for listening.'

'Oh, it's not so unselfish as you think. These little natters are very instructive. I hope we may have them again from time to time.'

He got up, but he seemed reluctant to go from the room. He glanced at the telephone.

'The small mammals, remember, if there's a message for me.' At the door, he said, 'You see the trouble with that story is that it's all too peculiar. A man kicked in the balls by a giraffe, or perhaps not. A giraffe that thought he heard a lion or perhaps not. There's an awful lot of "perhaps not" about it. Do you know what I'd call that story? I'd call it a tall story.' He opened the door, then he added, 'You think that's a cheap little joke. I meant it to be so. We may all have to get used to being callous in the months ahead. It won't do us any harm to start now.' He glanced anxiously again at the telephone and ambled off.

I was glad that I had already made this joke in bad taste

that Godmanchester thought so vital to my moral health. My reaction to his advice, of course, was resentment of its patronizing air. I determined to disregard it. But so obvious a reaction to so crude a manner seemed childish. To avoid appearing absurdly touchy I was almost obliged to consider the advice more seriously than I should have done had his manner been more tactful. Had he perhaps foreseen this, offered it in that way on purpose? I did not believe him to be so subtle. In fact I ended by suspecting that he had only consented to listen because it gave him an excuse to be by the telephone whose summons he so clearly hoped for.

When the telephone rang, however, it was no dramatic call for Coriolanus. It was instead Pattie Henderson.

She said, 'I say, I was pretty bloody rude on the phone yesterday. But I hope you realize that it was only because Newton and Nutting had got my goat by saying they knew you'd play safe. You can imagine how I've been chortling over them this morning when the news got round that you'd been dressing down that awful fat henchman of Falcon's. Remember we're all behind you if you want to have a showdown with the old boys.'

I said, 'Thank you,' but in a voice that I hoped mocked the pretensions of the revolutionary opposition as much as it did my suitability to lead them. Pattie in her simplicity was puzzled. She found nothing to say; I made no effort to help her out. Then made nervous by this silent communication, she shouted:

'I suppose old Leacock's bogging you down with a lot of fuss about his music hall turn on the television. Anything to stop chaps getting on with their proper jobs.'

I said, 'I imagine rather a lot of people are being distracted from their proper jobs today by the thought of what a war might entail.'

Pattie's answer came as immediately as I had expected.

'Oh, I suppose people like Leacock and Falcon who've lost all contact with the real work are bound to have the jitters. Down here in Research Block we haven't given a thought to it.'

'Like Queen Victoria.'

History had little call to Pattie. She said, 'Well it's all a lot of newspaper bilge, isn't it?'

'Oh, surely. So long as Newton is busy with marsupial placenta and Nutting has not satisfied himself about the fertility cycles of the common shrew, war is an unthinkable interruption.'

Now Pattie was really angry.

'If you haven't any appreciation at all for serious research work, then the sooner you get out of this place the better. We're carrying enough passengers already.'

She rang off. To a great extent she was justified.

The only apology appeared to lie in getting on with my work. The quarterly estimates for expenditure presented by the various curators lay before me ready for assembling into a single report to be submitted to the Finance Committee. The report would be made in the Director's name, but, unless there were items that seemed to him to relate to his National Reserve scheme, I knew that it would be useless to ask for his full consideration of them. The preparation of the reports would devolve entirely on me. Such a task gave me some conviction that my job was worthwhile. I knew the Committee well enough to make sure that tactful presentation would give to each request the highest chance of acceptance. However much my knowledge of the curators made me sceptical I genuinely tried to retain the urgency of each demand while remembering the limited resources available. When the curators got what they wanted, they took my work for granted. When their requests were refused, they either accused me of insufficient enthusiasm for the Zoo's welfare or complained that, forgetting the automatic rubber stamp nature of my post, I must unconstitutionally have favoured some other department's demand. This is the bureaucrat's lot. Those who like to feel conscious of hiding such light as they possess under a bushel get satisfaction from it. On the whole I did so; although on occasion I wished for the immediate applause given to the acrobat, the pop singer, or the tennis star. But perhaps the paid administrator has a more continuously pleasant sense of not being truly appreciated than any of these. At any rate I enjoyed such work. So long as one does not become a confirmed addict to virtue, I don't know why one shouldn't have the odd kick out of it now and again. Certainly few things made me feel so good as the occasional conviction that I have of doing some good.

No doubt it was some reflection of all this in my face that caused Bobby Falcon so completely to lose his temper in my office when he came in a quarter of an hour or so later.

He began with that sort of facetious severity often supposed to make unpleasant remarks more palatable.

'Look here, Simon, I've got a bone to pick with you. You were appointed here as secretary not as private investigator. I don't know how the other chaps regard it, but as far as *I'm* concerned you must keep your inquiries – morphine needle, violin, and deerstalker – out of the Mammal Houses.'

'I know I owe you an apology, Bobby. I should have come to you first but by an unfortunate chance I came face to face with Strawson this morning and simply let fly.'

Bobby began to relax the tense face he had prepared in order to carry through a 'difficult' interview.

I smiled and said, 'All the same, I have to tell you that I wasn't very happy about his attitude.'

Immediately the dark pouched skin beneath Bobby's left eye began to twitch, drawing up his flushed cheek and the corner of his mouth. He was a quick-tempered man. Since I know my own occasional rages to be no more than a failure to control childish frustration, I can never treat other people's loss of temper as seriously as they want.

I said, 'Oh, Lord, Bobby, I've said the wrong thing. Please don't take it so seriously.'

Such friendly levity had always proved effective before in assuaging his anger. Now my self-satisfaction must still have lingered in my smile or else my contempt for loss of temper must have lent a sneer to my voice; his left eye above the twitching cheek stared out at me like a frightened savage horse's. Beyond our knowledge of mental pathology, I suppose, we each have our folklore, nursery picture of madness. For me, people who look as though no word or gesture of mine could prevent them from doing me a physical injury are 'mad'; of such people I am very frightened. I thought at that moment that Bobby Falcon was going to hit me with a chair or with his fists. Instead he swept all my papers off my desk on to the floor. Immediately he appeared ludicrous to me. My main concern was to prevent him seeing this.

'Who the hell cares whether you're happy or not? That's the trouble with you, Carter. You've been state nursed from the cradle, without even learning to do your own flybuttons up. Not content with that, you had to find Martha's money to provide your bony rump with extra cushions. I suppose she believed that somewhere you had the makings of a real man. At any rate as soon as you tried to prove it, you fell ill. They didn't have any panel doctors or trick cyclists in the African jungle, so Master Carter had a nasty amoebal tummy and got sent home!'

I was surprised and a bit shocked to realize how pleased I was that in uncontrolled temper his language should so quickly acquire a vulgar slangy tone.

But the impetus of his anger had soon passed; the mood was now synthetic. I could almost feel the effort with which he was sustaining a rage from which he could see no escape without loss of face. I had no means of assisting him. The best I could do was by sharpness to cut his dilemma short.

I said, 'This is intolerable, Bobby. You must get out of my room.'

He slumped into a chair, and his invective began to grind down to a halt.

'Why the hell should I get out of your room? I brought you to the bloody place. God knows why! But then God knows why Martha married you. Good administrator? All right, so what? You've cut yourself off from real life for years with your reports and your files. And now something unpleasant with all the muddle that goes with real life happens outside your window; and *you're* not happy about it. You've got to put everybody's actions under your own twopenny halfpenny little home-made moral microscope.' He sat back almost at ease. 'My God, Simon, you are the most bloody awful prig. And if nobody else will tell you so, I must.'

It would have done no good to say that, on the contrary, hundreds of people had told me so, from my schooldays on. It would have been more priggish still to say that I had tried . . .

Bobby it was who did the right thing. 'I'm sorry for that exhibition, Simon, I ought not really to be here. I don't like the way things are going in this place and I keep hoping that I can save something of the old Zoo. But it's self-deception. Leacock's got it all his own way.'

'That's not true, Bobby, as you know. I'm on his side in my view of the Zoo's future, although in some ways he's both an ass and a bit of a fraud. But I'm very much in a minority. Some of the most important Fellows . . .'

'Oresby, old Dr Peasegood! No, Simon, I'm not such a fool as to think that *they'll* move mountains, let alone hold back the tide.'

'All right then. Look how much the *younger* people here – Newton, Nutting, all that crowd, dislike Leacock . . .'

'Don't remind me, Simon, that they wouldn't bother to dislike *me*. In any case I'm not going to pretend I'm in sympathy with them. Oh, I dare say they'd be happy enough to let anyone run the place as he liked, so long as he didn't interfere with their research work. It isn't good enough, Simon, they've no real care for the Society or the Gardens.'

'Research *is* a primary object of the Society.'

'Yes, and thanks to good higher education there are hundreds of young Newtons and Nuttings ready to come along and carry it out.'

Suddenly I was bored with the whole affair, with all these arguments I had heard so many times. Bobby's self-pity, his despair seemed to be coiling round me, suffocating me, pulping my lungs. The air of the room was stale, fetid like the breath of the great cats in the Lion House. I felt myself not a guardian but a prisoner of the caged beasts. My delight had been in their free movements, their untamed terrors and cruelties, the slow discovery of a pattern of life as I watched it unfold for hours at a time had freed me from all consciousness of self. There in the Suffolk beech copse or the Norfolk pine-wood, I had myself known life only through my senses – through the pungent scent of pine needles, crushed under-foot, in the sudden stirring of the green bowl above me and by the flash of a ragged russet tail curved umbrella-like over a fat, white-fronted squirrel. There were red squirrels in a cage near the Rodent House, pretty pets from a Victorian keepsake to gladden Bobby's heart; but I found no freedom in their charming, scurrying, captive antics. I was in the wrong place and for the moment I could bear to hear no more about it.

Attempting to turn Bobby's tide with a joke, I said, 'May be hundreds of Newtons and Nuttings, but never, I think, another Pattie Henderson.'

Bobby looked at me with surprise. I realized that during my reverie his familiar discourse had moved far on into the charms of the Victorian Zoo.

'What can have been more delightful,' he asked, 'than Obaysch when he first arrived here? Have you seen the wonderful *Punch* cartoons of him? H.R.H. – His Royal Hulk. *Punch* of 1850 was no respecter of the Crown. And the crowds that gathered round him – their first chance really to take a look at a hippo in captivity? No wonder the delicate crinolined young ladies risked the stench that came from the coster donahs with their ostrich plumes and fresh young gents from counting houses risked their watches among the light-fingered gentry of Seven Dials? Think of it, Simon. We've never seen colour or movement like it in *our* time, and I can remember the vast crowds that lined up in queues to see the polar bear cub Brumas. Queues! No, the crowd that surged round Obaysch wasn't orderly – it was the good old stinking Victorian mob full of wonder and awe still. And the stink that must have come back to them from His Royal Highness's

Pool! And then the delicate lines of Burton's Houses, the refinement of the shrinking ladies and the eau-de-cologne and the cigar whiff of the gentlemen at their sides. It's something of that mixture of grace and wonder and common orange peel holiday fun that I'm fighting to maintain. We could be one of the last colourful places left in London, Simon.'

Carried away by his own word picture with which he had escaped from the embarrassment of our scene, he sang a line from some Victorian music hall song. 'Roll up and see the hippo. Where better than the Zoo?'

I said, 'In its native rivers of Africa.'

Then I remembered Bobby's rows with the Republic of Tanganyika and the People's State of Uganda over preservation of wild life. These as much as his age had put an end to his famous career of exploration and collecting.

He said, 'You're not exactly tactful, are you?' But he was too elated to be much concerned. 'That's why I wanted Smokey to appear in this show of Leacock's. I could have got the crowd together and, if it lacked the colour of Obaysch's mob, Smokey at least drew children from everywhere. Set against the Burton House, even without the smells, I believe the movement and colour of that scene might have brought back memories to some older viewers. And Leacock believed it would make them cry out "Away with such cramped quarters! Down with Regent's Park!" Oh, he's probably right. We shall see. He's showing the old Eagle House and the ravens, but that's Price's stuff. It was Smokey I counted on.'

He paused; and I was about to make the protest that I now felt opportune, but his wound-up elation had to uncoil itself back to his usual depressive mood.

'I suppose,' he said, 'you wonder why I don't get out of a place where I'm so little at home. But where the hell could I go? The Chinese put an end to my old hunting grounds. I tried to swallow that little change. After all what was Asia? There was still Africa left. I did my best to save the game reserves there but these damned nationalist governments wouldn't

listen. Economic development before preservation of species!
Claptrap slogans! And those that are more enlightened have
their own collectors and wardens – Mr Tlumpumba and Mr
Nkekwe. Well, good luck to them! In any case, I'm too old.
I've got most damnable weak hams, Simon. Though I suppose
I could move in on your territory. Watching native species! A
nice summer studying the digging methods of the Thameside
mole, I'd almost do it if I could find a pretty girl to go with me.
A summer at Henley, I shouldn't mind that. Do you know any
girls who'd make a nice lay on a molehill?'

He came to a stop on a familiar sensual, grumbling note.

I said, 'I ought to tell you now, Bobby, that this question of
your agreement with Leacock not to have Smokey destroyed
will be raised by me at the next Curators' meeting.'

To my surprise, there was no storm in answer. He got up
from his chair and, as he left my room, he said,

'I still think you're a ghastly prig in many ways, Simon.
But you're probably very good for us.'

I wondered as I reflected on it, whether he had only responded so mildly because he had not fully registered my
declaration. I doubted whether, in fact, he had properly heard
anything except his own voice during the whole interview.

If I had been disposed to muse on my dissatisfaction the
morning's chain of self-centred interrupters shamed me into
closer application to work.

I opened the door that communicated with my secretaries'
room. Rackham was once again holding forth to them.

'Ah, they can have as many meetings as they like,' he was
saying, 'but when things have got this far, there's no going
back. No. It's war this time.'

The relish of his tone obviously played on Mrs Purrett's
nerves. She said assertively as though Rackham were a political
expert who needed serious refutation,

'If you read the papers properly, Rackham, you'd see that
every effort at agreement is being made on both sides.'

Rackham said cryptically, 'Ah, it's got beyond them now,'
and was gone.

I said, 'Rackham seems to be getting in your way a lot these days. Tell me if he's a nuisance.'

'Oh, no, we can manage him, can't we, Marian? It's whenever there's a war scare, Mr Carter. I suppose it's in the blood of these old soldiers. Poor old thing! But isn't the news good, Mr Carter?'

When I showed uncertainty of its nature, she said, 'Oh, you haven't heard. The Prime Minister's to meet the European heads at Innsbruck. We've insisted on Scandinavian representation to balance Italy. And the French and Germans have agreed quite readily. I think that's so promising.'

Meetings formed so regular a part of these periodic crises that I could neither share her elation nor refute it.

I said, 'Oh, good. I was thinking that as you have the Nuffield reports to do, Mrs Purrett, I should dictate the preamble for the Finance Committee.'

'Of course,' she said, 'I'm always glad when the Finance Committee's done with each quarter. I think figures are so dreary after staff matters. Human beings for me every time, they're much more real.'

Luckily Mrs Purrett's capacity for vague generalities in no way impaired her capacity as a secretary.

The Director shoved his ugly mug in at the door.

'What's the office programme of work this week?' he asked.

I gave an outline of the main tasks. He did not listen.

When I had finished, he said, 'Scrap the lot. I've just told Miss Chambers to cancel all my meetings. We've got exactly nine days to zero hour. The programme's scheduled for 9.15 p.m. on Friday week. They tell me that's the peak viewing time. But that's by the way. The point is that these television people are now asking for a whole mass of detail which anyone would have reasonably supposed was the business of their research department. However, I don't want to quarrel with them at this juncture. So I've told them that the Secretary and his staff will fill out any details they require in the outline I have already given them. In fact I've properly sold you up the river.'

He grinned at me, and then took Mrs Purrett in as an additional precaution. I had suspected for some time that, essential though he believed his television programme to be as propaganda for the central scheme of his life, he had not, as he would have put it, 'done his homework'.

I said, 'We can't scrap everything, I'm afraid. The Finance Committee and the Nuffield Reports must go in on time. I must also give preliminary seeding out interviews for Beard's four new lab assistants. On Monday next the Cromwell Road people are bringing the secretaries of the Latin American Natural History museums round to us. They're here for the Museums Conference. I promised to give them an outline talk on our functions.'

'I'll see them. I think they should see the man at the head in any case. One simply can't over-emphasize the importance of these American republics in relation to the future.'

'Then,' I went on, 'I shall have to be away on Saturday morning to represent you at young Filson's funeral.'

'Is that necessary?'

'Yes. I think it is.'

Leacock glanced at me, 'Well, as long as you know your "musts",' he said. 'Then I'll leave this with you.'

He handed me a folder of papers and was about to leave.

I said, 'I think I ought to grasp the general shape of this before you move out of questioning range.'

He responded to my humorous manner with some impatience.

'Mr Carter has all the traditional tricks of the Civil Service up his sleeve,' he announced to Mrs Purrett.

He spoke as though I had proposed a Commission of Inquiry. I flicked through the pages of his sketch for the visual track of his programme until I came on a careless, incorrect statement.

'I'm not sure,' I said, 'whether it's quite accurate to say that the Mappin Terrace does not provide satisfactory conditions for the breeding and rearing of mountain goats. The ibexes, at any rate . . .'

He could no longer hide his impatience.

'If there's one thing we must avoid, Carter, it's letting this really important occasion get bogged down in inessential detail. You getting along all right, Mrs Purrett?' he asked, but was gone before she could answer.

'I'm glad I'm more essential than the breeding habits of mountain goats,' Mrs Purrett said.

As I allowed myself to return her smile, I felt rather guilty. The carelessness and inaccuracy involved in the statements about the rearing of mountain goats were in fact very small, almost, as Leacock had said, inessential. But, of course, Mrs Purrett didn't know that.

At lunch time I made a complete tour of the Gardens. Nowhere could I find any further evidence of dangerous negligence. The houses under Strawson's charge were a model of order now. There would be no need further to exceed my powers.

That night, Martha and I drowsed our way to sleep in our usual desultory chatter about the day's events, an exchange that was no more than the last dying extension of our physical embraces. Announcement of the Innsbruck meeting had exorcized her fears. She dwelt dreamily on Maximilian's vast bronze figure, on the funicular railway and on the *Goldenes Dachl* as though vividly to recall these objects remembered from our holiday visits might in some way guarantee success to the ministers when they came to talk there. I let my fingers run backwards and forwards down the smooth firmness of her thigh, dissipating the last tingling searches of my lust, wondering whether similar superstitions lay deeply embedded in my own intelligence. And now, freed from paralysing visions of imminent nuclear annihilation of the children, her conscience, active even then when a hundred other consciences would have lulled into sleep, turned to Filson's death. I told her of the action I had taken. She kissed me.

'Thank God, they've got you there, darling,' she said. 'But you can't stop at that, Simon. Whoever's responsible, must be shown up. I don't care who it is,' – I wondered which of my colleagues she baulked at as a scapegoat – 'if someone has blundered, if anyone's inefficiency or pomposity was responsible, then he deserves to be exposed. You must go ahead, darling. It's only another example of British make do and muddle. It has to be fought.'

My fingers came to a stop in their caressing rhythm. It was not that I minded her sudden moral alliance with her American mother; Martha's powers of national bifurcation on ethical issues often enchanted me. It was rather that something in her demand recalled Pattie Henderson to me. I would act; but for no example, only on behalf of the young happy and living Filson whom I had known so slightly and who was now dead.

I said very sleepily, 'One's as bad as six hundred.'

Martha did not get the allusion, and we faded away together and from each other into sleep.

The Times at breakfast next morning carried a leader in which demands for strengthening the Government were sharply rebuked. But it suggested that 'responsible opinion' was moving against Godmanchester's inclusion in the Cabinet. I remembered that no telephone call had come for him yesterday.

I had no time however to dwell on Godmanchester's disappointment during that week. Leacock's neurotic anxiety about his programme spilt over and flowed around the whole office; we worked obsessively and continuously as though we were seeking opiates from alarms of our own and not simply being driven on by his. War talk, it is true, drifted in now and again like plumes of fog from the world outside; but the impression we formed in our anthill was of an ever clearing sky outside. Martha's tender soothing of my exhausted spirits each night only seemed to confirm this. In any case, Leacock was adamant against all breaths of air, foggy or fresh, that might ruffle the papers and photographs that now seemed to pile up around him in increasing quantities.

Once Mrs Purrett, seeking, I think, to laugh away any remaining war fears that might still disquiet us, said, 'Poor old Rackham's looking quite down in the mouth now that we aren't all going to be atomized into eternity.'

Leacock turned on her, 'I wonder if some of you people realize how impossible constructive work is in an atmosphere of uninformed gossip and rumour,' he said.

He looked at her as though some familiar chair or table in the room had revealed itself to be a hidden foe. For some days after his outburst he was quite unable to accord her the automatic smile he gave to the lower staff who, as he often said, 'it was our duty never for a moment to forget we're human beings'. He looked at her during those days as though searching beneath her pneumatic form for the disguised contours of some familiar, leaner enemy.

So strong indeed was his will to avoid all outside alarms, so deep his more immediate anxieties for his programme's success that I was not altogether surprised when one day he said,

'I hadn't thought it necessary, Carter, to rope Godmanchester in on this. A public figure of that sort might tend to blur the picture I want to convey. But I'm not so sure now. He *is* President and his absence may look a little peculiar. It occurs to me that in the section devoted to Man restored to Nature, it might be very telling to show Godmanchester with his llamas or his wallabies down at Stretton Park. I have no doubt at all,' by a searching look he tried to reassure any that I might have, 'that a great deal of that man's extraordinary vigour and – to permit myself what I know you think to be a bit of jargon – psychic health, comes from his hobby of studying animal behaviour. We couldn't find a better example of a sophisticated man, a man deeply committed to the modern world who has seen the need of losing his own complicated pattern in more simple rhythms. And . . . and then he's a figure who impresses the public. I think we ought to have him.'

I tried to find the easiest way of reminding him of Godmanchester's own preoccupation.

'He was in here a few days ago finding calm in the small

Mammal House with the binturong and the kinkajou. I think he was a good deal exercised about a possible invitation to join the Cabinet.'

Leacock mistook the emphasis of my remark. He said good-humouredly, 'Now don't try to sabotage my programme. I've no intention of showing him here at Regent's Park. I doubt if his visits here are more than – '

'That wasn't my intention. I was only suggesting that in the present political crisis he may not be prepared to give his mind to Zoo matters.'

'I think you make him out a smaller man than he is. In any case what is all this crisis stuff? We're not in the position to judge. I hate all this amateur politics. See if you can get hold of him, will you?'

I pursued Godmanchester by telephone and eventually tracked him down to the Tate Gallery, of which, by virtue of his wife's collection, he was a trustee.

The secretary at the other end said, 'Lord Godmanchester wants to know who is calling?'

I said, 'The Secretary of the Zoological Society.'

There was a pause, then she said, 'I'm afraid Lord Godmanchester can't take any calls.'

I imagined him pacing up and down before Turner's seas and sunsets or stopping to return the ox-like gaze of Madox Brown's immigrants; hoping that Turner or Rossetti would ensure him better luck than the binturong or the kinkajou. Leacock, however, despite all my attempts to dissuade him, insisted on getting through himself to the great man. Since he never again referred to his conversation I imagine that it was as discouraging as I had expected.

The Director's power of evading the impact of public events at this time was deeply impressive. My own detachment, I knew, was simply an inertia bred of a surfeit of crises. Yet Leacock, I am sure, was as deeply anxious lest annihilation or even lesser disaster should destroy his still unborn child as Martha and a million other mothers were about the fates of their living, breathing progeny.

Poor man, his task was a hard one, especially when that week the Russo-American Declaration burst upon an unexpected world and divided the opinion of every West European country with excited, hopeful, or apprehensive arguments. On the whole Leacock managed even this well. I thought at first he would try to ignore what all the world was talking of; had he done so he would have over-reached himself, for not only I, but the television engineers and programme planners with whom the office now seemed filled would no longer have found his enthusiasm infectious but embarrassingly dissociated and insane. In fact, at five to six that evening he appeared at the door of the huge Committee Room, to which we were now driven by our swelling numbers, and said,

'What about knocking off for half an hour? The Prime Minister can be seen making his statement for those of us who wish to hear it on the set in my room.'

I admired him particularly for the 'of us' by which he marked the norm of measured interest which outside events should command. I worked very hard for him in those weeks, for I could not imagine that I should ever myself know enthusiasm that would demand of me his degree of self-control. Yet those days of the Russo-American Declaration undoubtedly taxed him severely. To know that everyone whom his enthusiasm had pressed into his service had a part of their minds elsewhere, to hear on occasion the doubts of technicians or planners whether, in view of the crisis, his programme would even go on the air, were sometimes greater stresses than he could bear. His absurd round eyes looked hysterically unsure as he said to me each day, 'These chaps from the B.B.C. have got real loyalty to this programme, Carter,' or 'It's only cynics like you that can't see when they're up to their neck making history, as we are this week.'

Though Leacock almost insulated himself from events, nobody else did. Even Matthew, who had evolved a wonderful power of hearing, reading and knowing nothing about a world he had long since decided was 'not for him', was forced to complain about the Declaration when he rang up to tell me the arrangements for young Filson's funeral.

His reference was characteristically cryptic, 'It's rather hell those shits talking all that balls, isn't it?' he said.

I said, 'Matthew, Martha's half American.'

'Well, I had a Welsh grandmother but I don't boast about it.'

'I'm afraid Martha *does* boast about her American mother.'

'Oh, God! Well, of course the Americans are better than the Russians.'

Matthew's opinions if he was forced to voice any were always 'correct'. Now he took and indeed shared, the official Government line.

'I mean anyway – Americans or Russians – we can't have them telling us what to do.'

'They're trying to stop a war, Matthew.'

'Yes. Well we're not children, are we? We've had wars before, and we'll have them again I suppose, if it's necessary. Anyhow it's hardly for the Russians or Americans to tell us what we're to have.'

I saw no sense in arguing this.

I said, 'You're like the Prime Minister. You don't want any bullies showing you the big stick. I'm surprised. I must say that I should have thought that was just up your street.'

Matthew crowed with delight.

'It's nothing to do with you what's up my street. I *could* tell you a *very* peculiar story about the P.M. now you mention it. But I'd better not. At any rate not down the telephone. Well anyway I don't *really* care what the Americans or Russians declare, do you? And they talk such balls. I mean it's a matter for the Foreign Office people isn't it? Anyhow I hope no one will mention it at Filson's funeral luncheon.'

'What luncheon?'

'Well, the funeral baked meats, of course. Actually, Diana's getting them sent round to Mrs F.'s from Jackson's so it'll be all right.'

I suppose my anger now was in proportion to my admiration for Matthew's kindness on the day of young Filson's death.

I said, 'You forced those wretched people into this, Matthew. It's disgraceful. It's bad enough that they should have to put up with us at the funeral but to obtrude extra embarrassments on to them.'

Matthew's voice was alarmed. He disliked people being annoyed with him. I was surprised that he didn't run away from the telephone, but he said, 'Well really. Filson wanted to do the right thing. And I told him.'

'The right thing! At this moment! I suppose Falcon'll be there.'

'Well, naturally. He was the poor boy's Curator.'

'And what those poor people must be feeling after that ghastly coroner!'

'But surely all coroners are ghastly. I don't know any. But aren't they doctors or something?'

'That fool never questioned for a minute the responsibility for the boy's death.'

'Well, thank God! We don't want the Society's dirty linen washed in public.'

'Perhaps not, but I warn you I shall raise it at the next Curators' meeting.'

'I don't think you will, Simon.'

'Why shouldn't I?'

'Because you're not an absolute shit.'

Continuing calmly he said, 'Well, they live at Wembley so that'll be perfectly convenient for the R.C. cemetery at Kensal Green. Diana will drive us.'

'I had no idea you knew the North West London suburbs so well, Matthew.'

'Oh, well, I do you see. Our governess lived there for years.'

He rang twice again that afternoon. Once to tell me that the Filsons' parish priest would attend the baked meats.

'So that's all right,' he said in comment.

The second time it was to tell me that Bobby Falcon was uncertain whether Jane could attend.

'She has to go to a read-through whatever that may be,'

he said. 'Anyway the Filsons won't understand what it is, so maybe they won't be offended.'

I had to check through the camera arrangements with the Director so I told Mrs Jamieson that I could not speak to Mr Price again that afternoon. Twice Matthew appeared at the open door of my room where I was talking with Leacock. Each time on seeing Leacock he stared for a moment and then disappeared. On a third occasion, the Director said sharply, 'Yes, what is it, Price?'

'I just wanted a word with Carter, if that's all right.'

'Yes, yes, go ahead.'

'I was just wondering, you see, Simon, since Jane Falcon isn't going to be there whether perhaps you could persuade your wife. You see, it would be a compliment to the Filsons and then Diana wouldn't be the only lady.'

I suddenly felt deeply ashamed of this gross snobbery.

I said sharply, 'I really don't know.'

'Oh, well, I'll get Diana to ring her and ask.'

He scuttled away like the White Rabbit on an errand. Realizing a moment later that his snobbery which usually made me laugh had only caused me unease because of Leacock's presence, I was annoyed with my lack of self-assurance.

When I was leaving the Zoo late that evening about half past eight, I found a note that had been left in my secretary's room: 'Rely on you at tomorrow's baked meats to keep the conversation off dreary Declaration and Falcon's boring balls-up of boy's death – Matthew.' He seemed to me like a spoilt child who was out to annoy and I felt glad that I had snapped at him in front of Leacock.

I was exhausted when I reached home; I felt apprehensive about the next day's gathering. Then despite all my admiration for Leacock's scheme and even for the general outlines of the television programme by which he hoped to further it, I was increasingly irritated by the arrogant slipshodness which had left all the detailed, hard work to me and my staff. I was embarrassed too at being associated with such muddle in the eyes of the B.B.C. staff, many of whom I knew; and even more by what I felt sure they were thinking of the second-rate generalizations with which Leacock tried breezily to make light of his mistakes and omissions. Through everything else the thought that I must soon take action to avenge young Filson or else leave the grievance to poison my relations with my Zoo colleagues for good, nagged away at me. I was in the mood in fact to be both a snappish, tired husband and a pernickety, exacting civil servant.

I was not in a mood for the suffused, instinctive gaiety with which the Declaration had filled Martha's American liberal heart. That this light-heartedness made her younger, more attractive, more sweetly and gently asking to be loved than I had known her for some considerable time only made me feel the sourer. I thought of myself as a man who, always carrying last year's diary and an erratic watch, would for ever arrive at his appointments too early or too late.

Martha, indeed, was so happy, her fears so exorcized that her gaiety had no need to spill over me as I set foot in the house. She was ready for my exhaustion, quiet without any nerve-teasing ostentation of hushedness; she had seen that Jacqueline's silly brightness was not there to disturb me, had arranged with Grazia my favourite meal – osso buco, a light red chianti, zabaglione. I tried very hard but I could not purr. For more than half an hour Martha continued to keep silent, then suddenly she cried.

'Oh, Simon, I know how tired you are, darling. And I know you were wise and level-headed all along, but please rejoice with me that there isn't going to be any war. Oh, Simon, you don't know how awful it's been this week for people like me.' I had my own ideas of the motives for the Russo-American Declaration: Russia's preoccupation with Asia; America's distaste for growing British neutrality. But I did not harp on such cynical views.

I said, 'I'm very glad. I think it may go a long way to making us see reason. That is, if it doesn't cause too much resentment here or in France and Germany for that matter.'

She cried, 'Oh, phooey to Western Europe in that case. They'll just have to toe the line if the big Powers say so.'

'I hope so,' I said. 'Déclassé nations are very touchy you know.'

I tried not to exaggerate the measured reasonableness of my tone, but I failed.

Martha cried, 'Oh, for God's sake, Simon, it *is* the most wonderful thing and I don't care a damn for your European cleverness, seeing this side and that and spoiling every hopefulness with your doubts and despairs. It'll be about the only good thing the British and French and all the lot of you have done with your backyard squabbles – to make us see sense once in a while and break through that damned Iron Curtain.'

I said, 'You'd have agreed with Sanderson at lunch in the canteen: "So it's taken us little ones to bring the big chaps together."'

I caught the absolute fatuity of Sanderson's voice to a tee. Martha's hands trembled; she picked up a coffee cup. For a moment its olive green and gold shimmered in the light of the lamp behind her; I had already seen it shattered, even ducked my head to avoid the coloured splinters, when she put it down again in its saucer very determinedly.

'I don't mean what Sanderson means and you know it. Or maybe I do too. All I know is that the great shadows that have been hovering over us for so long – the great good shadow My country 'tis of thee – and I mean that, Simon, it is my country – and the great big bogey shadow that's been glowing a lurid red over there ever since I was a kid and frightening the life out of me – have come together for a moment. If they never come together again, it doesn't matter. They've done it. And they've done it for the right reasons. To stop all you little whiners from blowing up the civilization that you're always boasting that you alone have made. That's history, Simon, and no cavilling can stop it from being so.'

I thought of Edwin Leacock's remark; it seemed that everyone was determined to accuse me of failing to see history. I got up from my chair and put on a record of the Italian Symphony. I wanted something familiar, good and yet not profound, to purge me of all these enthusiasms and anxieties which people had been unloading on me for the last few weeks. I wanted more immediately to prevent further possibly disastrous talk with Martha.

But she had to pursue me.

She said, 'The only comment you can find on a great moment in history is to repeat an idiotic remark of an old fool like Sanderson.'

I said, 'I'm not very good at historic moments, darling, you know that. I was taught history on a different principle. In any case it's people that interest me, that concern me if you like. That's why Sanderson's reaction fascinated me.'

'People? People seem pretty dumb by the time you've finished with them.'

I got up and stopped the record.

Martha said, 'Oh, darling, I'm sorry. But you know how I think you're wasting your spirit away on a lot of people that aren't worth your while. You weren't meant to be involved with people. And even if you had the gift, so have millions of others. It's a feminine gift. Most women have it. I have. But you've got quite another thing. You can observe creatures and things. That's much rarer . . .'

I cut her short. I simply could not hear again the story of her disappointment with me.

I said, 'I am not a trained zoologist, Martha. And it's too late for me to be so. You must accept that finally.'

'All right, Simon, you aren't. But you were only the best naturalist on television when I married you. Only that. Was that nothing?'

'I'm a respectable man, Martha. Not a popular entertainer.'

She refused to let me off with a laugh. At times like this I hated her integrity and her innocence. I did not want to be saved from myself. She was seated on the arm of a sofa looking away from me, her head down, her whole body slumped in disappointment. I had taken away the beauty bred of her gaiety which had greeted my homecoming. I could with pleasure have hit her.

I shouted at her, 'I'm sorry that you feel you've wasted yourself. I'm sorry if your money could have been better spent. It so happens that I've been working very hard. But of course seeing that an organization is run properly isn't among your duties as a hero. Nevertheless I *have* been working very hard, I'm very tired and I'm going to bed.'

Much later that night I woke from a heavy sleep to feel her buttocks pressed taut against my thigh. I could tell by the tension that she was awake. I turned her towards me and began to kiss and caress her, hoping to relax her tension. Martha's was not the only *naïveté* in the home. She held rigid against me, and, having failed to force her to surrender, I fell into sleep again.

Martha was up next morning before I had woken. I did not see her until I came down to the breakfast table. All the radical fighting egghead manner of her American mother had gone from her. She spoke in that strange social English voice that she must have learned as a child from her father's mother. It rang bells of long ago, recalling my great-aunts or rather the grander of their county friends – voices that had been trained and nuanced before Victoria died. She seemed to be embattled behind the toast and tea and Seville Orange Marmalade.

'Will you call for me for this funeral, darling? Or shall I make my way there with Jane?'

'Good God! You're not coming are you? There's absolutely no need.'

'But Matthew Price telephoned and asked me . . .'

'What if he did? For once I'm quite sure he's got the protocol wrong. There's no call for wives to be present. In any case, it was only if Jane Falcon wasn't going to be there. To keep Diana company. In Matthew's phrase "so that she won't be the only lady".'

'But, Simon, surely Matthew wouldn't make a mistake of that kind. You've often told me how much you admire him for his social sense, and how all that snobbery of his is rather endearing.'

I pushed my plate away in what I have no doubt was a very petulant manner.

'To my taste,' I said, 'scrambled eggs should be scrambled, not cooked like a face flannel. And people like you whose charm lies in being ingénue shouldn't try to be bitchy. It doesn't suit them.'

'I don't think Grazia understands very well. But I'll tell her.'

I tried a desperate retrieval by whimsy.

I said, 'I shouldn't say the bit about bitchy to her. She might not understand.'

Martha ignored this. 'If your work at the Zoo is so important, then I think I ought to play my part as the Secretary's wife.'

I tried to give her the serious reasons.

'Matthew is a fool to have arranged the party. And more than a fool. What are the wretched Filsons going to feel like entertaining Falcon and, for all I know, Strawson after what happened to their son?'

'Oh, my dear, of course, they'll take it as a compliment. Their emotions can't be judged by ours, you know. I'm sure Matthew's told you that.'

I restrained myself from saying, 'What do you know about the British?'

I said, 'In any case, if I'm to continue with my inquiries into what really happened it will be a great embarrassment to be forced to be there with the Filsons and the people who may have been to blame.'

'*If* you're going to continue?'

'All right, *since* I'm going to . . .'

'Well, having your wife there will help,' Martha said. Then she asked, 'I've only got two black hats, darling, that large straw I bought for some unaccountable reason for the Garden Party and a silly little one with some nonsense on it that I could take off. Which would be correct for the Secretary's wife?'

I threw down my napkin and walked out of the dining-room.

Wanting formal etiquette, respect for the old Filsons alone could guide our behaviour. It was no help to me that, although my liking for the old man increased with the occasion, I took an instant dislike to Mrs Filson.

She was not old, hardly perhaps sixty, but she was formidable and square and deeply unsure of herself. She sat a massive figure in their lounge, receiving court and yet not quite knowing what to do with it. She sat too in a tight short skirt with thick legs wide apart, showing her underwear. I dislike above everything old women who obtrude what I wish to associate only with the young and desirable. That she was shy I could tell from the momentary tremblings of her square untweezered jaw; but she disguised her shyness in an aggressive jollity peculiarly inappropriate to the occasion and more inappropriate still, I am sure, poor thing, to her real emotions.

Matthew decided on the 'correct' means of dealing with the gathering. In ordinary circumstances it would have been a good one. He pursued memories of Zoo 'characters' both human and avine, or rather he encouraged Filson, who had a fund of stories, to tell them, confining his own part to comments that seemed like the responses in some litany – 'Oh God! The woman with the eagle owl. Yes, do go on about her', 'the Amherst's pheasant that killed the tragopan. Have I forgotten? My dear Filson, the sheer beauty of that fight. Yes, do tell.' 'Oh, Lord! Hastings, you see, the worst keeper we ever had. I'm sure he killed that condor.'

Matthew's *idea* of a common topic indeed might well have succeeded. Strangers – the Filson relatives, the parish priest, Father Hansford – were like most of the public fascinated by Zoo talk; this public interest is something that those of us who work there find hard to remember. All Zoo womenfolk – Martha, Jane, Matthew's sister Diana – have been conditioned over years to make the right faces at the birth of the tigon, the death of the okapi or the kiwi, and the unsatisfactory reactions of walruses or sea elephants to captivity.

All, it seemed, save Mrs Filson. Like many a Zoo wife – like Martha, God help me – she held the purse strings. The large nineteen-fifties house with its lounge and model kitchen in which we were met was hers, a legacy from her well-to-do builder father. From her unsure domination Filson, it became obvious, took refuge in the Zoo, a world that he kept apart. And so apart that she was clearly not just bored, but angrily ignorant. Would I, would Martha fight such battles in thirty years? The thought did not lessen my dislike of Mrs Filson.

'Is it true,' asked Father Hansford, 'that the snakes are still fed on live rabbits?'

'Now, Father,' Mrs Filson protested, 'I'm surprised at you. Encouraging him to talk about the nasty things that happen at that place.'

She looked around the room with a certain triumph – to demonstrate, I think, that devout Catholic though she was, or rather perhaps since she was, she was no particular respecter of Father Hansford apart from his office.

Father Hansford was also the jolly sort, but altogether more agreeable.

He said, 'Oh come, it ill behoves us to criticize the brute creation, Mrs Filson.' In mock horror, he turned to the old man. 'Come on now, Mr Filson, come straight as they say, do you feed poor live creatures to those horrible beasts?'

It was obvious that old Filson was a favourite of the priest's, and that in turn he loved to be teased in this way.

'I'm sorry I can't oblige you, Father. That was all put an end to in my own father's time. That was the work of Sir Peter Chalmers-Mitchell, I believe, wasn't it, Mr Price?'

'Oh,' said Matthew, 'Chalmers-Mitchell!' His voice had a note of deep veneration. 'I don't know anything about him, do you?' he added.

'I can't see Dr Englander allowing anything of that kind. Not him,' old Filson chuckled.

I wondered at his image of Englander, who I could easily imagine reviving 'live' feeding if he felt it was in accord with up-to-date continental methods.

'We'll have to put on an exhibition for you with live

rattlesnakes and Percy, Father.' Percy was a secretary bird and clearly a great favourite of Filson's. 'Now that would be something to see.'

'Charlie, you've talked enough. Make yourself useful with the wine.' Mrs Filson's tone was not playful.

Old Filson's little head on its scraggy wrinkled neck seemed to slip back into his slumped old body like a tortoise.

Matthew, ignoring his hostess, plunged on with Zoo reminiscence, while Diana Price tried to distract Mrs Filson with admiration for the lounge. Mrs Filson was momentarily pleased, but her misery combined with her unease would not allow her to leave her husband unbridled.

'I'll never forgive that man. "Neither grapes nor carrots," he said to me. "Neither grapes nor carrots, Mr Filson. There's a war on."' The old man was in full spate.

'Oh, God!' Matthew cried. 'Men from ministries. Like Mr Carter.'

'I'm sure Mr Carter would never have been so awkward. There was you away at the war, Mr Price. And what could I do? "Neither grapes nor carrots," the man said. And twelve of the toucans died. I'll never forgive him.'

'Toucans!' his wife cried, 'It's shameful of you, Charlie. Twelve toucans dead! Is that all you can find to mourn at the present time?'

He must have thought, as I did, that she was about to burst out in grief for their son, for he murmured, 'I was only talking, Dot, to help.'

But she had turned to Matthew now, as though he were responsible for the whole affair – as indeed in some ways he was.

'*You* may not see, Mr Price, what it means, but it's all too clear to many of us. Those devils have got what they want. A Declaration to stop war. The cunning of it! Well the Yanks'll soon see what they've done. It's not so clever to sit down to a table with the Devil. He has a long spoon. The Church has always told them what would happen.'

Father Hansford moved uneasily, and perhaps one felt that

she had been carried away to speak out of turn, for she asked, 'Has the Holy Father made any pronouncement yet?'

It was clear to me that she was addressing her priest, but Matthew chose to take the question to himself.

He said, 'Oh, Lord! I'm afraid I don't know. My allegiance is to Canterbury, you see.'

I think it unlikely that he had attended any religious service since his schooldays, but there were echoing overtones of historic and social rebuke in his answer. He went straight on. 'Did you ever hear how I nearly procured a moa for the Gardens? Well, that's what the dealer claimed it was.'

We all laughed. But we had reckoned without Martha. She came across from the other side of the lounge and sat down beside Mrs Filson.

Very quietly but with intense urgency, she said, 'Perhaps I shouldn't speak to you like this on today of all days, but how can you talk like that?'

Some deadness in the old woman's face seemed suddenly to anger her, for she cried, 'All right you and your generation don't care. But I do. I've got children.' Then, as suddenly, she seized the old woman's hands and held them tight in her own. 'Oh, please forgive me. I had no right. No right at all.'

Whatever Mrs Filson's reaction may have been, my attention was entirely distracted by Diana Price. She got up from her seat and spoke in that loud, clear voice which people 'in the body of the hall' are always urged to use.

'I sometimes wonder,' she said, 'what these extraordinary people think we are. Or what they think Europe is, for that matter. If we do this or that, *they* will annihilate us with their combined strength. Like a lot of self-appointed nannies! As though countries that have had centuries of diplomatic experience couldn't settle their differences without outside interference.'

Matthew said, 'Oh God! Diana darling, please.'

I felt I could not leave Martha to answer so ridiculous a challenge.

I said, 'You say "if we do this or that", but the Declaration is quite clear, Diana. It says that if, in European quarrels, we, the French or the Germans resort to nuclear weapons of any kind, then the Great Powers will retaliate upon the culprits. If they can't stop us from the madness of fighting, they are determined to limit our mischief. For myself, I must say that I agree with Martha – that West and East should together make this clear may force us to think twice. And, if so, it may have saved the world.'

To my surprise I did silence Diana; but to my even greater surprise I found that my words had loosed the tongues of everyone else. Filson relatives – and there seemed suddenly to be a host of them – were clucking and quacking, gobbling and hissing like some great poultry market or Goose Fair. It was only then that I realized how, in my absorption with Leacock's programme, I had been cut off from the general noise. This was not Matthew Price's echo of the official voice, or Martha's human cry of hope, but a noise of panic. I have written poultry, but it was the terror of ostriches whose heads have been rudely pulled out of the sand.

'I think it's shameful to talk like that. *They'll* drop a nuclear bomb on *us* if we don't – '

'I didn't know what to do when little Gwenda came home and said the teacher had told them the Americans and Russians were going to drop the bomb on us. She was shivering all over.'

'Poor little mite. Some of them teachers forget what it was like to be a child.'

'A child! I think it's bad enough for us. I was under the drier when this girl started on about it. And I said don't tell me . . .'

'Mind you, there's no agreement between these scientists that it would do the harm they say it would. They're all at sixes and sevens.'

'Don't talk to me about sixes and sevens! That's been half the trouble.'

'A chap I know was saying that the trouble is that as soon as these technical blokes try to put things into the plain man's language, they're up against it. As a result we get a very distorted picture.'

'Of course, mind you, half the trouble has come from calling it "the bomb" like that . . .'

'Well, of course, the sensationalism's appalling. But then some people just get a kick out of making other people's flesh creep.'

'I must say that I think this is a very unsuitable occasion to raise the subject.'

'It's not as if it's not in all our minds, but what can we do?'

'That's one of the troubles, people have become bomb-conditioned.'

The buzz around me grew until it seemed to come from everybody in the room. Everybody except a rather pretty blonde girl who was sitting on the edge of a chair in the corner of the room. She stood out from the rest of the company, for her deep black mourning had a sort of chic, but she looked so haggard and tired and washed-out that her smartness seemed somehow disreputable. Perhaps it was the black suit she wore, against which her white face, pale lips and green eye shade stared out so macabrely. She, at any rate, was free from the general chattering, commonplace panic, but she gave me little comfort – shut off so far away in her little universe, she might, I thought, be mad. Bobby Falcon was staring down at a dumpy, middle-aged woman who was saying to him, 'I may be unimaginative, but the road deaths seem far more real to me.' He looked down at her with undisguised contempt, but he was not, I felt sure, free from the general distress. Only Jane, sitting so unusually silent and unsociable, was really aloof and calm, yet her expression suddenly irritated me – she seemed complacent.

I went across to her and said, 'I suppose the state of the nation hasn't percolated to the green rooms of England yet. After all, the show must go on.'

'Not up to your best form, Simon,' she said smiling, 'You're rattled. Anyhow everyone knows that theatre people will respond down to the last and oldest trouper if the country calls.'

She followed my still questing gaze round the room. Near to us a stout man said, 'Of course, a lot of the experts says the nuclear threat is very exaggerated. I'm perfectly convinced myself that if the newspapers talked less about it . . .'

This so relieved the woman to whom he spoke that she cut him short.

'Oh, I do so agree with *that*,' she said and sighed with relief.

Jane smiled, 'Dear Simon, always so good with people. This afternoon is a triumph.' Then almost angrily, she added, 'Go on. Do something about it. I challenge you.'

I felt obscurely that to ignore the challenge would somehow endanger my future, 'spoil my luck'; the superstition annoyed me, yet it was too strong to resist. I had no other opiate to offer the company but the one that had drugged me all the week. Seeing Filson and Diana silent for a moment, I went over to them and spoke loudly to gather if possible the attention of the whole party.

'The cameramen were delighted with your waders, Filson. The Director was as pleased as Punch. After all a large scale waders' sanctuary will be one of the foundations of his Reserve when he gets it. I must say I was a bit reluctant to involve myself in this T.V. thing of his, but the more I work on it . . .'

I sounded to myself a little like an encouraging hearty parson.

'Do you think you could get me another glass of wine, Mr Filson?' Diana said. 'The rosé, as I'm driving.'

Then when he had moved away, she turned to me and spoke in a markedly quiet voice to emphasize that there was no return of her hysteria.

'I don't want to criticize Dr Leacock in front of Filson, but I'll tell you now that in my opinion he ought to be put on trial. I think it's appalling, at this moment in our history, that he should be devoting all his efforts to a self-advertisement campaign of this kind. Talk of fiddling while Rome burns. We deserve to be annihilated!'

Her determination had broken down and her voice had risen. Bobby Falcon smiled at her across the room and drawled loudly, 'Annihilated, Miss Price? Of course we do. Any society that tolerates houses as ugly as this, for example...'

Even Jane's composure was broken.

She said, 'Bobby darling, you're drunk.'

But it was Martha who went over to him and took his arm. She seemed to be smiling.

She said, 'Dear Bobby, just because your travelling days are over, or you like to think they are, you're quite happy to have everybody blown up to comfort you, aren't you? Or rather it makes you feel a devil to think that you are. You are a dreadful old poseur.' She squeezed his arm and he smiled down at her.

'And you're almost as ghastly a prig as your husband, my beautiful Martha,' he said.

Martha's behaviour astonished me: she was usually either respectful or impatient of her distinguished godfather, now she seemed lovingly patient and entirely disrespectful. And he, in his turn, showed a happy acceptance of her manner. What perhaps was more mysterious to me was that all the tension of the gathering seemed to vanish with the spectacle. The dirty word 'nuclear' might never have been spoken – family gossip, eating, drinking, commonplace discussion soon made the scene all that Matthew might have expected, all that I dared not hope for. I embarked upon one of my best Zoo stories, that of the French lady who erupted into my office one afternoon: 'I 'ate the 'ippo that 'as eaten my 'at.' A small group were enjoying my imitation. Mrs Filson was having a last confidential word with Father Hansford who announced that he must leave. Soon the whole thing would be over. The explosions had been disconcerting but not devastating. We should have performed Matthew's idea of our duty without too disastrous a result.

Then into the gentle, decorous chattering there crept another sound, also gentle at first, but frightening – a little stifled moaning that grew higher and higher until it broke into a hysterical, hiccoughing sobbing. There, more isolated than before as people seemed to draw away from her uncontrolled grief, sat the blonde girl, screwing her handkerchief desperately in her fingers, tears pouring down her cheeks. She was not I saw now, a girl, but a ravaged-looking thirty-year-old woman. Filson walked over and, putting an arm round her shoulders, helped her from her seat.

'Come along with Dad, Kay. There's been too much of it all, hasn't there?'

The eyelids came down over his little tortoise eyes as though to shut us all out; and yet, I think, he was quite unconscious of the emotional scene he was involved in.

The girl began, 'I'm so sorry, Mrs Filson. I tried. I did really.' Then she started to sob again. 'I thought you'd all forgotten Derek. And I want him. I want Derek. I want him.'

Mrs Filson got up from the sofa with surprising speed. Her eyes were quite wild. I thought she was going to hit the girl.

She cried, '*You* want him! What do you think I felt when you'd taken him away from me? A woman old enough to be his mother! And where did he find you? You were never our sort of person!' Father Hansford came up and touched her arm. She seemed at once to soften. She cried, 'Father, I can't like her. It's no good.'

The girl said, 'You were jealous. You couldn't let him go. But you've never thought of him today.'

'We have some sense of how to behave.'

'Silly snobs! What do I care for this lot?' She looked round at us disgustedly, 'I want Derek. That's all.'

Old Filson led her away out of the room; Father Hansford took Mrs Filson back to the sofa, where she sat, red-faced, trying not to burst into tears.

Matthew came over to me. 'Oh, God! The fiancée you see,' he said.

But I think most people were as overcome as I was with misery and guilt, for they began almost silently to make their departures.

Just as I was leaving, old Filson reappeared and, speaking

in an embarrassed whisper, asked me if he could have a word with me. He took me into the large back garden and we paced the lawn between the vegetable plots and the flowerbeds. Moments of moral decision play a ludicrously large role in my life. Each has left its associated images superimposed upon one another like a Victorian scrapwork screen. Now for some time there have loomed over all other objects, fleshy leaves of onion, minute lettuces, like specks of marzipan upon a rich chocolate earth, and a peculiarly hideous khaki and purple early lupin.

'Mr Price tells me you're not happy about the coroner's inquest, Sir,' he said. We were clearly back on an official level.

'I thought it was perfunctory.'

'Ah! Mrs Filson and I were very satisfied. We wanted to thank you for the way in which publicity has been avoided.'

'You have the Director to thank for that.'

'Derek hadn't been there long, Sir, but he'd already got a great feeling for the old place. Of course, it was in his blood. But you've no idea how proud he was to be working at the London Zoo. It brought him near to quarrels with his mother, I'm afraid. He wouldn't hear a word said against it.'

I tried to speak gently but firmly, 'Look, Filson, if you're wanting to tell me that your son would not have wished to look further into the causes of his death, I can't accept that as a reason. It may seem presumptuous of me to say it to you, but the truth is that no one however close can tell what the dead would have wished.'

'*I* should like you not to do so, Sir. The Zoo means a lot to me.'

'The Zoo should be run properly and competently. It's surely our duty to see that it is.'

'Yes. I've thought of that, Mr Carter.'

The change of his address seemed to suggest that he was both easier and less patient with me.

'To be honest, it's the point of view I first put to Mr Price. But he pointed out that no good can come to the place from a lot of unpleasant things being said.'

'I believe you know how fond I am of Mr Price. But you also know as well as I do that he doesn't like anything unpleasant brought to his notice. That isn't a good enough reason for leaving this business alone, is it? In any case, I want to hear about your feelings, not Mr Price's.'

The intolerable thought came to me that I should have to hear myself speak in these housemasterly tones many times before I had done with the business. Yet that sad blonde's accusation sounded in my ears set against the cackling panic of the ostriches. Before Filson could answer me I went on.

'No, nothing's going to alter my resolution, Filson. I'm sorry, but we're all too busy these days forgetting what we don't want to remember.'

The old man stopped for a moment. More than ever he brought back the good old gardener of my boyhood, as he bent to pick a fat green caterpillar from one of the young lettuces. Squashing it between thumb and forefinger, he wiped the remains off on a blade of grass.

'*I* shan't *forget*, Mr Carter. I told the man he wouldn't be welcome here today. I shan't forget that he failed in his duty to my son.'

For a moment I was puzzled, then I said, 'We can't be sure that Strawson was to blame.'

'The young keepers that work under me are in my charge. I see to it that their conditions are as good as I can make them. I see to it that they get all the training they need before they're left on their own. Yes, even when it's against their temperament, I check them. Young Larkin'll tell you that. I'm not boasting. It's the duty of any good head keeper. Barrett in the Big Cats would do the same, or Kennedy with the reptiles, any of the lot of them. I shan't forget Strawson's neglect of Derek, Sir, you need not worry about that.'

'But you have to consider the orders the man may have been given. I don't want to make accusations, but . . .'

'You'd best say no more. In any case a good head keeper sees that he *does* get the right orders. It's not my affair to look higher than Strawson.'

This mystic N.C.O. stuff was beyond my powers of refutation.

I said, 'Well, I'm afraid that I think it is *my* affair.'

As though continuing with a story already familiar to me, he said, 'You don't know *how* hard it's been for her. She always thought Kay was too old for him and not serious enough. She called it an infatuation. To tell the truth it was a strange thing. She's a dance hostess, and, though she's a good girl and it's no criticism, she won't see thirty-five again. And Derek had such different interests, singing with the choral society, singing good stuff. She refused to recognize the engagement. And then she hated him being at the Zoo, she thought it was a waste. They were always rowing in the last months. You don't know what she's going through now. Her only child. It's no good my telling her not to blame herself. Do you think it'll help her to know that he needn't have died?'

I said, 'There's no reason why anything that happens in the Society's meetings should reach your wife's ears.'

'Strawson'll see to that. He's said so. If there's any blame put on him, he'll give it all the publicity he can. It's natural enough he should.' When I did not answer, he went on another tack. 'You haven't seen Dot at her best. She seems hard with Kay, but she doesn't find it easy to show soft feelings where she hasn't got them. She's a shy woman, Dot is.' He was talking fast now, as I am sure he never did normally, but he was pleading his wife's case desperately. 'She doesn't find it easy to get on with people. But she's been wonderful to us – Derek and me – Mother has.'

As we turned back to the house, he asked, 'You'll think about it, at least, won't you, Sir?'

I answered, 'I shall not be able to think of anything else.'

I had taken an instant dislike to Mrs Filson for her charmless lack of assurance. It was clear that this had been her normal lot in life. How could I further hurt such a person? In any case I should at least let my conscience ponder over the problem until the television programme was out of the way.

3

LIMITED LIBERTY

BACK at the office, Leacock ignored the cause of my absence.

He said, 'Oh, there you are, Carter. They're filming the coypus up at Oulton Broad on Thursday. I think you'd better go up with them. I've got to be here to check the final scenes of this place at night. I've set a lot of importance on showing how much wild life really comes alive at night time and what the public fail to see by having no National Reserve.' A little later he said, 'It's rather a nuisance your having to go up to Norfolk on Thursday, I'm having a tremendous tussle over music and commentary. These television people are so dyed in the wool. But you seem to have a way with them.'

I said, 'If I could be in two places at once, believe me . . .'

'Yes. You don't seem to have been able to be in one today. There have been a hundred things I have wanted to refer to you.'

'I was at young Filson's funeral.'

He stood still and looked straight into my eyes.

'If we can pull this thing off, Carter, a shocking thing like that boy's death will be an impossibility in the future. It's worth fighting for, you know.'

I am sure that at that time I did not question this or a score of other battle slogans with which he urged us on during that week. Mrs Purrett came increasingly to resemble a fervent and highly coloured blancmange as she carried out her manifold small errands at the double; Rackham was forever bringing the last message that had got through to the beleaguered fortress, and thoroughly he enjoyed the drama of his role. As we worked late each evening over our coffee and sausage rolls or sandwiches we did not care, for there was our Chief working as late, indeed later, and encouraging us now and then with a word of thanks. I describe it with irony and yet at the time I was in a strange double mood that matched the Director's; to his egotism, his spurious self-dramatization, I presented a detached amusement that canalized my anger away from the thought that competent preparatory work could have avoided the whole 'strafe' as he liked to call our excessive labours; to his enthusiasm, his belief, his suddenly released imagination, I returned such powers of suspension of disbelief as I possessed. I found myself a more zealous believer than I had supposed possible; or perhaps he was a more potent spellbinder. In either case by the eve of the programme belief had driven out irony. I was already encased in his woven cocoon, although I knew it only in single threads and had no idea of its total form. I suppose I had composed it in my own ideal shape, for I responded to Leacock's constant self assurances that it was 'as good as he could make it' by a belief that it was probably perfect. None of the senior staff had been asked to take part on the night; and I found myself childishly envying Rackham who was to make a brief appearance opening a gate – gates in large numbers were to heighten the prison-like image of the Regent's Park set-up that viewers would absorb.

When I departed that evening, dispatched early by the Director on the ground that I must be fresh for his finished product, I left behind a mass of cables and cameras and microphones that seemed already to hold in their impersonal womb the foetus of Truth; outside the Zoo I crossed the road and at once knew Doubt. This Truth I was so eagerly awaiting was not the child of these careful precise machines; it had been conceived in the reckless, imprecise mind of Dr Leacock. Yet if only to justify my own weeks of zealotry I determined to hold my disbelief suspended. I deserted Martha and the children for the safe inertia of a very hot bath; to avoid the embarrassing faith of Leacock's naïve family and the deadening scepticism of the Falcons I insisted that we should arrive at Mrs Leacock's 'do' only a few seconds before the programme began. In fact the lists of technicians' meaningless names were already slowly pursuing one another off the screen when we tiptoed to our chintz-covered seats before the telescreen in the large drawing-room of the Director's London flat.

I tried to create around myself a desert, in the full knowledge that, on one side of me sat Martha ready to stiffen with boredom, and that, on the other, the Leacock's eldest, most priggish of sons was already swelling with vicarious importance from the sight of his father's name in white block capitals. Into this rather self-conscious desert loomed the face of a well-known young commentator, eyes a little too saxe blue, mouth a little disconcertingly vermilion.

He said, 'Men have dreamed dreams, strange dreams. Dreams, some of them that have vanished into the limbo of cranky illusion, dreams, others that have changed history, have altered the patterns of what men and women – you and I – think and say and do. In this series we shall try with the aid of all that the modern telescreen can do to give life to some interesting dreams of some interesting and unusual people.'

As he talked on I felt the bitter testiness of every bureaucrat who sees for a moment the feeble policy to which his hard working accuracy has contributed. Then I heard the voice continue, 'The first of these dreamers gives you his dream tonight – Dr Edwin Leacock, Director of the London Zoo.'

I waited for the well-known ugly mug, the strabismic beady eyes to peer at us down the long pointed nose, but instead I saw in quick succession flashes of many English cities, of the congested streets, the overcrowded buses, the lunch-hour restaurants, and then, at a slower tempo, short scenes of life on various social levels in flats, houses, factories, offices, and cafés. The scenes were familiar, the dialogue not new in its evocation of a modern strangled, frustrated existence; yet the total scene produced a most powerful effect of dismal, hopeless claustrophobia. What added to this effect was the total absence of the familiar otiose commentary or musical sequence, only the noises and voices came to us that related to what we saw. All the cloying irrelevance of so much documentary had vanished. I knew now what Leacock's tussle had been about and I honoured him for his victory. Then came Leacock's voice.

'I call that, the death of man's soul.'

There was a touch of didactic self satisfaction that inevitably jarred after the excellent pictorial statement, but it was a little palliated though not entirely erased by his adding, 'The phrase isn't new any more than the idea. Lots of people have used it before. I tried to think of a better, simpler one, but I couldn't find it.'

Now suddenly we saw photographs of the Zoo – animals, birds, reptiles, fish, even insects, he had managed to direct the camera at all of them so that they were seen cornered, cramped, monotonously pacing backwards and forwards across what seemed minute spaces, flying to the tops of oppressively low cages, swimming in desperate circles, jostling one another at the corners of dwarf rockeries or midget pools. It was grossly unfair and immensely effective. Then followed a sequence of what might have been called a satire on Bobby Falcon's dream – hideous, tired, Bank Holiday crowds moronically looking through bars at creatures they could hardly discern, creatures as listless, dragging in their steps and whining in their cries as the children that watched them. The total picture was pathetic and funny and also very off-putting; I wondered if perhaps Leacock had overreached himself here, for its caricature quality must surely strike many of the viewers who had visited the Gardens. Finally in this section came Rackham's little moment. One after another, as the visitors departed, gates clanged to, locks were secured, keys swung from chains, a whole sense of prison house came out of the screen. And suddenly, as night came and the public was gone, animals everywhere began to wake up and cavort in delightful antics, display their intricate lines and gaudy or subtle colours, no longer to live what had seemed to be a feeble, dejected life in anthropomorphoid guise; yet even this life was subtly seen to be less than full by reason of the bars and ditches. It was a distorted picture: some of the less interesting nocturnal creatures like the viscacia were simply not shown, some of the star turns like gibbons that weaved in patterns and howled were as much to be seen by day as by night. Even so there were enough night creatures – owls, flying foxes, aardvarks, bushbabies – to make a substantial claim to truth. Leacock's voice came, and I dreaded some underlying truism.

All he said was, 'That is Regent's Park. Since the closing of Whipsnade Park five years ago for reasons of economy the sole place where the truly remarkable collection of animals in the possession of the Zoological Society can be displayed to the public. Those of you who know the Zoo well may think that it is hardly a fair picture. It is not. This is my dream and that is my nightmare. However, on reflection, you may well decide that it is a more meaningful picture than that of the guide books and traditional stories.'

Now to my surprise there appeared a series of pictures of the former Green Belts around our cities. And then a delightful series of satirically chosen shots of cabinet ministers, speculative builders, estate agents, suburban householders welcoming the final legal abolition of the Green Belt zones in 1967 – a wonderful display of greed, philistinism and smug complacency. Especially pleasing was a shot of the Minister of Housing addressing the first group of building labourers to 'march in' as 'our new pioneers, our men of the covered wagon'.

'That countryside,' said Dr Leacock, 'was sacrificed in the name of boom and expansion. Whipsnade Park was abandoned in the name of slump and retrenchment.'

Now an air survey took us over the British Isles, highlighting its four preserves 'Zones of Scenic Beauty' – the Scottish Highlands, the Welsh Marches across to Snowdonia, the Northern Marches, and the little Norfolk Sanctuaries.

'Until last year,' Leacock's voice now had the denunciatory accents of Jeremiah or Habakkuk, 'there was a fifth area of countryside in our land, but Exmoor and Dartmoor have now gone the way of the South Downs. I did not think it necessary to bring to your notice the miraculous housing developments, the grand factory sitings that private enterprise has provided in New Taunton, Exeter West and Plymouth Drakeville.

Advertisement has already more than familiarized us with them.'

It was a momentary flash of his youthful socialism and his voice suggested to me that he had once been a fiercer man less padded with spurious *bonhomie*. And now we saw flashes from a variety of Brains Trusts and Face to Face interviews covering a large percentage of our better known intellectual and academic personalities. Inconclusively, feebly, despairingly, they discussed or answered questions upon either of the two themes of our deadened soul and our lost countryside. And then Dr Leacock's voice came through theirs suggesting that perhaps the two subjects were not so separate as they supposed, that perhaps these intellectuals could not answer because the developed intellect had crowded out their senses and their intuition, that perhaps man's soul could only be healed by replenishing these deeper sources of cognition. And so we came to Leacock's dream. From the mammal life selected by me, films of marten and badger, wild cat, coypu, red deer, and mole, we passed to avocets, ptarmigans, reed buntings, bitterns and crested grebes; and on through the reptile, insect and fish worlds we surveyed British fauna. Then we saw the wolves and wild boars, the wisents, bears and rebred aurocks, the bustards and storks of historical times. Then Whipsnade and Tring and Woburn were called in to show how wallabies, elands, zebras and gnus could live among us. The diminishing game reserves of Tanganyika and the Dingaan (formerly Kruger) National Park, Tserengeti, the reserves of India and Sumatra, Yellowstone, Yosemite, the Soviet Arctic Animals Park, the new Jungle Paradiso of the Amazon passed before us – their methods of security, their varying freedoms and the amenities for visitors. We took a look at some of the new vast acred aviaries controlled only by devices of lighting and at insect reserves seen from above through vast magnifiers; we went down in diving bells in the Ocean Parks of the Caribbean and of the Ionian seas.

'In every part of the world, something is being done to keep man in touch with the life of the instinct,' Leacock told us. 'We can't do all the things you have seen tonight; but we can have our own animal world here among us – smaller or greater, to include more or less. And I make a plea now, an earnest plea that, before it is too late one at least of our four "Zones of Scenic Beauty" be given over to the preservation of wild life, the gradual replacement of Regent's Park by a free, natural reserve. It can be done now and be within the range of visitors, restricted at first to those who want to train their senses and their instincts, to cultivate the patience, the awareness, and the tranquillity of those who learn to live among wild life.'

We saw them at work then, myself among them – the naturalists, and the ecologists; and a miraculously sensitive, dedicated, yet fulfilled lot we appeared to be. I felt almost embarrassed as I sat in the darkness, for this, in my depths, was how I liked to think of myself. A warmth of affection for Leacock welled up in me, and an extra affection for the fraud in him. He was giving me a chance to help build a Reserve where people who lived for the work that I wanted to live for would have the highest respect. I could happily throw him a conspiratorial wink for this that would make me accomplice to his sketchy science and his even more sketchy administration. Or rather I was happy to work hard to supply what was deficient in his work if I could.

'Of course,' Leacock told us, 'this does not mean that the intellectual workers with all that they have done and will do for humanity do not still have a central place in zoological studies.'

And there we saw the anatomists, the biologists, the bacteriologists, the biochemists and a legion of others in their labs and their lecture rooms. We saw, we admired, but after the field workers we somewhat doubted.

'I believe that they too will only find benefit from the Foundation of a National Zoological Reserve in Great Britain.'

Then a laugh came into the voice that was reaching us through pictures of such an imaginary reserve.

'What about the ordinary man in the street who wants to

pay his half-crown and see his hippo? I think that if we're really to get this thing going, he's going to have one of the most exciting experiences of his life. Not straining through bars but looking down on a whole animal kingdom through the magnifying glass floors of our hovering helicopters.'

And so we saw him, the ordinary man; he looked a trifle uncomfortable because a line of vision below one is never entirely satisfactory, but still the magnified herds of reindeer and yak that were all that proved available from the Soviet Arctic Animals Park were a beautiful and impressive sight.

'All the same,' said Leacock, 'I should hope that as many *young* people as possible' – and young faces studious and gay were flung at us from every angle – 'would try to profit by the naturalists' way of life, to go in parties or singly, and come to know animal life as it should be known through the senses and the instincts. Not just those who are going to become professional zoologists, but young people destined for all walks of life. They will be the pioneers in our society carrying the developed instinctual way of life to balance the top-heavy intellectual growth of today. After all because we do not want to live in chaos' – scenes of mobs looting, crowd panic, peccaries over-running yam plantations and elephants trampling rice fields – 'there is no reason why in our fear we should die in captivity' – factories, canteens, crowded transport, deadened genteel homes once more and shots of the Decimus Burton Giraffe House and Raven's Cage – 'Liberty we can find if we accept some limitation in its definition, liberty thus limited we may feed on' – shots of the naturalists again in the great reserves – 'Only so I believe can we restore the psychic balance, the soul's health of a very sick civilization.' And now suddenly and for the only time the ridiculously ugly features came to us in close-up; the effect somehow was to command respect.

'That,' said Dr Edwin Leacock, 'is *my* dream. Good night.'

One of the young Leacocks got up and switched off. I could feel Mrs Leacock's nervous movements behind me. And now I caught a glimpse of her straggly grey hair and foolish, hearty red face. She had just returned from a camping holiday with some of her grandchildren; her back and chest glowed scarlet, against an unfortunately chosen applegreen evening dress.

She said, 'Well, did anyone think that Daddy was as good as I did?' And then as she saw the glowing, admiring faces of the family, she said, 'That was something we'll always remember, wasn't it, children?'

It was no doubt a measure of my great enthusiasm, that, despite the many reserves and embarrassments I had also felt, I answered now before any of the Leacock young.

'It was very good indeed,' I said, 'I've absolutely no doubt at all, Mrs Leacock, that its effect will be to push the Director's ambitions out of the sphere of dreams into the sphere of active politics.'

She was surprised at my answering her remark to her children.

She said, 'Ambition? Politics?' with a nervous laugh. But she had so long heard her husband's complaint of me as 'a jolly good man but horribly casual' that any unexpected enthusiasm gave her real pleasure and she added, 'Thank you, Mr Carter. I know how much Edwin counted on your appreciation.'

And now all the Leacock sons and daughters-in-law, and daughters and sons-in-law, and even one or two of the teenage grandchildren gave their rousing applause to the programme. And by the time they had finished, under Mrs Leacock's approving eye, there seemed nothing much left for us others to say. But since they were all rising young architects, and young stockbrokers doing extraordinarily well, and young advertising agents writing brilliant copy, and young doctors and dentists with futures, and since their wives reposed on status, their acclamations lacked one thing – knowledge. Mrs Leacock in her childish way seemed aware of this. She looked at Bobby for over a minute.

Then she said, 'I was so sorry Lady Falcon couldn't come.'
Bobby bowed his head slightly.

'She too,' he said, 'but a new play she's interested in took her to quite another theatre.'

Martha said, 'I was really angry with Dr Leacock for working Simon so hard in these last weeks. But now I know it's been well worth while.' She took my hand, 'I see now exactly what you mean by the Zoo job, darling.'

She really meant it for me, but in the circumstances, she offered a part of it to Mrs Leacock.

'Edwin's appreciated it so much, my dear,' Mrs Leacock said. She gave Martha a look that almost included her in the family. 'I wonder what I can offer you to eat, Sir Robert?'

Bobby looked at the food laid out on the table.

'A chicken sandwich would be delicious,' he said, 'but let me help in handing round.'

The young Leacock males wouldn't hear of this. Public school manners towards older men were a hallmark of their status. I was angry enough with Bobby to point the situation.

'Sit down,' I said, 'and let us young ones do the running about.'

Mrs Leacock looked at him twice in hope and then turned away in anger.

'I think I'll ring Daddy at the studios. He'll be tremendously bucked by all you've said.'

I had hoped to escape early, but when she returned, she said, 'Daddy thanks everybody. The viewer response so far is jolly encouraging, he says. And you've all got to stay. He's having a quick whisky at the studios and they're sending him back in a Rolls. I suppose that's what they call V.I.P. treatment.'

She gave a little laugh. We seemed to wait hours for Leacock's return. In the first half hour we had telephone calls of congratulation to discuss – from friends of the family, other zoologists, important Fellows of the Society, even, to my surprise, from Godmanchester's secretary. Sanderson had telephoned his intention of coming over from Wimbledon to Finchley Road in person to congratulate his chief. Mrs Leacock had tried to dissuade him, but he was intent on the act.

She said, 'Funny little chap! We must save him a bone for his trouble.'

Under the strain of waiting I could feel my enthusiasm ebbing, and it seemed unlikely that anyone else's would be more enduring. Martha found a daughter-in-law, whose children went to Reggie's kindergarten. They talked child psychology, trying to avoid any serious engagement on the subject since their views were clearly divergent. Bobby made flirtatious chat with the teenage granddaughter.

Once Mrs Leacock said, 'Well, what shall we do children, while we're waiting for Daddy?'

I felt, looking at her family, that it would not be long before we were involved in paper games or even a sing-song round the piano.

I said quickly, 'How was the Garden Party this year?'

I had chosen the right topic.

She said, 'Oh, the Queen looked so pretty and she had a word for Daddy. A lot of people,' she went on, 'find official social life an awful fag, but I seem to thrive like the wicked on it. Of course I was a bit shy at first, but I soon found that other people are shyer than I am, so now I just barge in and talk. Mind you, a wife can make or break a man's career, so I always make a point of doing my homework first.'

It was only when in fact she began 'to just barge in', when she talked about Zoo policy, international Zoo matters and the characters of eminent zoologists, that I realized that like her husband she was incapable of doing any homework at all.

My lukewarmness at last got through to her, for she said, 'But, of course, you're terrifically off shop talk, aren't you? Though I don't mind telling you, you've confounded all the critics by properly putting your back into this business.'

Then she talked interminably of her grandchildren, their prowess at games, the public schools for which they'd been entered, and the extraordinary powers of improvisation they had shown during the recent family camping holidays when 'poor old Grandad had had to stay in mouldy old London'.

At last I heard the sounds of a latchkey, but as it was

immediately followed by the padding of animal's feet on the hall parquet, I conceived the notion that the Director had followed up his plea for intuitive living by bringing home a leopard or a puma. I smiled at the thought. Mrs Leacock looked at me angrily.

When the door opened a very large Alsatian dog walked in. If like me you find cats and pumas beautiful, you will probably agree that wolves and Alsatians have the wrong shape of face. But this was a very fine specimen of its tribe. The young woman who followed it was not a fine specimen of her tribe, if by that was meant a typical member of the Leacock family, nor in their eyes was there much fine about her, for she was Harriet, the eldest girl they'd had such a lot of trouble with. I knew her because, shortly after I arrived at the Zoo, she came to see her father, and, finding him absent, had borrowed five pounds off me and tried to get me to make a pass. All in a quarter of an hour. Dr Leacock had asked me never to lend her money again; he had even mentioned her other weaknesses: 'I'm afraid she's rather silly where men are concerned,' was what he said. It had struck me at the time that he had come, over the years, too readily to advertise his daughter's weaknesses. I felt sorry for her. Also she *was* rather fine to look at, tall, a little square-jawed perhaps, but with large blue eyes that had a pleasantly vulgar sexy glint and a large mouth to pattern, also her legs were promising. She seemed gentle, which was a praiseworthy characteristic in such a family.

Mrs Leacock said, 'Daddy's had a great success, darling.'

'Oh, good.' Harriet's voice was soft and deep and her tone completely casual.

One of her brothers said, 'It seems a pity you couldn't have stayed to see it, Harriet.'

She didn't answer him, but seeing me, she smiled and said, 'Television gives me claustrophobia.'

Then she turned to her mother. 'I shan't go to that man on Monday. You'd better cancel.'

Mrs Leacock looked horrified, 'But of course you must. Daddy's fixed the appointment.'

Harriet smiled, 'Well, if he's had such a success, he can take a little disappointment.'

One of her younger sisters said sharply, 'But Harriet, you promised him. You can't.'

'Oh, I think you'll find I can.'

There was a terrible family silence. I saw no way of breaking it, so I talked to Martha.

Then at last once again I heard the latchkey.

'Ah, that's Daddy,' Mrs Leacock said.

There was a general stir among the family.

'Well, I'll be off to bed,' Harriet announced. 'Come on, Rickie,' she commanded the huge dog.

Under the cover of the scratching and padding of its departure, I heard Martha say to Bobby, 'I think you've behaved absolutely bloodily, Bobby.'

But there was none of the warm teasing with which she had rebuked him at the funeral wake. He too reacted quite differently. He merely shrugged his shoulders and turned away.

As Harriet opened the door, she said, 'Oh, by the way, the French have sent a tremendous climbdown note or something. So we can all forget our fears.'

'How did you know, darling?' Mrs Leacock asked.

She spoke to Harriet in a less determinedly jolly voice than to other people, I noticed.

'Oh, it was on the tele news in the pub I was in,' Harriet said, and was gone.

A second later Dr Leacock appeared. He must have passed his daughter in the hall without speaking.

I did my very best, as did Martha, to communicate our enthusiasm. But beside the eulogies of his family our remarks appeared a little pale. One of his daughters, a young athletic version of Mrs Leacock, went out into the kitchen and returned with a parsley crown to put round his head. And, before we knew where we were, Mrs Leacock had formed us into a circle holding hands and around his grotesque figure we moved singing, 'For he's a jolly good fellow'. Leacock seemed some hideous Easter Island god in a tribal rite. Bobby somehow avoided involvement. As soon as this embarrassment was over, Martha and I made attempts to take our leave and sweep Bobby off with us. But Edwin Leacock in his triumph was not in a mood for dissent.

'Well, what did you think of it, Falcon? Has Saul been turned into Paul?' he asked.

Bobby's drawl was terrific, 'I'm never frightfully good with pictures, you know, so I think a lot of it passed over my head. But your voice came over naturally. *I* used to be so infernally nervous. I don't think your cameramen quite did justice to your material. Some of the shots of Regent's Park were shockingly bad. But there you are, if you hand yourself over to the technicians and ad men of today you can never hope to convey the real thing.'

Martha, in her nervousness said, 'It would make a wonderful film, Dr Leacock.'

Bobby said, 'Oh, yes, yes. I think it would do that all right.' We were saved by the bell.

'That must be Mr Sanderson. He's come all the way from Wimbledon to congratulate you, dear.' Mrs Leacock almost skipped out to open the front door.

Sanderson immediately shook Leacock by the hand.

'My dear friend,' he said, 'you gave us a wonderful glimpse of your splendid spirit.'

I had never seen the Director completely nonplussed before. He simply shook Sanderson's hand again and said, 'You must have a whisky after coming so far.'

Sanderson was not in the mood to be content with whiskies, although he took the one that was offered.

'I must see it again, you know. I missed a good deal, telling poor old Miss Delaney what was happening. Mrs Blessington does that as a rule but she couldn't keep up with it. She's got quite a bone to pick with you. She says you must think of the old people's slow wits next time. Of course, that's only her joke. She's very far from slow-witted. But there you are, the great thing is that you gave us that glimpse of your splendid, almost childlike spirit.'

I propelled Martha by the elbow to the front door, leaving Mrs Leacock to find a bone for Fido.

May came to an end in glorious sunshine, and in Zoo crowds large and congested enough to delight even Bobby Falcon's heart. The Innsbruck Meeting was held in hot June weather that must have been trying to the nerves in that somewhat shut-in town. However the tempers of the European heads of government were equal to it. Accord was complete; the war clouds were banished from the bright blue sky. It was almost as though there *were* a friend for little children above it. At any rate Martha and a million other mothers felt so. Everyone breathed again; a good number only in order to say that this merely showed how impertinent the Americans and the Russians had been to interfere in affairs that could perfectly well be settled without them. Lord Godmanchester's papers warned against optimism for ten days and then banished Europe from the scene in favour of an all out attack on the National Trust, the lazy porters of the People's country houses. Silly season was upon us. At first Edwin Leacock shared in the general carefree mood. Letters came pouring in from viewers of his programme, and, if there were some that did not make him feel loved, all of them made him feel interesting. The clearing of international tension augured well for governmental attention to his scheme. The Press had been friendly towards the programme; two of Lord Godmanchester's papers had run features on it. Eminent English zoologists, like his colleagues at Regent's Park, were enthusiastic about the programme as a model for the use of television. Pattie Henderson, who had watched in company with Newton and Nutting, told me that they had thought the old boy definitely had something as a speaker. Couldn't he, she suggested, barge off and become one of those quizmasters. They all seemed more concerned with the presentation than with the scheme itself. However, Leacock was a happy man. I did not like to intrude a discordant note into this deserved happiness, especially as all his energies had been brought to life by success and now, if ever, he seemed likely to have the determination for the hard slow work needed to drive home his gain. I decided to defer my confrontation of him with his possible part in the Filson tragedy.

But as the days went by, it became clear to me that the Director's picture of what he had achieved differed very much from mine. It is true that he was active day after day, to the detriment of the regular Zoo routine affairs, with seeing this and that Fellow of the Society, with wining zoologists from the Universities, dining chaps from the Natural History Museum, lunching so and so of the Treasury or so and so from the Ministry of Education, getting people on the grants committees of various scientific Foundations along for drinks. Mrs Leacock, he told me, was being absolutely splendid, doing her part in these social chores. This was disquieting, but it did not really matter, for I soon discovered that *his* part was in any case not what it should have been. The truth was that he had set complete store by the success of his programme. If it had not been successful, he might well have started work all over again to get his National Reserve in some other way. But it had been successful and he seemed to think that his work was done. People were either for the programme or against it; this seemed to be all that his round of contact making was concerned to discover, and if they were for it, they would no doubt set about giving their instant aid to the plan. It was childish, of course, and bit by bit, as this childishness showed, the important people he lobbied treated him as a child. He had done very well with his little play, but he mustn't expect them to talk about it for ever – they were busy people with work to do, and if he hadn't got any he should find some.

Poor Leacock became very depressed; as June's lovely weather continued into July he could not share in the carefree holiday mood of the country. He began like Lord Godmanchester to mooch. Indeed, I only once saw him at all content during that time and that was when his mooching had brought him to luncheon with the equally mooching Lord.

'One's really glad to be with somebody adult,' he said. 'Godmanchester agrees with me that the slackness in this country at the moment is almost pathological.'

I suppose I ought not to have been sorry for him, but I was; or perhaps sorry for a good idea that seemed every day less likely ever to be realized. On the other hand I found him an intolerable burden; it was not so much that he put all the work on to me, but that he constantly interrupted my attention to it by his incessant grumbling. I was heartily relieved when the time approached for him to leave for the International Congress of Zoologists in Rome.

'I'm not at all sure,' he said, 'that the right way to stir up British inertia is not to get to work through some of the foreign societies.'

It was a sentiment to appeal to Dr Englander. He, as usual, was attending the Congress at his own expense.

'Where are they putting Leacock up?' he asked me. 'At the Excelsior? I thought so. Ruggiero's got a very good method of putting all the clowns and bores together out of harm's way. I'm stopping with Felletrini at his house in the Urban hills. It'll be cooler. And he's got Scheiner from New York, old Sieffens from Amsterdam, Paladie and this brilliant young Indian Subhas Rao. It means we shall get away from the herd and have some serious talk. By the way,' he added, 'I hope we're stumping up with a proper allowance for Leacock this time, if only for the sake of British prestige. I remember in San Francisco he and his missus had to walk when everybody else took taxis. She was in bed with bunions by the end of the Congress.' I did not for a moment believe this to be true, but Englander loved to invent such occurrences and always chuckled to himself over them for some time afterwards.

It was a good time for me, that week of the Director's impending departure for Rome. By the time Leacock returned, I should be off on my own vacation. My full five weeks in one spell this year – time enough to reconsider my attitude to Leacock, to weigh Mrs Filson's unhappiness against justice on behalf of her dead son. I had even promised myself that I would seriously rethink whether I really wished to stay at the Zoo although I was determined not to let Martha know of this until I had decided. We had arranged that she and I should go for a week to Janice Earl's in Somerset, to the setts I already knew so well. Janice had reported a case of melanism among the badgers there. I should watch badgers in the evenings and early mornings, laze all day and ponder; it would be hot, Martha and I would make love. Then in the other weeks we were to take the children to the sea; but to Blakeney, where I could watch the birds and laze and ponder, and again make love to Martha. With the agenda for the last General Purposes Committee meeting of the summer complete, I seemed already to be living a little in my holiday. I took many walks in the less visited North side of the Gardens, looking at Amherst's pheasants or Stanley's cranes or ortolans – birds that were all dazzling colour or slender shape or sudden piercing screams, recalling nothing human. And in the evenings Martha and I read or listened or viewed, and I knew that later we should make love. Yet the tense urgency for sexual relief which had so dominated the last months seemed relaxed. We came to it surely, but we came to it easily at night and in the morning. Growing up amid the dedicated 'trampiness' of her mother's progressive bohemianism, Martha, when I met her, was horribly sexually shy. It had been one of my greatest happinesses to break this down – one of my greatest happinesses and, by now, my strongest self-confidence. I owed her so much; this, at least, she owed to me.

The sun streamed into our large bedroom picking out my determined neatness and Martha's easy disorder, waking me to some highlit angle of her sleeping face that would tease and arouse my desire. It was my free Saturday and there were hours before me in which to caress and awake her gently and slowly. Stroking her temples, her shoulders, her breasts, her buttocks, I would try to lose myself in the senses that never failed me, all my doubts would die away, and all my fussy primness leave me. I licked the glossy smoothness of her eyelids. She drew my mouth to hers, sucking in my tongue between her teeth. The telephone rang. We paid no regard. I moved my lips across her cheek to her ear; I bit the lobe. She cried with pleasure, 'Oh!' And then again as the telephone continued ringing, 'Oh no!' in American protest. Her arm leaving my shoulder, moved the telephone from its rest. But already there was a brisk knocking at the door. Martha pulled my mouth again to hers. But it was no use. Jacqueline's voice came sharply to us.

'Please, Mr Carter. I suppose you must answer the telephone. I have spoken on the other line. Dr Leacock absolutely demands some conversation with you.'

Martha held her hand over my mouth.

She shouted, 'Mr Carter absolutely can't talk now, Jacqueline. Tell Dr Leacock he will call back in half an hour or so.'

But even at that moment I did not feel happy to let Martha belittle the importance of my work.

I said, 'I'll answer, Jacqueline,' and with some difficulty, still straddling Martha, I manoeuvred the telephone.

'Carter here.'

The voice came back vibrant with self-importance.

'Edwin Leacock speaking. This is a pretty urgent matter, Carter, so I make no apology for my early call.'

Above me I could hear the children's feet pattering like a stampede of hartebeest. I knew it to be seven o'clock. It seemed unwise at that moment to let Leacock feel at any advantage.

I said, 'Oh that's all right, I'm usually up and about by seven.'

But he was too excited to be scored over.

'I tried to reach you a number of times last night.'

I knew that this was untrue. Perhaps like another old man's his mouth was full of dough. This thought and Martha's tickling me in the armpit made me giggle. I disguised my laughter in a fit of coughing and so lost the core of what he had to say. When I could hear him fully again, he was saying,

'But despite the shortness of notice I've managed to get a quorum.'

'What's he talking about?' Martha whispered.

'He's got a quorum.'

'Well of all the disgusting things to ring up about.'

I put my finger to my lips and said 'Shush!' with mock severity. She buried her face in my shoulder to stifle her laughter.

I said into the mouthpiece, 'Is Godmanchester able to be there?'

'Look, if you'd prefer me to ring back when you're more able to take in what I'm saying . . .'

'I think the line's very bad. So Godmanchester *is* going to be there.'

'He would hardly be absent from a meeting summoned to discuss his own very serious proposal. Yes, Lord Godmanchester will be there.'

I asked, 'Who forms the quorum?'

Martha began to giggle again helplessly into my shoulder. My phrase indeed sounded to me like one of Black Rod's or Herald Extraordinary's traditional rhetorical cries at Coronation time. I half thought Leacock would suppose I was being facetious, but he gave me the name of the five committee members he had summoned. I noted that all were his supporters. Perhaps that was why he had not been able to contact the Secretary the night before.

'We're bound to come up against a lot of opposition in the next few weeks,' he said, 'so I am anxious to avoid any time wasting this morning. I don't think any of the five I've named are likely to listen to red herrings.'

He gave a hard little laugh of triumph, to which, before I had thought, I had responded. But I was not going to be associated with a conspiracy before I knew its purpose, so I pretended a different cause for my laughter.

'Listen to red herrings! Ha! Ha!' I cried.

He was furious.

'I'm afraid, Carter, that at a moment so vital as this I'm

not always able to command perfect English. Nor for that matter to find verbal slips very amusing. However perhaps you'll appreciate the full seriousness of the business when I'm able to speak to you in more detail than for obvious reasons I can on the telephone.'

That at least meant that I should not have to confess to my ignorance.

I said, 'I shall be all ears.'

Martha pulled them both and I gave a squeal.

Leacock said, 'Yes, well clearly this telephone isn't very satisfactory. Anyway I want to go over the whole thing with you and Godmanchester before the others arrive. Shall we say nine o'clock in my office?'

Another play to make me a conspirator, I thought.

I said, 'Well, I'm afraid at this short notice . . .'

'Look,' said Dr Leacock, 'this is not a time to consider personal matters. In view of Godmanchester's remarks, I regard this as the amber warning. I'm afraid you must make it a must.' He rang off.

I had not really expected to see Godmanchester in the Director's office that Saturday morning at nine. I could imagine important events that might have brought him to Number Ten or even to Buckingham Palace; otherwise he would surely refuse to leave Stretton. However there he was looking like Kipling's Baloo, wise custodian of The Law. His only mark of the occasion, perhaps, a light seersucker suit such an emergency might have caught him in aboard his yacht at Antibes or at his favourite Tenerife; though he had not, I knew, left England since the beginning of the recent crisis. Leacock wore the formal clothes in which he always appeared before the General Purposes Committee.

He said, 'Both Lord Godmanchester and I felt it most important to take you into our fullest confidence, Carter. Simply because, to be perfectly straightforward with you from the start, your co-operation is going to be invaluable to us. Without you, I don't really see how . . .'

His voice tailed away; but I felt that I could supply the rest. Whatever the project might be, he was by now entirely dependent on someone else to do the detailed work. For the moment that person was me.

Lord Godmanchester heaved heavily from one massive buttock to the other.

'Don't make the chap feel too important, Leacock. Tell him what we're going to do.'

'Well, the scheme is actually yours, Lord Godmanchester.'

'Yes. But I'd like to see how well you've understood it.'

Leacock's face suddenly changed from the harassed man of affairs to the shy schoolboy.

'Really, honestly, you know, it's a bit embarrassing for me. But still, here goes ... It seems, Carter, that my television programme had a very powerful effect on our President. He – very characteristically if I may say so and also very wisely – decided to say nothing of his enthusiasm until he'd had time to think the whole thing over very carefully. Having done that, he, also very characteristically, decided on a scheme as generous as it is bold.'

I ought to have looked at Godmanchester while Leacock was saying all this, it might have told me much that I wanted to know; but, very characteristically, I was so embarrassed by Leacock's manner of speaking that I could only stare at the ground.

'He has offered the major part of the Stretton Estate including his own private menagerie to form the nucleus of a British National Zoological Park. It is difficult for me to find words to express my gratitude for an offer that is so completely magnificent. I can only say that I ... I haven't slept since he told me last night.'

For once Leacock's ugliness and lack of charm were most effective. His absurd words seemed to me genuinely touching. Yet his enthusiasm was wholly reasonable. It would not have been completely disproportionate if he had prostrated himself on the floor before his benefactor; for, after all, Godmanchester had not been named 'The Marcher Baron' by his political opponents without malicious reason. His estates, the largest in the country, sprawled across two English and two Welsh counties. I found no easy words myself.

I said, 'I'm very pleased indeed that your efforts should have been so wonderfully rewarded, Leacock. Of course, it's a very great moment. And I suppose our difficulty in thanking Lord Godmanchester comes from the inherent improbability of such a vast donation.'

Godmanchester chuckled. 'Are you blaming me for being a landowner on a large scale? Or are you saying that you don't believe what Leacock's told you? If you mean the second, to a certain extent you're right. I told Leacock to explain the thing to you, because I wanted to see how much he'd exaggerate it. People on the receiving side of the counter always do. There are modifications to what he's said. In the first place this is no hand-over. The suggested arrangements for the first two years will run like an ordinary lease and not an advantageous lease for the Society at that. It'll be purely experimental on both sides, and if either side is dissatisfied, a month's notice. Given, of course, that either side has serious ground for complaint. On the other hand if everything goes right, at the end of the two years I shall hand over something like three times the land of the old Whipsnade Park; and what's more I shall make a very substantial financial donation towards the support of the place. Although my own belief is that what with breeding for other Zoos, increased helicopter communication and one thing and another, the thing'll rapidly pay for itself in purely financial terms, let alone the moral or social or whatever terms Leacock made so clear in his television programme. I opposed the sale of Whipsnade on exactly those grounds but, you know what the general panic was in the '67 slump. I don't imagine my wife will want to go on living at Stretton when I die. She prefers a more cosmopolitan life. So that there seems no reason why the Reserve shouldn't expand to a very substantial size as my various tenants' leases fall in, provided we can get really good security arrangements to satisfy the rural councils about some of the villages in the area. You'll have at least two rivers and a lake to play about with, and a range of chalk hills with quarry workings and caves.'

'It's magnificent.'

'Yes. Leacock's already said all that. What we got you here so early for is to hear how you think the Society will receive the news.'

'There your financial offer will help a lot. It means that if the Treasury or the Minister of Education don't agree at first, we can afford to go ahead without them.'

'I don't doubt we'll have to do that anyway.'

Leacock nodded his head in agreement with such brave defiance.

'I think you underestimate the flexibility of government departments,' I said.

'I'm only happy with government departments when I'm in charge of them.'

Leacock's face took on an even tougher expression to keep up with Godmanchester's attitude.

'Whatever,' I said, 'your promise of money will satisfy the main part of any would-be critics on the Committee and, for that matter, it will help immensely when putting the scheme before the Society as a whole.'

Leacock said, 'There's nothing that won't give way before the old recipe of tact and firmness.'

Perhaps the same immediate doubts visited Godmanchester as came to me.

He said, 'I don't believe in old recipes, Leacock. Every new situation calls for a new way of cooking. Do you think it'll only be a question of money, Carter?'

'I think many people will be anxious that this should not prove a preliminary step to the abandonment of Regent's Park.'

Dr Leacock said, 'There will be no need to suggest it. History will eventually decide that.'

Godmanchester looked at him.

'Until history does, I'd advise tact rather than firmness, Leacock.'

He smiled as he spoke but hardly enough to disguise the short rein which seemed to accompany his new benevolent mastery.

'In any case what I'm offering won't allow for that in our life time, unless you're scrapping the aquarium and most of the tropical exhibits.'

I responded to the limitation of the objective; the whole thing at once appeared to me more practical, even more genuine. I determined to clear up what remained to puzzle me.

I said, 'With careful preparation I believe that we can get past all opposition. I hope that not too much will be said even to the favourable quorum you've summoned for this morning. With a lot of care and the right canvassing I should have thought we could come out into the open, or rather begin to do so, by the end of the year.'

'I have no doubt at all,' said Dr Leacock, 'that the English Civil Service training has more completely corrupted the élite of this country than any other single influence.'

'No, no, Leacock. We've got to hear what people have to say. And Carter's one of them. What would you say, Carter, if we told you that my offer was dependent upon an immediate start?'

My first thought was – not on your life, you old buggers, you're not going to mess my holiday, I'll leave the bloody place first.

I said, 'It wouldn't be for me to say . . .'

'Oh, for the Lord's sake, man, don't quibble.'

Leacock, seeing that Godmanchester was again about to rebuke him for his impatience, got up and went to the window.

'Yes, you look out of the window, Leacock. Carter's face won't annoy you so much then. You forget that to any man over sixty a man under forty looks self-satisfied. It's the price we pay for having the young about us.'

I hoped that the new proposal would not lay me open too much to Godmanchester's wise old man of the world stuff in the coming months.

'What do you think my reasons are for making this offer, Carter, apart from sheer generosity?'

'Belief in Leacock's scheme, I suppose.'

'Excellently cautious. Now try again.'

Young in his eyes as I may have seemed, I found this intolerable.

I asked, 'If the matter is so urgent, have we time for this guessing competition approach, Lord Godmanchester?'

Godmanchester flushed.

'Yes, I think we have. In any case I always do things the way I want to, Carter.'

I laughed to ease the tension.

'I suppose you might be going to invest in running a Zoo as an insurance against old age without political office.'

Leacock swung round from the window, his toucan eyes rounder than ever with anger. But Godmanchester was rumbling away with laughter.

'You're perfectly right. Everybody has a purely selfish thought on such occasions and you've hit on mine. Of course I shall never be idle enough to do no more than potter around with Zoo affairs. So you people don't have to be afraid. But I'd like to increase my interest – yes . . . That's not quite all though.'

He waited a moment, then he sat back, his short, stubby arms resting on those of the armchair.

'You're right. Enough of this "viva" stuff. I'm in a hurry with this business for the sake of the Zoo. In my opinion we shan't have any too much time to evacuate the more valuable specimens before the country finds itself at war. Well, what about that?'

So here it was at last – not in the usual newspaper scares, but from the fount of all newspapers himself. My first thought was – well, if he says so, then here it is. I was alarmed that I should show my fears, but strangely, confronted with such a sense of certainty, no physical symptoms seized me. Too many thoughts occupied my mind at once – Martha, the children, the still beauty of the woods that could then have been my surrounding instead of Leacock's strutting stance and Godmanchester's flabby old face. Detestation of the old man for being perhaps my herald of annihilation made me unable to speak for a moment.

Finally, I said, 'Do you suggest that the next war can be evaded? Or are you anxious to inspire confidence in phoney evacuation schemes? I'm not going to be party to using the Zoo for pretences of that sort.'

To my annoyance, he smiled, but as though to himself.

'Quite the contrary,' he said; then he looked serious. 'You don't really think, Carter, do you, that after the Russo-American Declaration even our Prime Minister would risk nuclear weapons. And luckily, however much he bungles, others won't risk launching them at us. No, thank God, I feel pretty sure that we shall be spared that. But unless something happens to shake this present crowd up, we may have a terrible enough war on our hands anyway. I'm not giving anyone here my reasons for saying so. Some people would consider that I had gone too far in my position and with my knowledge in saying what I have. And after all it doesn't matter if I'm wrong; because we shall be laying the foundations of something very fine. Will you help us to get this thing through as quickly and as easily as possible? You've made a good impression here with the staff and with the members of the Committee, if you throw yourself in with us, we shall make a strong team.'

I stared at Leacock. For all the solemnity he assumed at that moment, I felt he was really taking such things very lightly.

He said, 'Yes, Carter, there *is* this additional grave reason. Of course I couldn't tell you without Lord Godmanchester's agreement.'

As I looked at them both, they seemed for a moment like two very old irresponsible boys pretending to be adults. I had a moment of panic as to where they might be leading me. I determined to remain silent, but Godmanchester heaved himself breathily out of his chair and straddled his great bulk in front of me. His thick eyebrows went up in imperious demand for an immediate reply.

'I am thinking,' I said, 'of some weeks ago when I spoke to you. You described what I told you then as a tall story. There's too much in it of "it may be this or it may not", you said. Now we seem to be on the brink of war or we may not be. And again, we may be at the great beginnings of a British National Zoological Park, or we may not.'

Edwin Leacock said sharply, 'Luckily the alternatives demand the same actions from us.'

'Luckily!'

Godmanchester answered my angry scorn with a patronage even more scornful.

'Yes. As Leacock says. In any case we're simply concerned to know whether you'll co-operate or not.'

I had to try once again.

I said, 'I take it that there'll be little or no publicity in your papers for our move if we make it.'

'You take it wrongly. Anything to do with me automatically gets some publicity. I also intend that Leacock's great scheme shall not go without recognition from the public.'

He looked at me very deliberately.

'My whims, Leacock's vision. Anything more would be a breach of my idea of security.'

Leacock began to pick up sheafs of papers from his desk.

'If we're going to take on the running of Lord Godmanchester's papers as well as our duties here, we shall be very busy indeed.'

Intuitive suspicion cannot stand up long against authority's arguments. I agreed to assist them. After all either alternative – evacuation of an old Zoo or foundation of a new – was a large enterprise. How could I be sure that my doubt was not simply a product of my general mistrust of the declaredly important?

We did, as Godmanchester predicted, make a very strong team. Our first committee meeting, of course, had been rigged so that I found it difficult to judge what might be coming from their enthusiasm. But when the full Executive Committee met, I was surprised how little my disquiet was echoed by anyone else. Members who were sceptical of Leacock or Godmanchester, or of both, were clearly impressed by my adherence. Nicolls, the Zoology Professor from Oxford, said afterwards to me,

'Well, when I saw that *you* didn't deflate the idea, I took it that it was administratively possible.'

Old Miss Braithwaite, the great Amazon collector, said, 'It's on your head, you know, Mr Carter; you're the *sound* man, so I hope you haven't let us down.'

The old men, it seemed, had been right to fuss so much about my agreement. I had anticipated expert opposition to the haste and the arbitrary legal foundations of the new settlement; but I had forgotten how much we are confounded by sheer scale today. Godmanchester was making an offer worthy of a Renaissance prince, even canny lawyers and demanding civil servants seemed to expect him to behave with an appropriate imperiousness. The arbitrary manner, it seemed, established the sincerity of the act.

There was, as I had foretold, some opposition from those who suspected that the whole thing was the beginning of the end of Regent's Park. Old Lord Oresby, in fact, in particular, whose father had been sacked along with Asquith when Godmanchester's father had been raised to the peerage by Lloyd George, assumed an arrogant, contemptuous stance towards what he even openly called 'some bit of caddish sharp practice'. Yet much as he hated Godmanchester, he altered his view after talking privately with him, although he refused to say why. He quarrelled with Bobby Falcon over his change of mind: 'I'm not quite sure that Falcon's sane,' he told me, 'he seems to be preaching the millennium.' Bobby, on his side, told me, 'Oresby and his crowd aren't aware that we're on the brink of Armageddon. Their mental attitude is about appropriate to Gladstone and the Ashanti wars.' I saw clearly then that Godmanchester's ideas of security were flexible.

By early August the Committee had authorized our move. Leacock and I had already laboriously gone through all the records of transportation, organization and staffing in the early Whipsnade days. But life had changed since then and the tough work of organization was still before us. It was going largely to be a two-man job, for although we had secured the formal support of the Curators, they could none of them be said to show enthusiasm.

Leacock, on my advice, had discussed the motion before the Executive Committee with each Curator in turn. I truly believe that left to his own inclination he would have funked the interviews and tried to bluff his way through the opposition of his staff by presenting them with a directive. I was present by his request, at all the interviews. But let me say now that his request was prompted by my own suggestion. I had for once engaged myself; I was determined not to evade my responsibility. I invented a special mock-pompous voice which I used when office life became unbearably high motived; no one else seemed to notice when I put it on, but it gave me some release from my distaste for the grandiose.

For the first time I found myself fully on the side of action. I quite understood all the Curator's mistrust of Leacock; after all I knew his weaknesses far better than they did. But I also knew his virtues. In any case I thought they should at least have seen a little beyond the man to the ideas he proposed. Their involved distrust and apathy irritated me. Yet, in the end, all of them for various reasons, accepted his proposition. I don't believe that Leacock noticed these involutions; or, when he did, he called them 'an awful tendency to fuss that men acquire who are protected from facts by specialization'. When however, in the end, he got a sort of agreement from them all, he told me confidentially,

'Despite all Godmanchester's grim forebodings, you know, Carter, I'm inclined to take a more hopeful view of world affairs. This experience has taught me a lot. I don't mind saying that I anticipated some very rough passages with one or two of the Curators, but when it comes down to it, it's amazing what a deal of horse sense there is in most human beings.'

He was, or course, under the new scheme to preside over Stretton in the inaugural years, away from the horse sense of his Curators who were all for the time being to continue in London.

I, who was to divide my time between London and the Welsh Border, saw the interviews with the Curators with a less favourable eye, for I should now be the sole representative of central administrative authority with whom they would have to deal at Regent's Park.

I say the sole representative because the manner of Bobby Falcon's agreement to deputize for the Director in London gave me little reason to think that he would take his job very seriously. The whole course of his response to the news was so erratic that I felt very disturbed for him. Leacock insisted on a different approach to Bobby from the simple interviews he gave to the other Curators.

'We must be civilized with Falcon,' he said, 'none of this modern office formality. I shall lunch him at the club and tell him there. After all he's a very distinguished man.'

I tried everything I could to dissuade him; I knew that Bobby would regard such behaviour as very bad form. But success with the Committee had increased Leacock's belief in his knowledge of men. I proved to be right. As we slithered about on an American cloth sofa with our after-luncheon coffee, Leacock outlined his plans.

Bobby said, 'I take it I'm not meant to comment now.'

Leacock was a little surprised, but he agreed.

'My dear Falcon, yóu must say what you feel right when you feel right. Though I shall be anxious, you know. Between ourselves, yours is the only Curator's opinion that counts.'

He received it the next day in the form of a note.

Dear Director,

The proposal you made yesterday seems to me as wild as it is undesirable. The haste with which you and Godmanchester are trying to force it through gives one some doubts of your motives and greater doubts of your capacity to realize such a grandiose scheme, even were it desirable. I do not know how far anything "matters" much more today. But I have the wishes of those who have stood by me in my views – Oresby, Peasegood, and others – to consider as well as my own. I shall therefore use all the influence I can to frustrate the scheme.'

Edwin Leacock was very angry.

'I'll tell you this, Carter, I'm not going to let that man's arrogance and folly put the clock back.'

But he was also clearly very apprehensive. I imagine that it was then, at his request, that Godmanchester revealed his full views in conversation both with Bobby and with the Oresby group, for, shortly afterwards, the split occurred that I have already reported. Bobby wanted to resign from the staff.

'In view of everything,' he said, 'I really don't know why I shouldn't do a last bit of exploration. It can hardly matter if it kills me.'

He seemed extraordinarily ebullient and carefree. Leacock would, I think, gladly have accepted the decision, but God-manchester was appalled.

'Falcon's a name,' he said, 'and we don't want names walking out on us at a time like this.'

I saw the letter that he wrote to Bobby.

'Whatever happens we need a man in charge of Regent's Park who cares for the traditions of the place. And you're that man.'

I should have admired Bobby more if he had refused such cheap flattery; as it was, he accepted very perfunctorily.

'Just as you like,' he said, 'but I hope Simon's ready to do a good deal of deputizing, because I may still go on my travels again.'

I was glad at that moment that against Martha's wishes I had insisted on receiving a salary; to have an honorary status as Bobby had, simply removed all sanctions and shape to ones actions.

Dr Englander, the only other honorary Curator, clearly felt even more free of sanctions. Leacock tried twice to summon him back from Rome, but he paid no attention to the letters. Finally when he did return, he expressed interest only in the financial extent of Godmanchester's offer.

'I'm surprised he's got as much as that,' he said. 'I've always thought he was a fraud. Mind you he's not in the class of Berard or Huebsch or even old Masiello – you'd be surprised how much that old chap's got, by the way. But by English standards he's obviously rich.'

When Leacock said he had no intention of attempting a reptile display at Stretton as yet, he answered, 'I suppose not.'

We left the Director's office together and the old man laughed.

'He's got pretty puffed up about the whole thing, hasn't he? I'd better send a couple of bullfrogs down there to keep him company.'

The next day, however, he came to my office and questioned me in detail about the terms of Godmanchester's offer.

Finally he said, 'No, it obviously won't do. Of course I'm not concerned with all this nonsense of Leacock's, but it did occur to me that the place could be kept in mind in case this country's silly enough to run into war. I can't believe even our rulers will be that crazy, but you never know. If it comes, mind you, it will be a pretty quick walk-over for our friends abroad; but though short, it may not be altogether sweet. It might be as well to have some plans, for a temporary hide-out. I don't want all my research work upset by some idiotic English politician who's trigger happy. But this place of Godmanchester's won't do. The man himself will be hanging around interfering And then look at the terms of the tenure – no security at all. Leacock must be mad! But then he *is* mad. No, I'll talk to some of my friends in industry and see what they can stump up.'

I heard no more from him until the first dispatch of mammals had begun. I think that an accident which had occurred to one of the mountain goats from the Mappin Terrace when it was being rounded up must have disturbed him. Twice during our interview he swallowed a digestive tablet from the small silver box he kept in his waistcoat pocket.

'Look here,' he said, 'I suppose Leacock isn't going to start any of this nonsense with *my* collections, is he?' And he refused to be reassured. 'I'll tell you what. I'll make a list of some surplus specimens and offer it to him. It's always as well to get in first with these maniacs. Flatter him a bit. What's that phrase of his, "learning to live with wild life"?' He went out chuckling to himself.

I don't know how far Charles Langley-Beard fully took in the change. Leacock was so determined to protect him from its impact.

'I should never forgive myself if that man's work was disturbed for a moment, Carter. And by his work I mean the very delicately balanced genius that controls it.'

One of Beard's assistants was to carry out the veterinary work at Stretton.

'I'm expecting the other Curators to visit us from time to time to familiarize themselves with our progress, Beard. But I know how your work keeps you at it, and for the moment I shan't expect you to be there at all. We can always send you any corpses you want up here. Not, of course, that we shouldn't welcome a visit from you, if you felt like getting a little country air.'

Dr Beard considered this from afar.

'I've had very little to do with the country,' he said, 'my life hasn't taken me there much.'

Dr Leacock signalled to me the pathos of this.

'I've often hoped that it isn't blasphemous,' Dr Beard went on, 'but I find the natural scene part of God's creation I can do without.'

Matthew, of course, was as unattracted by the countryside as Beard. It belonged, I imagine, to the time of his childhood and his public schooldays before his egoistic will had hardened. At any rate he had banished it from his carefully protected world. When, however, it became apparent that he was not expected to reside there and that his classifying work would not be interrupted, he became almost enthusiastic about the move.

'I believe Godmanchester has some very passable landscape gardening and a very pretty formal garden too. They would make an excellent setting for aviaries.'

This was not quite Leacock's conception of the National Park.

He said, 'Nothing can be too elaborate at this stage, Price.'

'Oh, I don't think anything can ever be *too* elaborate at any stage, do you? We shall have space for the most intricate and curious aviaries. And then the construction of artificial islands in the lake. I see a sort of miniature Japan with beautiful wading birds instead of all those tiresome little people. Completely charming.'

Dr Leacock was always uneasy with Matthew; he thought he was 'pulling his leg'.

He laughed and said, 'Well, I'm only too pleased to find a loyal supporter in you, Price.'

Matthew drew his willowy form to its considerable height, and said stiffly, 'I hope I've always been loyal to the work of the Society.'

Leacock was taken aback. He even mused for a moment after Matthew had gone, and said, 'Funny chap, Price.'

'He's an extraordinarily honourable man,' I said.

It was a juggling use of the word, but, after all, I had as much right to try to poise someone on a pedestal as Leacock had.

My pedestal crashed very soon after. Leacock, only too willing to leave the Curators behind, was determined to have his full share of head keepers to do the work for him. As yet only 'Mammals' and 'Birds' were much involved. It was proposed to offer their head keepers a house and an increase in salary to encourage them to leave London. When I realized that this meant the confluence of Strawson and Filson in the remote countryside, I protested vigorously to the Director; I told him of Filson's declared hatred for Strawson. But I chose the wrong moment. Excitement, anxiety, unfamiliarity with such hard work, and doubt had already made Leacock's temper very uncertain. Was it guilt that now toppled it over the edge?

He turned on me savagely, 'If you have to gossip with every underling in the place,' he shouted, 'I'd be obliged if you'd keep your findings to yourself. I've heard about as much as I can take of your sickening moralizing about that wretched Filson business.'

'You'd have heard a great deal more,' I shouted back, 'if I hadn't been forced to consider the feelings of the underlings you despise so much. Yes, and your own.'

We stood, our faces red, our bodies shaking, facing each other across his desk. I think that anger had loosed in each of us the clamped suspicion that the other was taking him for a ride. Then we realized that the journey had already begun, it was too late to climb out.

Leacock said, 'My dear Carter, you don't suppose I'm going to *force* either of these men to go down there. And if they do agree, I shall bear in mind what you've told me. Whatever my faults, I'm not an inhuman man, you know.'

It wasn't entirely the point at issue, but it sufficed to let us out of the quarrel.

Strawson agreed to go down for a trial period. If after six months, he liked it, his wife would put a manageress into her shop and join him.

'I wish she could give up now, Sir,' he said to Leacock, 'but, as Mr Carter knows, a lot of us find a little help towards the Society's wages no bad thing.'

I truly believe that he chose to go to Stretton, when he knew that I should be mainly in London. Filson was a little more concerned – they were old, there was his wife's house, he would like time to think it over. Later that afternoon Matthew appeared in the Director's Room where we were busy comparing railway and air estimates for transportation of the wolves and jackals. I thought he had come to gossip with me, but he addressed Leacock in a purring drawl.

'Oh, it's just to say that Filson's decided to go to Stretton. I've got a letter here from him confirming it. I thought that best.'

Leacock said, 'Well, that's excellent news, Price. He seemed very doubtful this morning.'

'Oh, well, he's one of the old school. He didn't like to act without consulting me.'

'Well, I'm very grateful to you for agreeing to let him go.'

Amazed, I said aside to Matthew, 'How on earth will you manage without Filson?'

He looked annoyed. 'Perfectly well, thank you, Simon. I think he could do with a change of scene after that business with his son.' He looked at me challengingly, 'And then quite frankly it's a crashing bore for me to hear about it all the time.'

When Matthew had gone the Director gave me a frank apology. 'You're perfectly right about Price, Carter. He's not a Langley-Beard of course. But he's a *very* good chap. And he's got a deal of horse sense under that airy fairy manner.'

With this I agreed. Sanderson, I regret to say, showed qualities the Director admired less. Since no entomological collections were as yet to be included in the National Reserve, Leacock was almost disposed to leave him out of the interviews; I persuaded him that this would be unnecessarily wounding, tedious though the old man might be. Yet when Sanderson appeared, he seemed quite uninterested in all that the Director had to say. Future hopes for carefully controlled displays of agricultural pests, for observations of insect life under magnified conditions, of butterfly gardens in summer, and for special crepuscular displays of moths, brought only the most perfunctorily characteristic comments from him.

'Yes, that's very fine,' he said. 'It's a wonderful conception. My dear friend, you've got the creative gift.'

Only as he was leaving did he turn, and, his plump cheeks pink below the blank circles of his glasses, ask in a trembling voice,

'Is it true what they say, Leacock, that you intend to desert the old place altogether in the end?'

Leacock came out of the entomological spins he had been weaving with a nasty bump.

He said, 'We can't predict the future, Sanderson. I think it more than probable that this sort of menagerie will become obsolete. Probably in our life time if you want my candid opinion.'

Sanderson walked back towards the Director's desk.

'It's absolutely damnable,' he said, 'absolutely damnable. There are hundreds of old people and poor people for whom this place is a second home. And lonely people too. People who don't find it easy to make contact with other human beings, but who have found friends among the birds and animals. And you propose to cut them off from the source of their living.'

Leacock was amazed.

He said, 'Come, Sanderson, there are thousands of people, you know, who never get near Regent's Park and who may find it easier, not to say more satisfying, to see the animal world in greater freedom.'

Sanderson considered for a moment, then he announced,

'Yes, that may be so, but I don't know them. I *do* know the people who come here.'

He went out of the room at a slow, sad pace. Leacock was disgusted.

'Making every allowance, you know, Carter, there's no doubt that he's impossible. Thank God, he's only got two more years to go.'

The most discouraging reaction, however, came from Harry Jackley, the Curator of the Aquarium. Godmanchester already had a small freshwater aquarium at Stretton; it was proposed to enlarge it with additional species from Regent's Park. Leacock was all for doing this without consultation. He poohpoohed my insistence that to antagonize Jackley would be to antagonize the younger generation of the staff and to jeopardize the future of the Reserve.

'There'll always be a younger generation who don't like what's being done because they aren't doing it. You're too easily influenced, Carter.'

However, we wrote to Jackley in New Guinea where he was collecting, only to learn that he was on his way home – they understood he was stopping off in Bahrein to see if he could replace the two dugongs that had recently died.

'Good God!' Leacock cried. 'Why on earth can't Falcon manage his own mammals?'

It was not the time to remind him of mammalia that needed aquarium conditions. I was forced to agree that, as deputy for Jackley, Leacock should go ahead with his own schemes. It was on a very hot August 12th, I remember, that I sat, looking for a moment at Mrs Purrett's copy of Lord Godmanchester's chief daily. The Prime Minister, it seemed, and the paper suggested how irresponsible it was, felt happy enough with the state of world affairs to be shooting grouse. The telephone rang, it was Mrs Leacock to say that Dr Leacock would not be in until late that afternoon, he had been called away on family business. I cursed his guts, for we were desperately busy. Yet when he turned up at five o'clock, he looked so tired and old that I felt sorry for him. He began mechanically to deal with the questions I put before him, then he suddenly broke off.

He said, 'I'm sorry to have left you to all this work today, Carter. However, perhaps what I've been engaged on is not so different from my aim of doing away with the old Zoos with bars. I've been saving my daughter Harriet from being sent to prison. Apparently her tastes now lead her exclusively to associate with the criminal classes. Only the employment of a first-rate counsel saved her from a conviction on a charge of receiving. Receiving of all things! I don't know of any other time when she has failed to *spend*. But still, to be perfectly honest I'd have let her take her chance. After all there are open prisons nowadays. But Mrs Leacock felt differently. So we've accepted the stipulation that she should live with us down at Stretton. It should be most pleasant for all of us. Limited liberty, you know!'

He paused, and when he spoke again it was with less bitterness.

'Nobody,' he said, 'is going to turn this dream of mine into a nightmare. That I'm determined on.'

As he spoke Rackham came in and handed Leacock a cablegram. Leacock read it and passed it to me.

'REFERENCE YOUR LETTER AUGUST 6TH THE ANSWER IS NO, JACKLEY.'

I bit Pattie Henderson's head off two days later when she telephoned to me.

'Isn't it splendid,' she asked, 'about Jackley's cable? Simply "no". Newton and Nutting have just told me about it. Of course it's the only answer to give to all this time wasting nonsense.'

On August 20th Dr and Mrs Leacock and their daughter Harriet left London to take up residence at Merritt's Farm, a large eighteenth-century red-brick house on Lord Godmanchester's estate, only a mile from the Stretton Private Zoo.

'From now on,' Dr Leacock said to me as he left, '*you'll* be my link with the past.'

The equinoctial winds blew fiercely that autumn. After the stuffiness of my office and more still the numbing sense of never-ending, self-renewing, detailed work, their freshness would have been welcome to me, but the railway detective and the guard obviously felt otherwise. The guard had been stoking up the small stove in the centre of the brake van ever since we left Paddington, and by now the air was stale and stifling. Yet from crevices and doors freezing draughts sped down my back and crept round my ankles. I sat on my air cushion on the minute wooden seat that was hinged to the wall of the van; I clutched the thermos of rum and coke that Martha had made up for me; and I dozed on and off as it seemed for hours. It was the third journey I had made since a fortnight earlier the escape of a skunk had led the railway authorities to insist on the presence of a senior officer with every trainload of beasts. They agreed that it was a futile precaution, but it satisfied the insurance law. Apart from my illness in Africa I had not been used to much discomfort in my life; I had never known insomnia. But now I sat shivering through the night, so sleepy that at short intervals the guard and the detective and the fug and the red glow would swim in front of me, revolve rapidly and turn to some nightmare in which a hundred voices and faces that I knew, seemed to be chivvying me, and this dream in turn would dissolve and, with a crack that seemed to tear my head apart, I should be woken again by a whistle or a sudden jolt. Through it all, through all my tired, muddled, and anxious thoughts, went the low, steady drone of the two men's conversation, only on occasion breaking into my exhaustion with a sudden chance flow of meaningless words. I smiled at them now and again to palliate, if I could, whatever might seem snobbish or frightened or morose in my silence. But after my first two trips I had decided to give myself the luxury and them the peace of not attempting to make conversation.

That evening, however, though I felt tired and jumpy, the whole scene seemed to flow over me. Tomorrow I was to begin a five-day stay at Stretton. Five days without any office work. Five days to see what Leacock's new-found energy and determination had created for the grand opening next spring. The Exotic Park with its prairie herds of zebra and hartebeest, eland and giraffe, I had already travelled through in one of the Society's buses; it had promise, but would always be only a glimpse of what the richer or more leisured or more interested could see in a visit to Africa. Behind this, stretches of pine forest provided the Historic British Reserve soon to be closed to all but the guided and the armed; for here in ten years we hoped for increase of deer that would maintain carefully limited packs of wolves and in the mountains that stretched beyond into Wales, golden eagles and the brown bear. Here already in patches of brown scrub great bustards roamed, and in the forest, wild boar were finding cover. But it was in the deciduous woods and chalky downland that I hoped to find the end to the bifurcation of my life; for eventually I was not only to be Administrative Secretary of the whole Reserve but also Warden of this region of fox and badger and marten – the British Reserve. There, in company with other selected naturalists, I should pursue the pleasure of my life, but free from conscience because I should also be giving the Society my cursed administrative skill. The good and the bad fairies at my cradle had embarrassingly both provided themselves with the same gift – a power to make patterns out of muddled details; they had squabbled over this social gaffe ever since; perhaps now they would be appeased. Then Martha could see me do what she knew I wanted to do and I could know myself to be doing my duty. I now knew that the success of Leacock's scheme was as crucial for me as for him. Yet my cautious nature still only allowed me timidly to hope and plan for a future that Leacock's stout, absurd and scheming, egoistic dreamer's heart already declared to be a reality.

It was easier, of course, for him than for me. He had made Stretton a Castle Faithful where treacherous voices of doubt were instantly silenced, where only Godmanchester, in his rare appearances from the London political waters in which he was still angling, talked of 'evacuation' rather than 'foundation'. At Regent's Park all was quite different. With Leacock gone, it had amazed me how quickly war had become the general topic of the day among the staff, when everywhere else in the country, save in Godmanchester's unreliable 'rags' *The Advertiser* and *The Globe*, the sunny mood of Innsbruck, the Prime Minister's slogan 'Dover and over, not Dover and under' reigned in happy, peaceful sloth.

I sat that evening on the little seat trying to adjust myself to the rhythm of the guard's van, yet every so often it jolted and shook violently. I summoned up the country scene that awaited me at Stretton – underfoot the beech leaf mould, hanging above the graceful snake head buds like paint brushes dipped in water; the sudden flashes of jayblue or pigeon opal – but the idyllic vision was constantly shattered by memories of Rackham's persistent war chatter, of Bobby's increasingly carefree last trump laughter, of Englander's canny estimates of this and that blast proof material. In vain I assured their haunting voices as I had their solid presences that this was a great beginning, not a melancholy, long-expected ending. As an inspirer of confidence, I was, as Jane Falcon would have said, 'acting against the grain'. She would never have cast me for the role. Yet, just as by persevering in my vision of the Stretton countryside I was able to endure the fug of the van, so by hoping against hope that Leacock's scheme was a reality, I had been able to support the tedium, the three men's work, the petty squabbles and the sea of papers that nowadays filled my office. I had even found some balance on the crazy seesaw of evacuation-foundation which Godmanchester had offered us; and, believing that Godmanchester's fears were justified, could carry out the evacuation single handed. But, as constant icy draughts made the van's inferno almost intolerable, so the chilling winds of my doubts half-spoken in the interview with Leacock and Godmanchester returned again and again to make my work days at Regent's Park seem meaningless. Why, whenever I heard that our President had been pottering or mooching in the Gardens, did it always seem that yet another member of the staff had become assured that the National Reserve scheme was a cover for evacuation? Why did poor Mrs Purrett, alarmed for her ageing mother in London, assure me that a secret with her was as safe as with the Bank of England? Why did Matthew become a model of soldierly discretion, assuring me that he knew how important it was that the rank and file shouldn't panic? If Godmanchester was so gaga that he blabbed like this, then our prospects were alarming. If, as I believed, he was not, what was his motive in telling all and sundry what he had so solemnly asserted was only for Leacock and me? The answer I hazarded to this question was cynical, intuitive, and malicious; it had been met already by his almost direct negative. I could not voice it to anyone. Least of all to Martha. With her I had to hide even Godmanchester's prediction of war, until I had decided whether I credited that enough to tear her out of her present happy calm.

Yet I almost forgot my anxieties, grievances, and discomforts when we arrived at Stretton. There on the platform stood Edwin Leacock ready to receive me. A regenerated old man is a sight to banish self-pity. He was always bouncy in his movements, springy in his gestures, of course; but, as I had known him, the vigour had been curiously wooden, the ebullience forced and impaired by a certain shiftiness. Now, with a change from the not very good formal suit which marked in his eyes the man at the top to an old man's grey flannel trousers and sports coat, he seemed suddenly fifteen years younger, more honest, more likeable. Filson and Strawson, out of uniform until we opened to the public, were on each side of him. A group of young keepers and labourers stood by. It was the very picture of some inspiring, able colonel-archaeologist with his assistants at a dig.

With confidence and happiness Leacock had also acquired consideration.

'I'll take on from now, Carter,' he said. 'You go and have a sleep. And then you can tell me what you think of everything.'

He summoned one of Godmanchester's chauffeurs to take me to a waiting Bentley. It was evident that his command extended over more than the Zoo staffs. As I left him he was briskly and jovially giving orders, checking railway clearance sheets, even giving a hand to move some of the crates of porcupines. Speeding across a lush countryside of rolling farmland and oak-filled parks, I saw in the distance the hills and forests of our National Park. I thought of the leisure of the next few days and moulded my aching limbs into the soft upholstery of the car. This, at last, was the holiday I had hoped for before Godmanchester's offer; and, since it gave hope of such happiness to come, I was able to accept even the absence of Martha and the children that would otherwise have marred it. Able? Perhaps willing.

Before sleep I had breakfast in the little inn parlour that was to be mine for the week.

'Would you care to look at the paper?'

'No, thank you, I'm too tired. But leave it with me.'

The decision was unfortunate for my peace of mind. The paper was Godmanchester's *Advertiser* – a rag I seldom saw – and a large portion was given over to rumours of war. Although the Zoo was not mentioned by name, there was a special word of praise for those London institutions which, despite the Government's lulling words, had decided on evacuation. I lay on my bed for more than half an hour before my aching desire for sleep could swallow up my growing certainty that my suspicions of our President were well grounded.

At first I felt I could not puncture Leacock's new-found zest in living; then I became irritated with his evasion of reality; at last, I decided that I must not again let my dislike of doing hurt absolve me from a larger duty. But not until I had slept, I thought, not until I was rested enough to be as kind and as serious as I knew how.

It was midday when I woke, refreshed and resolved. I was to meet Leacock at the old Stretton Private Zoo now used for the resting and treatment of new arrivals from Regent's Park. Then, sauntering through the Exotic Park, we were to make our way to Merritt's Farm for luncheon. The motor car dropped me at the entrance to a paddock which might have been the scene of rehearsal for some County Agricultural Exhibition or even the Royal Show, if it had not been for the rarity of the creatures being groomed. In the foreground Filson was superintending the feeding of some emus, a crane, and an adjutant stork that had just been released from the loose box in which I had brought them down. In the distance, half a mile away, Strawson's fat figure was being shaken into melting jelly as he helped a young keeper to exercise a llama.

Concerned for Filson's welfare and anxious to postpone my meeting with Leacock, I asked the old man how he found life in the country.

'It's a new life, Sir. I'd never have believed it. But I feel as I did in the first days when I was put in charge of the humming bird house just after the War. There seems something to do all the time and something worth doing too. Mind you, it's not for me to say, but it's the Director that does it. It's an experience to work for him. Nothing's too much trouble to help you, but nothing's too much to ask you to do. I said to Mrs Filson last night, "I've never been driven like it and I've never felt more equal to it, though I'm turned sixty." Of course, there'll never be anyone like Mr Price, as you know, Sir. But . . . well, working with the Director is a different sort of thing. As I said to Mrs Filson it's like a mission sermon – like the Dominicans or the Jesuits give in our church, you know, Sir – after the usual sermon by Father Hansford. I can't do fairer by Mr Price than make the comparison.'

I wondered what either party might have made of it.

But I asked, 'And Mrs Filson?'

'Marvellous, Sir. She's learning to drive the little car Lord Godmanchester's given us, to go into Hereford for Mass and that. And though she misses her lounge, she's got it into her head to start collecting antiques to furnish the cottage. Black and white it is. With the old beams. And she's hoping to pick things up here and there, you know, as the fancy takes her.' He paused. 'And the dahlias in our cottage garden, Sir, are a picture. I hope you'll come to see them.'

I hesitated, then I asked, 'It doesn't worry you working with Strawson?'

The old man looked down, then taking a handful of grapes from his pocket, he appeared to be intent on feeding the crane.

'I haven't forgotten,' he said, 'but time will do it. And everything tactful to make me feel easier the Director's done. I'm sorry you had to tell him by the way, Sir, of what I'd said, and yet I'm not, for it's taught me the fine cut of the man's character.'

This information further complicated the feelings with which I saw Leacock get out of his Landrover and come towards me from the distant road. As I advanced towards him, I tried to avoid Strawson, but he bore down upon me.

'And how may I ask is the old place, Sir? As smoggy as ever if I may judge from the London look you've brought with you.'

Luckily Leacock hailed me at that moment. As we walked back to the Landrover, he said, 'Of course, I've been very cut off from the uniformed staff in the past, but I'm getting to know them now. That man Strawson's a humbug, as you said, but he's not altogether incompetent and I work him hard. Filson's the best chap – a bit slow but utterly reliable. There's no doubt your friend Price has done a good job of training there.'

I gazed out of the window until I no longer wanted to laugh at this judgement, then I took a gulp and said, 'Before you talk about the wonderful progress you've made down here, will you forgive me if I tell you something that's worrying me greatly.'

'Of course. But you shouldn't worry. You can never do the best work that way. Of course with Falcon and Sanderson round your neck, I'm not surprised.'

'It's not that. I am overworked but that wouldn't upset me if I felt sure of what I was working for.'

Leacock turned on me with a hurt and puzzled look.

'Don't judge what we're doing here until you've seen everything, Carter.'

'Oh, please, I've judged it in essence already and I mean all the praise that I've given. No, it's Godmanchester's motives that I'm worried about. There's hardly a member of the staff at Regent's Park who hasn't come somehow or other to think that the move to Stretton is an evacuation in the face of threat of war. And though I can't prove it, I believe Godmanchester has told them so.'

'Well that's what he believes. He told us so.'

'He also told us that his belief was not to be murmured to anyone. Now it's more than hinted at in his newspapers. What is one to think?'

Leacock laughed. 'That he's trying to create a war scare, of course. I've never had any doubt that that was one of his motives.' He began patiently to explain to me, 'You know, Carter, there are more sorts of men than one. Now I'm an entirely single-minded chap. But Godmanchester's got multiple aims. Take his attitude to this place. I think he was sincerely impressed by my ideas. But he's an amateur and his vision is elsewhere. Then again, as *you* told him, he's got it into his head that he may have to retire from the political scene and that zoo-keeping would be a nice hobby. I doubt if he thinks of it as more than a very remote insurance. We must hope he's right. Then he truly believes that the Government's incompetent so he's not exactly lying when he says that he thinks we're in for trouble. But I've felt from the start that he was exaggerating that. I don't feel war in the air myself.' He sniffed the breeze that came in through the swivel window as though to reassure himself. 'No, far more important to him is that he should be in power. Not selfishly, you know, he genuinely thinks he's the only competent man for the job. He may be right. That's politics, I don't know. Being, as I say, a single-minded chap, I don't too much like the devious way he goes about things and the lack of concentration of effort. It looks to me too much like old age, but there you are.'

I burst out laughing. Leacock flushed red.

'I'm sorry if you find my views ridiculous.'

'No, no, that's not it at all. It's only that this has been my suspicion all along and I've thought it too disgraceful to mention to you.'

'Unprincipled more than disgraceful, don't you think? But then we know he's not an idealist. At least not in the sense that we understand it. But in any case ours is only one of the enterprises he's interested in. I read his rags down here, you know. I'm too tired for *The Times*. Business firms, factories, archaeological expeditions, sports events, everything he's got a stake in, even the pictures his wife has lent to the Tate, are being used to point the same moral – Godmanchester for Prime Minister or else. And we must hope he gets his way. The Prime Minister for our honorary President would give the Society great prestige and it would also bring the Reserve government money. And it would keep him too busy to interfere.'

My amazement at his new-found confidence must have

reached him. For a moment the old high-flown, preaching note came into his voice.

'And he's been generous beyond belief, Carter. If anything I've said suggests that I've forgotten that, I'm sorry for it. I shall never forget it.'

We were approaching the red-brick farm-house. One wing was covered with the grey green of wistaria, the other with the glossy green of magnolia grandiflora. With its elegant white porch and shelled cupola it seemed to me everything that was desirable. My anxieties were forgotten in contemplating it.

'It's a bit square and characterless, isn't it?' said Leacock. 'But Mrs Leacock's made the rooms very cosy.'

I said, 'I simply don't understand how you can calmly accept all you've said about Godmanchester and place any reliance on his word. The gentleman's agreement you've accepted for the Reserve . . .'

He braked suddenly, jolting me against the car roof, turning the bonnet close up against a rhododendron bush, so that its rare autumn crimson blossoms were pressed ridiculously against the windscreen.

He said, 'I'm sixty-two, Carter. I haven't time to hang about. This is the greatest chance I've ever had and I assure you that I shan't easily allow anybody to take it from me.'

I did not feel much happier, though I recognized in his new manner some basis for reassurance. As we drove up the gravel drive towards the porch, where Mrs Leacock in cinnamon jumper and purple tweed suit awaited us, I could say no more than, 'I'll do my best to help you.'

Inside the house my spirits were at once depressed. What Dr Leacock meant by 'cosy' was clearly no more than the presence of his own furniture from the London flat. Armchairs and sofas upholstered in wine-coloured rep and with wooden arms, a wine-coloured carpet flecked with almond green, and an oval mirror with beaten silver frame – they had always saddened me in their old surroundings, now they seemed to make these well proportioned rooms cheerless beyond hope.

Madge Leacock, indeed, unlike her husband, did appear a little dimmed in her bright spirits by the move.

She kept patting the chairs and saying, 'We're not quite straight yet, Mr Carter. But Edwin's out such a lot and I'm more used to camping when I'm in the country.'

Dr Leacock gave me the smallest glass of the driest sherry. 'They say this is rather good Tio Pepe,' he said, but he did not take any.

Mrs Leacock cried, 'Oh, none for me, Daddy. It would make me tiddly at lunchtime, I'm sure.'

I had a feeling that she was not exaggerating.

It would only be pot luck she told me, she was not used to cooking.

'Our Mrs Coppard was such a real cockney; we couldn't persuade her to leave London. Sometimes Harriet cooks us something special, doesn't she, Daddy?' Dr Leacock didn't answer.

The dining-room furniture was of a standard antique oak kind that has been machine made now for many decades; it did not even claim to be imitation Jacobean. Its very lack of pretension was depressing. Nor were the jug of water and the small squares of cut bread beside each place more cheering. The shepherd's pie was of the very worst sort – with lumpy mashed potato and the minced meat swimming in a strongly flavoured gravy. Mrs Leacock said that the house would be nicer when they had some of the family down to stay – Elinor was coming shortly with the twins, and then Michael and his pretty little wife. She also said that, if she knew herself at all, it wouldn't take her long to get to know everybody round about. Leacock talked of the acclimatization of agouti and hyrax. But he was less entirely happy. He was clearly waiting.

We had already begun to eat the apple crumbly when Harriet came in, preceded as she had been on the night of the programme by Rickie. Both dog and mistress looked the worse for wear. His coat was mudcaked and she had put on too much make-up too carelessly. Her eyes were great dead sapphires; at the sides of her large sensual mouth misplaced lipstick emphasized lines of discontent. She gave a scowling look at her father, a contemptuous look at her mother and the food, a hungry look at me.

Dr Leacock said, 'Harriet, I must ask you to have some consideration for meal times.'

He would have gone on, but Mrs Leacock made absurd little signs at him to stop. Harriet sat, crumbling her piece of bread. I made a selfish resolve that the Leacock family troubles should not spoil my visit to Stretton.

Mrs Leacock said, 'I hope they've made you comfortable at the Crown. I believe it's a nice old pub.'

'I was worried when I heard that they'd got young children, Carter. That sounded too much like home from home to me. You need a rest.' Dr Leacock seemed really concerned.

'I hate children,' Harriet announced defiantly.

Mrs Leacock began nervously to scrape out the remnants of the apple crumbly from the dish.

'Harriet lost her only one,' she said in what I think must be termed a half-aside.

'Mummy always thinks that will make people like me better. It's rather odd really because the thing only lived two days. And I had a miscarriage as well in my first marriage but that's never been expected to endear me to anyone.'

Mrs Leacock gave a little embarrassed laugh almost before Harriet spoke so that it struck me that they must have had this ghastly conversation many times before in company. The thought did not endear them to me.

'Actually I had two abortions in my second marriage. But I suppose they would be considered downright off-putting.'

Dr Leacock said, 'As you will see, Carter, Harriet likes to show off in front of visitors. She's never really grown up.'

She turned to him and said very quickly and quietly, 'That's marvellous really, coming from someone who still calls his prick his weewee.' Then she turned to her mother and, as though she had never made the remark, said, 'They hadn't the green wool, darling. They wanted to sell me something of a sort of dark sage green which I didn't think you'd want. Horribly dingy!'

Her father was forced to accept the escape she offered him. He too said as naturally as he could manage, 'You're going to give Carter coffee, aren't you, Madge dear?'

Harriet now turned to me. She gave a kind of wink. Then she asked me what I was going to do at Stretton.

'I can't say I like being surrounded by all these captive animals,' she said, 'I suppose it's all right with a very few – the tortoises and things, though even then ... But with the beautiful strong ones it horrifies me. One could forget them in London even though Father was their keeper. But here one seems surrounded by them. I think of them at night. The wolves and the pumas – all the lordly ones. They ought to be free.'

She was talking, I thought, to give her mother time to recover from her embarrassment. The old woman's head seemed to shake involuntarily when she went out to the kitchen. She returned carrying cups of some pale brown liquid with a strangely iridescent surface. She was composed enough to make an effort.

She said, 'For all their quarrels Harriet and Edwin are so alike. Those are just Daddy's ideas, dear!'

'Limited liberty!' Harriet laughed as she said it.

To prevent a fresh outbreak of the feud, I said, 'What about your dog?'

'Oh, Rickie! That's different. He's my man. Aren't you, old darling?' Then smiling almost happily, she said, 'But you really are concerned with *wild* animals, Mr Carter. I remember you on television some years ago with those badgers. That *did* seem to be a thing worth doing.'

I told her then of my excitement about the British Reserve, of how I hoped during this week to prospect and chart the whole area, of how I knew already of at least two groups of badgers' setts, and that they seemed to be independent colonies. I wanted to talk about it and I wanted to help. I managed somehow to include all of them in the conversation, but, although she talked with her mother, she completely ignored anything her father said. As she relaxed, I thought that I liked her rather better. After all, if she was what most people would have called 'impossible', she was also, from another angle, in an 'impossible' position. I did not know to what degree she was held there, whether by indigence or laziness or by a promise or possibly by some legal control. If her weapons seemed crude and cruel I had no means of knowing what ancient feuds she was fighting. Perhaps she guessed that I was not 'against' her, for she smiled and said,

'Well, I must see that Rickie doesn't play havoc with your wild life. Not that it will be possible to lay blame on him, that's one thing. There's sure to be some dangerous beast escaping all the time from this prison without bars. So any shambles that Rickie creates on the local farms can be put down to the escaped hyena or what not, thank God.'

Dr Leacock said coldly, 'I hope you'll keep this kind of frivolous nonsensical talk to yourself, Harriet.'

'As I don't know anybody here to talk to I shall have to, shan't I? In any case if they do escape, good luck to them.'

I tried to take a hand, 'I'm afraid it wouldn't be good luck. An escaped captive animal is simply a hunted and terrified creature.'

'Oh, I dare say it would have some fun before it was shot. Getting its own back by eating some fat, juicy little child.' She was silent for a moment and then quite abruptly she asked, 'Would you take me with you to watch your badgers?' She sounded desperate.

It was the last thing I wanted, I thought it unfair, and yet at that moment I felt that I couldn't let her down in front of her father.

I said, 'Certainly. It's tiring, you know, keeping still and absolutely quiet. I shall verify the setts today and if the wind's right, we might go at dusk tomorrow.'

Mrs Leacock said, 'You'll have to behave yourself, Harriet dear.'

She looked at her mother for a moment and then burst out in laughter.

I said, 'I'm afraid you won't be able to bring Rickie though.'

'I've got some sense of the *convenable*,' she replied.

In for a penny, in for a pound. I tried to be interesting. I sketched the future Reserve for her on a scrap of paper, marking such fox earths, badger setts, squirrels' dreys and so on as I had already found. She leaned over my shoulder, her dark hair tickling my neck and cheeks; she seemed completely happy and relaxed; but, attractive though I had often thought her, her physical touch somehow repelled me. However I was now committed. Mrs Leacock condemned me to a further decrease of my privacy.

'You must join Daddy and me this evening,' she cried, 'we're being shown round Stretton House by Lord Godmanchester's private secretary. The lords and lordesses are away so we common mortals are to be let in.'

I was amazed that they had not yet been invited to the house; I expected a note of bitterness in her voice but there was none.

'Don't say you won't come or I shall think you like Harriet better than me.'

I wondered how Martha and I would ever support the Leacocks if my dream came true.

I spent the whole afternoon charting the Reserve, verifying the observations of my previous visit, noting what might have been the runs of various mammals, looking out for fur caught on twigs, for dropped feathers, for spoors and for excrement. One of Godmanchester's keepers had told me that a polecat had been shot there some months before and twice that afternoon I thought I detected their scent. In fact I returned to the pub feeling that the British Reserve had an exciting future.

I had already seen Stretton House from a distance, and, of course, in illustrations. The late Victorian architect, in choosing the French château style, had included every sort of tourelle and spiral staircase, every carved dormer or chimney; no colour was missing from the tiled roof, no possible inset medallion or carved heraldic device from the staring white stone surface of the walls. It was only admired by a very few extremist neo-Victorians – Bobby Falcon had professed some interest in it. I found it absolutely repellent.

Mrs Leacock said, 'Isn't it a lovely old place? A change after *our* terrible barracks.'

Her husband said, 'I fancy it's been added to.'

This hint gave no warning to his wife.

She said, 'All the carvings and little creatures! They couldn't do it now, of course. We haven't the craftsmen.'

Ashamed of myself I nevertheless became taut with embarrassment, wondering how the secretary would receive Mrs Leacock's *naïveté*. All was well; a young woman from the village had been deputed to deal with us. She recited the details of the house in a flat singsong voice and neither listened to nor waited for comments. She seemed mainly to be concerned with questions of size – Stretton was larger than Chambord and Chenonceaux combined; there were twelve more turns in the staircase than in that at Blois; the mansards copied from those at the Louvre were twice as high; and so on. Here and there were paintings and pieces of furniture that interested me and I soon fell into an easy enough daze. Mrs Leacock asked whether Lady Godmanchester stayed there often; no, said the girl, her ladyship didn't care for the country, though she was now having her collection of pictures brought down there from London.

When Madge Leacock was expressing her interest in a portrait of Godmanchester's grandmother by Jacques Emile Blanche, there was a sudden clatter and a high angry foreign voice shouting orders. The village girl looked alarmed, but, before she could move us on, the double doors at the other end of the long gallery opened and Lady Godmanchester walked in followed by footmen carrying three large pictures. I recognized her at once – she was every bit as pretty and as hard as her Press photos showed her, only whereas I had thought of her as perpetually the twenty-five-year-old penniless country girl Godmanchester had married in the sixties, she was now much nearer thirty-eight and lines of boredom rather than of bad temper showed her age in her face. At first the Leacocks didn't recognize her and I breathed again; then Mrs Leacock suddenly made a little nervous girlish run towards her.

'Lady Godmanchester?'

'Yes.'

'I'm Mrs Leacock – this is Dr Leacock. And this is the Secretary of the Zoo, Mr Carter.'

Lady Godmanchester said again, 'Yes?' and went on giving orders about the paintings.

'We're so grateful,' Mrs Leacock said, 'for all you've done to settle us in here.'

This time Lady Godmanchester only turned her head slightly towards us.

'Just tell the housekeeper or my secretary, will you?'

Dr Leacock tried to help his wife out.

He said, 'We've been most interested in your pictures, Lady Godmanchester.'

She turned with faintly more interest.

'Oh, when did you see them?'

The Leacocks looked puzzled, then Mrs Leacock said bravely, 'The hands are so finely painted. That's the real test, isn't it?' She pointed to the Blanche portrait.

Lady Godmanchester didn't laugh, it would have been better if she had.

She simply said rather angrily, 'Oh, these are dreadful things, they're nothing to do with me. I wondered how you could have got into our London house.'

The village girl clearly detected Lady Godmanchester's mood for she tried to move us on; but Mrs Leacock was dauntless, she went up to a picture that the younger footman was carrying. Bending down to look at it, she said, 'Ah, these are *your* famous pictures, Lady Godmanchester. May I?'

Lady Godmanchester said, 'Nothing good is down here yet. I don't want to move the Delacroixs and the Ingres until I have to. All this war is so infuriating.'

Mrs Leacock said, 'You must have great fun picking them up.'

'Picking them up?' Lady Godmanchester seemed genuinely puzzled, then she said impatiently, 'Oh, I buy through dealers, of course.'

Even Madge Leacock was aware that they were not getting very far. She bent her head round to look at another painting.

'What's that?' she asked.

'Well, a nude, I suppose.'

Dr Leacock laughed as well as he was able.

'My wife meant who's the artist.'

'It was painted by Etty.' Lady Godmanchester sounded desperate.

Dr Leacock said, 'I believe you collect Turners.'

'I have some paintings by him, yes.'

I said feebly, 'I love the late Turners.'

'Well, yes, I suppose so. They're very good.'

But Madge Leacock had moved on to the third painting. A light seemed to dawn in her childish eyes.

She said, 'Look, Daddy. One of the old Victorian pictures.' I caught a glimpse of a genre painting by Wilkie or someone of that kind.

'Well, that is amusing, isn't it?' She had found the 'smart' word; she knew now what Lady Godmanchester was up to.

More confidently she said to her, 'You certainly have found some amusing things.'

Lady Godmanchester's romantic urchin boy's face set in fury, her eyes blazed.

'They are not very good paintings, but they are certainly not amusing. I don't buy amusing paintings. And now I'm afraid this room is closed. Good-bye.'

Poor Mrs Leacock was near to tears on the way home.

'Oh, dear, Edwin. I'm afraid I put my foot in it badly. I do hope I haven't done any harm.'

Dr Leacock took one hand from the wheel and squeezed hers.

But it was Mrs Leacock who unwittingly said the right word, I believe. 'You know I really think,' she said, 'that the trouble was that she wasn't too sure of her own taste.'

After dinner I was enjoying the luxury of reading *Tarka the Otter* quietly in the pub parlour when Dr Leacock appeared. He accepted a brandy and then said nervously, 'Carter, I think you saw something at lunch of what we have to put up with.'

I wasn't having that. If Martha and I were coming to live here I had to watch what nets of intimacy I involved her in. So I answered, 'It's really entirely a family matter, isn't it, Leacock?'

'I had hoped we could keep it so. But she seems determined to drag others in. I want to ask you a favour. Don't let her come with you tomorrow night.'

'I'm sorry. That's nothing to do with you, I think. May I be frank? I don't think you'll help your daughter by treating her like a child.'

He got up from his chair and paced up and down the room; he came to rest before a large stuffed salmon at which he stared.

'You know, I suppose, that she's only after one thing with men.'

'Well, it isn't such a bad thing as all that, is it?'

He looked so upset, that I cried, 'Look, I'm thirty-six, and she's not so much younger. As it happens I believe in being faithful to my wife. But on any grounds we're adults. It's for us to decide.'

He said, 'You don't understand. Wherever she's been involved there's been trouble. So far she's kept away from my colleagues. But you don't know how much I value your co-operation, Carter. And if she starts anything with you, I don't know where it will end. She hates me, you know.'

'You don't exactly love her.'

'No. I dislike her very much. Mrs Leacock thinks we're to blame. God knows why. The others have done well enough in life. But Mrs Leacock is very fond of her and that's that as far as I'm concerned. Though, of course, Harriet trades on it. Anyhow these are all *our* troubles. I'm only asking you, and asking you very seriously, to do an old man who values you very much the favour of not involving yourself.'

'I think she may be very hurt.'

Dr Leacock wouldn't listen.

'Will you just do me this kindness, Carter?'

He sounded so desperate that in the end I agreed. I wrote a note there and then to Harriet Leacock telling her that I was not after all going badger watching. I made it as cold as possible – in for a penny, in for a pound. I posted it that night in the village. I had no intention, in fact, of changing my plans.

I tried the next day to give myself up to the pleasures of the place. Indeed it's only a sort of inbred puritanism that makes me write 'tried'. I separated myself completely from the Leacocks that day and made my tours with various members of the uniformed staff. They were enthusiastic and I was so with them. The place had enormous potentialities and not only in my field of British fauna. The reconstruction of our historic wild life seemed to present fascinating problems. Even the exotic park would do much for the preservation of foreign species that were threatened. And there was the overall excitement of design. At the end of the day I felt that my life would really make sense if I could settle down there.

As I was returning to the pub, I met Mrs Leacock.

She said, 'I had a mouldy night, I don't mind telling you, thinking about the way I'd dished Edwin with Lady G. But do you know what I've done? I thought at first of just leaving it, but problems don't get solved by forgetting them. I'm no good at writing apologies and anyway letters often do harm. So I just popped a pot of the bramble jelly I've made into a bag with a little note saying that it was a poor thing, but my own. You see with someone so rich there's nothing you can do for them. But I dare say they never think to give her anything homemade. Then I just added casually that I wanted to be friends. I hope it works, don't you?'

I could have shaken her soundly, old innocence and all; but I could only say that I hoped so too.

She said brightly, 'This is a place where I'll have to watch my ps and qs, I can see,' and set off gaily for home.

It was growing dusk already, when with a torch and field-glasses I made my way through the deep bracken towards the bank where I had located the second group of setts. They were the newer of the two, I had decided, with few entrances; the sandy surface that here covered the clay subsoil was less worn with seasons' digging than the larger group at the edge of the beechwood. There the ground was so worn and slippery that the setts might well have become disused; a scent of fox seemed to confirm this. But here among the oaks the setts were so recent that only a few of the huge knotted tree roots had been laid bare. At the side of the clearing too there was a fresh-seeming midden. There were only three entrances to the setts. Not too many to observe. Yet the setts had been used for more than two or three seasons, I felt sure, and were likely to house more than one family of badgers. I avoided carefully the beaten tracks in the bracken that showed where they passed to their feeding grounds – one, I thought, to a small hazel copse, the other, perhaps, to a nearby field of stubble. The light was fading as I stationed myself against an oak tree, laying my torch and glasses in a gnarled hole and so scattering a colony of woodlice. A light breeze blew dead against me. The bracken's scent brought serial memories stretching far back into my childhood. There would be a full moon up in an hour. The situation was ideal.

I had been there about twenty minutes. Occasionally the breeze stirred the leaves like waves on a distant sea shore. Otherwise the noises in the absolute stillness came harsh and exaggerated to the ear – even the movement of what might have been a rat or a stoat two hundred yards or so away from me in the bracken. Once a jet overhead scraped the nerves of the silence. Once, too, a barn owl had clattered overhead in the trees – there was still light enough to see the buff of its wings as well as the white of its breast. I thought once that I heard a slight snuffling sound at the entrance to the setts which suggested that I might not have long to wait. All the echoes of past happiness were setting up their reverberations in me; yet, and this was the anticipated glory, I was exactly in *that* wood opposite *that* sandy bank behind *that* oak tree at *that* moment only.

She made, I must admit, professionally little noise in approaching me. So little that she must have been only a few yards from me, when I caught a glimpse of a black and white snout sniffing the air at entrance B. Then suddenly I knew that someone was moving up behind me. She stood very close to me and began to whisper.

'I looked for you at the other place first by the beechwood.'

I put my finger to my lips. She was here, that was irksome enough; but if I could possibly prevent her, she should not spoil my pleasure. It was clear that my letter had not yet reached her; I pushed out of my mind the thought of how it was at all possible now to prevent her from getting it – her mother's aid? I would not think of it now. This was my well-earned evening. She took my hand and pulled it under her skirt; she had nothing on underneath. A moment later I felt her hand against my thigh, and then on my crutch, and now her fingers were dexterously opening my flies. My only thought was that in this place anything we did would inevitably make noise enough to scare the badgers for nights to come. Lust and anger and a sense of being made a fool of fought together in me. Then she pulled her hand away and with the other smacked my face hard. The noise echoed through the wood. She spoke in a violent intense whisper as though the wood's silence made her afraid to raise her voice.

'You needn't have been so frightened,' she said. 'You and that old bastard! You'd have to have something much bigger than that to interest me.'

I saw her face for a moment as I turned; she was not in the slightest degree hysterical, and only wish-fulfilment could have told me that she was mad. She was just a very angry, unhappy woman who for years had fought every discipline. I put out my hands towards her shoulders. I wanted to shake her if I could not comfort her. But she was gone, crashing her way through the bracken, rousing woodpigeons and owls and jays. The setts by the sandy bank would yield nothing again for some nights.

I walked slowly back to the pub, cursing all Leacocks as I went.

I had at that time experienced very little melodrama in my life. I had no simple prescription for banishing its after effects. For the remainder of my stay at Stretton, I soaked myself in the new organization. To my good luck, I also found that the old sett under the beech trees was, in fact, occupied by two families of badgers. I watched them regularly and was even rewarded by seeing a cub ejected by its parents from a nest it had outgrown. The autumn departure of the cubs was one of the least documented aspects of the badger life cycle. I should have been deeply satisfied. Yet the scene with Harriet hung around me in part anger, part shame; it was as though I was constantly finding by some mischance that my private parts were showing in public. I also did all my watching in great inconvenience at dawn, as though the dusk had somehow become tainted. I didn't see Harriet again, but, not long before I left, Mrs Leacock said she hoped her daughter hadn't been a nuisance to me.

'Poor old Harriet,' she said, 'I'm afraid life's a bit mouldy for her here. But then she shouldn't have been such a naughty girl. She's always been rather the odd one out. Of course, she had rotten luck both times she was married. Edwin says she's got a natural flair for picking up duds. The thing is she's never been as go-ahead as the rest of the family. And Daddy's so brilliant, he gets impatient. But you mustn't think she's really bad. That's just talk and showing off.'

The day before I left there was a sudden alarm. An opossum had got loose from the Exotic Reserve, climbed into a farm-house window and given an old woman a nasty scare by feigning death on her bedroom floor. It was easily recaptured and could in any case have done no harm, but Dr Leacock was nevertheless extremely angry, particularly when he discovered that the loss had been reported to Strawson three or four days before.

'The whole foundation of a National Park in a populous

country like ours must depend upon security. People will only welcome liberty when they know it means safety. The natural life can only grow up among us when all suspicions and fears have died away.'

Without identifying myself with his form of words I was in complete agreement with him. Lord Godmanchester, who had just come down from London, was less helpful. As the local landowner and a former M.F.H., he was all against coddling complaining tenants.

'You ought to have talked to my agents first, Leacock,' he said, 'before apologizing too profusely. They know these people and it just doesn't do. If we're going to grovel every time a tame mouse gets under some old woman's skirts, we shall lose all face. I suppose Strawson didn't fuss about this 'possum because he knew that the most it would do would be to pinch an egg or two out of the chicken runs? You'd have taken quite a different line if it had been a kodiak bear or a wolverine, wouldn't you, Strawson?'

'That was exactly my meaning, Sir. I never care to raise an unnecessary alarm. *Parturiunt montes* I've never studied Latin, but certain tags stick.'

Dr Leacock cut right through all this.

'There's absolutely no excuse, Strawson. And I don't want to hear any. You're very lucky, you know, to be associated with a scheme of such revolutionary proportions, you will do well not to try to measure it by your own inevitably limited standards. Rules have been laid down, if you follow them, you will at least have an excuse.'

'I think the chap was trying to use his initiative,' Lord Godmanchester put in.

Dr Leacock entirely ignored this.

'I accept your excuse, Strawson, for this time. We shall make a complete check of all boundary wiring, exits and so on. I don't want to blame you for what may be the fault of the workmen. But I do blame you for taking the escape casually, and I shall blame you still more if it happens again.'

When Strawson had gone, I thought that Leacock would

offer some excuse to Godmanchester, instead he turned sharply upon him.

'Running an estate and running a National Reserve are two quite different things, you know. I didn't want to put you in an embarrassing position in front of subordinates, but I must ask you to keep right out of all questions of staff discipline.'

To my surprise, Lord Godmanchester only said, 'You and Carter both let that chap's way of speaking prejudice you against him. But still that's your affair.'

Before I returned to London, he took me aside and asked me how I thought the Director was coping with the situation. I replied that I was very much impressed.

'Yes, that's what I think. He's nothing like such a windbag as he was, is he? That's why I'm letting him have his head.'

I was not altogether convinced now that he could have held Dr Leacock's head even if he had wished to do so. But I didn't say this.

It had always been agreed between Martha and me that we should tell each other everything, especially anything that concerned our sexual life. As Martha said, 'It'll either be so important that we must talk about it; or else it'll be so unimportant that it'll be funny. That's how sex is.' Like a lot of Martha's sayings, this was an over-simplification. But it was fundamentally what she had learned from me. With modifications, and with due allowance for the pathology that asked our compassion etc., the Harriet episode fell into the funny category. Yet I had some hesitation in telling Martha. I wasn't altogether sure that I could not have behaved better, but still that was a poor reason for concealment. More disturbing to me was its effect upon Martha's attitude to our moving eventually to Stretton. I was so set upon this now that I could not bear to unearth any opposition; yet Martha had a horror of the 'crawly', and there seemed no doubt now that there was something 'crawly' about the Leacock family life that in the enforced gregariousness of rural isolation might become a problem. I compromised by telling her first of my happiness and excitement about the Reserve; only when we were firmly relaxed after dinner, did I retail the Harriet story.

Martha said, 'Oh, poor thing! What can be done for her, Simon?' Then, 'Ugh! It's rather crawly, isn't it?' And at last, 'Well, phooey to her, she doesn't know what she's missed.' And she walked over to me and kissed me.

Yet, in a fashion, she seemed a little detached from the whole of my Stretton adventures.

She said, 'I'm so happy for you, darling. So truly happy. This could be it, you know, the beginning of what we hoped for when you left the old Treasury!'

I felt sleepy and contented and very ready to take her to bed; but she was restless. She put on the banquet scene from *Don Giovanni*, but I thought she was only half listening. Then she came and sat on the floor at the foot of my chair and put her head in my lap. I stroked her hair, but I was disturbed – it was a posture that so often preceded confidences of varying discord.

'Isn't it awful,' she asked, speaking as though she was very far away from me in a beautiful deep sea cavern, 'that just when everything seems right for someone, it seems all wrong for someone else?'

I said, 'Yes. But stop talking in that far away voice. You're not a young actress with her first part in *The Seagull*. What's wrong for who?'

She laughed, 'All right,' she said, 'it's Bobby. After what Jane said I've been seeing quite a lot of him. I suppose I've always taken him for granted, Simon. He was the great figure of my childhood, my godfather whose pictures appeared in all the papers. At every school I went to I was the envy of all the other girls – my godfather the great TV star, the man who found the abominable snowman, the man who exploded the myth of the Nandi bear, so handsome and sexy, a sort of pin-up boy for the girls of our social class. I was even more flattered than embarrassed when he made a pass at me on a ski-ing holiday. Then I had a period of being against him. I suppose I was upset when I found out that he and Mummy had been lovers. And I used to rather like Jane. But just lately after he found you the job at the Zoo, I've thought he was a nice old thing, rather pathetic and absurd. Simon! I didn't know how pathetic!'

'My dear, I've told you often enough.'

'Yes, darling, but everybody you describe is ridiculous and a bit sad. Oh, I don't mean that nastily. You do see very funny things in people and you have got a feeling, but you paint the whole world that way. Anyhow I didn't take it seriously. But now I've seen more of him, I feel miserable. Simon, one shouldn't ever take human beings for granted, however long one's known them. And that wretched marriage of his – I've just found it easier to say "that wretched marriage" and leave it at that. They don't even hate each other, they're just that awful thing – "good pals". I must say I hate Jane a bit for it now. All that competence and fun out of life and so on. I thought she was a martyred brave wife, she's just a cold bitch, I'm afraid. I can't do anything for him really. Except that I *have* made him think that he's not too old to explore again. Apparently he's always wanted to search for some sort of armadillo in the Amazon. Anyhow I've got him round to the idea. Oh, it's interfering of me, I'm sure, but if I can't get *you* to do what I want. But he's only agreed, I'm afraid, out of a sort of desperation. And I think if he could get away from that place . . .'

'And leave me all the work to do.'

'Oh! I know, darling, that's exactly it. And that's why he won't go. He says it's not fair on you. Of course, I can't say it to him, but surely he's more in your way than anything . . .'

'You want me to urge him to go. Of course, I will, if you think I should.'

I smiled to myself and Martha cried, 'Well, aren't I right?'

'Yes. I think you are. I was only remembering how you urged me to act against anyone whose muddle might have led to young Filson's death.'

'Oh, I know. But muddle it is, Simon. I've taxed Bobby and

all one can get is guilt and self-accusation. I suppose it's best to let sleeping dogs lie.'

'Remembering only Don Giovanni's misery, let the Commendatore moulder.'

Martha flushed scarlet round her neck. 'You speak as though Bobby had murdered the young man. If you're sure, why don't you face Bobby and tell him? Anyway what *have* you done about it?'

'Oh, for God's sake, Martha. It hasn't been easy for me. I've taken what practical measures I can. But there's the happiness of so many people to consider.'

She kissed me. 'I know,' she said.

I agreed to urge Bobby to go.

'It'll mean late homecomings and an overtired husband.'

'I know, Simon. And that makes me feel more awful because . . .' She paused and then went on, 'or rather it would, if you'd been honest with me, but you haven't. I don't understand how you could have kept from me this business about old Godmanchester's belief in a war.'

'After all it's there to read in his papers every day.'

'Oh, that! Who takes notice of them? Don't try to evade, Simon. You know that this is more serious. To evacuate the Zoo!'

'Well, there are two or even three views about that.' I told her of my conversations with Leacock.

She listened carefully, then she said, 'Yes, I see. That makes it seem more remote. But it's no good, Simon, I can't take any risks over Reggie and Violet. We've been given a warning and we must act on it.'

'Do you suppose I haven't been thinking about that? But one must use reason.'

'Not me. I won't use anything except caution where the children are concerned. I shall take them to Hester in California. God knows Bobby may be right and the whole world's going to blow up. Then they'll simply die quickly or slowly away from us when we could have all died together. But I must take a chance on that. I shall go as soon as I can get a flight, Simon. I'll settle them in there with Hester and then, of course, I'll come back. But meanwhile . . .'

Meanwhile we eased away our miseries in bed as best we could. And very well we could do it, if there need be no tomorrow. As Martha lay back from me with a sigh of content, she said,

'I can't think how anyone else could give that pleasure except you.' Then as she rolled on to her side, she added, 'My God! That poor Harriet just wanting it from anyone, anywhere. The people she must go with! The love she must do without!'

'Darling Martha, I could hardly have taken her out of pity. That would be the worst caddishness of all.'

Martha sighed and rubbed her face in her pillow.

'I suppose so,' she mumbled.

'Well, would you have wanted me to have had her?'

'Oh no, Simon, no, of course not. I should have hated to hear it. One just wishes that everybody could be happy, that's all.'

So Bobby Falcon, with the agreement of the Committee, went off to the Amazon to hire guides and make preliminary charts for his expedition. Godmanchester was a little disturbed, at first, at the disappearance of so famous a man from the scene; but, as Bobby would have resigned had he not received permission, there was little that anyone could do. The God-manchester Press, in fact, decided to back the inevitable heavily. They provided money for the expedition, arranged for a famous cameraman to accompany Bobby, and altogether went out for exclusive rights on the story. For weeks they carried gossip about Sir Robert and Lady Falcon. Jane was asked whether she would not have liked to have accompanied him and was reported as saying, 'Blissful, but you know what the theatre's like. No Amazon this year, I'm afraid, for me.' She took the opportunity to expatiate on the brilliance of her newest playwright. Bobby was photographed looking every sort of soldier-explorer, introspective, reckless and dashingly lecherous in a presentable sort of way. He declared, 'Now war's off the map, thank God, I need a bit of hardship to use up my energies.' It was unlikely that he said this; and it was extremely inconsistent of Lord Godmanchester's papers to call it 'An old soldier's tip to youth', since they were prophesying war in most of the other columns – but truth and consistency after all . . . I was not altogether sorry to see Bobby's neurotic energies out of the way. It was agreed that though I should, in fact, fill the Director's role at Regent's Park, a more senior member must act as titular deputy for Leacock. After much debate, Langley-Beard was chosen; and, irritating though I had often found him, it seemed to me that the Prosector was the man least likely to interfere. Also I was intrigued by the idea of getting to know this saintly man a little better.

In any case the Zoo's affairs came to me through a fog of personal distress at that time. Either the children were going away quite unnecessarily or else it might well be that I was seeing them for the last time. For Martha I had always found a way to express my deep love; but for the children never, and consequently to see them go – despite all the jealousies and irritations that their presence caused me at times – roused an agony and remorse and longing in me. It was not helped by the manner of their going. Naturally war was not mentioned to them, it was simply a holiday with Aunt Hester. We caught their imaginations with a fantasy of cacti and tumbleweeds, of cowboys and Indian Reserves, of dustbowls and canyons; but Reggie, at any rate, I think, considered the whole affair rather strange and my part in it rather callous. Only just before he passed from me beyond the passenger's barrier at London Airport, he said,

'I should think if we stay long at Aunt Hester's, we shan't even remember Daddy's face when we get back.'

And Martha, of course, was only going to settle them in. But what might happen in that time? And how would she find the strength to leave them? In any case, I knew that to be without Martha – especially her physical presence – for even a short while, would prove intolerable.

4

WARS, DOMESTIC AND FOREIGN

WORK, they say, is the best physic of grief. It is not, however, an opiate, merely a counter-irritant that keeps one alive. I got through my work, got through it competently, but it was only with the surface of my mind; my body and my spirit were smothered in a fog of unhappiness that seemed to seep into me from the unusually thick and yellow smog that had settled upon London in those early November days. I could find my way home or, on occasion, to the little Greek restaurant around the corner in Camden Town, through the thickest peasouper – how blessed not to have Bobby in Victorian cockney hailing 'the London pertickler'! – without mischance, if other less sensitive persons did not blunder and bump into me; so I could get through my work and my depressed days were it not for the sudden incursion of the muddling, maddening, blundering of people around me. But such incursions into routine are the very essence of an administrator's day. And many came to irritate and grate upon my tensed up nerves, to send me home each night ready for nothing but to feel and deplore the emptiness of the house.

Only a day after Martha and the children had flown, Godmanchester padded into my office to encourage me in my new authority.

'I know you're not ambitious,' he said, 'but you realize that you've got it all your own way here, don't you? All the rest of them are over sixty.'

'Harry Jackley's only forty.'

'Yes, but he's away from the scene too much. No, no, you're pretty certain to be the future Director. And a very good thing too.'

It was all well-meant Napoleonic stuff, yet I could not but say,

'I'm much more interested in running the British Reserve at Stretton.'

He seemed a little non-plussed.

'Oh, you'll do that all right,' he said, 'but I want to see you make a success of this in the next few months. You're rather a favourite of mine, you know. And I may not have a chance to encourage you too much, because if everything goes right I ought to be pretty busy. For the first time in my life I shall accept office if it comes with a certain reluctance. This business of Leacock's could have been a real interest for me. But still it would have been an old man's second best. In any case there are more important things than my comfort. I believe I can galvanize even this Cabinet into action enough to pull us out of this mess. No, I don't mind saying that I feel a certain real chirpiness these days. I haven't liked playing the role of Cassandra, especially as I've had to overact my part a bit all the time. But I'm beginning to think that we shall avoid war now. Mind you none of this is in the bag, so you'll not say a word about it. But I know you won't. You're one of these efficient people whose feelings don't run away with them. That's why I can afford to let off steam with you.'

I said, 'I've just sent my wife and my children to America. Your papers convinced us that we ought not to take any risks.'

He raised his eyebrows, 'Don't be sarcastic about my papers. That's intellectual claptrap. They're the best value in the market.' He folded his hands across his great paunch. 'Well, let's hope you'll be able to bring them back again in double quick time.'

He was evidently set on the role of being my benefactor; yet it was all I could do not to kick his huge shapeless rhino's bottom as he ambled out of my room. As it was I was too livid with anger that my family should have been pawns in some political game of the old man's, to think out clearly what that game meant for the future of the National Reserve.

The menace of Beard was less expected. He appeared nervously in my office two days after Falcon's departure.

'I'm leaving everything to you, you know, Carter. Apart from anything else I'm engaged on a very interesting histological problem at the moment – the optic nerves of the loris. Some of the people at the College of Surgeons believe I'm on the right lines. However I can't quite stomach being a captain who's never acquainted himself with his own bridge. These war service maxims stick, I suppose. The only experience I had, of course, of this sort of admin thing was as a young sub-lieutenant in the last war. I volunteered, you know. Wavy navy, of course.' He seemed overflowing with confidences, then he looked away from me. 'I was unhappy at home. However they hauled me out again after Dunkirk. Back to research work. And they were quite right. All the same I enjoyed that time at sea. I liked the neatness and order of the Navy, you know.'

It was a new Beard that I introduced to Mrs Purrett and the girls in the typists' pool.

'You won't see much of me, I'm afraid,' he said, 'anyhow you've got Mr Carter. But if there is anything that you want to talk about, I shall always be available between fifteen hours and sixteen-thirty.'

When he had gone the pretty little typist said, 'Good heavens, are we going to be put into uniform? I thought Dr Langley-Beard was so shy. He looks to me to have a nuisance-value.'

Mrs Purrett didn't agree. 'I thought he was charming,' she said, 'so unassuming and helpful.'

Yet it was she who first began to complain. Two or three times in the next few days I found him in the Office Records Room.

'I'd no idea all this stuff was here,' he said.

'Yes, we've often thought of junking it. All the important stuff's been incorporated in published documents.'

'Yes,' he said, 'I know. Except what's been left out.'

Then he seemed to feel the difference in his own manner, for he blushed, dropped a file and began feverishly to collect the spilt documents together again.

'I'm awfully sorry,' he said.

That did not deter him. Now whenever I went into the secretaries' room, he seemed to be there asking Mrs Purrett some question about documentation or filing, dangling some paper in front of her.

'Look, this is duplicated in the "Memo: Finance" files,' or 'This letter should never have got into "Correspondence: Curator", surely. It's a purely external letter from the Director of the Dresden Zoo. Whoever put it in there *did* make a howler.' Then he took to bringing large files to her, saying, 'Mrs Purrett, I'm not a bit happy about 1908. I think I'll have to ask you to re-file the whole year.'

When this happened once or twice, Mrs Purrett said, 'This was all done a very long time ago, Dr Beard. It's hardly my fault.'

To which he only gave a nervous laugh and said, 'The sins of the fathers, Mrs Purrett. Unto the third and fourth generation.'

At last he began to take files home, even quite recent ones, and the office work was thrown into disorder.

At first I tried making fun of Beard. Mrs Purrett, however, did not share my frivolous attitude to the Prosector. She asked for a special interview and presented an ultimatum.

'I know Dr Beard makes you laugh, Mr Carter. And nothing gives me more pleasure than to hear you laughing. But I really don't know how long I can go on working here if he's going to fuss about like this.'

I represented Beard as a mere child in authority, as a dedicated scientist deserving of humouring, as a man of suffering whose life made him a law to himself. It was no good, Mrs Purrett's maternal instinct was not awoken.

She said, 'I don't see that any of that exonerates him from showing a little consideration.'

I was fond of Mrs Purrett; in any case, as we all know, it is difficult to get good secretaries though not perhaps as difficult as to find good anatomists and animal physiologists.

I was a little alarmed at speaking to Beard; I had no idea

how he would react. Luckily the Prosector broached the subject himself.

He said, 'That Mrs Purrett isn't a very quick worker, is she? I asked her to re-file the Statistical papers for 1898 and '99, I showed her exactly the system I wanted, but that was two days ago.'

'She's a first-rate secretary. And she's extremely busy, you know.'

He considered this carefully, then he said, 'All the more reason for working a bit faster surely.'

I was annoyed. 'The office staff here have a great deal of work to do. You can't suddenly start asking them to rearrange the archives and you certainly can't take away files that may be needed for current work. I'm not fussing or anything, but Mrs Purrett's already complained, and she's invaluable to us.'

He looked down at the ground, 'Oh Lor'!' he said and went out of the room. I thought how easily I had put him in his place. But he came back that afternoon.

'Look here, Carter,' he said, 'I've been thinking about it and I'm afraid I can't accept what you said earlier. These files are absolutely vital to the history of this place and at the present moment they just don't make sense. Now, I don't know how much you're told but I dare say you pick up a good deal in your position so that it won't altogether surprise you when I say that the move to Stretton is in some degree an evacuation. War is nearer round the corner than the man in the street knows. Now if it does come, one thing that must be preserved is some record of the work of the Society, even if we're all blown off the face of the earth. But that record's not going to be of any use unless it's in proper order.'

'As I've said, I don't believe that anything essential in those records is not reproduced in published series of the Society.'

'Essential? I'm afraid I'd have to verify even that before I could accept what you've said.'

His nervousness was such that he blushed violently and even stammered as he said it; but he did say it.

'I shall have to go on as though that Mrs Purrett had made no complaint.'

This seemed to me ludicrous and I laughed aloud; then I saw his jaw was set in angry determination.

I said, 'Well, will you take them to the typists' pool instead?'

'I was under the impression that this Mrs Purrett was the senior. That's why I went to her, Carter. But, of course, if she's simply a cypher, I'll go to the other women.'

After that he never appeared to notice Mrs Purrett's vast presence again. The girls grumbled a bit at the extra work, but they seemed to find a way to satisfy Beard's fussing without allowing him grossly to overwork them. Or so I thought.

Beard's fussing, however, continued to run in and out of all the pleasures of that time. Yet I could get no serious counsel from him, nor, for that matter, from Leacock so long as it concerned Regent's Park. There was the matter of the Aquarium, for example; during Jackley's absence, it was under Leacock's supervision. He had neglected it shamefully and only its excellent keepers had insured its maintenance. But they could not be expected to make decisions of major policy. Yet since Jackley's famous 'no' cable, Leacock could hardly allow the word 'aquarium' or 'fish' to be mentioned to him.

I did not care for the little I knew of Jackley, but it seemed to me that, however Leacock and I might discount the war aspect of the Stretton foundation, the Curator of the Aquarium ought at least to know that Godmanchester had given us this warning. I had not so far worried too much, for Jackley was supposed to be returning from abroad at the end of October. Then we heard that he had been injured in a collision between fishing boats in the Tyrrhenian Sea when collecting data about dolphins. He had serious head injuries and a crushed leg; he was likely to be in hospital at Palermo for some months. I immediately urged upon Leacock a provisional plan for the Aquarium in case of war; but to admit this eventuality, and to concern himself with a branch of the Zoo unlikely to form part of the National Reserve for some time to come, were together more than he could face. He simply ignored my

repeated questions on the subject. In the end fairness to the
absent and uninformed Jackley became a pressing point of
honour for me. I read up in detail the management of the
Aquarium in 1939; I had talks with the two keepers. Only the
freshwater fish, it seemed, could be preserved; but prompt
action in storing the ocean water had made reopening an
early possibility after the last war. My task was more difficult,
for I could not well denude the Aquarium of its present water
supply and order the destruction of all marine fauna on the off
chance of a war in which I hardly believed. Yet Jackley, had
he known the facts, might have decided otherwise. I could not
risk informing him of a security matter while he was in a
hospital of one of our potential enemies. It wasn't even my
affair. In the end I took upon myself for the first time in my
life an illicit decision. I arranged for transport to the Gardens
of some 200,000 gallons of sea water from the Bay of Biscay
which alone, I was informed, provided the environment
necessary for all marine species. And I ordered the construction
of underground tanks in which to conserve it.

To organize all this was vexatious enough on top of my very
full programme of regular work, but what at once alarmed and
yet somehow roused my depressed spirits was that I, the man
dedicated to carrying out other's decisions, had made one of
my own, and that in a field in which I had no specialized
knowledge. I needed all my irony to protect myself from the
absurd pretension of the action. And sure enough it exposed
me to the criticism I feared. Pattie Henderson rang me one
afternoon.

'I say,' she said, 'you're making rather an ass of yourself,
aren't you, storing all this ocean water without having a word
with Newton?'

'Why should I have a word with Newton, and how did you
know anyway?'

'Oh, Nutting heard about it. These young chaps are more
on the beam than you think. And as to Newton, conditions of
water storage happen to be his hobby. The younger men are
rather all round sort of men, you know.'

'I don't call knowing about water storage being all round. I think it's a ridiculous sort of thing to have as a hobby.'

Pattie laughed loudly, but she said, 'Unfortunately the last laugh's on you, isn't it?'

I ate humble pie and consulted Newton, only to find that he had not taken into account the action of blast. He withdrew his criticism but I doubt if he informed Nutting and his other friends that he had done so. As he said, 'It never does the administration any harm to be criticized even when it's done the right thing.'

Criticism seemed to be my lot at that time, for a few days later, I received a letter from Leacock.

'I am worried to hear from Langley-Beard that he feels you don't take the Society's work quite seriously enough,' the Director wrote. 'I have come over the last two years to know your worth, and I shall not quickly forget the hard work and the loyal support that you have given me in the move to Stretton. But as you see, I write that "I've come to know your worth" because it took me some time to realize that your ironic approach to much that we do, and the ingrained tendency to abide by the formulas which you've acquired through your years in the Civil Service, were only an unfortunate surface. My own very liberal supply of faults has given me a degree of humour and an acceptance of others that a dedicated scientist like Beard cannot be expected to have. I'm afraid you don't realize how easily your manner seems mere flippancy and how shocking that can be to a senior man for whom the Society's work has perhaps become almost too sacred a duty. I hope you will forgive me for writing like this, but, as an older man and your Chief, and as one who believes that you could come to serve the Society in the highest capacity, I feel that I must draw your attention to those superficial qualities that so often do you injustice.'

I used the letter to wipe my arse. I then wrote a memorandum to Leacock setting out shortly my grounds for considering that the Prosector's virtues and experience made him unsuitable to deputize for the Director. While I agreed, I wrote, that my

very short period of service for the Society and my junior
status made it impossible for me to have final control, there
were, I thought, good reasons for increasing my authority in
all administrative matters. The deputy, should, in fact, be
all but titular. It was not easy to find any of the old men competent and reasonable enough to fill the role. I was forced in
the end to suggest the unpopular Dr Englander.

Hardly had the memorandum gone to the post, before Mrs
Purrett introduced a heavy, square-jawed, youngish man,
unusually for her muddling his name. I believe it was the look
in his clear blue eyes, at once friendly and absolutely without
warmth, which made me immediately think that here was some
sort of policeman. Or it may be, more simply, that it was his
blue gabardine raincoat so tightly belted at the waist. At any
rate I congratulated myself when he corrected Mrs Purrett's
deficiency by announcing himself firmly as 'Detective-
Inspector Martin'.

'Dr Leacock?' he asked.

'No. I'm Simon Carter.'

'I asked to see the Director of the Zoological Gardens.'

'I'm the Secretary.'

'I understood that the lady who has just left us was the
secretary.'

'No, no, she's my secretary. I'm the Secretary of the
Society.'

He looked very dubiously at me.

'The questions I have to ask are highly confidential, Mr
Carter. I think I should prefer to put them to the Director.'

'I'm afraid you would have to go to Herefordshire to do
that. Dr Leacock is at the new National Reserve at Stretton
Park. May I ask the general nature of your inquiries?'

'I think there could be no harm, Mr Carter, in my saying
that they concern the activities of a member of the Zoo's staff.'

My mind ran over all the possible misdemeanours of all the
many people in the Zoo's service – it surprised me how
potentially criminal everyone suddenly seemed to be. I was
not going to let Beard in on this if I could help it.

I said, 'I think you may safely put the questions to me, Inspector. Staff matters are entirely in my hands.'

Inspector Martin considered for a moment, then he said, 'Very well, Sir. In any case this is a purely routine inquiry, although, of course, you'll regard it as confidential.'

He paused and I bowed my head slightly. I wondered if all interviews with the police partook of this ritual element.

'I believe you have a Mr Emile Englander on your staff.'

'Yes.'

'Can you inform me whether he has been abroad on Zoo business in the last two or three months?'

'I can. And he has. He attended the International Zoological Congress at Rome. Not as the representative of the Zoological Society, but as a world famous herpetologist invited by the Committee of the Congress.'

For some reason I could feel a desire to discomfort the Inspector creeping over me; an irrational bond with Englander I had never previously known.

He asked, 'He was not engaged on any work for the Zoo during his visit abroad?'

'I don't think so. He may have visited other reptile gardens or collectors or natural history museums in connexion with his work here. I can't say.'

'Would it surprise you to learn that in addition to Rome, he had made visits to Milan, Munich, Frankfurt, Zürich and Brussels?'

'No, no. It wouldn't. He's very fond of being abroad. He thinks very highly of it.'

I remembered Leacock's charge of frivolity and I felt determined to live up to it. But the Inspector, if he was nettled, didn't show it.

'You mean that his work here takes him abroad a good deal?'

'Not more than anybody else's. It's entirely up to him. Dr Englander is an honorary Curator. That means to say, you know, that he receives no pay.'

Only then did the frank blue eyes look faintly less friendly; and for some reason I felt a little appeased.

'Provided that he leaves the Reptile Collections in competent hands, which of course he does, Dr Englander is free to be absent from the Zoo as much as he feels necessary. He's a very rich man and so he travels a good deal.'

This was substantially true, yet even here I found myself stressing the permissiveness of Zoo rule to this representative of law and order.

He said, 'Thank you, Mr Carter. Just one or two more points if I may. Is the Zoological Society considering any loans or gifts from European sources at the present time?'

'No, I don't think so.'

Once again a certain chauvinism, as it seemed to me, in the man's tone annoyed me. After all, the Prime Minister had only recently made a speech extolling the real sense of unity with Europe that had resulted from the Innsbruck conference.

I added, 'Of course we should always be glad to get money from any source however foreign.'

'But there is no such negotiation at present? For buildings or anything of that kind? Nothing that might demand consultations with government departments of foreign countries?'

'No.'

I was puzzled by what Englander might have been up to, but once again I felt an impulse not to desert him too easily.

'Any Zoo Curator, of course, is greatly interested in new types of Zoo buildings abroad. Foreign architects have contributed most valuable ideas to modern methods of housing animals in captivity. Indeed some of our best houses were built by foreign architects. The magnificent Lemur House, as you possibly know, was a gift from the French government.'

If I expected him to spring up in horror, I was disappointed.

He said, 'Well, thank you, Sir. I suppose Mr Englander has been with you a long time.'

'Dr Englander is seventy,' I said. 'He's a very eminent man, Inspector, you'll find a full account of his career in *Who's Who*.'

As he rose to go, I got up and we shook hands.

I said, 'Despite his sinister name, he's not in fact a foreigner, you know.'

'Oh, no, Sir. His grandfather was German Swiss and his wife's family was Austrian. We have a record of all that.'

I wasn't quite sure whether the Inspector smiled.

'I see. And I'm not to be told what sinister things Dr Englander's been up to.'

'As far as I know, Sir, he's not been up to anything. But there are certain people abroad who rather interest us at the moment and it may be that Mr Englander can tell us a little about them.'

'Ah! Well the person to question is Englander himself.'

'I dare say we shall, Mr Carter. But I shall ask you to say nothing of my visit at the moment.'

'I see. Not to the Director whom you intended to see?'

'Well in fairness to the gentleman concerned, I should say the less people who are informed the better.'

'I see.'

I did see. I had no intention that Englander should be surrounded by a vaguely sinister light in the eyes of his colleagues. I decided to tell no one. On the other hand it was unfortunate that I had chosen this moment to urge his claims to be made Deputy.

I need not have worried. When Dr Leacock came up from Stretton for a week's visiting of Society committee meetings, he was in a hearty, jollying-on mood that made little of my memorandum. At first he did not refer to it and I was forced to raise the question myself.

'My dear chap,' he said, 'I've got far more important things to do than run around refereeing fights between you and Beard. An experiment is experiencing its birth pangs. It's annoying enough that I should have to come up here for all these committee meetings, but I don't want to ride members too hard at this stage by making them come down to Stretton. Though that's what we must aim for. Meanwhile you and Beard must behave or I shall knock your heads together.'

'So you don't accept any of what I suggested?'

Dr Leacock smiled. 'Now don't be touchy, Carter. Of course I do. I accept it all,' he paused, 'in principle.' Here he burst into a loud laugh. 'But seriously – when Falcon comes back, we'll go into the question of the Secretary's exact functions and establish a wide range of authority for you if your Civil Service mind insists on putting everything in black and white. But for the moment you must just get along as best you can. And very well you can do it, if you don't start having all sorts of notions about reorganizing the place. Putting Englander in charge! Do you realize what the Committee's attitude to that would be? But, of course, you don't, you haven't been here long enough. No good asking me why the old chap's so disliked. It's a case of Dr Fell. You know the rhyme? There's something circuitous about him and then he's never really been part of the place. Oh, he's a good zoologist all right, but he's never tried to get on with his colleagues or accept anything we're doing here. Strictly between ourselves if there'd been another herpetologist in the country to touch him, he'd have been sent packing long ago. And having all that money doesn't help. He's been inclined to think he can buy his way in here and the Zoo's too old an institution for that. He should have been in one of these commercial foreign Zoos he admires so much. Englander! I'd like to see the disasters that would follow that suggestion of yours,' Dr Leacock ended in loud laughter.

Yet, if he was unwilling to take seriously any of the duties that lay outside Stretton, on that subject he seemed confident and convincing. To me, remembering the committee meetings of pre-Stretton days, it was amazing to hear him giving facts and figures instead of blustering his way through with pious hopes, moral generalizations, and evasions unsuccessfully disguised by the hearty, downright tones in which they were uttered. He was willing to discuss shortcomings, to defer hopes and express doubts. He admitted that, until the two years of provisional agreement with Godmanchester were at an end, much of his work must inevitably be limited in scope; in particular, he was concerned lest Godmanchester's autocratic attitude to his tenants and neighbours should make for a hostile local atmosphere in which minor breaches of security would be met with disproportionate alarm. The building up of the Historical British Reserve, which in his opinion was the most important experiment, he admitted would inevitably be slow; the Exotic Park needed constantly renewed imaginative approach if it was ever to be more than a conventional Zoo without bars. Yet, given continued public support and the goodwill of Lord Godmanchester, he seemed absolutely sure that, in the ten years he intended to continue in office, he would realize the beginnings of a new and revolutionary relationship between wild life and the British public. I was particularly struck by his saying that for the next two or three years, while the project became reality, he would be glad to see as little publicity as possible.

Lord Oresby noticed this too, for he said to me, 'Living in the country's made Leacock a much more sensible, modest chap. But then town life these days is the ruination of everyone.'

We were all able to agree in Godmanchester's absence, that the only addition *he* could make to his munificent gift was to avoid interfering with it.

Lord Oresby said, 'Well, I suppose, Leacock, we can say that if the worst happens to the country and Godmanchester's made Lord Privy Seal or whatever they'll give him to keep him quiet, the Zoological Society at least will profit. I'm told the P.M. thinks it worth putting up with his presence at Cabinet meetings to make an end to this constant war scare newspaper campaign which is having such a shocking effect abroad. Foreigners still think of Godmanchester as the great English statesman, although, in my opinion, his reputation has always been overrated. He makes an excellent President for us, of course, because most of the time he just sits and looks wise and nods off to sleep. But you can't run a modern government that way. At least I don't think so. I've never been a politician so I can't say.'

Lord Oresby was always modest. Dr Leacock had no wish

to be involved in talk against Lord Godmanchester, so he hastily agreed.

'If more people,' he said, 'would realize that politics is essentially a craft and a very specialized, professional craft at that ... But there's no doubt that Godmanchester has the stamp of statesman upon him. It's really grievous to see him down there at Stretton eating his heart out because he can't get his hand on the wheel, and trying to fill his mind with the little details of Zoo work to which he can't give proper attention. It's pathetic to watch. Like a giant trying to play with a doll's house.'

I could not let the Director's flight of fancy pass altogether unnoticed.

I said, 'We surely shouldn't compare the National Reserve to a doll's house.'

He attempted a laugh. 'I was carried away,' he said, 'but compared to world affairs, you know, it is. Again and again I've told Godmanchester, "Don't bother yourself with all these details." I said it only yesterday. I've left a first-rate man Filson in charge. But the tragedy is that a great man and a great benefactor should seem to be in the way; that I should still have to ask myself, what is Godmanchester up to?'

We were soon to know. Leacock, anxious to naturalize the wild cat at Stretton, had gone up to Perthshire and Argyllshire to interview local gamekeepers. I found to my surprise that I was jealous of this visit, so proprietary had my interest in the British Reserve grown. In Leacock's absence Filson telephoned me to report that a young mountain lynx was missing from its cave in the Exotic Park. I was struck by the confidence that authority had given him; his voice, as he assured me that all was under control, carried conviction and even an independence of my opinion. He would always be a 'respectful' man, but, even at his age a little command seemed to have transformed him from an old retainer to a man of action.

'You can tell the Director, Sir, that if it causes any trouble in the farms or so, I shall have it destroyed. As much to give confidence to the local people as for anything else.'

Leacock, on his return, was more than content with this.

'This security problem's absolutely vital,' he said. 'Whether Godmanchester agrees or no, I'm having the whole place reviewed from that angle. Meanwhile Filson's quite right, confidence is what we must aim at.'

He was full of fascinating information about the home range, mating, and nesting of the British wild cat. Seeing my enthusiasm, he suggested that I should go down with him for a day or two to study Stretton's terrain in relation to these data.

'It'll mean,' I said, 'that licensed naturalists will have to go armed. But the interest of getting the wild cat to breed outside Scotland would be tremendous.'

The night before we left London saw a very severe frost. The morning produced the unusual sight of a heavy December snowstorm. But I wanted to get out of London. Dr Leacock was unwilling to pilot his aeroplane in such weather and I was able to indulge my eccentric weakness for a luxury train. As I gazed from the window at a whitening world, I felt that now the testing time of all our hopes was to begin. How would the Exotic Park stand up to winter conditions? How would the keepers and wardens maintain their surveillance of the Reserves under snowbound conditions? How would the high spirits of Leacock and his cockney staff react to the isolation and monotony of a severe English winter in the country?

Filson at the station seemed more bent than ever. His eyes watered and his cheeks and nose were blue with cold. Leacock met the crisis at once.

'Did you recapture the beast?' he asked.

'Yes, Sir.'

'Good chap! Had he done a lot of damage?'

'No, Sir. But I'm afraid it was known locally that he'd got loose before we recaptured him. I gave strict instructions but you know how talk spreads down here, Sir. He hadn't gone beyond the Reserve limits I'm happy to say. He made his meal off a pair of Egyptian geese, the property of the Society. All the same local talk's been bad.'

'Damn,' said Leacock. 'Damn. Did you give the news of his recapture plenty of local publicity?'

'Yes, Sir.'

'And that he had been destroyed?'

'I sent the information to the local farms and to the Stretton District Council and to Colonel Shipley's agent at Swart Hall. But he cancelled my instructions.'

'Colonel Shipley's agent cancelled your instructions! What do you mean?'

'No, Sir, Lord Godmanchester.'

'Good Lord! I see.' Leacock led us towards his Landrover in the station car park. 'Come on, Carter. Pile in, Filson. Now,' he announced as he drove us through the thickening white flurry, 'the sooner we're back the better. Tell us exactly what happened, Filson.'

'Well, Sir, as soon as "Marmie" – that's what Strawson and his keepers called the lynx – was traced, I gave orders that he was to be shot. He was seen crouching high up in one of the chalk quarries. He'd found himself a cave and I reckoned it was just a question of keeping a couple of men there until hunger drove him out and they could pick him off. Strawson was all against it, he reckoned that they could lure him out with bait and net him. But if the beast was to be shot anyhow, that seemed to me an unnecessary risk. Ah, that was what brought him out so strong against me.' Authority had given Filson decision but not command of language. He seemed to become as clogged with words as the windscreen wipers with thickening snow. Both obstructions were beginning to irritate the Director.

He said, 'Who? Lord Godmanchester?'

'No, no, Sir. *He* knew nothing of it then. No, it was Strawson. It was the first he'd realized of my determination. He came out strong against me, as I said. No knowledge of mammals, rare and costly beast, criticism of his management, slip that wouldn't happen again – I had the lot of it. But I wasn't going to budge. He begged me for that animal, Sir. He bred it himself, Sir, at Regent's Park. And from what he'd always said they're not easy to breed in captivity. But I simply said to him, "You're not taking risks with human life again." He understood all right. Well he disregarded my orders, Sir, and caught the thing in a net. I shouldn't have known of it but one of the young keepers found out and told me. When I knew, I went straight for Strawson and gave orders for its immediate destruction. What I hadn't reckoned with was his going to Lord Godmanchester. And before I could say another thing, Lord Godmanchester cancelled my orders. I was very angry, Sir, I must tell you. And I had words with him. I dare say that did more harm than good.'

The old man must have been reliving his anger, for I saw his body shaking as he sat back in the seat. Leacock said nothing.

It was I who asked, 'But why was Lord Godmanchester against the animal being shot?'

Leacock cried, 'What on earth does it matter?'

I realized that he was in an almost hysterical rage. I reflected that with these frozen roads covered by a light snow an angry man might kill us all before we had a chance to do justice to the errant lynx. But it seemed no time for frivolous observations.

Filson said, 'Well he didn't like it, Sir, because it was climbing down to local opinion and it seems he's always refused to take notice of them. A lot of nobodies, he called them. There's been rows in the past both with him and her. And from what Mrs Filson hears they've never been received by the county, for all his being so famous. Of course, he justified his view by distances. "No possible danger," he said, "nearest farm nearly fifteen miles away, Colonel Shipley's estate over thirty!" But that wasn't it, Sir, I'm sure. Well to tell the truth I think he liked Strawson appealing to him.'

Leacock said, 'You did quite right, Filson. And you can take it from me that the animal will be destroyed.'

He dropped me at the pub and, when I asked if he wanted me any more that day, he said,

'No, Carter, but I shall ask you to be at the Great Cat pits at eleven sharp tomorrow morning.'

I was not the only person present at the appointed hour. It had stopped snowing, though the sky was grey and heavy with promise of more snow to come. The air was cold and damp with a white mist that crept into every fold of one's clothing. I was in a depressed, irritable mood. I had tried the evening before to reconnoitre in the larch woods that covered the slope of the hilly land to the west of the British Reserve, but gusts of sleety rain blown into my face by the strong south-west wind had sent me back to the pub. The parlour had provided me with a fire that scorched my face and draughts that sent cold water running down my back. My bedclothes seemed to me suspiciously damp. There was no prospect of watching the badger setts during that visit, for the ground, it seemed, had been hard frozen for over a week. I longed for Martha and home; or, at least, for the office and the cup of coffee that I took with Mrs Purrett as 'elevenses'. An array of mackintoshed men, a few furcoated women, and a huddle of shooting brakes and two motor cycles were no substitute. The scene was that of a point to point on a really bad winter's day, and I had never been one for intrepid outdoor sport.

Dr Leacock was bustling about like a housemaster encouraging his fifteen on the touchline. And Mrs Leacock, clapping together her hands in their fur-backed gloves, was chatting briskly with the strangers like a good housemaster's wife. The uniformed keepers were drawn up in a line – with Filson, a proud old prefect and Strawson, his doughy face white and blue, the fat boy in disgrace. But when one looked towards the field, as it were, to the pits in which the great cats were housed, there was nothing whatever to see: the lions and leopards and pumas had all sensibly withdrawn into the depths of their caves. The great Siberian tiger perhaps might have put on a show for us in the snow, but he was as yet in London.

I stood withdrawn at the side, sketching this school fantasy, because I had an uneasy sense that the Director was about to do something foolish and embarrassing. My instinct was right.

Getting up on to a little wooden platform that had been erected in front of the ditch that divided us from the lynx's pit, he addressed the company.

'Ladies and gentlemen,' he said, 'I have asked you to be here on this very unfriendly morning because I am anxious that we here of the National Reserve should demonstrate to you, our neighbours from Stretton and the surrounding country, the very great friendliness that we feel towards you, and the real concern we have that our presence here should never endanger your interests. I think you have all heard that a lynx escaped from captivity a few days ago. I have every hope that with the extra precautions now being taken no beasts are likely in future to go beyond the very extensive liberty they enjoy in this place. Even should they do so, as you will see in this case, the chance of their passing the Reserve boundaries before they are found is very small. But an animal that has found means to escape is properly an object of suspicion. For this reason I have given orders that all such animals shall, on recapture, be destroyed.' Here he turned to the staff. 'As in this case there was some misunderstanding, I want this order to be clearly understood.' Then he addressed himself directly to Strawson. 'Have you carried out the orders I gave you now, Strawson?'

I thought for a moment that Strawson was going to walk away; but he mumbled something in reply and then spoke to the younger keeper who was in charge of the Felidae. Both men disappeared to the back of the caves. As we stood there in the cold, I hardly knew where I dared to look – at Leacock erect on his platform like a leader of men, at Mrs Leacock still doing the lady bountiful, at the farmers and odd gentry frozen, impatient, and amazed, at the nervous whispering villagers, or at the younger keepers who were nudging each other with embarrassment and smothering their guffaws. But we had not long to wait. From the cave at the back of the pit emerged the lynx, its tapering ears and slanting eyes, its slender form and dappled colour beautiful even in that dead grey light. It seemed so little ferocious, more like a poor house cat dazed from a glancing blow of a bicycle wheel. It stretched a little in the cold air, then rose, wobbling on its legs. A moment later the young keeper appeared with a rifle on the rocks above. He fired and the beautiful animal coiled back for a second in the air, gave a faint mewing cry, and fell dead. A village woman screamed and a child began to howl.

Dr Leacock got off his platform and began shaking hands and talking to people in the crowd.

'You'll come back for a snifter, won't you?' he said, 'I'm sorry it was so abominably cold, but I believe Mrs Leacock has some coffee ready for us all at the farm, haven't you, Madge?'

And Madge Leacock said, 'Yes, Daddy.' She turned to me, 'So jolly to see you down here, Mr Carter.'

Most of the crowd had packed into their brakes or had mounted their cycles and were gone before invitations could reach them; some refused in a numbed manner that could have been due to the cold; others again seemed too numbed to refuse. I felt completely sick. I could see Strawson coming back from the caves. I wanted to say something to comfort him, but I was frightened that he might reveal himself as aggrieved rather than sickened. Then from between two snow covered rhododendron bushes at the side of the roadway Harriet appeared followed by Rickie. She went straight up to Strawson.

'I believe you're the man who tried to save that wretched beast. Will you shake hands?'

Mrs Leacock began to talk loudly to cover her daughter's voice. Dr Leacock's eyes blazed with anger.

Harriet saw me. 'Well, look who's here,' she said, 'on this big day for limited liberty.'

Leacock tried to come to my rescue. 'You hop into the rover, Carter. You're frozen.'

But I turned my back on both father and daughter, and walked away.

With no daytime exploration of the Reserve tolerable and no evening watching likely to be productive, I did not see how to avoid entanglement with the personal feuds of Stretton. Yet I was determined to have no more to do with them all until their insane angers had died away. I decided to take the evening train back to London. Meanwhile, with no books provided, I sat in the parlour turning over bound copies of *Punch*. I was lost in the jokes about servants having cars that marked our triumphant victory of 1918, when a lot of clatter, banging of car doors and stamping of snowy shoes announced a new arrival.

'Snowing pretty badly, Sir?'

'Oh God, yes. But then I suppose it always is in the country.'

As companion for a short stay on a desert island I could have thought of no one preferable to Matthew. I got up and greeted him with real enthusiasm. He seemed faintly disconcerted to see me.

'I had no idea you were coming down here, Matthew.'

'Oh, well, the birds, you know. After all I am responsible for them. And then I was a bit worried about the old Filsons in all this weather.'

At the most Filson could have been two years older than Matthew; Mrs Filson certainly younger.

I said, 'But Matthew! To choose weather like this for your first visit to Stretton.'

'Well, I haven't come to *look* at it. I hate the French Renaissance anyway.'

'I mean the country!'

'I'm hardly going to look at *that*, am I?'

'No, I mean the discomfort in this cold.'

'I don't know how it was at Winchester, but at Eton we soon learned never to think about the weather.'

It was true. Even in this deep freeze he was wearing only the very lightest overcoat.

Obsessed by the macabre events of the morning, I found myself recounting the scene to Matthew.

His only comment was, 'Yes, I can't say I feel this *poésie du lynxe* as you do. But then, of course, I'm a bird man.'

'I'm more concerned about Leacock. I know you hate psychology, Matthew.'

'Oh, very much. Yes. All the balls our nurses told us long ago dressed up in German-English.'

'All the same Leacock seemed worryingly round the bend this morning. After all his daughter . . .'

'Oh, God! I've heard extraordinary things about her. I had a beer up at Stretton station with one or two of the younger keepers. And naturally we talked a good deal of smut.'

'I don't know why you say naturally. They never talk smut with me.'

'My dear Simon, I dare say you're not very good with the men. After all army life . . . Anyhow she seems to have been after most of them. But you know what they're like. They don't like a lady to use whore's language. Anyhow she seems to go rather far if the stories are true. I must say I never thought Leacock would have a Messalina for a daughter. In fact she seems to start where the Empress left off. As I said she couldn't be better placed than in a Zoo. But still we mustn't gossip about our Director's daughter, must we? Will you dine with me, Simon? I asked at my Club and there's apparently an excellent roadhouse as they call them about five miles from Hereford.'

Depressed at the thought of a late return to empty London, I agreed.

'Good. And now if you'll excuse me, I have two cockatoos to describe before I walk up to see the Filsons.'

The car Matthew had hired was very comfortable and his roadhouse turned out to be a large country hotel with excellent food. Even he praised the burgundy, although he said, 'I don't know that I want that naval commander fussing round my table all the time.' He revealed a vast knowledge of nineteenth-century explorers and talked of them in a mixture of genuine admiration and salacious Gibbonian mockery that was very entertaining for one evening. We drank a good deal, but at last Matthew said, 'Well, I hate to break this up, but we have to go to the Mule's Head.' He studied a scrap of paper. 'Yes. The Mule's Head. I took the name down when Filson was talking. That's where he and Mrs F. go.'

'But surely not on an evening like this.'

'Oh, I don't know. They're cockneys. I imagine they'd go to the nearest town if they could. I know when we were stationed in the country, the men all traipsed miles to the nearest town in the evenings. What else could they do?'

'It isn't the same thing at all . . .'

'Do allow me to know my own head keeper, Simon. After all I'm devoted to you but it was him I came down here to see.'

I was a little too high to care much what happened, even to mind about Matthew's driving, which usually wildly haphazard, acquired an appearance of extreme caution when he was drunk that would have normally seemed to me most sinister. I must have dozed off once or twice, for there were many gaps in the anthology of quotations about parrots or popinjays from Ovid through Skelton to Masefield to which Matthew treated me on the journey. Once he was singing, 'I don't like food for parrots boiled beef and carrots,' and I heard myself say aloud, 'You may think that driving with you and Leacock like this I have a death wish but I haven't.'

'Oh! You must be very drunk, Simon, Leacock isn't here, you see,' he said.

By the time that we arrived in the deathly quiet streets of Hereford I was quite sober. It seemed to me that Matthew himself must be very drunk to have driven to this town where nothing stirred even on a Saturday night. Even more did I feel this when we entered the Mule's Head, a pub in a little side street near the Cathedral, where through the dense smoke I could vaguely see a man in shirt sleeves playing an old honkytonk piano, and a huge blonde singing 'The St Louis Blues'. The bar was packed with people. It was, I imagine, what my grandmother who lived in Salisbury would have called 'the seamy side of the town', and if by that she meant that it had remained petrified from some more remote age, she was right.

At first Matthew said, 'Complete hell!'

Now I could see through the haze that apart from a sleazy sprinkling of tarts and Irish casual labourers on the booze, most of the clientele were family parties. Among them, Barley, the sporty keeper of the wolves, and his more sporty wife. He waved a glass at me.

'Matthew,' I said, 'there's Barley, the keeper of the wolves.'

'Well, that's nothing to do with me. Wolves aren't birds.'

'All the same we must speak to them now we're here.'

'I can't see why.'

'Well, I must, if you don't.'

'Oh, very well. It's really Bobby Falcon's job, isn't it? But still since he's not here.'

Mrs Barley, all good fun and gin-and-It, in slacks, said, 'Looking for something to keep you warm in this snowy weather, Mr Price?'

And Matthew answered, 'Judging by the local girls I've seen, I think I'd rather sleep alone. That's unless Barley waives his claims.'

Mrs Barley said, 'Now *then*.'

And Barley, 'Hands off, Mr Price. I'll tell you what, Larna, though, we'll fix Mr Price up with old Harriet. She's sure to be coming in.'

Mrs Barley looked towards me, but Barley was just tight enough not to care. I went to buy a fresh round of pints and whiskies and gin-and-Its.

When I returned Barley was saying, 'The latest is Strawson. She come up to him this morning and shook him by the hand. All the boys have been on to him now, stringing him along, she wants to be in his bloody album. You know he takes these nature photos, or at least that's what he calls them. Mostly he has to take Mrs Strawson, God help him! Mrs S. among the daffodils showing her tits.'

Mrs Barley said, 'Now, Arthur! Don't be disgusting. Anyway she's a fine looking woman.'

'Well fine or not, it's all he's got. Then he has Mrs S. all backside among the brussels sprouts. Part of some religion of his, he says. Dirty old man, that's what. Anyway the boys have told him Harriet wants to be in it. And he's all set to take her. I can just see old Harriet, if she thinks he's going to have a bash and then he takes out his bloody camera instead. She'll hang it round his neck and all.'

Matthew hooted with laughter. 'Oh, God! Well he'd better not show the album to the faithful dog or he'll tear it to pieces.'

Barley suddenly looked very prim.

'Disgusting. They oughtn't to let that sort live. Well, come on, Larna, we must be moving.'

It was a frosty ending.

Matthew said, 'Oh, God! I said the wrong thing.'

He looked so sad that I went to the bar to get him another whisky. And then I saw Harriet come in. She was rather tight and on easy terms with everybody, and yet she seemed to me like a much younger girl who was shy but too tired to care. If it hadn't been for Barley's and Matthew's talk, I should have avoided her; but, as it was, I felt impelled to show her some friendship.

I said, 'Would you let me buy you a drink?'

'I'll let anybody buy me a drink and I'll take a double brandy neat.'

When I returned from the bar, a stocky Irishman with bloodshot eyes was steadying himself by holding on to her arm.

'What do you say, Harriet my darling? What do you say?'

'I say, fuck off. I want to talk to my friend,' she indicated me.

The man immediately let go of her arm, though he stood a short distance away, muttering to himself.

Harriet said, 'I hope you're not slumming or being broad-minded or something, because that won't be necessary.'

I said, 'Oh, for God's sake, let up, woman. Either we're going to talk or not.'

She said, 'I'm not very good at talking, but let's do that.'

She wasn't very good.

She said, 'If I could any longer taste brandy, I should say this was filthy.'

Then she remained silent for five minutes while I tried to be funny about people in the room. She didn't appear to hear me, not because she was drunk, but simply because she was too abstracted.

Then she said, 'Isn't that Pansy Price you're with?'

I said, 'Well, I call him Matthew. And he's not a pansy at all.'

She said, 'Don't tell me about him. He looks like one. And I can't bear them. It's such a waste.'

This seemed illiberal, but, in view of Matthew's attitude to her, only just.

Then she said, 'Do you know much about dogs?'

'Not a lot. No.'

'Well you'd have to know a lot to talk to me about them, so that rules out most of what I can *talk* about. I could tell you about my life. How I shouldn't be like this if my parents weren't so bloody. No, it's a bore. The only thing is that when you see what bloody little twerps all my good little brothers and sisters are, it *does* lend me a slightly rosier glow. I shine by comparison. But as nobody has to make the comparison, there's not much point in it.'

She stood silent for a moment, then she said, 'Mummy isn't wicked actually – she's half-witted. But the old bastard is an absolute fake from start to finish.'

'I don't believe that's true. Neither start nor finish. Only at some points along the line.'

'That sounds clever, but I'm not going to work it out. I think he's off his rocker. Look at this morning's little ceremony. Anyway he's so hideous. I'll bet you didn't know that he has an absolutely hairless body. Isn't it ghastly? That's a good enough reason for any girl being down the drain. And if you're thinking of trying to haul me out, don't bother, because I'm wedged as hell and mediumly happy there. But you could get me another brandy.'

When I came back with it, she said, 'This talking idea of

yours hasn't been a very good one. It's made me feel sick.'

I said, 'Why not sit down?'

She put her arm round the Irishman's neck, and, turning to me, said, 'Oh, fuck off. I want to be with Paddy.'

When I returned to the other end of the bar, Matthew, red-faced and flustered, was involved with a circle of old women out on the spree who were doing 'Knees up Mother Brown'. Matthew's feeble lifting of his knees was exciting not derision but compassion.

'Poor old dear,' one of the women said, 'he's doing his best.'

I wished that Bobby Falcon could be in Matthew's pre-dicament, it would teach him a lesson about old-time crowds. With difficulty I rescued Matthew, and, as he seemed very drunk, I took charge of the car myself and had a most un-pleasant drive back to our hotel on slippery roads through a white mist. Matthew sighed deeply as we went in.

I said, 'Thank you very much for a lovely evening, Matthew.'

'Delighted to have entertained you.'

'I'm afraid the last part was a bit depressing.'

But Matthew was not prepared to receive sympathy.

He smiled vaguely and said, 'Oh, well, in the country it's all rather hell, isn't it?'

On this occasion I was forced to conclude that he was right. I decided to return to London the next morning; but first I had to inform the Director. I expected to find Leacock at home on a Sunday but his wife told me that he now worked every weekend. I went to the little temporary administrative office – no more than a large wooden hut – that had been erected near the entrance to the Reserve. Godmanchester was there with the Director.

'Did you see this grand guignol of Leacock's yesterday morning?' he asked.

I pretended not to understand him.

Leacock said, 'Godmanchester thinks that the destruction of the lynx had a morbid effect on the spectators.'

'I don't think. I know.'

Godmanchester's tone when he was being deliberately offensive was not a nice sound.

'Despite the fact that you don't believe in bothering with the opinion of the neighbourhood.'

'I've got the opinion of my own men. You forget, sometimes, Leacock, that we had a sizeable collection of animals and some first-rate keepers before you came down here. But it doesn't matter where I heard it from. The fact is that you set out to kow tow to the locals, to invite every little grumble they like to make. And now on top of that you scare them out of their wits.'

'I don't accept that. But in any case the whole demonstration need never have taken place as I told you on Friday evening, if you hadn't unwarrantably stepped in and over-ridden my delegated authority.'

'I happen to be the President of the Society, you know.'

'Yes. And I am the Director appointed by the Committee to run the Zoological Gardens. If you want to get me dismissed, you're at perfect liberty to put the proposal before the Committee! Until then I'm in charge.'

Lord Godmanchester gave his famous chuckle, but, I thought, a little ostentatiously.

'My dear Leacock, in your obsession with your very fine scheme, you've rather lost a sense of reality, you know. I'm a very busy man and my time is not, strangely enough, entirely free to hatch schemes for controlling the Zoo. Even if it were, I shouldn't be interested in trying "to oust you from your authority" as you call it. Why should I? You're a very good Director. You think I shouldn't have countermanded the orders to shoot the lynx. I think I was right to do so. In your place even if I'd thought as you did, I'd have let it ride. But still, you felt a principle or something was at stake ... However one thing nobody in their senses would have done was to stage this ridiculous spectacle simply in order to snub me publicly. Because that's why you did it, Leacock. And it was childish, wasn't it, Carter?'

'I can't measure how a child would have acted in a situation where only adults are concerned.'

Again he chuckled and rumbled, but I thought how little I should want him to hug me at that moment.

'Good enough,' he said, 'but you take it from me, Leacock, you won't hear the end of this business from the local people. You've got them jittery and you'll have a hard time calming them down. Can I take you up to London, Carter?'

'Thank you. I think I'll go by train.'

'Ah, well, I shan't come with you. Very picturesque and all that. But I don't like public transport, train or plane.'

He got up with his usual heavy, slow, and soft movements.

Leacock said almost casually, 'I'm afraid it isn't enough, you know. I've got to ask why your newspaper this morning has given wide publicity to the escape of a dangerous lynx at Stretton.'

Lord Godmanchester blinked and then said, 'Sunday papers take a lot of filling. I don't interfere with my editors. Two can play at being spiteful. Take your choice of reasons and welcome. In any case, wide publicity is not the right word for a ten-inch column. If you want to know what wide publicity is you ought to look at the space we've given to Falcon's expedition.'

Leacock pursed his lips and the end of his long nose twitched.

'Yes. And now it seems it will have to be called off.'

'Well, you can hardly blame him for a nationalist *coup d'état* in Brazil. However he's gone off to the States to collect support. It's amazing the contacts that man's got. And, of course, he's an adventurous personality. I blame myself for overlooking him recently. We're going to need a sense of adventure in this country in the coming years, once we're out of this trough we've fallen into.'

He turned to go, then with difficulty he screwed his thick neck round, until his fat, surprised old face was staring at us.

'By the way, Leacock,' he said, 'Katie's coming down here

for Christmas. So I'd be obliged if you'd keep Mrs Leacock away from the house. She gets on my wife's nerves.'

Leacock's Adam's apple bobbed twice as he swallowed. Then as easily as he could, he said, 'I'm sorry for that. I'm sure Mrs Leacock would never wish to go where she's not wanted.'

'No? Well, that's all right then.'

When he had gone, Dr Leacock swivelled from side to side in his chair.

Then he said, 'Firmness and tact, Carter, firmness and tact. I told you that's what we should need. Well, you've seen me use both this morning. We're in for a fight, I think; but this has been my great chance and I'm not going to give up easily.'

Ten days or so before Christmas, Martha wrote as though I were desperately urging her to come home. She must have read between the lines of my letters, for, although I longed to do so, I had carefully refrained from mentioning her return.

'I *do* want to come back as soon as possible, darling. But Reggie won't settle in. And Hester spoils him. Also I'm afraid she's not taken to Violet. And then you know how when I'm in England, I'm always wanting the children to have a good American education. Well, now I'm here, of course, I don't feel so sure any more. It's no good pretending that we binationals are not schizoid because we are. And there's no good starting them here unless we're going to leave them for a while. Anyway I thought I'd stay here at least over Christmas for them. I suppose you couldn't possibly come out; I know you're so busy but just for the few days. Who in the hell cares about the money if we're all going to be blown up? Not that anyone here thinks that we are, but then they don't know how mad the British are. Oh! Simon, even though I did write that about American education, you don't know how good it is to be in a country that's big. May God and my liberal ancestors forgive me for writing it. Bobby still expects the end of the world. He was at San Francisco seeing some Exploration Fund and I went over and spent the day with him. Poor old Bobby! I really believe he had snapped out of those long years of manic-depression or whatever it was. And now this lousy Brazilian government won't let him in. But he's being pretty tough about it. Of course he's quite a different kind of person away from Regent's Park. I always reckoned he would be. Why don't you try it some time? There's an awful lot of mammals waiting to be watched over here. Then we could all be together without anyone feeling mean.'

I wanted very much to join her; yet I replied almost at once that I couldn't. The British Reserve really did seem worth fighting for, to offer the useful happiness I'd never quite dared to believe in; and I surely could not desert Leacock at this moment. All the same I could have flown over for Christmas. Pique stopped me, I'm afraid. I'd written so much in my letters to Martha about Stretton, about our future happiness there and the genuine value of the work – and yet she could so easily ask me to give it all up. But pique wasn't all. As I read what she wrote of Bobby Falcon, jealous waves rolled over me and knocked me silly. I couldn't go out to her with this suspicious motive hidden in my visit. Without Martha and the children, however, approaching Christmas seemed a phoney time of commercialized goodwill. I had occupied myself a lot with choosing presents for them, but these had to be posted so early that the weeks before the holiday were an anti-climax. It was among Mrs Purrett's stock of commonplaces to repeat over and over again that 'Christmas is a time for children really'. This year, to my embarrassment, her words threatened to bring tears to my eyes.

I was not helped by Beard's treatment of the typists in the pool. Mrs Purrett first drew my attention to the fact that four out of our seven girls had reported sick. She was certain, she said, that Beard's lack of consideration, niggling, and constant demands upon their time had made the feebler girls ill and the stronger ones rebellious. I put this down to her animosity, and accounted for the spate of illness by the claims of Christmas shopping.

Then one evening I heard him at it bullying them.

'Oh dear, Miss Dargie, I'm sure you're missing things. Do

please remember that every dead animal counts. The death of a liver fluke is every bit as important as that of the most advanced primate. And a great deal more important than either of ours.'

I could not tell if he was joking; I doubt if he was. Certainly to the girl he seemed like a monster.

Then to another, he said, 'I do hope you haven't raced through this box, Mrs Dunbar. We need toothcombs. I'd rather take them home at night myself than risk missing a recorded death.'

It was true, of course; he would undertake unlimited work. He never neglected an autopsy, never failed to treat a sick animal, supervised the research work of five or six students, worked away on the loris's eyesight and, I believe, the histology of the gorilla's testes as well. But all that was no comfort to the typists. Nor to Mrs Purrett or me in organizing the office work.

Two days before Christmas he drove one of the remaining girls too hard. He was quite oblivious of the unwritten law that the days before Christmas should be slack. I passed through the pool room to see him standing erect, a little red in the face, before the desk of a girl who was crying.

'This really isn't good at all, Miss Bates,' he was saying, 'you've typed moose for mouse. It would be ludicrous if it wasn't so serious.'

The girl banged her fist on the table. 'Oh, go to hell,' she shouted.

Beard said, 'Oh! Lor'!' and fled.

But later he returned to me and announced that we couldn't keep on a woman who was insubordinate.

I said, 'She's not. She's ill. And I'm not surprised. We shall lose all our typists if you go on overworking them.'

We received a doctor's certificate after Christmas giving her leave for nervous debility; and shortly after this she resigned.

These tedious office problems only added to my depression over the Christmas season. I tried work and a little dinner in Soho and the theatre; I tried work and a delicious partridge cooked by myself followed by an evening's L.P., *La Sonnam-bula* and *Manon*; I tried work and dinner at the pub round the corner followed by the local cinema. All were evenings such as periodic fits of misanthropy extending even to my family had often painted in golden colours. Now they were drab and seemingly endless. Ridiculous jealousies of Bobby Falcon rushed around my head and kept me awake at night. Under their influence I rang up Jane, half possessed by some incoherent plan that by involving myself with her I would rouse Martha's jealousy in turn, half hoping that in con-versation she would betray similar fears to my own. To get her on the telephone proved a formidable task: she was always at rehearsal. But each time that I failed it seemed more vitally important to succeed, as though Martha's innocence depended upon Jane's answering the telephone. When I finally contacted her, she was off to Liverpool for over-Christmas rehearsals.

She said, 'Poor old Bobby! I can't say I shall be pleased to have him back a failed hero. I love Bobby discovering things up the Amazon, but I loathe him hanging around the house. Damn the Brazilians and their revolutions!'

'Martha's been holding his hand in California.'

'Yes, I know. He wrote to me about it. I'd write and thank her, but with two authors' new plays coming on, I haven't a moment. Why did you ring me?'

'Oh, I was at a loose end. I wondered if you'd care to come to the theatre with me.'

'Darling Simon! How enchanting of you! Young men never asked me out as a rule unless they have some stinking plays to get rid of. I'd love a busman's holiday too, but unfortunately Liverpool calls in all its ghastly Liverpudlian gloom. Poor darling! Being at a loose end. I always forget what turtle doves you two are. I tell you what, I'll send you some tickets for that new musical from Angola. It's rather heaven. And you can take what Bobby calls a cutie. I'm sure Martha wouldn't mind for once.'

I didn't take a cutie. I took Mrs Purrett. And on the whole it was my most enjoyable evening of the Christmas season.

Martha and I had a lot of friends – mostly young married couples. Two or three of these asked me for Christmas dinner, but I realized how little I liked social life without the post-mortems Martha and I indulged in on our return home. I refused, and spent Christmas and Boxing Day going over some field notes I had made for a book I had planned on British mammals. If I had been in the country, I thought, I should have had no difficulty in passing my solitary time.

On the whole I was glad to be back at the office, though I awaited Bobby's return with mixed feelings.

Despite the fact that the new Brazilian government was still proving intransigent, Bobby seemed extraordinarily buoyant.

'California's done wonders for Martha. You can imagine that the last thing I should want is for anyone to settle out of England, but she needs to live America out of her system, Simon. After all it was her mother's country. I think you ought to give up here and go out to her. It's a beautiful country tho' I shouldn't want to live there. And they'd welcome you at the San Diego Zoo or better still on one of the Reserves.'

I explained that the British Reserve at Stretton seemed likely to give me all I needed.

'I see. Well you know your own mind. All these escapes down there look pretty bad, don't they?'

'All? One lynx!'

'Oh, I think you'll find there are more than that. Even *The Advertiser* got worried about them and, since it's Godman-chester's place . . .'

I asked Mrs Purrett about it and found that, immersed in my loneliness, I had missed a lot of news. I studied the accounts of escapes from Stretton in *The Advertiser* and in rival papers. They came, it seemed to me, to very little and that rather absurd: an escaped wombat found by a well-known sculptress in her garden shed, a llama belonging to a travelling circus that scared some race horses near Hereford, and a small girl's very dubious report of a leopard glimpsed in a wood. I pointed out to Bobby how feeble the stories were.

'All the same, I think Godmanchester's rather worried from what he told me.'

'I don't believe a word he says.'

'Oh, that's rather steep about our President.' He laughed. 'Perhaps you're right. He's an old scoundrel. But we need a scoundrel to save us and I think he'll do it.'

'To give him his due, he's done it already by giving us the National Reserve.'

Bobby scowled, 'I meant a bit more than that. I think he may save the world. Oh, only like Justinian – for a breather. The smash is bound to come. But, if we've got to go, we may as well go with all lights blazing. And I don't mind if it's by courtesy of Godmanchester or of any other scoundrel.'

I found Bobby's apocalyptic talk no less tedious now that he was buoyant.

I said, 'Gas lighting, no doubt.'

He answered with great excitement, 'Good man! You see the point. Yes, by God! Gas lighting!'

A few days later the world was saved. At any rate Godmanchester was appointed 'a Lord Privy Seal, with what the Prime Minister called 'a roving commission to put our house in order'. *The Advertiser* told us that all our troubles were over. And Edwin Leacock's troubles really began to get serious.

A wisent escaped. In view of the extreme rarity of these beasts, I was neither surprised nor unsympathetic when I heard that Strawson had resigned because the Director had refused to spare its life. It was only a few days later that I saw in *The Advertiser* that Strawson had in fact refused to carry on at Stretton because he felt unhappy about the security there. He was described in the newspaper as 'the jovial keeper of elephants, a "character" beloved by generations of children, not least of the grown up kind'. There was a photograph of him with open-necked shirt and sandals. He was quoted as saying, 'I've come regretfully to the conclusion that what we are doing at Stretton is wrong. An animal that cannot trust in the surety of its own confinement is an unloved animal.' He intended, he said, to devote himself to photographing the human form as it blends with the changing Mood of Nature. Apart from his joviality, his resignation took the colour of Krishnamurti casting off the rule of Mrs Besant, or a serious split in the ranks of the Goetheaneum. I warmed to Edwin Leacock when he told me on the telephone that, he was 'heartily glad to be rid of the humbugging mountebank'.

Bobby Falcon, however, was not prepared to take Strawson's departure lying down – 'My own head keeper . . . an invaluable man.' It was a sign of the times that, despite the Director's disagreement, the Committee agreed with Bobby that Strawson should be asked to return to the Society's service. With difficulty he was persuaded to leave his photography; indeed, the wooing of him, in which I refused to take part, was long and, for his hurt pride, no doubt, delicious. However in the end he returned to Regent's Park. To this also *The Advertiser* gave full publicity but in a wholly sentimental vein: 'Trunk Call's keeper returns to the Zoo he loves'. Sir Robert was quoted as saying, 'The place has not been the same without its landmark, Strawson. He was part of the old Zoo which is a happy rock in a world of bewildering shifting sands.' Wisely Strawson was not asked to make any metaphysical pronouncement on that occasion.

But that was only the beginning of Leacock's worries. Godmanchester, of course, was too busy to concern himself or even perhaps to care what happened to the Zoological Society. But just as he had been active in bullying galleries, libraries, museums, factory units, schools to leave London in his campaign of 'no confidence' in the Government, so, now that he had got office, his henchmen were equally busy urging these bodies – including us at Stretton – to return. The campaign to destroy confidence in government without Godmanchester had, after all, been a touch unethical and had been carried out covertly; but the restoration of confidence in government with Godmanchester was patriotic and needed shouting. The publicity could now be loud and open.

Only Dr Leacock withstood the pressure. Every Committee member of the Zoological Society, eminent Fellows, the senior staff, even the rank and file were approached in an attempt to bring pressure to bear upon him.

But Godmanchester's aides were not Godmanchester and their effect was not so happy. Leacock, too, emerged well as a man with a purpose, reasonable about what had gone wrong – a lynx and a wisent did not make a ravening horde; Godmanchester began to appear inevitably as double-faced and unreliable.

'After all,' said Lord Oresby, 'supposing war *did* come.'

These reactions were enough to decide Godmanchester. The campaign was called off. There was enough other evidence of returning confidence. It was not worth while forcing a show-down with Leacock, or, by seeking to annul the lease, risking a scandal. Stretton and Leacock's work were quietly forgotten; where the Zoo was remembered at all in Godmanchester's Press or on the television channels on which his companies advertised, it was as the famous London Zoo, the happy, cheery family binge Zoo of Falcon's dreams. Sir Robert's, indeed, was fast becoming one of the best revived faces of our day. In all this victory of Leacock's, I hope and think that I played my part.

What we had not reckoned on was that the Press *opposed* to Godmanchester would not let him alone. Finding little else in the domestic field to attack, Godmanchester's critics began to look round for signs that he was not so confident as he pretended. They found a reddish, angry-seeming spot to test in the affairs of the Zoo. Everyone, their articles told us, recognized the remarkable venture upon which the Zoological Society and, in particular, its Director had embarked in founding the Stretton National Reserve. The public, it predicted, would be amazed at the success of this enterprise when in April the Reserve was opened to visitors. Even the most obstinate critic of the Lord Privy Seal must concede his splendid generosity in making this imaginative project feasible; it could indeed be that when the noise of party politics had died away, future historians would find in Stretton Reserve the finest monument to Lord Godmanchester's name. Nevertheless it was an open secret that, in some part, the decision of the Zoological Society to send so many of its valuable specimens to Stretton, in particular the exotic animals which could never be acclimatized, had been actuated by a strong suspicion that affairs in the hands of the Prime Minister and his government did not give promise of lasting peace. Fearing, at any rate, a limited and conventional war, the Society had decided on a limited and conventional evacuation from London. At that time Lord Godmanchester, as President, had no doubt only been acting on what Lord Godmanchester as politician and newspaper proprietor had been prophesying. Now, however, Lord Godmanchester's newspapers one and all gave us to understand that with their proprietor in office the danger was over, the government, otherwise unchanged, had overnight become an assurance of peace. Yet, if actions spoke louder than words, it was curious that Lord Godmanchester as President of the Zoological Society did not this time follow up the words he uttered as statesman. None of the exotic animals had returned from the inclemency of the Welsh Border to the assured safety of Regent's Park. Some liaison had broken down between the split personalities of the noble lord; he should not be surprised if the public drew its own conclusions.

Having touched this spot, and found from a rather injudiciously scornful comment in *The Advertiser* that it hurt, the opposition newspapers pressed on it continually. Yet even the report that Godmanchester was very angry, did not frighten Leacock into giving way. If Godmanchester cared publicly to break the lease with the Society, let him do so and give his reasons. Godmanchester did not so care.

In this atmosphere I went down to Stretton for a few days to encourage and abet Leacock, to get away from Falcon and Beard, and to devote my time to the pleasure of the British Reserve.

December's snows had been unseasonable, and we now had an equally unusual February, mild though wet. Heavy rain had turned the crumbling bracken fronds from cinnamon brown rust to a blackened mush, the wet orange stalks and the

bruised purple of the remaining bramble leaves alone gave
colour to the undergrowth; yet the scent that came up from the
sodden bracken where I trod on it was as acrid as that given
out by the tender green fronds of spring. Too early yet even
for precocious aconites, the woods were a black skeleton world
of branches and trunks and twigs in the early dusk. Now and
again the snuffy, catarrhal scent of crushed acorns came to me,
nauseous and quickly gone. Since the importation of a pair of
wild cats from Scotland, I was setting the example of carrying
a revolver as well as my field-glasses and my torch. Yet the
woods were filled enough with deer and hares and pheasants
to satisfy the needs even of so fierce a pair.

I made straight for the badger setts; I was to be in place
by the beech tree half an hour or so before the first came out
to sniff the evening air. I was anxious to establish my suspicion
that last year's young had already begun the establishment of
new setts. I heard once or twice the retching bark of foxes;
and before me on a long witch-fingered branch of an oak tree
sat a little owl who let me go by as happily as though I had
been a passing motor car and he perched on a telegraph pole.
There was no other noise. I was only a quarter of a mile from
the setts when I heard at a long distance shrieks and howls that
seemed to come from within the woods, yet might have been
the strange calls of forty different creatures in the Exotic Park.
I strained to identify them, but an airliner bound for Ireland
and, no doubt, the U.S.A. blotted out the sounds with its
throbbing hum, and switched my thoughts to Martha and the
children. My mind had then only one thought – 'They must
come back, they must come back, they must come back' – and
to the rhythm of these words I tried to adapt everything around
me, even my own breathing. To my superstitious distress the
pace of my breathing would take only the words, 'they must
come' – 'back' I could not fit in. Then into these obsessive
thoughts there came the sound of heavy panting and of feet
rapidly padding upon the soft surface of rotting leaves. That,
at least, was no wild cat, perhaps a fox, but strangely noisy for
such. The sound gained upon me. I thought with increasing

nervousness of escaped wild beasts – a wolf, a lynx, a jackal, what? Was I to die for my own cause? Then through the tracery of bare boughed brushwood I saw the long muzzle and blazing eyes of what? a young wolf? a jackal? In two seconds I was up six feet above the ground among the branches of a huge oak tree, sending some wood pigeons crashing and flapping through the nearby branches. Danger soon renews agility. From above I saw clearly the creature that was padding through the undergrowth, on a blind path that would certainly pass beneath my oak tree – a large Alsatian dog, Rickie, his muzzle flecked with foam and, as I saw in the torch light, with spilling blood. I flashed my torch directly in his eyes, he paused for a second, but then came on. I think it was only fear that made me draw the revolver; and yet, six feet up, I had nothing to fear. But I aimed as he came within yards and shot him in the left foreleg. He came, howling and limping, towards me. Now kindness as well as fear made me fire again and this time the bullet passed into his narrow skull and, with a shiver running through his shapely body, he fell dead.

It was not, I thought, going to be easy with Harriet Leacock. She was lost, friendless and bitter enough. If gossip was correct ... well, then, I still felt the terrible guilt of cruelly hurting a woman who in her disorder had almost destroyed herself. I got down from the tree. I dragged the carcass under the cover of some thick ground ivy. Then, confused, I decided to leave it there, and cope with Harriet in the morning. The best excuse that I could provide now was that, if the dog had killed sheep, she would, of necessity, have had to shoot it. I had saved Leacock from the public scandal. Neither of these reasons would either soothe or satisfy her. Perhaps during the night I could think of a more comforting story. I made my way to the setts.

I had only been there a quarter of an hour, when I was rewarded by the sight of a white snout sniffing at the air. A moment later the greyish mask of an old dog badger appeared and at last the heavy beast came out, sniffing around the well worn earth at the mouth of the setts. More suspiciously the bitch followed him two minutes later. For a short while the two creatures sat licking at their paws and then trotted off in the direction of a clearing where I had suspected bluebell bulbs. They would not probably return from feeding until dawn. I wondered at the female's presence at that breeding season, but a certain heaviness in her gait suggested that she was perhaps pregnant. I still waited and then to my excitement the process was repeated, but this time the dog badger was, as I had hoped, a young male of the previous year and no bitch followed him. I wondered if she was within, suckling new-born cubs. I promised myself an interesting spring watching the cubs in their early days of freedom in the open air. I knew then what happiness the prospect offered me. By the time that I had made my way back to bed, I had almost banished Harriet from my thoughts.

But the morning brought anxiety and remorse. I set off for the farm with little creatures scrabbling in my stomach. Lord Godmanchester's chauffeur sat in a Bentley drawn up before the porch; somehow the luxurious car seemed to spoil the simplicity of the house's lines, turning the scene to gracious living. I had known that our President was down at Stretton for a weekend's rest, but he showed so little interest now in the affairs of the Reserve that I had not expected to see him. Yet there he was in the hall in heavy overcoat more than ever like a menacing grizzly. Dr Leacock stood foursquare, his absurd face quite drained of even its ordinary grey-brown colour. In an armchair Mrs Leacock was weeping. There was a youngish man in country tweeds seated on a long high backed 'old oaken' seat.

'Carter,' Leacock announced, 'something very terrible has happened. My daughter has been murdered.'

He said this with a sort of calculated defiance which I did not understand. All that I remembered of Harriet – revulsion, compassion and liking – assailed me at once. And yet the news did not really touch me. Mrs Leacock seemed to be trying to protest at what her husband had said, but her words were swallowed in sobbing.

The youngish man said remonstratingly, 'Now, Dr Leacock . . .'

But Godmanchester interrupted him, 'I don't know what you're at, Leacock,' he said, 'your wife's broken enough as it is. Do you want to drive her out of her mind? Dr Wainwright,' he turned to the youngish man, 'take Mrs Leacock up to her bedroom and get her to lie down until that nurse comes.'

He had clearly taken charge. After the doctor had led Madge Leacock upstairs, Godmanchester turned on Leacock.

'My dear chap,' he said, 'nobody's sorrier for you than I am. But you've heard what the Inspector said and the doctor. You're only hurting your wife by making these ghastly suggestions.'

Leacock looked as though he might strike the fat old man, but he said only, 'I don't want to talk to you about it. But I shall make myself perfectly clear to the doctor when he comes down again.'

He walked away from us into his study. Godmanchester shrugged his shoulders.

'It's pathetic, Carter. The wretched woman was killed horribly last evening in the British Reserve by some escaped animal – from the doctor's description of the wounds it sounds to me like a wolf. But Leacock refuses to face it because of course it's bound to put an end to his project here. It would be a fascinating study in egotism if it weren't so horrible. His daughter's good name, his wife's peace of mind, everything sacrificed to –'

It had taken me a moment to grasp what he had said.

Then I burst out, 'God! That must have been the screaming I heard in the distance last night. And of course that dog of hers must have been wounded by the wolf or whatever it was. It was bleeding heavily from the muzzle and I thought it had killed a sheep. That's why I shot it. Instead of that, the poor beast had been fighting for its mistress.'

I stopped, horrified. Then, as I looked at Godmanchester, I saw that the same thought had come to him as to me.

He said grimly, 'I've heard the same stories that you have, Carter. Talk here travels fast.'

'I shall have to speak – '

'You don't *have* to do anything. You don't know where this is going to lead, Carter, or who's going to be hurt. Don't say a word until you know the way things are moving.'

Doctor Wainwright came down the stairs as the nurse arrived. He said a few words to her and sent her up to Mrs Leacock.

'I've given her a sedative,' he announced. 'There's no point in my being here any longer. I've told them all I can and I shall repeat it at the inquest.'

Godmanchester nodded. But Leacock came out of his study.

'Look, Dr Wainwright. My daughter was a whore. I believe medical science would say she was a nymphomaniac. I use a more old-fashioned word. I sent her to psychiatrists, analysts, I did everything I could. To no purpose. You're a local man. I have no doubt the scandal has reached you. If it hasn't it's a miracle because she gave herself to every man in the area she could find willing to take her.'

Dr Wainwright interrupted, 'Please, Dr Leacock, you shouldn't be saying all this. In any case it's nothing to do with what's happened. As I've told you already many times the wounds in your daughter's throat and in particular the gashes on her cheeks and thighs could only have been made by the teeth and claws of an animal.'

'But you admit that she'd been with a man.'

'Yes. There were evidences of sexual intercourse at some time during that evening. But that's irrelevant.'

'To anyone who knew my daughter's life it's far from irrelevant. She picked up with any casual man, the lower the better. Good God! Do you think I don't feel the horror of it? Whatever I say of her, she *was* my own daughter. And for any human being to have suffered at the hands of a maniac. For that's what it was. Find the man! Hang him! That's what I demand.'

I tried to make myself heard above his shouting.

I said, 'Leacock, please try to argue all this when you've rested a little.'

He answered brusquely with a return of his old manner.

'Thank you, Carter. I can manage my own affairs. I am not going to let that man,' he pointed at Godmanchester and began to shout again, 'ruin this great scheme. My daughter was murdered.'

Godmanchester said, 'Tell him I want a word with him, Carter. Tell him he'd be wise to talk with me.'

I hesitated.

'Well, wouldn't he?'

I said, 'I think you should, Leacock.'

'I have nothing private to say to Lord Godmanchester, Carter.'

Dr Wainwright put on his overcoat and scarf.

He said, 'Well, I'll be round again later to see Mrs Leacock. The coroner will inform you of the time of the inquest.'

Leacock said, 'If you won't listen now, Doctor, you'll force me to speak publicly.'

The doctor turned to me, 'Make him rest,' he said and was gone.

Immediately Godmanchester told Leacock brutally what he believed had happened. I saw then how deeply her father's sexual childishness must have aggravated Harriet's erotomania, for, at first, he just did not understand and then he supposed that we were trying to make some horrible joke in bad taste. He looked at me in bewildered appeal, but it would have been no help to him to prolong Godmanchester's determined attack. I said as kindly as I could that I believed it to be true. He laid his arms on the chimney piece, buried his head in them, as though he would blot out our existence.

Then he turned to us, 'What can we have done to have given birth to a monster?'

I said, 'How can anyone have become so desperately lost?'

Godmanchester dismissed these moral judgements brusquely.

'It's an appalling tragedy. The sooner we get this inquest and so on over the better for you and your wife, Leacock.'

But now Leacock's eyes assumed a childishly cunning look.

'Well, I've always thought these creatures were treacherous. I'm glad you killed it, Carter. It obviously had the rabies.'

Godmanchester's comic eyebrows went up.

'No, Leacock,' he said very deliberately, 'your daughter was killed by an escaped beast. A wolf I should think. If it wasn't so, you know, I should have to insist on a further examination.'

I shouted, 'What you're doing is disgusting and wicked. You're blackmailing Leacock. You've never intended to let this place succeed. You've cheated us all through.'

'You're a very romantic sort of chap, Carter, aren't you? I've let Leacock have a run for his money and I'd gladly go on doing so, but I can't afford it now. The confidence I need to save this country is more important than anything else at this moment. The opposition's got on to the Reserve as a weak link in my armour.'

'Well, if you aren't strong enough to smash that . . .'

'I am, thank you, Carter, but I don't believe in running any risks that I don't have to. I tell you what, Leacock, if we can put the blame on a jackal or such, you can keep your British Reserve with its wolves. All we need do is scrap the Exotic Park – that's the crux of the opposition's attack.'

There was a note of conscious magnanimity in his voice that maddened me as he made the offer.

'Don't bargain with him, Leacock.'

'You'll be a fool if you don't,' Godmanchester said. 'Half a fine scheme is better than none at all. But I shan't press it. I haven't time to waste.'

'You needn't worry, Carter, I shan't. You're perfectly right, Lord Godmanchester. My daughter was killed by a wolf.' He spoke with hysterical deliberateness that changed to an equally desperate irony. 'We must suppose that despite all Barley's competence, one has escaped.'

'Oh, you needn't worry about that. I settle all that. You must bury that dog quickly, Carter.'

I turned in horror to Leacock, 'You can't capitulate to blackmail like this.'

'I can't do anything else, Carter. Harriet and I in our selfishness – God knows how alike we were, she was my favourite when she was a child – have hurt Mrs Leacock enough. She's had to know too many humiliations. I will not have her told this disgusting thing.'

'Do you think she wouldn't prefer anything to your sacrificing all you're doing here?'

'I don't know. Yes, or course, she would do anything for us, for the family. But I don't want her to know this.'

'I think it may be my duty to take the decision out of your hands.'

I hoped that I detected an alarmed tension in Godmanchester's solid mass. Leacock came over and faced me. He looked more than ever ridiculous, his eyes in his tense emotion more squinting.

'I don't believe,' he said, 'that you would like to take into your own hands the decision of an old man's honour. For that's what it is, Carter. Whatever schemes and hopes and ideals I may have and that we may share, the security of Madge's world, of her life, are my affair, and my affair alone. She is a simple woman and if I can't protect her simplicity, if that's taken out of my hands by anyone, even by you with the best motives, I'm reduced to nothing. You will have taken away my honour, made me nothing as surely as if I had a stroke and were reduced to being fed like a baby again. I don't believe you would do it.'

At last I said, 'I ought to. I've made too many concessions of this sort already. But you're right, I can't.'

So it was settled. 'The Stretton Experiment' as Godmanchester's papers now called it – and 'experiment' in their columns was a very pejorative noun – came to an end. I went out that evening with a spade and buried Rickie. Only Mrs Leacock ever mentioned him again.

'Poor old Rickie, he was a one-man dog. I don't suppose we shall see him any more.'

Both Lord and Lady Godmanchester came down for the funeral; and Lady Godmanchester even found time to say a few words to Mrs Leacock. It was lucky that I was not carrying my revolver, for I should at that moment have liked to kill both the Lord Privy Seal and his decorative wife. Practically all the staff of the Reserve attended, but not those of Regent's Park. As the ceremony ended everyone seemed to feel the embarrassment so acutely that they made almost *en bloc* for the cars and taxis at the churchyard gates. I know that I feared lest Madge Leacock in her *naïveté* should feel it her duty to arrange some grim meal for the mourners. I think others must have felt as I did. At any rate I became conscious as I reached the gates and looked back that the Leacocks had been left with only the Filsons for company. There they stood, two battered old couples, blown about by the high wind, their loneliness outlined against a luminous, pearly sky. Two drab old pairs they seemed – the gnarled wronged old men, and their charmless heavy wives for whom they lived. Everyone had drawn away from them as though they carried a dangerous infection. It was, I knew, the most dangerous of all infections for me – pathos.

Just as I was leaving, Mrs Filson, who now appeared to be an expert and devoted driver, called to me out of the window of her Austin.

'Mr Carter, don't blame Charlie for handing in his notice, will you? Mind you, it's broken his heart the Reserve coming to an end. But it's my decision. We've made a life down here and here we shall retire. It's a sad business for Mrs Leacock, this. But I can't help wondering if they all remember how their muddle cost my Derek his life.'

I was angry that the Committee didn't press Dr Leacock to stay on, although he would not in any case have done so. He seemed to have acquired once more the hollow, rhetorical enthusiasm that had marked him in the old days before he went to Stretton.

'I don't feel finished yet, you know, Carter. So I've accepted a job at this new North Western University at Carlisle. My marine biology's a bit rusty, of course, but it's a small faculty as yet. It's mainly a question of building it up, building it up. And there's no doubt, I think, that the Lake District's the place of the future.'

Mrs Leacock thanked me for all I had done for Edwin.

'How little we know even our dearest,' she told me, 'I never realized how deeply Daddy loved Harriet. But this has nearly broken him, Mr Carter. In any case this place has not been lucky for us. Do you remember how I put my foot in it with Lady Godmanchester? Though I must say she was kind enough to say a word to me today. But I think it's just as well we're leaving. As I told Daddy, we're starting all over again, just as we did when we were first married. And I have high hopes, Mr Carter, though the Lake District is rather damp.'

I wished so much then that I had ever been able to believe in Mr Micawber's success in Australia.

As, so often, a leader in *The Times* spoke the knell of Leacock's great hopes – 'It has been the fate of the National Zoological Reserve at Stretton, with its sad loss both in human and animal life, to write finis to all dreams of large-scale preservation of foreign wild life species in natural surroundings. Our island, it would appear, is too small to allow even for the controlled return of the wolf, the bear and the boar.' On the day that this leader appeared, *The Advertiser* published the first of a series of popular, nostalgic articles on the 'London Zoo' by Sir Robert Falcon.

5

A GOOD OLD, RARE OLD,
ARMAGEDDON

I STILL, of course, had my own future plans to decide. Leacock, when he said good-bye, urged me, despite my great distaste for doing so, to stay on.

'But I think you've been abominably treated, Leacock, and in so far as it counts with the Committee, I should like to register my protest.'

'No, no, Carter, we've had enough gestures. Besides you don't owe me any loyalty. I misled and deceived you at the beginning as much as Godmanchester did. I foresaw much of this, but as I've told you I couldn't afford to wait. I was determined to fight it out and, frankly, if this ghastly blow hadn't hit me, I think that I'd have won. But you're badly needed here. *I* can testify to that. The orders you were given may have been wrong but nobody could have administered them more efficiently.'

'Thank you. But I've had the idea of leaving for some time. I'm so much happier when I'm simply working as a naturalist and I'm beginning to wonder why I shouldn't indulge that happiness.'

'I've never been happy, Carter, so I can't advise you about that. Oh, of course, I'm happy at home, gloriously so. But I've always been an ambition-driven man and always shall be. So *happiness* in work isn't quite my field. Pleasure in work at times, of course; I've had great *pleasure* down here. But I've always expected trouble, you know, in my life. Now I don't think you're ambition driven, but you are a man with a strong sense of duty. I don't think you'll be happy if you neglect it. And your duty's here. As to field work, Godmanchester'll want to keep you, and if you insist on retaining the British

Reserve here, he won't be able to say no. After all with the exceptions of the Scotch wild cats and a few red deer, all the fauna were here before anyway.'

'I couldn't be beholden to him.'

'Well, that I understand. But if you're worrying about having to deal with him, I shouldn't. He won't have time for Zoo affairs again in his life, I'm sure. Anyway I hope you stay. I'd like to think that you'll be Director in time.'

Bobby Falcon gave quite other advice. He begged me not to waste my time in administration. Of course, he'd be delighted to have me work with him, but frankly he had never thought of the Secretary's job as one for a man of real ability. He felt sure he could do it all himself with the assistance of a couple of good old-fashioned clerks, if such could be found nowadays. He must tell me honestly that he proposed to put the clock back at Regent's Park a good deal, to a more leisurely and most especially, a more colourful age. Godmanchester was giving the world a bit of a respite, God knew for how long, and the least he, Falcon, could do was to try to bring back the good old days while it lasted.

I was strengthened in my impression that since his return from America, he had been ill at ease with me, no doubt because he knew me to be a Leacock man.

I was angered by his low estimation of administrative work; I was horrified by what might happen to the administration if he were in sole charge; I did not really see why he should get rid of me so easily. On the other hand it might well be as unpleasant as he predicted, and why should I go on seeking discomfort. I told him that I should not decide until I had consulted by letter with Martha.

'Well that's all right then,' he said. 'You've as good as gone. I know what she thinks.'

I wrote a full account of my dilemma to her that night. Three days later I received a cable which read, 'AIR PASSAGE BOOKED RETURNING WEDNESDAY DO NOTHING UNTIL I ARRIVE CHILDREN STAY ALL MY LOVE MARTHA'. That morning one of Godmanchester's secretaries phoned me, requesting that I should visit the Lord Privy Seal's office the next day at 11.15 a.m. precisely.

Godmanchester's personal office was sumptuous in the most old-fashioned, late Victorian sense of that word: good leather everywhere and an array of inkstands and cigar boxes on his desk that looked as though they had been the gifts of Indian Rajahs to the Queen Empress Victoria. I was reminded of a story of some Foreign Secretary – was it Curzon? – whose first act in office was to have the silver inkstand replaced by one of gold. Waiting for Godmanchester, I wondered whether, in fact, he was the saviour that England needed. Or whether senile megalomania had imposed itself upon a desperate people. However politics were not – I had never allowed them to be – my concern. In any case my reflections were interrupted by the flushing of a cistern and, a moment later, Godmanchester ambled out from behind a concealed door, doing up his fly-buttons. It was clear that his manner of enhancing grandeur was by treating it with contempt.

'You're a very lucky man, Carter,' he said, 'I've no time for business like yours at the moment. But I've heard you're thinking of resigning from the Zoo service and I don't want you to do it. Now I've got exactly ten minutes I can spare for you. Do you think you can come to your senses in that time?'

'I'm waiting for my wife to come back from the States before I decide what I do. She'll be back here next week.'

'I take it that you're not such a fool as to be ruled by your wife's decision so we'll regard that as an evasive ruse. Now I've told you before that I think you're very good at your job and that I hope you'll be Director later on. I think you've been a fool in fighting Leacock's battles for him, however loyalty's a fault I've no objection to so long as it's not persisted in ridiculously. You tried to help Leacock, so did I. We failed. Forget it. It's over. He could have kept his Historic Reserve but he wouldn't play ball. Now you can have *your* British Reserve, more easily in fact than his historical one. Badgers and polecats are one things, wolves and wild boars quite another. I know you've imported those Scotch wild cats, but

I don't see why the people of Hertfordshire shouldn't face the same remote dangers as the people of Argyll. You want the British Reserve. We want you at Regent's Park. All right. Will you stay?'

'I've told you, Lord Godmanchester, I shall consult my wife.'

'Look! Is it my treatment of Leacock that's sticking in your gullet? Or is it that you think I made my own uses of an important zoological venture? I don't know why I should have to argue with you about it. I'd like to tell you where to put your moral scruples and kick you out of the room. But I can only say to you that I wouldn't have done a lot of the things I've done in the last year if I'd seen any other way of campaigning myself into office. And if you say – who cares whether you're in office? – I can only answer that no one in this country will ever know how much they ought to care, because they'll never know the ghastly things I shall save them from. But, if you can waive your glorious disbelief for a moment, I'll tell you what is true – that I'm particularly upset about the Zoo. In point of fact there are many other places, yes, and people, some of them old friends, who have as much reason to complain of my treatment of them as the Zoological Society has, but I happen to feel more about the Zoo. And that's why I want you to stay on and give the place the administration it needs.'

'I don't think I can order my life to help settle your conscience.'

Godmanchester rolled back in his padded leather armchair in disgust.

'Go on. Get out,' he said, 'I don't believe that anyone as priggish as you can be indispensable. I just can't believe it.'

'I'm sure I'm not. Sir Robert Falcon will tell you that the work can be done by a couple of clerks.'

'Yes, yes. Falcon's just the man that's needed there at the moment, thank God! But he doesn't understand the first thing about how any organization works. Why should he? His *métier* is being a colourful personality.' He paused, then leaning his short stubby arms on the huge desk, he loomed towards me, a blubbery shapeless old mass. 'Will you stay on for this year, Carter? After that we can train somebody else. Particularly for this spring. I want to have the biggest show put on in London this spring that we can mount – tradition, art, sport, enterprise, everything we've got – to show the confidence we feel. Economically we need it, politically it may save us. There isn't a famous building or a celebrity that I don't intend to rope in. But my name's particularly associated with the London Zoo and for that reason I want to stage a fine show there. Falcon's got ideas. Will you stay at least until the British Day, as we're going to call it, in the first week of June, and help him to put his ideas into practice?'

'I don't know. You've given me some reason for thinking that I may be very useful, if that gratifies you. But I still intend to talk to my wife before I make a decision. I'll let you know next week.'

Godmanchester began to study a memorandum. He said in an offhand way,

'Tell one of my secretaries. I shan't be on tap for this sort of thing in the future. Anyway you've had more than your ten minutes. Good-bye.'

When from the balcony overlooking London Airport, I saw Martha stepping briskly across the tarmac from the aeroplane gangway, outpacing in her eagerness even the commanding air hostess, I felt such an upsurge of love and lust and reproach and remorse for my reproach that in dizziness I had to steady myself by holding on to the railings. In her turn, when she came out of the customs room and saw me standing, as she said, like a puppy ready to bound forward at a look of love or backward at the raise of a correcting arm, Martha felt, she afterwards told me, exactly the same turbulent swell of emotions. We silently concurred, too, in letting our remorse and reproach lie unspoken in the hope that a few days' happiness together would make them seem too paltry even to be thought of. I had taken a week off and we gave it up to trivial talk and happy reminiscence. We wanted nothing more than a flat, brightly painted backcloth against which we could express unimpeded our pent-up love and desire. It was a sunny, gusty March week, where even from Primrose Hill or Regent's Park the stiff puffy white clouds could be seen scudding across the pale blue sky, pursuing one another at irregular speeds and intervals like tableaux trying to catch up with the main procession in a splendid but ill-rehearsed pageant. Just to walk out in the parks or on the Heath under such skies banished the sense of London's confinement and gave the illusion of open plains or mid ocean. I felt more than ever at such a time that my hope of blending town and country, the Zoo's office life of human contact and the Reserve's peace of heightened sight and sound was not an absurdity. On the last evening of that week we sat on a seat near the Open Air Theatre, sheltered from the wind by a magnolia tree already coming into flower. The dying sun was almost fierce on our faces for a while. I looked in turn at the strolling crowds, the scudding clouds or the white crocuses frosting the bank beneath the magnolia; and, wherever I looked for those few minutes, the world seemed to have some secret unity. Pleasure and duty need not, I thought, tear me apart.

Martha said, 'I haven't said anything yet, darling, about the job. I believe *you* want to stay at the Zoo. And that's all that matters to *me*. I felt sick when I read your letters about the end of Stretton and I only wanted you to get away from the whole lot of them. But something I learned from seeing Hester again, I think, is that one can live with the past and disregard it. She was just the same – all the small things that maddened me and seem to spoil a very nice person – and yet I could manage to think of her simply as someone I was visiting with a view to leaving the children in her care. The truth is, Simon, that I've come back feeling exactly about her as I did before, but quite sure that the children will be happy and safe with her. She's two people – an infuriating sister from the past and a decent guardian for Reggie and Violet if war comes here.'

I spoke through a haze of happiness, as though I knew everything would be all right from now on.

I said, 'I trust you know best, Martha. And about my work too.'

But she cried, 'No, no, Simon. That's just it. You must do what *you* want. I only told you about all that because I thought maybe you were anxious lest the past, all that horrible business at Stretton, might dog your life at the Zoo in the future. And from my visit to Hester, I could say to you that it *would* always be there but that you could go ahead and get what you wanted out of the place all the same. Yes, I know, darling, and *give* what you wanted too.'

'I want to keep the place running properly and I should like, too, to make a first-rate Reserve available to British naturalists. But at Stretton, Martha, and by Godmanchester's courtesy! It's not easy to swallow.'

'Oh, phooey to Lord Godmanchester! He's made use of you. You try to make use of him. But I'm not going to give advice, Simon. I've gone on far too much wanting this and that for you. You know best. What I know is that I want to be with you, and, as soon as we feel able, to have the children with us too. I've been too goddamned pleased with myself, fussing about whether you're fulfilling yourself. You are you and that's that.'

'I like you to approve of me.'

'Approve! Simon. Approve, pity, admire, despise, revere – I suppose I shall come around to the lot of them in the years ahead.' She touched the bench on which we sat, 'Given any years that is. But let's call it love and not start sorting out the bits. Whatever my immediate emotions I shall love you as . . . as, well, as Jane doesn't love Bobby.'

I took her hand in mine and stroked it.

'Thank you.'

What she had said seemed part of this sudden sense of unity, of allrightness that had settled upon me. I did not need to sort out her words. Stroking her hand, watching a lion shaped beast hurrying across the sky to join (as it never could) a grey white map of Australia, I made casual conversation – or was it casual?

'Bobby seems thriving at the moment anyway. Heaven knows what jubilation he's concocting for the Zoo. I can't get as enthusiastic about it as I was about Leacock's Stretton scheme. But I think I can help him, even if I'm only an amused observer, because whatever he intends will presumably need organizing and I doubt if he could organize a church bazaar.'

'He's organized some important expeditions in his time.'

'Yes, God knows how. I may be wrong. In any case the Society's affairs have to be looked after, jubilee or no jubilee; and I'm quite sure that he'll never attend to day to day work. The only trouble is that he doesn't want me there. He says it's a waste of my time. But in fact I think he really does believe he can do it all himself. He's quite wrong of course . . .'

Martha broke in fiercely, 'Bobby's a stupid coward. You *must* not take any notice of him. If he looks like being a nuisance *I'll* deal with him.'

I laughed. 'First steps in the policy of non-interference. As a matter of fact I hadn't *intended* to take any notice of him now that I know you agree with my decision to stay.'

Australia had blotted out the sun, the wind came fiercely through the shiny magnolia leaves, whipping up dust and a discarded cigarette packet around our feet, the crocuses still seemed like snowfall, but cold and dead now without the reflected light. Martha got up.

'Well, that's all right then. We must move on, darling, I'm getting cold.'

And so I telephoned to Godmanchester's secretary to say that I was remaining.

Bobby Falcon was absolutely charming, once he had gulped down the news.

'My dear Simon,' he said, 'if you and Martha are happy about it, nothing could be better than to have you holding my hand at this critical moment.'

It was a strange régime that we entered upon, ironically as like as two peas to the days before Leacock's television programme. Bobby transformed the Director's room into a symbol of all we stood for. He moved in furniture of the eighteen fifties and decorated the walls with his collection of Victorian genre paintings of the Zoo, including the vast canvas of Frith's 'A Ride on Jumbo', and the series of sketches of mountain goats on the Mappin Terrace made by Holman Hunt before he left for the Dead Sea. Deposited around the room were a model of Steller's sea cow, some authentic dodo feathers, a Victorian card case covered in quagga skin, the thigh bone of a moa, and a genuine stuffed Great Auk surveying the world with great surprise from its viewpoint of extinction. There was also a case containing broad-sheets and comic songs that referred to the Zoo. Against this background he carried on his remarkable manic-depressive Directorship – elated, lively, charming, competent, and above all imaginative when preparations for the British Day were under discussion; morose, rude, inattentive and sometimes surprisingly obtuse when other business had to be done. He only became really angry, however, when Stretton was mentioned; and once the animals, including Godmanchester's so generously given own private collection, had arrived safely in London, Leacock and the Exotic Reserve were banished from all tongues.

Pattie Henderson, once, at the Staff Restaurant, pouring down her usual lunch-time two pints, did say to me, 'Is all that business down in Wales wound up now?'

And when I said that it was, except for my own proposed Naturalists' Reserve, she said, 'Do you mean the creatures that were there anyway? The whole thing seems to have been rather a sweat for nothing, I must say. But of course you admin boys have to think up these bright ideas to keep yourselves busy, I suppose.'

Then she told me that she was only chaffing.

The only person who confronted Bobby with criticism of the move was Sanderson. He came into the Director's office one morning when I was there.

Gravely looking down at the ground, he asked, 'Is all this moving of the poor animals over yet, Falcon?'

Bobby, whose mind was on a scheme for rehousing the

species most popular with the public in special replicas of the Victorian cages, said,

'No. We've hardly begun, Sanderson. But I don't think we shall trouble you much. I've got one or two ideas for showing the ants and the butterflies with moral texts, but I'll let you know about that later.'

Sanderson grew red in the face.

'I don't only think of my own exhibits, you know,' he said. 'It seems to me completely damnable the way these poor beasts have been moved down to Wales and back again. And you say it's not even completed.'

I intervened. 'The Director misunderstood you. All the exhibits were back from Stretton a week ago.'

I said it with a certain fervour, since the operation had fallen almost entirely on me.

'Well, I only hope they won't be moved again. After all, they're in our care and we ought to consider that. By making them captive we take their welfare on our shoulders for good and all. Otherwise we've no right to deprive them of freedom.'

Bobby leaned back against his chair and gave a sort of jaunty twist to his moustache that always indicated an attempt to mask rising anger under jocularity.

'My dear Sanderson,' he drawled, 'have you ever thought how damned lucky the animals are that fall into the hands of the Society? By and large, that is, unless climate's against them. No ghastly search for scarce food or water in times of drought! No relentless native huntsmen! No jungle rivalry! No old age, tracked down, feeble and desperate! I *know* the jungle and I can tell you this, that if our beasts here were shunted back between Wales and London for a year they'd be better off than the old lion or the sick rhino in their natural state or the giraffe separated from the herd. Think of *them*, Sanderson, before you bleat about our chaps' cushy little troubles.'

Sanderson said, 'I'm concerned for the animals here because they're the ones I know.'

Afterwards Bobby reacted much as had his predecessor.

He said, 'I haven't seen much of Sanderson in the last few years. He appears to have become gaga.'

But I reserved my opinion. And Bobby sulked on and off for the rest of the day.

But as the British Day drew nearer, he was transformed. The old sick puma became visibly a sleek, handsome young leopard. The downward curving lines, the flabby bags and pouches, the grey that suffused his tanned skin had seemed less striking when he returned from America; now they were suddenly gone. Mrs Purrett said he looked every inch the soldier; Rackham said he'd like to see some of these young chaps today under Sir Robert's command, they wouldn't know whether they were going or coming; Jane said that she'd forgotten that she'd married such an old charmer; Sanderson announced that there was a strange, spiritual strength about our new Director that perhaps came from his knowledge of the East; Englander asked me if Falcon had come into money; Lord Oresby wondered if Falcon had been cutting down on wine and women, he looked so well; Strawson said there was something about the leadership of a gentleman; and Matthew, when I drew attention to Bobby's dandyish military appearance, said,

'Yes. He's a terrible bounder, isn't he? Like an advertisement for whisky.'

It was a unanimous verdict. With his refreshed appearance came a new and extraordinarily lighthearted energy that bowled over even those of us who were amusedly scornful of his schemes. He laughed at himself all the time for being such an anachronism in this earnest age, yet he laughed at us even more for taking the age so earnestly. I saw in those weeks the secret of the success of his expeditions, that he made it all a game and, in so doing, assured everyone how tremendously serious it all was, for, after all, games were the only things worth doing well. It was an arrogant charm and I watched fascinatedly to see how he got away with it. For instance, there was an electrical engineer, the principal representative of the firm concerned with the lighting 'on the great night' whose pomposity soon became a bait of Bobby's. He was, funnily enough, a heavy, handsome matinée idol sort of man like Bobby himself but several social or sophisiticated rungs (you could call it which you like) lower in the charm ladder. Perhaps that was what riled Bobby. This man whose name was Johnson-White became 'that charming fellow Bronson-Sprite' or 'that invaluable man Monson-Tight'. All this was as childish as it was snobbish, but it was done with such an air of enjoyment of what was known to be a cad's trick that one couldn't help joining in. Johnson-White, too, let himself in for it by suggesting, 'if I may venture, a pastel shade for the Humming Birds' House to tone down their somewhat strident tropical colouring'; now he could never set foot in the office without Bobby asking 'what was that frightfully good phrase about the humming birds, my dear fellow?' Or, again, Johnson-White, after much hesitation and archness, recommended an old rose lighting for the Ladies' Rooms on the night – 'the ladies like a kind lighting, Sir Robert. That's not my opinion, let me hasten to say, but Mrs Johnson-White's. The age-old wisdom of women about their own sex.' After that hardly a day passed that Bobby did not call upon Mrs Purrett for a spot of age-old wisdom, and he even insisted on a tray marked 'For Mrs Bronson-Sprite' into which problems of entertainment or colour scheme were placed. Yet when Johnson-White might have expected to smell a rat and become offended, Bobby was to be found with him in real earnest, down on his hands and knees examining an angle of the tortoise house or a recess behind the pheasantry which opposed problems to effective wiring. His consumption of detail was alarmingly impressive and endeared him to all the technicians; so also indeed was his inventiveness and power to make do and mend.

'Look,' he would say to the works foreman concerned with the hydraulic problems of the 'Seashore of Britain' exhibit, 'we had a nonsense like this to sort out when I was pursuing the non-existent Nandi bear in Uganda . . .'

Or to the carpenters concerned with the trapdoors through

which young otters were to disappear when amusing the public with their antics, 'I had a problem a bit like this with a little racoon once, a lively little fellow. I constructed a box, a frightfully amateurish thing, but if I could just show you . . .'

It was not only his mental agility, however, that captivated; he was up and down ladders and across planks with the youngest workmen in the place. That he enjoyed all this exhibitionism he never for a moment hid. I have seen him leap from one scaffolding above the seals' pond to another; and, when the workmen half-ironically clapped, he bowed to them with an equal half-irony. Sometimes my annoyance or disgust was stronger than the charm he exerted and I tried to puncture his performance with sharp remarks. But to no avail.

'My dear fellow,' he would say, 'how frightfully good you are for me.'

Then a day later before a crowd of colleagues or visitors, he would say, 'Simon, for goodness sake say something good for me. I'm in need of it,' and, when, from laughing at the absurdity of the face he pulled, I could say nothing, he would cry, 'Nothing good for me! You're not fulfilling your function! You've run out of moralities. Shame! Shame!'

I have written 'visitors' and that was another matter for marvel. I had known that Bobby 'knew everybody', but not how devoted 'everybody' was to him. For the staff and the workmen every day was a field day, for Bobby brought television stars, Victoriana experts, stage designers, peers who were expert showmen of their gracious homes, actresses, ballet dancers, top journalists, explorers, gossip column financiers, Brains Trust scientists – anybody whose face adorned the popular dailies and the telescreen. He enrolled them somehow in his happy absurd antics and mixed them in with the staff and the contractors' men. Debs got tied up in tartan ribbon that was to grace the Highland cattle; an important and doubtful financier was persuaded into being photographed with a wart-hog that horribly resembled him; a veteran revue star did her famous imitation of a seal from the sea-lions' pool. Masons laying tiles for the Great Hall of Beasts found themselves cheek to cheek with beautiful starlets as they pondered over the William Morris patterns that Bobby had presented for their choice. As the Day grew nearer Jane, attracted by the theatrical atmosphere, became more and more involved. Indeed she and Bobby were photographed again and again as 'London's smartest Darby and Joan' – an irony that made me at times desperately sad for the Leacocks, whose dowdy devotion had never drawn the notice of even a passing camera. But it must be said that the Falcons did look extraordinarily elegant. And elegance was the keynote of the whole thing – elegance with a touch of chichi. Matthew thought it horribly vulgar. Lord Godmanchester, who appeared only once, looking tired and strangely purple in the face, hoped that Falcon wasn't forgetting the Commonwealth aspect; but Bobby reassured him.

'Good Lord! I should think not. We've got oodles of kangaroos and kiwis laid on.'

I ventured once to hint that the wonderful stink of the mob might be lost in all his wealth of stylized Victoriana, witty parody, Romantic charm and music hall pastiche, but Bobby took me quite literally.

'My dear fellow, you don't know the crush I've asked for the opening, half London, and in this boiling weather!'

Of course, in a sense he was right, so long as there was enough sweat, it didn't matter whether it came from the cockney crowd or the top people at play, the stink would be much the same.

And the weather that May was exceptionally hot. As the celebrities and the art students and the workmen took off more and more clothes, and Bobby improvised a bathing pool in the canal, where Jane's actresses served out chicken sandwiches and iced beer and even iced champagne, the whole place assumed more the air of a free for all *fête-champêtre*. Not that it was an idle one, enormous quantities of hay were made. And in the evenings a small knot of us would gather in Bobby's office – Jane, sometimes Martha strangely mute, a keeper or two, Mrs Purrett – and, eating a cold supper, we would work hard at the plans for the next day. Bobby, imitating the particular celebrated visitors of the past day, would draw me in to assist him, until all the work was carried on in a frenzy of mimicry and farce. On the whole I enjoyed myself very much, even when it all seemed to me most frivolous.

Bobby's frivolity, indeed, seemed to know no limits. One afternoon Inspector Martin appeared upon the scene again; and this time he was not prepared to be fobbed off with the Secretary. His manner with Bobby was grave and a little servile; Bobby's with him a schoolboy's acting in an Agatha Christie.

'I imagine Mr Carter has already given you some account of my earlier visit here, Sir Robert, with reference to a member of your staff, Dr Emile Englander.'

Bobby assumed an absurdly conspiratorial manner, his moustaches hunched up under his nose.

'I should *think* so! It gave us a pretty good shock, I can tell you.'

Inspector Martin gazed at me as at one he had always known to be unreliable.

I said, 'You told me to say nothing to anyone about Dr Englander's foreign associations, Inspector, and I have not done so.'

Bobby leaned back as though immensely relieved.

'Trouble abroad! Oh, I know nothing of that. I thought you were referring to the sinister affair of the two schoolgirls and the bar of chocolate. But if you don't know about that, Inspector, I'd prefer to say no more. It is after all entirely a Zoo affair. Perhaps you'd tell me something of the Doctor's clandestine activities overseas.'

The Detective-Inspector, looking puzzled, outlined what he had said to me.

Then he added, 'Since that time we have reason to think that Dr Englander may have associations with the Uni-Europe Movement.'

Bobby's manner changed to his most arrogant.

'Oh, I hardly think that's likely, Inspector. Surely they're all corner boys and anti-semitic loafers and scum, aren't they?

Englander has a lot of connexions with Europe certainly – he's a scientist with a world-wide reputation, but his friends are very distinguished people – European scientists, and businessmen and financiers. He comes of a big business family. He's a very rich man, you know.'

The real reverence with which Bobby said this gave me a sudden insight into the strange foundations of his 'patrician' snobberies. I understood more than ever why Matthew found him vulgar. The Inspector seemed more impressed by Bobby's *naïveté*.

He said, 'The two things are not necessarily contradictory, Sir Robert. The Movement has considerable funds, you know, although its membership is mainly confined to what you rightly describe as scum. I see,' he added suddenly, 'that two of Dr Englander's keepers are away on leave at the same time as he is.'

I said, 'Yes, I believe that is so. The summer leaves are often difficult to fit in and we like to get as much leave taken n spring as possible.'

The Inspector said, 'I was asking you, Mr Carter, whether Englander's principal assistants were away on official leave.'

'I imagine so, Inspector. I haven't the staff lists here . . .'

Bobby's voice interrupted me.

'*Doctor* Englander, Inspector, naturally runs the staff side of his department as he thinks best. We're concerned here, you know, with eminent people working in a world famous institution, not with the managers of branches of Woolworth's.'

'I have my inquiries to make, Sir Robert. It would help if you could understand that.'

'My dear fellow, go ahead.'

'Has the Zoological Society any particular interest in the Western Islands of Scotland at the present time?'

'We have interests everywhere, Inspector. And for the moment particularly everywhere British.'

'Is it possible that the Zoological Society might be concerned with certain building activities there?'

'Where?'

'In the Western Islands, Sir Robert.'

'Yes, yes, my dear fellow. But the Islands are numerous. Mull, Staffa, Iona, which?'

'I see that any such activities were *not* licensed by yourself, Sir Robert. Thank you. That's all I wanted to know.'

'You see no such thing, Inspector. As I've already said the senior staff here are internationally famed zoologists, not schoolboys. If Dr Englander is constructing some building for his work in the Western Islands then he's doing it for some very good scientific reason which I have no doubt that the Committee will approve. As a matter of fact, I expect he's making a hideout to watch these snake-worship ceremonies. There's a particularly bad outbreak of them in Scotland. I'm surprised that the Yard is not investigating that instead of the ridiculous antics of the Uni-Europe Movement.'

'Not everyone takes your view, Sir Robert.'

'Oh, Good Lord! Inspector! I have no view. But if the whole thing's going out with a bang, it seems rather a waste of time running around fussing about who's trying to put Roman Candles under the Houses of Parliament. But you don't want my views on all that, my dear chap. As I say Dr Englander's not a child, why don't you ask *him* what it's all about?'

'We should like to, Sir. But he left the country two days ago. I imagine on official leave.'

Bobby started angrily at the Inspector's sarcastic tone.

'As you say, Inspector. Well, you have work to do, as you reminded us. And I must remind you that we're very busy too. So if you've no more questions . . .'

As the Inspector went out, Bobby said, 'By the way do take my advice about this Scotch snake-worship seriously, Inspector. Now there *is* something pretty sinister going on, I'm sure.'

The whole interview seemed to fill him with delight.

'That chap didn't like me at all, you know,' he repeated again and again that afternoon.

Once he asked me what I thought old Englander was up to; and with a certain hesitation I suggested that from what he had once said to me, he might be engaged on some private scheme for the evacuation of the reptiles. Bobby seemed amazed.

'I say, that's pretty bad, when our President's promised us an era of peace.' He roared with laughter. 'I thought Englander was such a wise old bird. But what an optimistic chump he must be. The Western Isles of Scotland!'

It seemed a good moment for me to confess my own clandestine actions over the Aquarium. Bobby again laughed.

'Biscay water, eh? That must have cost us a pretty penny. But I'm not surprised at *you* being an optimist, Simon, you're such an innocent.'

'I'm a bit concerned about Jackley's reaction when he hears what I've done.'

'Are you? I don't care a damn. Just look at this letter of his.'

He took out a letter from his files and tossed it across to me.

Dear Falcon,

It is kind of you to inquire about my health. I am glad to say that I am now convalescent. You ask whether I shall be with you for the British Day: having been away from England for so long I am not quite sure of the nature of this celebration; events at home seem to move so rapidly and yet, to an outside observer, the crises appear without significance. However I take it to be some social occasion unconnected with the scientific work of the Society. I seldom distinguish myself socially, and therefore, with yours and the Society's permission, I shall absent myself from the junketing. Since I am unlikely to leave England again for some time after my return home, I should like, again with the Society's permission, to visit our Marine Research Station at Funchal before returning to my duties . . .

'Junketing,' Bobby said. 'He has the Society's permission to go and . . . And so I've said in my letter. If he doesn't want to be in on the Great Day, who the hell cares?'

A couple of days later Bobby told me casually that he'd looked into the Reptile House affairs.

'I suspect there are some of the most valuable specimens

missing. But the chaps there are frightfully loyal to the old boy.
They won't say anything. Anyhow that head keeper Kennedy
is a very good man and he's co-operating nicely with my
ideas for Reptiles on the big night. And the last thing we want
is that sort of scandal now. We can give the old chap a rocket
afterwards.'

I suggested that the Committee should be told of so serious
a matter; it was after all a grave misuse of the Society's property.

Bobby said, 'What about your Biscay water? No, all right.
I know it's not the same thing. As a matter of fact, I've discussed it with Godmanchester. It's frightfully difficult to get
hold of him these days. He seems to be in a perpetual political
flap. But he agreed. No scandal at any price, he said.'

The same afternoon he told me that Englander had telephoned from Zürich.

'I blew him up a bit about pinching our pythons. But you
know what he is, he just chuckled. The main thing of course
was to tell him that this inspector chap had been asking about
him.'

'Wasn't that a bit irresponsible?'

'My dear Simon, my responsibility is to my senior colleagues.'

He was so fierce that I drew back.

'I was only suggesting. After all Englander might con-
ceivably be mixed up with this Uni-Europe Movement and,
although it hasn't been declared illegal, it *could* obviously be a
danger to the State in certain circumstances.'

'I doubt if scum like that will play a large part in Armageddon.'

'They might bring it closer.'

He laughed, 'We've only got a fortnight to the British Day.
Surely Godmanchester can hold off the last trump for that
short time.'

'I'm not going to ask you to be serious, Bobby. It's no use
these days.'

'Good. Good. You're the serious man, not me. Though

mind you, I doubt if you have the faintest idea of what really ranks as serious.'

'Tell me then.'

'Good Lord no! It's not my job to spout metaphysics. We must leave that to the saintly Beard.'

Beard alone of the senior staff, as a matter of fact, incurred Bobby's real hostility at that time. He showed almost no interest in the preparations for 'the day'. That, as Bobby said, would hardly have mattered since there was no idea of having a post-mortem tableau; but he was still intent upon checking the statistical data from the office records. Since the row over the typists' pool, he had given up asking for assistance, but he stayed after hours to do the work himself. Many of our jolly evening sessions with cold duck and white wine, or *pâté* and claret, were marred by the presence of the Prosector inexpertly climbing ladders and dangerously balancing boxes of files one upon another. He seemed ostentatiously unaware of our presence, or perhaps he genuinely was so.

One evening when Bobby could bear it no longer, he shouted, 'For God's sake, Beard, pay some attention to what's going on, or get out.'

Beard looked down over his glasses from the ladder's height, blushed, and said, 'Oh, Lor'!' and fled.

Yet the next evening he was back again. From then on Bobby tried angrily to ignore him.

It was all the more infuriating then, when a few nights before the Great Day, Jumbo, our largest elephant, fell ill with some skin trouble. He had been re-christened from his more modern name 'Trunk Call' to prepare him for the tableau representing Frith's famous painting. Neither Strawson, Bobby himself, nor Beard's assistant hastily summoned from his home in Highbury seemed able to diagnose the trouble. It was nine o'clock at night and for once the Prosector had not stayed late. I rang his home number again and again, but it was always engaged. The operator, urged to test, reported that it was not out of order. There remaining nothing for it but to fetch him. His assistant was very unwilling to do this.

'Dr Beard's absolutely forbidden anybody to intrude into his home life.'

Should we send a messenger? Perhaps he would ignore the summons. Bobby clearly felt that he would lose caste by going to Beard's house. I set off myself in a sanctioned taxi for the gloomy reaches of Cromwell Road – since the rebuilding of North Kensington, West London's chief remaining slum. I had not before known where Beard lived and it came as a shock to me to think that my last visit to this area had been with European tourists who wanted to see how English people 'used to live'. The old Edwardian block of flats at which the taxi drew up was almost an exhibit of decay – I thought how Bobby had missed a ripe example of old England by not undertaking the mission himself. Yet Beard's salary, if not princely in Englander's terms, established him many economic rungs above the 'handicapped', that flotsam class which inhabited such areas as this. Perhaps, I thought, his living here was a mortification, or, perhaps, he was too dedicated to notice. I told the taximan to wait and going through the open front door, made my way up the uncarpeted stone stairs. The door of the first floor flat was opened by a fat, thirtyish woman with mottled bare legs and plimsolls. The crocheted jumper that covered her large, low-slung breasts seemed home made, as did the ridiculously short crimson silk skirt that was drawn tightly over her large hips and belly. Her dark hair looked as though it had been cut under a pudding basin. Her wrists were tightly bandaged.

She asked, 'Are you the nurse?'

When I explained, she said, 'Oh, well, you'd better come in then, Father's with Granny. She's had an attack and we're waiting for the nurse.'

I began to apologize for my unseasonable arrival, but she took no notice.

'Father,' she shouted, 'a man from the Zoo.'

There was no answer from the long, dark corridor down which she called, and she set off to fetch him. The large hall in which she left me was filled with the bric-à-brac of a middle-class household of half a century ago, a proliferation of cheap Asian objects suggested the sort of ex-Indian home which I seemed vaguely to remember from my youth (or was it from some novels? After the age of thirty fiction gets inextricably mixed into fact). The room was dark, dirty, airless, and infinitely depressing. Apart from its general gloom, however, I could see no object that connected with Beard the scientist or Beard the Christian. Two or three doors were banged very loudly. Miss Langley-Beard (if she was as fatly virginal as she looked) returned. She said, 'He'll be in in a sec.'

I began to explain my errand, and to suggest that if old Mrs Langley-Beard's attack was so serious, I should withdraw. She commented on this only by giggling each time I used the word 'elephant'.

Then she asked, 'Do you want coffee?'

Before I could reply, a door in the passage was flung open and from the room came a cracked contralto voice. It spoke with difficulty and with long pauses for breath.

'My dear Charles, you'd much better let them put me into hospital. I shall be less trouble to you all there.'

I began to speak again to cover what seemed a very private conversation, but Miss Langley-Beard said rather irritably, 'Ssh!' Then, repeating her giggle, she announced, 'They're rowing.'

They were indeed, for Beard's voice now came to us, loud and far more assured than it ever sounded at the Gardens. 'It's not help to make useless suggestions, Mother. They won't take chronic cases as you've been told again and again.'

'I'm sure they won't have me there for long, dear, anyway.'

'I'm afraid your assurance of that isn't worth very much. You've recovered from other attacks.'

A young man's voice, much deeper than Beard's, now said, or rather shouted, 'And we hope you do from this, Grannie. We know you will.'

Beard said, 'It can hardly help your grandmother to tell her what is not true, Alan.'

Then he appeared from the doorway and came out to me in the hall.

'I had hoped,' he said, 'to be left in peace in my home.'

I apologized and explained the nature of my errand. As I was talking a very handsome young man in his late twenties came twisting into the room on crutches. As with most spastics, the enormous breadth of his chest and shoulders were somehow more distressing than the twisted, puny shape of his legs. He swung himself with practised complication into an armchair. Striking out with one crutch, he tapped Beard on the ankle.

'That was disgusting,' he said, breaking through my speech, 'talking to Grannie like that. You know she's frightened out of her wits.'

'Pretence isn't going to help her.'

'Pretence! A little human sympathy!'

'Since you can do very little at a time like this, I would suggest that you at least spare us hysteria, Alan. If you want to help your Grandmother, you can pray for her.'

'If I had any prayers, I should offer them for you.'

The young man got up again, but as he twisted and writhed, Beard turned his back and spoke to me.

'I'll come straight away. Not that I was aware that we had an elephant called Jumbo.'

'It used to be called Trunk Call but Falcon's renamed it.'

Beard laughed scornfully.

'A most useful occupation for the Director.'

'Are you sure that you can leave here?'

'I suppose so. Why not?'

'Your mother . . .'

'Oh, she's been dying of cardiac trouble for some time.'

Alan Langley-Beard with difficulty twisted round in his walk and put his face close to his father's.

'If Gran dies while you're away, I hope you'll never forget it.'

'I asked you not to be hysterical, Alan.'

Now Miss Langley-Beard, who had been sitting, trying

hopelessly to mend the broken strap of her sandal by knotting together two very tough pieces of leather, looked up and said, 'Don't keep on at Alan, Daddy. He's only trying to help. You shouldn't call him hysterical.'

Beard looked at his daughter's bandaged wrists.

'I really don't think, Catherine, that hysteria is a thing that you're qualified to discuss.'

Her plain, fat face flushed and she bent down quickly again to her sandals. Beard spoke to his children in a firm tone but without bitterness, yet his remarks clearly evoked a fierce response.

'You have the doctor's telephone number, Catherine, if the nurse isn't here in the next half hour ring him up. Come along, Carter, if you've got that taxi waiting.' Going downstairs he said, 'Now you see why I prefer to keep my home life to myself.'

Once again he spoke without bitterness – as an observation. I made no comment.

In the taxi Beard expressed particular interest in Jumbo's symptoms.

'You were quite right to come for me. It may well be some inflammation of the hair follicles. What you'd probably call acne and no doubt suffered from as an adolescent,' he laughed delightedly. 'I shall be glad to have an opportunity of watching the course of the disease.'

I said that surely if it was only such an infection he should on no account have left his family.

'No, no, the doctor's coming. They must learn to manage. I'm not surprised that you thought to let me know.'

I emphasized that our anxiety had been to make sure of Jumbo's presence on the British Day.

Beard said, 'I don't make much of all that really, do you? We should be getting on with the plans for evacuation in the event of war. *I've* not been idle you know there. I've been listing specimens of particular anatomical interest.'

'Well, of course, we have always had perfectly clear plans for the evacuation to Woburn Park of the most valuable animals. Long before Stretton was ever mentioned. But the war scare has receded.'

'That wasn't the view at the time of all that move to Stretton. And I suppose we'd still be there if old Leacock hadn't upset Godmanchester or something. Not that that's my concern.'

'It was mainly our confidence that war was now far less likely that led to the return.'

'Was it? I don't understand that sort of thing, I'm afraid. Once I get working on an idea I very seldom go into reverse.'

We sat in silence. I looked out of the window, trying to decide what kind of a man he really was. Then suddenly in the light of Piccadilly Circus, I glimpsed a late night paper placard. It said, 'Godmanchester: Grave anxiety'. It seemed, I discovered, that the Great Reaper was working overtime. Not only Jumbo and Langley-Beard's mother, but Godmanchester too. He had had a stroke in his office. He was alive, but unconscious and paralysed. So we all moved into a new age.

For the next two days, however, Godmanchester rallied, and Bobby spurred us feverishly on to further preparations for the Day. The weather was still gloriously hot, and the nights were pleasantly cool. I remember well on the second evening walking round the Gardens with Bobby. He was in a peculiarly elated mood, for, to Beard's disappointment, Jumbo was much recovered and would now figure in the Frith tableau. On that clear, moonlit night, the extraordinary theatricality of the Zoo's new décor merged happily into the starry background. We wandered round looking at the great massed beds of auriculas and tulips and wallflowers that spelt 'God Save the Queen', and 'Norman, and Saxon and Dane are We', and the fountains playing in coloured jets. Here at the entrance to what was being shown as the Old Victorian Zoo were to be the recitations and the tableaux and later a show of fireworks with two set pieces – a British lion and an Indian elephant. The Old Zoo looked peculiarly charming with all the Decimus Burton Houses picked out with very subtle lighting (Jane's work), with a chalet for the old woman who was to sell fresh cows' milk and bags of buns, and booths for the peanut men and coconut shies, with goat chaises, and a wondrous bear pit. Beyond the Old Zoo, the Lemur House, its modern lines disguised with ferns and hothouse plants, had been converted into a *chef-d'œuvre à la* Paxton; and in this great glass palace, to Matthew's delight, were to be housed birds from every corner of the earth that was now or ever had been British. For, of course, it was only by cheating and taking in history, that a British Day could cast its net wide enough. From this show centre of the Old Zoo, the aviaries and the gardens, five separate roads led off each to a separate continent – to Stanley's Africa, to Botany Bay, to a Hudson Bay fur station, to the jungle of the British Raj, and, a little incommensurately (but by a determined whim of Bobby's) to the Apes of the Rock. Strictly European animals or those creatures such as lemurs, armadillos, Brazilian tapirs, sloths and manatees whose species had never known the glories of British rule, were temporarily banished to a remote corner of the North Side of the Gardens. Had Beard so wished, I think, he could have slaughtered them all with an easy nod of assent from our President or our Director. Their mere presence was in some sense a counter-demonstration.

'Well?' Bobby asked.

'It's all very enchanting.'

'We've made something beautiful,' he said. 'Never mind too much about all this British business of Godmanchester's. Commonwealth, Empires, all that stuff – it's always needed by men like him, whose memories have no deep roots. But once get the crowds in here, and it'll be English! A real night out, a lark, a spree, wakes week! Think of it, Simon, Hampstead Heath on Bank Holiday, Henley, Epsom Downs and the Colonial Garden Party all rolled into one. What fun it'll be, what beautiful, high old fun!'

It occurred to me that between Godmanchester's Wembley Empire stuff and Bobby's elegant Crystal Palace, and the cockney crowds, and Jane's chichi, the whole thing might somewhere have missed its mark; but I was too disturbed by Bobby's dissociated elation to give much thought to this.

I said hesitantly, 'Bobby! With Godmanchester so ill, you *have* considered that the whole thing may have to be postponed?'

My voice sounded over loud and dramatic as it carried away on the evening air.

'Oh, Good Lord! We shan't postpone. If the old boy's too ill, we'll have all the other old boys along.'

I was frightened and angry.

I said fiercely, 'What if war comes, Bobby? Remember how we all rely on Godmanchester for our peace. What if war comes?'

'Then we'll die merrily, like first-class passengers and not rats. Your cataracts and hurricanes, spout! And then, all shaking thunder, strike flat the thick rotundity of the world, crack nature's moulds . . .'

Before he had finished he had left parody behind. If I could have met him somewhere on his own dramatic level, I might still have found some way to ease him; but such histrionics made me shrink into myself with disgust.

I said in what I could hear to be my prissiest voice,

'Neither the *Titanic* nor Lear, Bobby, seem sufficient for the occasion.'

He looked down at me, his eyes puzzled as to what I was doing there beside him. Then he frowned impatiently.

'Oh, for Christ's sake go and boil your head,' he shouted and strode off into the darkness.

On the next day Godmanchester died. Whether he was a great man or not, I don't know. I'm not qualified to make judgements on public events. Some say now that he might, as he believed, have prevented war. Again I'm no expert. Certainly his death had an immediate depressive effect in England. But we soon had more to think about than 'the passing of a great symbol', as *The Advertiser* described it. I do not believe that any honest man who remembers that week can say that anything but terror – terror, to be fair, in varying degrees – possessed everybody. The reiteration of the Russo-American

Declaration, which once had seemed to me to banish war, now seemed to imply that the Great Powers feared its certainty. And once war really stared us in the face, who could stay reasonable enough to take comfort from the Declaration's restraining threat? We had so long associated war with annihilation that no reasoning could now banish that image. There were a few, who for different reasons, like Matthew or Bobby, behaved as though nothing had happened; but fewer than is now said, I suspect. I don't think I behaved more wildly than most. I was not involved in the various panic scenes that, as the current phrase goes, 'marred those vital days'.

For once I had returned home in time for tea on the day that we heard of the invasion of our ally Portugal. I took Martha in my arms, and for a long time we lay holding each other tightly, tightly enough to prevent the shivering fits of fear that seized us both. Every minute of that time, I think we expected intense agony and final extinction. Yet all the while, I could hear outside the ordinary street noises of the day. I now know that our moment of terror came to us earlier than to the greater mass of people – even death's terrors seem obstinately to deny my egalitarian feelings. For most people the overrunning of Portugal, even the fall of Gibraltar and the capture of Malta by the Italo-Greek forces soon after, meant no personal threat – meant indeed only an end of anachronisms, loved or despised. Strangely enough it was the news an hour later from the North of the invasion of Sweden by the Benelux-German troops that really struck alarm into the majority of people and caused the various panic scenes that so aided the Uni-Europeans.

By that time Martha and I had recovered from our terror – if annihilation were coming, we had decided, it would already have come. I see now that this was no more 'sensible' a view than any other taken then, but where could sense be when all was confusion, when the bogey had become real, when we had rubbed our eyes and woken up and found that the nightmare had come in through the bedroom window? Many people at that time ran away from London, but only the foolish thought that there was anywhere to run to. We decided to go about our business. I pulled my top lip down stiffly and said, 'If I keep a stiff upper lip, darling, will you hold your head high?'

And Martha said, 'Don't do it, Simon. You look exactly like a camel.'

I said, 'I'll just go across to the Zoo and see if the Home Office has anything to say about safety precautions.'

And Martha, turning off the television on which some 'splendid' woman was appealing for civil defence volunteers, said, 'I'll go up the High Street and see if I can get some asparagus before the shops close. It may be our last asparagus. And then I'll look in at the Town Hall and see if there's *really* anything one can do.'

Then she began to cry. By the time we'd gone out into the street, she had recovered. It was as I reached the Staff entrance that I suddenly thought we were mad: these *were* our last moments and we were wasting them in triviality. I turned round, almost knocking over a white-faced Sanderson who had arrived at that moment; I could see Martha walking away from me down the deserted street. I ran after her. Coming down Primrose Hill I saw a strange, broken down, slightly mad old man who was well known to the neighbourhood as a character. I reached Martha, held her tight in my arms and kissed her.

The old man called out, 'That's right. Bloody kiss. You'll be bloody dead tonight.'

It was my last moment of wild panic. We left one another and I walked into the Zoo.

Bobby Falcon sat at his desk making notes.

He said, 'Oh, Simon! What do you think of this? It's a little idea of mine for an addition to the children's exhibition. I thought, this afternoon, what about all the animals in children's fiction? You know – Black Beauty, Alice and the White Rabbit, Tarka, the Banda Log, Jemima Puddleduck, Badger and Mole, Wol and Pooh. Only, adapted like one of those Victorian screens so that the scenes fade into each other. To give a sort of fairyland pantomime effect. I think it could be done if one arranged the caging at various levels like this and then filled in with some sort of greenery, rather feathery and whispy, almost like a cloud, to give that strange dreamy feeling of Victorian childhood.'

I sat down opposite him and said as quietly as I could manage, 'Too literary, I think.' Then, trying to maintain the same tone of voice, I went on, 'Have any precautionary measures come from the Home Office, Bobby? I imagine that, short of a miracle, we are already at war and there must be immediate measures to be taken for public safety.'

He said shortly, 'Nothing's come through to me. The best thing we can do is to get on with our job. I've always hated all that theatrical cant of Jane's, but it has its points. "The show must go on", Simon; and again, "it'll be all right on the night".'

I asked, again trying to sound casual, 'Are you sure there's nothing from the Home Office? If there's not we'd better go ahead with the destruction of the dangerous species as we listed them two years ago.'

At last I forced his attention. He said, 'If you think you can identify the species that will be dangerous in an atomized world, you go ahead.'

He strode out of the room. I followed him to the typists' room where Mrs Purrett was taking off her hat.

She said, 'I didn't know what to do for the best, Sir Robert. The evacuation people have fetched my mother and I thought I should come straight round here.'

He said, 'Splendid. I want you to take a letter to the Victoria and Albert Museum. We'd better write to the Director. He'll know where to apply. What I'm interested in are these Victorian children's keepsakes. But with animal figures.'

I saw an expression of real terror on poor Mrs Purrett's fat face. I motioned to her behind Bobby's back to take the letter. I went off to my own room and rang Lascelles at the Home Office.

He said, 'We've been waiting for your confirmation that your safety measures have been carried out. I told Falcon an hour ago that if the European powers hadn't responded to the Russo-American appeal . . .'

I said, 'They're under way,' and rang off.

Before I could implement this, the telephone rang. It was Beard.

He said, 'I suppose the evacuation's started. I can't get any sense from Falcon. But I have a preliminary list of specimens vital for research work. Shall I bring it round?'

'Please. I would like to get all the Curators to my room within a quarter of an hour.'

Mrs Purrett met me in the corridor.

She said, 'I don't think Sir Robert should be in charge, Mr Carter. He doesn't seem to grasp . . .'

'I know. I'm going to try to bring the situation home to him now. Will you get Mr Price and Mr Sanderson round here as soon as possible.'

'Yes, Mr Carter. Oh! And Mrs Englander rang up. She was in a terrible state. The police have been round to arrest Dr Englander.'

'Well, as he's abroad, she needn't worry. But tell her as soon as everything's clearer, I'll find out what it's all about.'

'She sounded very foreign, Mr Carter.'

'That's not a crime yet. Now please get those Curators as soon as possible. And then contact Lord Oresby.'

She patted my arm. 'That's right, Mr Carter. We must all find plenty to do.'

I said sharply, 'I don't suppose that's going to be difficult.' But I put my hand on her shoulder. I liked Mrs Purrett.

I walked into Bobby's room. He was still scribbling drawings of cages.

I said, 'Bobby, you withheld from me the Home Office orders. I don't know whether you've gone out of your mind or what. But I must tell you now that unless you're prepared to take control, I shall act with the other keepers to give effect to what has to be done.'

His flushed face as he looked up at me was not at all wild, only contemptuous.

He said, 'Do whatever you like. But don't touch any of the show pieces, do you understand? If we can't open, we'll at least go out in a blaze of glory.'

I meant to say no more, but irritation drove me on.

'I shall take whatever safety measures are required for the public and for the animals in our care.'

He got up, 'If you touch my work . . .'

In my nervousness, I made a little smirking sound. He gave a roar like a lion and came for me. Youth tells and I had sprung aside before he reached me. I put out my foot, and, tripping, his heavy body crashed over a chair on to the floor. I saw that his nose was bleeding. He lay on the floor and groaned. So the age of violence had arrived, I thought; it seemed as ridiculous as any other. I wondered whether it was my duty to hand him over to the police or to the asylum authorities; but they were no less busy, I felt sure, than I was. Looking at him lying groaning there, I felt a strange and unfriendly sense of power. I think I could have shot him, if someone had told me that circumstances had called for it. Instead I put a cushion under his head and walked out of the room, locking the door behind me.

Matthew and Sanderson were in my room. I told them briefly about Bobby. Matthew was very evidently shocked. He was the complete officer now.

He said, 'Oh, God! Well, there you are, you see, it's what one would expect. But he *is* the Director. I should think he'd better report sick.'

Sanderson said, 'We must try never to mention it when the real Falcon comes back to us.'

Beard came in with his list. It took me nearly a quarter of an hour to convince him that the destruction of the dangerous species must precede the evacuation of the anatomically interesting ones.

'My dear Beard, poisonous snakes and pythons to say nothing of spiders could survive quite a while in this hot weather and the number of people they could kill is considerable.'

'But I suppose those people will be killed anyway.'

At last it was Matthew who said, 'Oh, God! Well they might kill *you*, you see, Beard. And then all the creatures we'd evacuated for you to cut up would be wasted.'

After that Beard agreed.

Before we separated to take up our tasks, I said, 'In any case if war is declared, we'll all be atomized in a moment. So I don't know what's the use, but still.'

Sanderson said, 'Oh! I'm glad to say, Carter, that they're not going to use those dreadful weapons. I heard it on my little radio set just before I came over here. There's been a Franco-German statement promising not to. It does mean we're fighting sportsmen anyway.'

Matthew said, 'Oh, God! It's always balls about the enemy being sportsmen.'

'I don't think you should say that, Price. Anyhow our Prime Minister's taking them at their word. We've promised to stick to conventional weapons ourselves.'

It seemed difficult to place all one's relief on a report of Sanderson's. However, the constriction went from my chest. I felt able to let in a new, less paralysing fear.

'God help us!' I said, 'we haven't got any.'

Matthew was in a transport of delight, 'Conventional? Oh, it'll be like the last war.'

Beard rustled the papers he held.

'Has everyone got a copy of my list?' he asked.

'Beard's the man of the hour,' Sanderson announced.

Before the Prosector left, he asked irritably, 'Why is the Director's room locked, Carter? I may want some papers from there.'

I explained the situation. 'He might do himself an injury if he wanders about in the state he's in.'

Beard said, 'Oh Lor'!' and went out of the room.

I had taken upon myself to superintend the Reptiles and the Aquarium. As I passed Mrs Purrett's room, I asked her to telephone all the keepers ordering them, transport permitting, to come to the Gardens.

When I reached the Reptile House, it seemed that only a very young keeper, a cockney boy of no more than seventeen, had reported for duty.

'I didn't know what to do, Sir, what with Mr Kennedy away and all. So I come along.'

He seemed either too frightened or too foolish to answer my questions. I had relied on one of the head keepers to destroy the snakes, but now it seemed that I should have for once to take an active part, for the boy told me that he'd never used a revolver. I told him to conduct me round the upstairs inner gallery that, running behind the show cases, is used for observation and feeding of the most deadly species. The boy was to operate the feeding shutters, I to fire through them. The priority on my list was the bushmaster. I stared through the aperture to see nothing but a small artificial tree trunk and some soiled grass and straw; the smell coming through the peephole was sweetish and quite sickening.

'I don't see the snake.'

'Ah! No. Mr Kennedy took him away Thursday when he come.'

'Took it away?'

'Yus. In a van he'd got with him.'

Fascinated to see how far Englander had taken things into his own hands, I went on to the black mambas – with the same result, but this time I was told that Mr Granger, the second keeper, 'had taken them away Wednesday'. Questioned further, the boy told me that they 'took away all the poisonous ones'. I went downstairs and walked round the fronts of the show cases. It was quite true – three quarters of the snakes had gone: rattlesnakes, puffadders, cobras, mambas, the bushmaster, the taipan, king snakes, whip snakes, and a dozen other species had simply vanished; so, too, had the great constrictors. Once the boy saw that I knew the worst, he became more communicative.

'The Doctor 'phoned Monday night from Germany, I think, and give instructions they was to be taken away to safety. I think 'e knew trouble was coming. Mr Kennedy and Mr

Granger was waiting for the orders so they had all the vans ready. But they don't tell me where they took 'em. They said if Sir Robert or you was to ask, to say Dr Englander left two of them British adders for Sir Robert's show. And frogs and toads, of course.'

And sure enough there the adders were. I had not the heart to destroy them. Compared with innumerable mammals and even birds that we must leave alive, their power to harm was negligible. My pent-up tension escaped in a wild burst of laughter. The boy was clearly much relieved.

'There's some alligators still here if you want to take a pot shot, sir. They're a sitting target, that's one thing.' He giggled nervously.

But neither friendliness nor show of authority could get him to say where the snakes had been taken; I doubt, in fact, whether he knew.

'I *know* they've gone North, sir. That I *do* know.' He repeated it again and again.

My work at the Aquarium was more easily done. Jackley's keepers were all in attendance. I gave orders for the destruction of the marine species and the siphoning of the ocean water into the additional subterranean tanks I had provided. Now, with the Biscay water I had imported, there would be enough sea water for Jackley to double his marine collection when the war was over, if the sea of destruction had not engulfed us all by then. It was nice to feel one's conscience clear towards at least one person. The fresh water fishes I ordered to be placed in Dr Englander's empty water snake pools. I remembered his telling me that some similar action in 1939 had been one of the greatest absurdities he'd had to endure in his whole Zoo career. It seemed reasonable that he should know that the administration could hit back, however feebly.

I was now free to see how the twin tasks of blast defence and of evacuation were proceeding. Yet first I thought that I should let Jane Falcon know of Bobby's condition. It was very difficult to make a telephone call at all at that time; even more difficult to track down Jane. I almost gave it up, for it seemed so monstrous a waste of precious time. Then Mrs Purrett came in.

'I've been to see the telescreen in the canteen,' she said. 'They're still talking. It's all a question now of our agreeing to some European control of our industries. I didn't quite understand it. But while there's life there's hope, isn't there?'

The reprieve seemed to justify my calling Jane. I got her at last at a rehearsal at a West End theatre; the box office people were very unwilling to disturb her.

She said, 'Isn't it all too sickening? This piece of Ronnie Stapledon's is to open on Tuesday. I'm quite certain it's the best thing he's done. But who's going to come with all this panic on? I don't think people realize what this kind of thing means to the live theatre.'

I said, 'Jane, I'm very concerned about Bobby.' I told her what had happened.

'My dear, whatever do you suppose *I* can do? After all, poor sweet, this thing couldn't have come at a worse moment for him.'

'Jane, I'm sorry. That sort of line may be all right for the theatre until the moment when you all start putting on shows for the forces, but the Director of this place has very serious commitments. We can't have Bobby here in his present condition. Something will have to be done with him until he comes to his senses.'

'Bobby come to his senses! My God, your conceit, Simon! Poor old Bobby, whatever he's not been, he's been more in one day than you'll ever be in your whole life. You leave him alone, do you understand? You Carters have done quite enough to hurt him. Don't bloody well interfere with anything until I come over. Ronnie Stapledon thought it was incredible that I should be called out of a rehearsal like this; but then ordinary people don't have to deal with maniacs who are trying to shut their husbands away. If nobody else cares what happens to one of England's greatest explorers then his wife does!'

I had stung her into action and that was the main thing.

I realized that I had longed for him to be taken away. The spectacle of his collapse filled me with repugnance, where I should have liked to feel compassion. I steeled myself to see at least that his injuries were not serious. When I turned the key of the lock in his door, I found that it was open.

I went across to Mrs Purrett.

'Have you unlocked the door of the Director's room?' I was angry.

'Oh, no, Mr Carter. It was Dr Beard. He said he wanted to get some papers. I told him of the orders you'd given. But he was quite determined. He made me give him the duplicate key. I am so sorry.' The poor woman was very distressed.

'But Sir Robert isn't there.'

'Oh, Mr Carter. Oh dear! I haven't seen him. Dr Beard said he was asleep.'

When I reached the centre of the Gardens by the tunnel entrance to the Old Zoo it was already getting dark. I could see no sign of Bobby. I went across towards the Parrot House. Matthew was busy there with a group of keepers. He had removed his coat, and his elegant willowy figure seemed more exotic than ever in a white silk shirt, the sleeves rolled up to the shoulders, and tight black evening trousers. He seemed to be everywhere at once, now consigning cages of colourful parrots to their lorries, now urging me over to see the netting of the wading birds and the luring of the graceful flamingos into pens on wheels. As he leapt, pirouetted, and generally danced his way from one spot to another he seemed like an eighteenth-century duellist; and yet from his constant screaming chatter, he might have been a gigantic magpie. As I followed him across to where the humming birds were being netted like butterflies and packed away into strange lobster-pot shaped glass and wire containers, we passed Beard. He was helping to head off the nervous okapi into a waiting loose box. With his extreme short sight I felt sure that at any minute he would be seriously injured by a kick from the beast.

But as Matthew said, 'Beard's got surprising guts for a man who looks as though he has worms.'

It was when Matthew and I stood surveying the emerald, ruby, topaz and gold shimmering flight of the humming birds as they flew wildly here and there among the thunbergia and the giant frangipani trees vainly seeking to evade the butterfly nets, that suddenly the whole Gardens seemed to be flooded with light of every colour – blue, rose, green, amber, purple.

'What bloody fool has turned on the illuminations?'

It was a rhetorical question and I waited for no answer, but ran full tilt to the power house down by the sea-lion pool. As I ran the whole place seemed to turn to a fairyland somewhere between a child's dream and a pantomime transformation scene. There was no doubt that Bobby and Jane had done just what they hoped with the lighting.

Near the power house, I came on Strawson's stout figure.

'It looks very fine, doesn't it, Sir?'

I thought he seemed to be laughing at me.

'What the hell are you doing? Turn those lights off, you fool.'

'Sir Robert's orders, Sir.'

I tried to push him aside, but his bulk was more than I could dislodge. Reason, I thought, before violence – in any case I was not sure of my strength against his.

'Look, Strawson. Surely you see that the Director's not in his right mind. This display of lights is madness when at any moment . . .'

'I doubt if the enemy would need lights to guide their missiles. You're living a little in the past, Sir.'

I realized then that it was the mood rather than the action that had appalled me.

'We're on the brink of a war, man.' This time Strawson really did smile.

'We may be on the brink of *eternity*, Mr Carter. But no siren has sounded yet. Meanwhile a little colour . . .'

The rest of his words were lost in music swelling out from amplifiers in every part of the Gardens. At the same moment floodlights were played on all the houses, tableaux, and pools.

Woken by the unnatural day, lions and tigers began to roar, birds to scream, sea lions and monkeys to howl. The fountains sent up their coloured showers. And now suddenly, to crown all, with a hissing and a crackling, the great firework set-pieces began to give out their showers of coloured lights – God Save Our Gracious Queen, the British Lion, and the Indian Elephant came alive in glorious sulphurous blue, and demon red and palest amber white. And through it all the music sounded – now it was 'Villikins and his Dinah' on what seemed a hundred barrel organs, then brass bands blared a selection from *The Gondoliers*, and now through a sudden stage stillness came a sweet soprano voice – 'Mid pleasures and palaces though we may roam, be it ever so humble, there's no place like home.' Everything that was absurd about Victorian England seemed to come from that genteel, sugary, drawing-room–parlour voice, and yet it filled me with a deep nostalgia, a willingness to surrender myself to the prettiness and to die. As the last 'Home, Sweet Home' died away, I saw Bobby Falcon mounting the high platform erected in front of the Lion House.

'Ladies and Gentlemen,' he cried into the microphone, and his voice echoed far away across the park, 'we are not as many as I could have wished.'

I heard someone running behind me. Bobby stopped speaking. I looked round. It was Jane, in sweating, dishevelled chic, toppling and teetering so precariously on her high heels that I thought she must never have run since she was a girl. Gazing round me, I saw that Bobby had spoken truly. We were not many – a dozen or so of staff, including a horrified Matthew, an angry Beard, a vaguely smiling Sanderson, and a weeping Mrs Purrett; Pattie Henderson stood red faced and foursquare flanked by Newton and Nutting. Suddenly from the Tunnel's gloom another young woman came running into the floodlit square. It was Martha.

'Simon! Bobby! What is all this noise? Are you all out of your minds? This isn't a time for music. Why! You can be heard way over in our house!'

She sounded as she so often did when she scolded Reggie or Violet.

Then, maternal still, she cried, 'Bobby, you're sick! Simon, he mustn't be up there. Come down, Bobby! Come down!'

But if Jane's arrival had silenced Bobby, Martha's cries woke him into speech.

'We're only a few,' he cried, 'but we're the lucky buggers. They'll all go out in their grey dreariness. We'll go out as a high old, rare old, bloody beautiful joke.'

Immediately his words were drowned in the belly-churning wails of a hundred sirens. Then there was an absolute silence, followed by cries of panic and some shouts of anger. One or two of the staff began to run towards the Tunnel as to the nearest shelter, others picked up stones and threw them at Bobby. Beard was on his knees in prayer. I saw Barley and the young keeper of the bears advancing towards the platform.

'We'll get you, you fucker!' Barley was shouting.

And then came the crackling, whistling thudding sound of an explosion that filled the universe. I pushed Martha face down on the grass and threw myself on top of her. There followed in quick succession four more such dreadful sounds but farther away from us; and then a vast whistling, rushing wind. We lay still on the ground, waiting as it seemed to me for hours. I held Martha to me stroking her arms. Against the shrieking and howling of all the captive beasts and birds, I could hear Mrs Purrett quietly crying behind me. At last here and there people were getting to their feet. In the distance ambulance and fire bells were clanging, and there were shouts and cries in the streets. I got up slowly as though I must take the world by surprise if I were to survive. Martha lay on the ground bruised and shocked. Whatever had fallen, must have been far off, yet blast had wrecked and twisted Zoo buildings; the Old Zoo was in flames and from it came the agonizing screams and roars of hippos, rhinos, zebras, apes and trumpeting elephants. The roof had gone from the eagle house and high above it great condors, vultures and golden eagles were circling and spiralling up into the sky. The trees were filled with chattering parakeets, and among the beds of broken, bruised flowers lay the little bodies of a hundred multi-coloured tropical birds; for the aviary had been shattered into a thousand pieces. Here and there men were writhing on the turf. In the floodlight the pools of blood stared in technicolour red against an emerald grass. A hundred yards from me lay the body of the boy from the snake house, his head nearly severed by a great sliver of glass. There above us on the top of the bronze lion that crowned the Lion House was Sir Robert Falcon, doubled up with pain, but still wildly shouting, blown on high by some freak of blast, whole though bruised and shaken.

In that next half hour, like all the rest of London, we worked like beavers to repair our dam against a tide that any minute would engulf us and all our works forever. Firemen, staff, wives, all worked like navvies. The wounded were taken in ambulances. Injured animals were destroyed. Fire had spread too far to save any part of the Old Victorian Zoo and in it died most of the giraffes, rhinos, zebras, deer and elephants crammed in by Bobby to make his Roman holiday. Two wounded hippos broke their way down into the canal and we could see them, lashing the bloodied water for a while, until Strawson's assistant picked them off with a gun and they sank to send a great tide of mud spilling over the banks. The Insect House was a hopeless wreck. Sanderson, tears in his eyes, came to assure me that we need not fear the poisonous spiders or any other venomous insects among those that were now crawling or flying in the ruins.

'I had them destroyed when you told me,' he said. 'In a way I'm glad I did it if only because they were dead before this awful thing happened.'

The Area Air Wardens appeared from outside and ordered us all to shelters. But Beard appealed to volunteers to carry on loading for evacuation. A good number of the keepers responded at once. And Matthew rallied the rest to Beard's cause by making them laugh.

'I can't imagine anyone will go to the shelters, can you?

Unless they want to be gassed by each others' farts,' he said.

All this while Bobby hung over the bronze lion, his sick old puma face staring out into the distance, as though he were already dead. Jane and Martha and even Mrs Purrett formed a knot in front of the tiger's cage, shouting, and imploring him to come down, above the roaring of the beasts. At last, when all else had been attended to, I gave orders to the firemen that he should be fetched down by ladder, but when they reached him, he clung wildly to the bronze lion's neck and resisted all attempts to move him. At last they were forced to play a hose on him. He was carried struggling and shouting to an ambulance, like a half-drowned old cat to the gas van.

Up to this moment, although they had been standing side by side, Martha and Jane had not exchanged a word.

Now Jane suddenly turned and shouted, 'Thank you. Thank you very much. You've randied him into the looney bin now. I hope that's satisfied you.'

'*You've* no right to speak,' Martha cried, 'you never gave him anything. At least I tried. I wanted to help.'

Jane stood squarely in front of Martha, looking at her with fierce contempt.

'Aren't you just a lovely person,' she said in a phoney American accent, 'the highest-minded little whore that ever almost gave herself out of charity. You make me sick.'

I said, 'Shut up, Jane.'

'Don't you start,' she turned on me, 'you're worse than her. You're too frightened even almost to give. A lovely pair of lovely people! Get radiant sex health the Carter way! She'll brush you up and he'll brush you off.'

I held her shoulders and began to shake her, but she was stronger than I had thought, she pushed me away.

Martha said, 'You gave him no life at all and you know it.'

Jane laughed. 'Oh you silly little bitch! Why, you don't even know what's twat.'

She ran from us, and a moment later, despite her tightest of chic skirts and her broadest of smart broadbrimmed hats, she had hoisted herself up the steps of the ambulance and was driven off, holding Bobby's hand.

Martha was trembling. I looked round apprehensively but everyone was working too busily to have noticed the scene, I think. I gave Martha into Mrs Purrett's hands and she took her off to the office cellars and gave her hot tea.

6

MASSACRE OF THE INNOCENTS

For many days after that first night we worked on, like all London, waiting for the next blow. It was not until news from the rest of England began to assemble that we realized that we had perhaps seen the end of active warfare. It took us even longer, a week perhaps, to discern the meaning of the news that was coming in; and even longer still to see that there was nothing we could do about it. We lived an improvised, all-hands-on-deck, air-raid shelter, darts and sandwiches sort of life that, as the days passed without further attack, seemed more and more senseless. Fresh provisions, of course, were soon in short supply; but it was surprising how little the government measures of food control carried real urgency to us who lived such a picnicking troglodytic life. The destruction of the ports from Southampton to Glasgow seemed far away; and for some time the Government ban on the use of roads and railways out of London except by special permit – a ban enforced by armed police – disguised from most Londoners the fact that few of these roads or railways still existed. Many, of course, had made this discovery, but they were not able, even had they wanted to, to return to tell us.

It is often said now that the riots that broke out in one district of London after another were fomented by members of the Uni-European Movement. I doubt this myself: if there was one thing in which the Government showed themselves absolute it was in the rounding up of suspected dissidents although their action was far too late. I discovered this when, a few days after the outbreak of war, I tried to contact old Mrs Englander. The procedure was a lengthy one, not because the bureaucrats concerned were inhumane. Indeed, although I was not related to the interned woman, had never even spoken to her, I was eventually able to send her extra clothing, books, and a small food parcel. No, the delay arose because of the vast number of people interned. Of the name of Englander alone there were some hundreds. The Government, in fact, uncertain of the extent of the underground movements, had on the basis of the census register made wholesale arrests, including, for example, all persons with European sounding names. From my observation, the rioting began solely as a result of even more stringent food rationing, insufficiently explained because the authorities did not wish to reveal the extent of the damage to our roads, our ports, and our shipping. Public disorder finally came to a head, when, with the idea of transferring popular anger from themselves, the Government released the text of the Melbourne Declaration. I remember perfectly well the arguments and discussions both at the Zoo and at my local defence post about the culpability of Australia, New Zealand, and our African allies. Nobody among us cared much to blame them for refusing to run the superior enemy atomic submarine blockade. We all found more reason to revile a Government that had failed to feed us.

For ourselves, however, I must say that it was a fortnight before we knew any serious want of food; a little longer than that before I saw demonstrations parading in the streets; and nearly three weeks before I witnessed police action against rioters in Camden Town. This was largely, perhaps, because I seldom stirred from the area around the Zoo. Martha, at first, did nursing work that kept her away from home. Then when there was no more nursing to be done, she worked at a Government food provision centre nearer our home. Somehow we managed to live our grey, somnambulistic lives apart. Yet all half designed measure smeet their end. One night I returned to the improvised inside cellar-bedroom which we still occupied to find that at last we had failed to be on opposite shifts. Martha was reading, sitting up, in an old sleeping-bag that survived from the days of my youthful naturalist expeditions. We were both intensely nervous. I strayed upstairs and fussed around in the bathroom far longer than I needed, hoping that she would pretend to be asleep when I returned.

When I came down she said in a hard, bright voice, 'I really wonder, you know, whether there's any point in this sleeping down here. Obviously nothing is going to happen and if it did, our being *here* wouldn't help.'

'The greater proportion of the people who were killed in London that night were killed by blast.'

'Yes, but it's rather absurd when we're about outside all day. I think all these precautions are imposed on us by left-overs from the last war who are so excited to get back to the old days. You should hear them at the Food Centre, old women gossiping about the last war. They feel young again, I suppose. I think I shall sleep upstairs tomorrow.'

'I should feel much happier if I knew you were down here.'

Martha looked up at me, but she changed the subject.

'You saw Hester's letter and the little notes from the children that I left in the hall?'

'Yes, I'd just written to Reggie. But now I've heard about his sore throat, I'll write again.'

'Oh, I don't think it's anything. Hester's very good about that sort of thing. She never pretends. But I'm trying desperately to get a phone call through . . .'

'So am I.'

'Oh! . . . Well, *I* went to the American Embassy. There's just a chance they can do it for me.'

'Martha, why don't you ask them to get you an air passage back? It can be done. I've found that out.'

'Thank you! I suppose that means you don't want me here.'

'It means, as you very well know, that I can't bear you to be in this danger.'

She had lain her head back on the pillow and closed her eyes. When she said nothing, I went on.

'And also I don't know that we have any right to risk leaving the children orphans.'

She was tense now, her eyes open but hard.

'You can't suppose that I haven't thought of that. Or is that a nice way of getting rid of me?'

'You speak as though only *you* cared for the children.'

'I speak because I want you to say you care for me.'

She began to sob, a sobbing that swelled and shook her whole body convulsively like a terrible fit of hiccoughs. I held her tightly, running my fingers across her shoulder blades down her spine, trying to relax her tension.

'Do you think I've bothered about what that bitch said,' I asked.

'But you thought it was true.'

'No. I didn't think anything about it. Jane just wanted to hurt that was all. Even then she couldn't pretend that anything had really been wrong . . .'

'But you thought it had. You thought I'd let Bobby seduce me, didn't you? Otherwise why have you kept away from me like this?'

'Circumstances have . . . Martha, what's the sense of dragging it all up? I was jealous when you saw such a lot of him in California, yes. I was lonely and unhappy. And I suppose when Jane spoke like that the other day, it brought it all up in me again.'

'But, for Jesus' sake, Simon, why couldn't you come and talk to me about it?'

'Because jealousy's a squalid emotion of which I'm ashamed. It was disgusting enough hating Falcon irrationally after he came back. But to suddenly find myself hating you!'

'Well, if there had been any truth to it, you'd have a right to hate me as much as Bobby. More really.'

'If it had happened!'

'Well, Simon, it almost did. At San Francisco. No, that's not true. I couldn't really with anyone but you. But perhaps it ought to have done. As Jane said, I led him on. Out of muddled feelings I didn't know I had. But I ought to have done.'

She was crying almost soundlessly now. I bent over her and ran my fingers along the line of her cheekbone. She kissed me excitedly, then she lay back.

'Come in with me, Simon,' she said.

It was a very tight fit in the sleeping-bag, and with the exhaustion of overwork and undernourishment, our love making was hungry rather than satisfactory. Perhaps happily I burst the rotted seam of the canvas, got my leg caught, then, trying to extricate it, I rolled the bag entirely over. We were released by farce, but when our laughter had died away, Martha said,

'He seemed so desperate. And you don't know him. You never will now. But he's far more than a pathetic buffoon. Anyone who's been something, I suppose, keeps some of it. And he certainly has been someone. Not just a figure, Simon, or a charmer or any of that, but somebody who'd realize a lot of what he'd always wanted. And he was desperate. And to have me seemed so important to him. I see now it was all part of the craziness. Do you know he thought you'd made fun of his being impotent? Something to do with what you said about that Filson boy's injuries. He couldn't forgive you. And it wasn't for me to deal with *that*. But, after I'd persuaded him to take an interest again – that old Amazon trip – I thought I couldn't let him drift back. I let him take me around, I made a fuss of him. I thought I could stop him going too far. But not before he'd humiliated himself.'

'Well, darling, you're not a psychiatrist. He was mentally sick.'

Martha giggled. 'Sometimes you seem like the comic American, not me.'

'All right, he was off his chump.'

'Yes. I know. But he was sexually starved too.'

I kissed her and said, 'We've talked about it enough.'

I tucked her into the sleeping bag and went to my own mattress against the other wall. Then a fear that she had gone to sleep seized me.

I whispered, 'Martha.' She did not answer. Then I said loudly and casually, 'In any case he was too old to be your lover.'

She said, 'Stop tormenting yourself, Simon. I couldn't with anyone. I don't think I care that much about sex with anyone but you.'

I sighed and relaxed.

She said, 'Anyway your old formula – no sex without real affection – wouldn't have kept me on the straight and narrow path. I truly am very fond of Bobby. I must tell you I went today to the hospital to ask about him. He's been allowed to go home. Oh don't worry. I shan't go near him again. I've done enough harm. But I am very fond of him, and I was very, very sorry for him.'

'But you can't mix up being sorry with sexual love.'

'Can't I, darling? I've told you I'm a very confused person. Awfully maternal anyway. I think I'm always very ready to be protecting someone I love. And when I feel protecting I want him to take me to bed if it gives him pleasure. I think that's the basis of all sex for me really. Oh, I don't know.'

She sighed and seemed almost immediately to go off to sleep. As for me, it was as though she had suddenly hit me over the head with a heavy stick. I lay confused and awake for hours.

Happily my life at the Zoo was still a very busy one. It was not the back-breaking navvy work of those first few days after the raid. Then, in the tension born of hourly expectation of long agony or annihilation, all personal differences seemed to be effaced, all identity almost to be lost in united toil. The closer the threat of general devastation, the harder we worked to preserve. Against a background of ruins and stench we banded together to save the collections – and for a week at least did not quarrel over priorities of what should be saved. Beard, with the support of Pattie Henderson's research boys, advanced the priorities of current research; Matthew preferred birds, and, within the bird kingdom, some mysterious parrot-crowned hierarchy of his own; it was left to me to put forward the twin claims of rarity and cost. Somehow in those first days of revolutionary fraternity, we made a blend of these claims that disguised all factions. Apart from the fear of further enemy attack, we worked already under a hot May sunshine that showed the ruins in all their grisly details and rapidly turned the carrion to a stench of putrefaction. Each day we could see the condors and vultures wheeling high above us in the clear blue sky.

Sanderson said, 'It's extraordinary, isn't it really? Like the prisoners who were released from the Bastille, they know no other home.'

I pointed out that they had come after food not home.

'One would like to say that Nature provides,' he said.

But even he could not say it. We were not on the Veld and we had to do our own scavenging. So for the first three days we buried our dead, or such as remained of them. More difficult proved the disposal of the huge, swollen hippopotamus carcasses that surfaced in the canal; and the vultures did aid us in this slow task before we had done. At last, the twisting, hovering, wheeling circles in the sky were seen no more; or only at a great distance. Sanderson remarked on this and hoped that they were getting fed. It was the only time when I saw Beard relax during those days.

He smiled and said, 'Oh, I'm sure people are feeding them, Sanderson.'

So, shirt-sleeved and short-sleeved, we worked. Huge and red-faced Pattie Henderson, in linen trousers and an odd straw sun-bonnet like a donkey's, worked side by side with Matthew, who in hot weather, trailed clouds of expensive scent behind him. Strawson dug and I buried. Newton netted and Nutting caged. Even the wives came to help – Mrs Barley, cockney in every crisis, got even Mrs Purrett laughing at her near-the-knuckle 'cracks'. How happy everybody was, we are told, and I suppose they were – some English love improvisation and 'do it yourself'. But I belong to the other English, who don't like the right pigeon-hole used for the wrong papers, or the wrong label on the right box. I chafed under all this glorious dissolution, chafed for law and order. Or perhaps it was that I had invented the old order, and now Beard – as Sanderson had said, 'the man of the hour' – was imposing his new order on the chaos.

'Get things away to Woburn' was his command – and,

given an orderly conventional war, he would have been right. But if annihilation did not come neither was the last war reborn. For a few days lorries managed to get through by roundabout routes to Bedfordshire. Then two returned because roads were impassable; then one because police had refused to allow it beyond Hendon. Then a lorry driver trying to get through at night undetected overturned in a sudden crater near Welwyn Garden City; by some mischance two leopards escaped and added panic to the neighbourhood. We received military orders that no more live beasts were to be evacuated. At first Beard seemed unwilling even to notice this setback.

'We must find someone to override this,' he said, 'we can't give up in midstream. You know the various Ministry chaps, Carter.'

It was true – I did and he didn't; I also knew that nothing could or indeed should be done. The Committee of the Society or such of them as were available in London had confirmed Beard as Acting Director; but they were too busy to do more than urge him 'to do his best'. With some difficulty he got through to Lord Oresby, who, on Godmanchester's death, had become Acting President; but – sign of the times! – that kindly patriotic old liberal Tory country gentleman strongly advised a quietist policy.

'My dear chap,' he said, 'quite frankly nobody knows what on earth's happening and the situation's so very fluid that I think it's most unwise for the Zoo to get mixed up in any sort of action. Between ourselves I'll tell you that, in my opinion, this is the time when the true patriot retires to his country seat and awaits events; but unfortunately there's not the faintest chance of my getting through to Wiltshire. But certainly my advice to you is to do nothing. And as far as day to day administration goes, rely on Carter.'

I think Beard would have contested even this if he could have rallied the support of the staff around him; but the same spirit of wait and see that had infected Oresby and most people in high places outside the immediate Government circle had now begun to spread to the population at large, and the Zoo staff was no exception. The glorious comradeship of the barricades was waning, a new feeling of sceptical boredom on which the Europeans were soon so cleverly to trade by withdrawing all their troops from England, was now in the air. Sanderson, for example, with his insect kingdom all but vanished, felt the pull of other ties.

'I think it's the turn of the humans now, don't you,' he said. The proposal he based on this was less reasonable. 'I wish you'd open to the public again, Beard. There's a hundred poor souls who'd find a walk in the Gardens something to take their minds off things.'

When this was refused, he began to appear less and less among us. I learned later that he'd collected a number of his protégés including Paper Bag Peter, and assembled them at his rambling old Wimbledon home. There, under protest from Mrs B. and Miss D. he managed somehow to keep alive a party of fifteen on the dwindling rations of three. Young Newton was summoned to military medical work, but Pattie Henderson and Nutting retired once more to their research. I was soon hearing new complaints from Pattie.

'I say,' she said, 'this chap Beard seems to be off his chump. He's evacuated all the wallabies. He must know that Nutting's working on Marsupials. But to crown all he has the cheek to tell me that the tachyglossus was killed in some lorry smashup. I don't know what Newton's going to think. I promised to look after his interests while he's away on this army business and now this fool's let the only living monotreme in the country get killed. Can't you suppress him or something?'

Beard was not checked by his staff's lack of enthusiasm any more than he was deterred by physical impossibilities or military vetoes; but for some days he looked anxious. I thought, indeed, that the responsibility of his family might be weighing on him – anyone with a family in London at that time was likely to be worried, but a family of lunatics, cardiacs, spastics and hysterics might reasonably be too much for any man. When I asked him how his family had fared, he answered,

'Thank you, Carter. People in that condition don't change, you know.'

'I meant rather what arrangements have you been able to make for them at this time?'

'Arrangements? They're on these borough evacuation lists, if that means anything. I suppose they'll have the same chances as anyone else.'

A few days later I learned what had been the real source of his anxious frown.

'I don't like doing it, Carter,' he said, 'but I think we may have to modify our plans. I've decided that we can't hope to evacuate live animals as things are except for a few essential breeding specimens and they've mostly reached Woburn. I don't know how much it matters really. The basic concern in my case is with the anatomical specimens, especially since South Kensington lost everything in that raid. I've secured the co-operation of a small refrigeration plant near Dunmow. I can work on them at leisure there for future preservation. It's too small to interest anyone militarily and it generates it's own electricity supply – that part of Essex appears to have been so devastated that it is unlikely to be brought into this war again. There are ways and means of getting there by side roads, I suspect.'

'Don't you think that we've gone beyond the point of evacuation, Beard?'

He said, 'Oh, Lor'!' and vanished.

I knew this well enough now to wait for his return. Sure enough he came back an hour later, and said,

'It's bad enough, Carter, you know, to have to alter my schemes without your backing out in this way. Of course, I'm well aware that things may get worse so we must be very selective in what we send.'

Thus began a massacre of the animals by selection. It occasioned a breach between our acting Director and his closest ally, Matthew. There *were* some patriots, of course, who even at that stage of the war refused even to consider defeat – Matthew and Diana Price were among them.

As Matthew said, when I asked him after Diana, 'My dear Simon, she's happy doing all the things that women must in war-time.'

For himself, he confessed, he would have liked to rejoin his regiment, 'only some ghastly man abolished it years ago'. Meanwhile Beard was his C.O. and I was soon to learn what that meant for Matthew. One morning I was imitating Beard's curious capacity to dictate absolutely in a hesitant and tentative way.

'Er, look, Carter,' I was saying, 'this is . . . er . . . something *I* want done. I mean it's . . . er . . . got to be given an absolute priority.' It could be a trial and a bore, I said.

Matthew snubbed me sharply, 'It's hardly a time to criticize the Director,' he said. 'In any case it's not a question of putting him up for one's club, is it? Though, of course,' he added, egged on by loyalty, 'I should be delighted to do that if he asked me.'

Their admiration for each other's single-minded industry in the face of the enemy was mutual.

Beard said, 'It's rather a pity Price has that foppish manner. He's done so very well during these weeks. We shall have to let the Committee hear about that when the time comes.'

Matthew, in his regard for his new chief, even showed him the little inner sanctum of the Parrot House, a favour reserved only for his intimates. In this room he kept three or four parrots bought in the Docks whose wide vocabulary of obscenities was a source of constant delight to him. Even this failed to alienate Beard.

'Price showed me what he calls his "special parrots" last night,' he told me. 'I'm afraid I'm not a good enough ornithologist to grasp what he thought important about them.'

Matthew, indeed, even postponed the evacuation of a large number of parrots, cockatoos, and macaws because Beard's list did not give them priority.

'Once you've been in the army, you see, you learn to take orders,' he told me.

Yet it was over these parrots left behind at the Zoo that the split between them now came.

'You might give me a list of the birds you want sent into cold storage, Price, will you? Then we can have them killed straight away.'

Matthew gulped. 'I don't think I quite understand what you said.'

Beard repeated his statement. Matthew swayed and went out of the room. I could see that for him Beard was now some Captain Bligh or Commodus against whom even the most loyal praetorian officer or first mate might be driven to mutiny. The next day he came into the office.

'About what you said, Director, there's no need for any further evacuation of my collections,' he said.

Beard was surprised, but he had other things to think of. A Ministry memorandum had arrived ordering us to hold ourselves in readiness to slaughter all the animals and to await the visit of an inspector of food who would decide what was suitable for human consumption.

Beard brought the order into my room. He read it out loud. 'I don't think we need pay any attention to it, do you?' he said.

As Rackham was in my office collecting the weekly pay cheques, I said only, 'You needn't wait, Rackham.'

But Beard went straight on, 'As a matter of fact, I think I told you, I always get my evening snack at the Lyons' at Earls Court. A chap there, who seemed to know, told me that this Government's rather insecure now.'

I waited until Rackham had gone, then I told Beard that, although he was probably the last person to hear this whisper, he was also probably the first to shout it out loud.

'It's very unwise, you know, to say that sort of thing publicly in a beleaguered city when a war is going rather badly.'

All the same I suddenly warmed to him for his *naïveté*.

'Oh, I'm not at all political, Carter,' he answered, 'I don't think as a matter of fact that it's ever been the tradition here, though we did get a bit too mixed up with that chap Godmanchester. Our job's to care for the collections. At the moment that means preventing some idiot from cooking them all. We shall have to get the vital specimens away before that inspector comes.'

'I'm not sure whether carcasses can be called vital,' I said. Then when I saw him frown at my levity, I felt remorseful. 'We may *have* to obey the order, but I agree with you that we shouldn't. After all it's only a propaganda token gesture on the part of the Government. And in any case there's shortage but no starvation in London . . .'

'That's hardly our concern,' Beard told me.

The next day my resolution hardened. One of the two 'independent' news sheets that was allowed to circulate carried a chirpy little note that read, 'Are we to eat Leo and Ebony ? Most London citizens would be sad to see the familiar lion and black leopard go the way of all flesh. Some would say we should all have to be a lot hungrier than we are now – thanks to our navy's campaign against the enemy's atomic submarine fleet – before we should store lion or leopard in our larders, though there might be something to be said for a gazelle or antelope steak. But Food Ministry officials, anxious to conserve any potential stores of food, have given the Zoo the red warning light."It's not only a question of eating lions," one official told me yesterday, "it's a question of what the lions themselves are eating. Wild beasts consume an awful lot of meat, you know, and a nation at war just can't afford meat for lions." Reaction of the average man: sorry to see old Leo go, but the family comes before the pets. Reported reaction of the Zoo: Acting Director Langley-Beard, concerned for his research – the Government demand is nonsense; they will take the animals over my dead body. Big words, but there's a war to win, Director Beard.'

My reaction was to write a full statement of the diet of our surviving animals pointing out that the carnivores were fed on a diminishing stock of smaller fauna. I asked Beard to sign it and sent one copy to the Ministry, and another to the news sheet.

'I don't see why we need bother with that rot.'

'Have you seen some of the crowds that have collected lately, Beard? Have you witnessed any clashes with the police?'

'My dear Carter, you seem suddenly to have turned into a politician. We've got a hard job on here without all this political speculation.'

'It isn't political speculation. I want you to send this notice in the rather vain hope of undoing the effect that that poisonous little piece may have had on a lot of angry, bewildered people who read it, and on any loose Uni-Europeans still not imprisoned who are out to find a cause for fomenting trouble. In fact, I doubt if we can do anything to counteract its effect. For that reason I want you to request a special police guard for the Gardens.'

Beard said, 'Oh Lor'!' but not this time in the calculated surprise that I had come to recognize, but with genuine alarm.

'I don't think we can do that,' he said, 'after all it's difficult enough to get the specimens away to the storage plant against official orders without surrounding ourselves with police. Do you really think anyone would take any notice of that column you've shown me? I should never think of reading that kind of stuff.'

'There are some millions of people in this city who will have read it. If only a few hundred decided to demonstrate against us we should be in a very unpleasant position.'

Beard smiled, 'The article certainly seems to have had its effect on you, Carter. I've never seen you so worked up. If that means I shall get more co-operation from you, it's not been at all a bad thing.'

'Will you allow me to get police guard?'

He said, 'I don't like it.'

I took this as permission. I telephoned to the local inspector and he agreed to send a small detachment of guards. Half an hour later, he telephoned, to say that he could not spare the men. I then telephoned to the Police headquarters, but they confirmed his view. Either, I thought, the London situation was less stable than the Government allowed us to know, or they were not unwilling to allow a discontented population to find scapegoats. In either case it was not a good look-out for us. It seemed to me that our first duty was to see that no member of the staff should run an impossible risk. Beard was too occupied with what he now called 'final evacuation plans' to pay any attention to my views. I took it upon myself to inform the staff. I telephoned to all the head keepers in the absence of the Curators ordering them to withdraw all night staff and to put all the animals under lock in inner cages from that night on. No animal was to be left in an open enclosure or paddock. It was the maximum safety we could ensure for the beasts without danger to the staff. I did not give the head keepers my reasons for these orders; but to Matthew, the only remaining active Curator, I explained the situation. His voice on the telephone was always peculiarly shrill, it came now to interrupt me as ear-splitting as the shriek of any of his parrots.

'Thank you, Simon. I think I know what to do.'

He sounded offended; but I felt that this was too important to neglect. I tried to reach him with some recollection from the last war, though I found it difficult to take all that officer side of him seriously.

I said, 'Matthew, you do understand that this is not a time for suicide pilots?'

'Oh, God! I'm not Japanese, you know.'

I was relieved to hear him chuckle; beneath all his absurdities, he was a very down-to-earth person. I was sorely tempted to put Rackham on a lone night watch. But perhaps he had anticipated trouble, for he suddenly went sick.

I worked late in the board room above the restaurant that night, disregarding the sirens which now sounded at dusk to send Londoners to shelters against dread raids that never came. I sorted out and collected Society minutes and correspondence that seemed to me essential for future historians. After all history had as high a claim as anatomy. I had a cold coming on, and with the low diet, I was finding it hard to fight off. I dozed over my work. My head seemed filled all at once with a roaring sound. I was back in my room at Oxford, shut in, but why? I must have sported my oak. Then it came to me, it must be bump supper night – the roar was that of the college celebrating victory, going perhaps to wreck some poor wretch's rooms. Then I was wide awake and rushing to the window. There across the Gardens coming from Regent's Park I could see a mass of electric torch flashes and great petrol flares, sweeping towards me, some moving steadily, others in sudden rushes, now bobbing low, now flashing up against the sky. Here and there the outlines of some square white objects showed up in the darkness. Soon the distant roar neared and split up into drunken songs and shouts, and into a sort of wild wordless yelling; and then again changed, perhaps at some commanding words, into a rhythmic chorus of slogans. Now I thought that I could distinguish the words – they could be 'We want Peace'. Perhaps it was some orderly anti-Government demonstration. But then I could hear more clearly – 'Men not Beasts'. The white squares no doubt carried similar slogans. Coming from men, the words had an ugly sound. I turned out my light. Now I could hear the thudding of steps, almost marchlike in their precision. Then for some moments all sounds ceased and the lights seemed concentrated into one glow. The silence was broken as suddenly by a loud clang of metal. Then came shouts of triumph and the glow shattered again into a hundred points of light bobbing towards me and the rhythmic march broke into a clattering, deafening, uneven run. The hoarse roar seemed to engulf the silence of the Zoo, though here and there the cry or scream of an animal or bird joined the human din. At least, I congratulated myself, there was no human to suffer, and, with luck, the crowd would reach very few of the animals. Then suddenly I was gripped with a terror of fire, perhaps my safety measures for the staff and the animals would prove my own roasting. The white gibbon – sole remnant of its tribe – started its melancholy howling. Immediately the crowd was diverted from its rush, away from my window. I crossed the room to follow its glow and, looking three storeys down to the ground below, I saw across the ornamental beds a tall blond figure standing in a

feeble pool of light from a small torch. The man held himself as
erect as his swaying willowy figure would allow him and held
– God help him! – a stick. Matthew stood alone in defence of
his parrots. I opened the window, but my voice could not
carry above the crowds' nearing roar. I could see that Matthew
had raised his stick above his head and was attempting to
harangue the crowd. I thought I heard that familiar voice
screech, 'impermissible trespass', but it was probably only a
sudden rush of wind. I ran from the window and down three
flights of stairs, stumbling, even falling once in my haste. At
the entrance I cracked my head hard against Beard's. Stars
exploded their pale silver lights before my eyes. Through thick
cotton wool I could just hear Beard ask,

'For God's sake, Carter, can you drive?' or so it seemed.

But I brushed him aside, fell over a low stone balustrade,
cutting my knee. I was up in a second and across the flower
beds to find myself part of the straggling tail of the crowd.
Next to me was a heavily built but baby-faced teenager who
was shouting hysterically,

'Do 'im! Do them! Kick the bastards in the balls!'

Part of the crowd was calling, 'Men not Beasts', but some
others chanted, 'We want Peace'. Then through the slogans
came a battering, hammering noise; and a sudden whisper
that rushed back through the crowd.

'Parrots.'

A big blonde woman turned to me, 'Parrots, dear,' she said,
'I can't see my lot making much of them.'

But a bobbing, cheering mass in front of me moved on.
On the ground, trampled and crushed into the gravel, lay
Matthew's body. Blood frothed from his mouth, streamed
from his ears and nostrils. I bent down and began to unloose
his silk shirt, I took out my little pocket mirror and held it to
his mouth; but he was dead. I tried to lift him, but dizziness
overcame me. So I dragged his body under a clump of
mahonias. A deep and jagged wound in his temple suggested
that he had been killed by a stone. I hoped so. As I pushed his
long, dangling legs under the shiny, prickly leaves, I remem-

bered suddenly Harriet Leacock's dog Rickie. I drew myself up straight and ran away from the shouting crowd and the shrieking birds into the darkness back towards Beard.

He was standing still, blinking in the doorway.

'Where on earth have you been, Carter? Can you drive a lorry?'

I must have seemed quite uncomprehending, for he suddenly shook me.

'Good Heavens, Carter! Pull yourself together. This is vital. That driver's not turned up. We must get the lorry away. Can you drive the thing?'

From behind us, out of the darkness came the shrieks of the birds sounding like a witches' sabbath, or perhaps with the shouts of the crowd, a holocaust of witches. I rubbed my hands on my trouser legs to rid myself of the feel of Matthew's sagging body. I was breathing hardly now, and suddenly I began to shake involuntarily. I wanted to run away from Beard, to go to Martha; I loved her more than anything in the world and now this senseless violence was going to separate us for ever. But I had taken on the Zoo job; to give up now would be to make nonsense of all proper order, of anything I believed in. Under my breath I begged Martha to understand why I had to go away from her. The roar and tramp of the crowd was now shifting across towards the Lion House from which came the answering roar of lions and leopards. There was little the mob could do there; for their own sakes I hoped they would not succeed in doing even that. There was little they could do anywhere in the Gardens, and that little we could not stop. I turned to Beard.

'I can drive,' I said and followed down through the Tunnel across the canal and out of the North Entrance where the lorry stood. I hoisted myself up into the driver's seat. As we left, some squawking, gaily-coloured macaws and lories flew across to the trees on Primrose Hill, and a flight of five or six cockatoos passed like a small, chattering cloud overhead.

At one time I had driven a motor car regularly, but a heavy lorry was quite another thing. It seemed to take all my strength to operate the wheel and the gears. My head was spinning, I felt hot and flushed, and my stomach ached so that I had often to stop and bend double in my seat. I wondered if the dysentery, so frequently announced by the doctors to be 'positively the last', was about to make one of its squalid reappearances. Beard said nothing, except to give me uncertain directions from a map which he held against the dashboard light and at which he squinted myopically. We got clear of Pentonville and then Walthamstow, districts that were deserted, but untouched by the raid. Then as the road climbed up to the edge of Epping Forest, the lorry swayed and jolted across holes, and I twisted and turned until my arms seemed ready to break avoiding craters that the headlights picked out before me. Ahead of us towards Epping we saw a cluster of lights across the road.

Beard said, 'Police! We must turn off.'

But I saw that he had no idea where to turn. I knew the area a little from a time when my mother had lived in an Essex cottage and I had driven to see her at weekends in the days before Home Counties private motoring came to an end. I turned the lorry off by side roads towards Chigwell. There had been bomb damage among the housing estates of this area, too, or could it have been looting and burning? We had constantly to turn off the main road but by a zigzag route we came at last into the flattish open country that stretches for some miles to the village of Abridge. Alone of all the immediate environs of London, this rich farming land had never been swallowed up by housing. Now it would be some time before it was farmed again. For miles the green spring shoots of wheat and oats had been charred black; the scattered farmhouses, too, seemed to have been gutted. Yet, by twisting off into side roads, I was able to drive on. I had grown more used to the lorry now. To turn my mind from the griping pain in my stomach, I spoke to Beard. I had meant to talk of other things, but I said:

'Matthew was there. Matthew Price! He tried to save his parrots. But the mob killed him. He had been trampled on when I found him, but I think he was already dead before they came to him.'

Beard sat muttering. I think, perhaps, that he was praying.

At last he said, 'Suffering is an impossible thing to measure, Carter.' Then he added, 'I had all these specimens to pack into the van myself. Not one of the night staff was on duty.'

I made no comment.

He said, 'You were rather a friend of Price's. It should help you to think that his being there may have deflected that mob from surging across to the North Side. I'm not at all sure that in that case we could ever have got away.' Later he said, 'You seem to have studied politics a good deal to have foreseen tonight's troubles as you did. I wonder you didn't go in for that sort of thing instead of mixing yourself up with zoology. You're the only untrained chap I've come across in our work.'

I wanted to break the silence between us. I needed desperately to make contact with another human being, but when I tried once or twice to speak, the words died away before I had voiced them. It was as though I were throwing a rope bridge across a chasm into a void.

In the high street of Abridge my pains became unbearable and I had to stop driving. I got down from the lorry and leaned against the bow-fronted window of a pub. I was bent double. In the headlights of the lorry I could see that there were two or three other people slumped against the walls of the houses – an old woman, her legs spread wide across the pavement, a boy with his mouth adenoidally open, and a fat man, whose neck and cheeks looked oddly green instead of flushed. I knew that I was entering a deluded world peopled by my fever and I shut my eyes.

Beard said, 'I'd better see if I can get something hot for that cramp of yours. We can't afford to hang around here.'

I heard him move away down the street. Hours later, as it seemed to me, he returned.

'The place is deserted,' he said. 'Those who are not dead are dying. You'll have to pull yourself together.'

I groaned that *I* was dying. I heard Beard give a prim little laugh.

'Oh, I'm afraid your sort of dying is in quite another category. That's just how you *feel*. But there's a young chap lying in the street here who really is dying. They've been without food in these parts for a week or more, I think. That's why we must get moving. Hunger makes people rather desperate and they may not be at all as near death as the people here.'

I found it difficult to focus my thoughts on what he was saying, but when at last I had done so, I was revolted.

'Surely there must be something we can do for them.'

'I'm afraid not.'

I groaned with a sudden surge of pain. He misunderstood. He said, 'I'm afraid I'm very used to the impossibility of doing anything to relieve pain.'

He put his hands under my armpits and began to drag me to my feet. I felt as though my arms were being torn from their sockets.

'Leave me alone, for Christ's sake.'

'Christ attends to his own concerns, but you must help me to get these specimens to Dunmow. All my optic work is there. And I've got material for work on the comparative histology of primates' testes that I can probably never amass again.'

His voice carried such urgency that I forced myself to my feet, but the pain made me cry out. 'Oh, God, oh God, let me die!'

'I'm afraid God doesn't send death to order. No bombs fell on Broadmoor or Cromwell Road to release me from my encumbrances. His mercy and his justice are beyond our understanding, Carter.'

Now suddenly as I stood straight I voided in my trousers and the pain died temporarily away. When we returned to the lorry, I opened the door at the back. Beard had not been entirely truthful: there ranged along one side were a row of cages from which stared great round living eyes. I flashed my torch – chocolate, black, cinnamon grey, ring-tailed, the graceful lemurs crouched, legs bent and tails coiled like a row of long-nosed cobblers; above them, greater eyed, were the more absurd tarsier, potto, and loris. But on the other side of the lorry the huge orange gorilla himalayensis lay dead, last monument to Robert Falcon, the end of the yeti, and sprawled above the carcass the dead body of a young African gorilla and staring at me, like a coconut ritual god, the fibrous fringed mask of an orang-outang. At the sight of the lemurs' beauty I almost refused to go on – but where else could I go? I got in the driving seat again. Soon our way became more impassable, and we had constantly to turn off by side roads. As we travelled it came to me that we could have fed the starving at Abridge. But we bumped on. At last it was clear that neither Beard nor I knew where we were. We turned off a cratered main road, lurching across a track through a charred field, and, twisting again, were suddenly confronted by the lamps and torches of a little group of people. In the headlamps I could see a tall, stout white-haired woman with some sort of heavy woollen shawl over her head and her shoulders. She was leaning on a stick. A thin young man in a hacking-coat and breeches, two other, older men, and a long-necked, pale-faced, blonde girl in jeans, completed the group. Behind them a large farm-house loomed out of the thickening white mist. I shouted to them for directions, but Beard gripped my arm tightly and said, 'Drive straight past them.'

Answering me, the old woman stepped forward. She said, 'You're not far from Chipping Ongar, but there's no way of getting there. All the roads are blocked.'

She spoke authoritatively in a deep contralto, redolent of garden fêtes, point to points, and the country magistrates' bench. She said, as though she were searching for a phrase that would give a peace-time normality to life,

'They could stay here tonight, couldn't they, Harry? But I'm afraid there's nothing to eat.'

The young man, equally grand but gruff voiced, redolent of the County Show and the Hunt, said, 'Depends who they are, Gran.'

The girl now spoke, in the voice of the Pony Club.

She said, 'Perhaps they've got something edible in there.' She moved forward but one of the older men held her back.

'That don't do, Miss Ann, to go mixing up with what you don't know about. Where do you come from?' he called.

The girl struggled with him, 'I'm hungry,' she cried, 'I'm hungry.'

Before I could answer, Beard had leapt from the lorry and was standing before them with a revolver in his hand.

'I shall shoot anyone who comes near.' His voice sounded higher than usual but even more prim.

I called, 'Really, Beard. Don't be ridiculous.'

With difficulty I lowered myself from the lorry, and stood behind him. The old woman was obviously relieved by the everyday tone of my voice.

She said, trying to sound as conversational as she could, 'The wireless said there would be helicopters from Norwich dropping food on isolated houses. But that was some days ago ...'

As she was talking, I saw that her son and one of the older men had begun to move out of the circle. Beard had seen it too, his body stiffened. I could not take any risks; I flung myself upon him and we fell hard on to the ground. His revolver flew from his hand, scudding across the ground to come to rest at the old woman's feet. She picked it up and came towards us. For a moment I thought that she was going to kill us, but, instead, she hit Beard sharply across the side of his head with her stick. He moaned and his head fell back on to the ground.

'That'll put him out,' she said, 'until we know where we are. Such a lot of people lose control at a time like this. Poor man.'

Meanwhile Harry and his companion had forced open the lorry door.

'Monkey!' the labourer cried. 'Now that is a rare old surprise.'

'Actually,' Harry said, 'I think they're lemurs.'

His grandmother took charge.

'My dear Harry, whatever they are, I've no doubt they can be eaten.'

'Ah! No! Monkeys wouldn't go down proper with my stomach,' said the man who had not spoken. 'That'd be a tough little old dinner.'

'Oh, nonsense, Palmer,' the girl said grandly, 'it's only a question of boiling the things long enough.'

I heard a shot.

'I don't think I'll shoot them all at once, Gran,' Harry said, 'they'll be fresher if we kill them as we need them.'

'My dear boy, I don't know what you think we're going to keep them alive on,' she answered. He had clearly been in the habit of bringing inconvenient pets home as a child.

I got up with difficulty and began to walk away into the darkness, shining my little hand torch before me.

'You're leaving your friend,' the old lady cried. I started to run.

'Oh, let him go, Granny,' the girl said. 'We don't want to feed half London.'

'Yes, for God's sake, let him go, Gran,' Harry said, 'who knows whether he's the forerunner of some bacteria infected invasion from London. You heard the last warnings they sent out.'

'In that case,' I could hear the old lady's voice say, 'you'd better get rid of this.' I ran on.

Some little while after I had crawled into the wood, I caught my foot under the thick sprawling root of a beech and fell, striking my head against an old tree stump. The wound on my temple stung fiercely, yet I think that I did not faint, but passed out into a sudden sleep from exhaustion and hunger. I came to once when it was still dark; and then with a cruelly aching head to a pale, white-misted dawn and a deafening bird chorus, yet not so deafening that I did not at once slide off into sleep again; when I woke fully the sun was hot even through beech leaves that cast a dappled pattern upon my naked thigh where I had torn my trouser leg in forcing a way through the undergrowth. Each time I had woken mysteriously to a stink of garlic, and now I could see the tightly furled white flowers and the shiny green leaves smashed and pulped by my fall. With my ball pen I dug up garlic roots here and there until I found a good sized clove, but, as soon as I had munched it, the sharpness burned my tongue and I felt sick. By pushing against the trunk of the great beech tree I managed to lever myself to my feet. For a few seconds the scene revolved before me and I thought I should fall. I leaned against the tree and then, breathing in the clear air, walked on. I heard a cock pheasant crow once, started some wood doves flapping above me, noted high up in a larch tree a squirrel's drey, but I had no gun with me. Once too a stoat ran across my path, heard me, coiled snakelike and hissed, and was gone into the bramble and the briar. Every now and again I had to cross the narrow beds of dried-up streams that seemed to me in my weakness like canyons. Near one of these where the yellowish clayey soil suddenly changed to an ochre sandy surface I saw what seemed to be long-used entrances to badger setts. And sure enough nearby I saw evidences of badger dung and there were flattened paths through the surrounding growth. There were no berries at that season, not even bracken fronds to be eaten. At last in a thicket of hawthorn I found a blackbird's nest of three eggs, and fearful lest the clumsy instrument should smash the delicate shells, I punctured each with the tip of my ball-pen and eagerly sucked two delicious yolks. The third had addled and the stench alone almost made me sick. At last I chanced upon a man-made path, dry and hard to the foot from the long season of hot weather. Water avens and some late oxlips flowered at its side; behind them the brambles and briar roses seemed impenetrable. From these thickets came persistent noises of birds stirring or even, perhaps, of some animal, although it was difficult to see what animal would be on the move at that hour. The path turned sharply round a clump of elms and there before me in a clearing was a small wattle and clay cottage, thatched, its white-washed walls pargetted with a small shell pattern. The garden was bright with early roses and oriental poppies, and at the side, above a plot of onions and potatoes some sheets hung feebly stirring in the light breeze. I could see no sign of life. I began to make my way towards its small iron gate, when, from the briars at my side, stepped a thin, sunburnt boy of about fifteen, dressed in faded blue jeans and a short sleeved flowered cotton shirt. He was pointing an old shotgun at me.

'Keep away from here. That'll be just bad for you, if you don't.' He spoke with a broad Essex accent. 'Mum. There's a man.'

A voice came from the cottage, shrill and even more broad in accent than the boy's. 'Ah! Well, he'd best keep right on walking. There's nothing here for no one.'

She came out – a white-faced, reddish-haired woman of forty in a bright blue sleeveless dress. Mother and son both had freckled arms.

'That's all finished,' she said, 'we had the last tin of baked beans Tuesday.' I pointed to the plot of vegetables.

'Ah! That's what it looks like coming down to,' she said, 'last we saw on the tele before that faded out was they was bringing proper tinned stuff from Norwich.'

'By helicopter,' the boy added.

'Ah, tinned soup, and that,' she announced, 'but nothing come.'

'I reckon old Norwich has about copped it,' the boy said and laughed.

His mother said, 'Ah, likely. Then what's to do, eh?'

I asked, 'Haven't you shot anything in the wood?'

She answered for him, 'Oh yes, he's brought back pigeons and that. One time it was a pheasant, wasn't it, Stanley? But I reckon that's got too cunning, that knows he's coming.' She suddenly smiled at me. 'We could about do with them rabbits now, couldn't we? He's never seen a rabbit, have you, Stanley?'

'Yes, I have. I've seen pictures.'

'Ah, pictures's not the same.'

'Well I seen them anyway.'

Their voices, hers shrill and his now falsetto, now in his

boots, echoed round and round my head. The pink daisies on his shirt and the bright blue of her dress pulled tight across her large breasts glared in my eyes, fused, drew apart, and fused again. The poppies blazed in fires of scarlet, pink, and flame. The fire flared up at me, licked my face and I fell.

When I came to I was lying on what had once been called a contemporary patterned sofa. I was aware first of its chocolate material with a design in pistachio green thread. Then I smelt hyacinths and moving my eyes with pain, I saw the tightly twined blue locks, now half dead, above a paper-frilled flower-pot. I turned my head and there was the boy, holding my coat with one hand, and going through its pockets with the other. I closed my eyes.

'You oughtn't to do that, Stanley, that's not right.'

'That's what they do on the tele.'

'Well, that don't make it right.'

'Well, it don't make it wrong, do it? Ah and that might be this travelling sickness that was on the tele that come from gas,' the boy looked very knowing. 'I reckon we ought to get rid of him.'

The woman said in a very final tone, of resignation and of determination, 'You can't get rid of a sick man, Stanley. That wouldn't be right.'

I thought that I should scream if I had to live with this cross talk act for long. I asked for water.

'Ah! Now the water all went when the soldiers was at Chelmsford.' I could make no sense of this. 'There's well water,' the woman added. 'Get him a glass of that, Stanley. But there's nothing to eat. That all went Tuesday when we had the last tin of baked beans.'

I did not believe her. I said, 'I think I could show your son where to get food in the wood.'

'In the wood?'

'Yes. I'm fairly sure there are badgers, but I'm too weak to get there unless you can find me something to eat first – the potatoes in your garden?'

The boy came back with the glass of water.

She said, "'E says there's badgers in the wood.'

'Ah, that might be, Mum.'

He sat down. The woman turned and hit the television screen.

'Still nothing out of that thing.'

'I reckon old Norwich has copped it.'

'Ah! That's what too.'

I said, ' You could live off badger meat for a long time. It's like pork.'

It took them a lot of talk to decide that my scheme was sensible. I lay back and closed my eyes. I was woken by the woman shaking me.

'Here,' she said, 'that's a last tin of steak. Or pretty well. What'll we do after that?'

The boy said, 'That could be something to have them badgers, but that needs a lot of digging out, don't it? I reckon we haven't got the strength to dig.'

I asked the time. 'That's after five now.'

'Wake me at half past eight and I'll take you there.'

She woke me with a plate of tinned steak and diced vegetables.

She said, 'That's seven o'clock.' Then she pointed to two tins of soup on the table. 'That's all there is and that's the truth.'

This time I believed her. The food brought back my stomach pains; but, with the sleep, I felt stronger. I did not intend to waste my energy by walking to the wood before dark. As the woman and her son ate, I read an old newspaper.

But at last the light began to fade, and it was time to set out on our errand.

We stood before an old ash tree with the breeze running in our faces. A hundred yards away across a patch of dying oxlips beaten down to form a path for the animals, I could see the openings in the yellowish sandy soil. The boy had a lucky and remarkable power of stillness; because of my stomach pains I found the wait more difficult. But we had not to wait long, not more than twenty minutes. First a snout, then a flash of black and white, then a heavy boar badger trotted out and stood sniffing the wind. He moved across to the midden. A few minutes later, came, more cautiously, his mate. She was followed by two young cubs who began at once to snap and roll over each other in mock fighting. The sow joined in the play, and soon even the old boar was sliding and rolling with his family. This was the happy family play whose healing innocence I had been cheated of again and again in the days of watching at Stretton. I nudged the boy's arm. He fired and the boar fell, screeching, on his side. Instantly the mate was down the sett, followed by her cubs. But before they had reached the entrance, the boy had fired again and one of the cubs lay dead. The boy walked over to where the old boar lay, only grunting now; he knocked it on the head with the butt end of his rifle, half crushing its skull. Even together we had not the strength to carry the body back. The boar must have weighed around forty pounds. So, for the next hour, in the clear light of the now risen moon, I hacked away at the carcass; and the boy and his mother made journeys to and from the cottage, carrying badger joints. The cub required only the one journey.

It was long after ten when we had done; and yet, I knew that until I had washed the slimy blood from my hands I could not sleep. To my surprise neither the woman nor the boy would let me carry the pails of well water to the detached bath house. Though they still talked to one another in endless desultory chatter, they seemed somehow to regard me as a part of their life there.

'That was a right little old job we had to do,' the boy said.

'Ah, that's brought us together like,' the woman added.

I tried to smile, but I felt I must be grimacing like the third murderer. After my wash, they settled me, dressed in some pyjamas that had belonged to her 'old grandad', on the sofa. They wrapped me in blankets, but I spent a weary night, journeying to and from the outside privy. At last towards six, I fell into a heavy sleep to awake to a smell more nauseating than I ever thought could be. Mother and son were feeding avidly at the table.

'That's proper good that old badger of yours,' the boy said.
'Ah, you'd best have a piece of that,' the woman told me.
Nausea fought with hunger in me. I sat up on the sofa, conscious of the ludicrous effect of the ill-fitting pink candy-striped flannel pyjamas. But neither of them laughed. The woman brought me a plate of what appeared to be pinkish, greasy, fried pork.

'That's real good,' she said. 'That'll put body in you.'

I cut a small piece, and, to my surprise, it tasted rich and delicious. In a short while I had eaten all but a small piece of browned fat. I speared it with the fork, felt its grease against my lips, and then suddenly I vomited. So violent were the spasms that it seemed as though my body were rejecting all its vital organs. I spewed a flash of light vermilion blood. The room span round. My head fell back on the cushions and everything became dark, became nothing.

7

THE HOOPOE LIES DOWN WITH
THE GROUSE

SOPHIE ENGLANDER, whose maternal affection for me seemed to increase every week, signalled to the butler to fill up my glass again.

'It came direct from Paris for Emile. Two cases of burgundy. In the French diplomatic bag. You see, they're making a fuss of him in his old age. You must drink it up, Mr Carter. It'll give you body. With the winter coming on, you need body. And you don't wear enough. After your long illness you mustn't take risks. You're very pretty, my dear,' she said to Martha, 'but that won't keep him warm. Or at least not altogether.'

Her heavily made-up old face creased and cracked with the sentimental chuckle that was now so familiar to my ear. Then, from laughing she began to wheeze and cough until her cheeks, usually a sort of dull orange from the peculiar colour of her make-up, turned almost as crimson as her dark hennaed hair. She signalled to the butler to fill her tumbler with water and she drank it in sips, still laughing until drops of sweat stood out from the thick powder on her rather bony bare shoulders and dripped down among the diamonds and sapphires of her neck collar. Though Martha was still guarded with them both, I was pleased to note that she liked the old woman enough to say, 'Well, Mrs Englander, I had no idea that Simon and I were that funny as a couple.'

Mrs Englander's dark eyes looked worriedly through a mist of blue eyeshade and mascara for a moment to see if Martha was offended, then, when she saw that it was a joke, she called down to her husband.

'Emile, these young people are trying to make me die of laughter. You're a naughty girl,' she said to Martha, 'but all the same, my dear, you must feed that husband of yours. He's eaten nothing this evening. Juicy steaks and red wine. That's what he should have.'

'Well, we could kill him off that way, certainly,' Martha said.

'Kill him! Nonsense, don't you listen to those doctors. Red meat never killed anyone. Emile'll get them for you. He knows where.'

I saw Martha's neck tauten, as it had already done at the sight of the huge saddle of mutton cooked French gigot fashion, that had appeared on the carving table.

I said, 'Dear Mrs Englander, I don't think I should be happy to eat porterhouse steaks, even if I were allowed to, so long as food in England is in such short supply.'

I hoped that my intervention would take the edge off Martha's anger. And so it proved.

'Many people who come to the Relief Office never see meat at all, Mrs Englander,' she said.

'Oh, my dear, I know it's terrible.'

I liked the old woman too much to let her off lightly. 'There's a lot of *real* starvation you know.'

She cried, 'Oh my God! Is there? That's terrible. You see, Emile always keeps sad things from me. He's always spoilt me terribly. You hear that, Emile? Mr Carter says there's real starvation. No more saddles of mutton, my dear. Not even for you, Herr Kästner,' she called down to the Second Secretary from the German Embassy, a frequent guest there. 'No, something light – that's what we'll have to live on. But not eggs because they make Emile look quite yellow. You would be getting jaundice, Emile, and then we'll have to send you to Vichy. Oh, how I hate it there. So dull, though the pastries are very good . . .'

Dr Englander cut into his wife's stream. 'Now, now, Sophie. Don't you take any notice of their nonsense. We shan't be going to Vichy and we shan't be having anything light. I've got a hard job of work to do and I need a proper diet to do it on.'

He looked indeed plumper and more comfortable than I

remembered him; like a tortoise in his thick protective covering of woollen waistcoats and a little padded satin quilt coat that he had put on over his dinner jacket because of draughts, though no one else could feel them. But central heating was not available then, even for the Englanders, so he was sure there must be some draughts.

'Anyway all this distress, it's bound to happen after a war. But the Government's got it in hand, don't you worry your head, Mrs Carter, it's much too attractive.'

Sophie Englander whispered with delight, 'Emile loves a pretty girl. Food and pretty girls! I don't think he could do without them. And his old snakes.'

'I'll tell you why your husband's got to put on weight and get really well. It's because I need him back with me to put the Zoo on its feet again. There's no use in our French friends and our German friends sending us valuable animals every day as they are doing,' here he raised his glass to Herr Kästner, who returned the salute, 'so long as there's nobody but an old man like me to run the whole place. That's my interest in Carter's health – selfish.'

Sophie was delighted with this, her old red head on which she had put some sort of sapphire ornament, bobbed about, as she cried, 'Oh, yes, that's it. Selfish, nothing but selfish.' She whispered to Martha, 'Emile's teasing you.'

'As a matter of fact, staff shortage is one of our worst difficulties, Harmer.'

He turned to a short, fat little man, who said, 'You'll get your staff, Englander, don't you worry. Now we've got a government that has foreign confidence, the whole prosperity cycle so far as businessmen are concerned, will start up again soon enough. And once that happens your technicians and scientists will start flocking back to the country. And we've got sensible men at the head of labour now too, chaps like our friend Tillotson here who will pool their labour with Europe, not kick against the pricks.'

And now around the whole long table there rose a familiar buzz of conversation – talk of renewed confidence, ancient

European culture, international science, sound economy and civilized living that played in and out of the massed chrysanthemums and antique silver to assure us that a new era of solid, adult, wide-horizoned, big men had begun. Indeed there they were, as Martha and I had seen them at five or six dinner parties now in the Director's ornate, heavily Empire dining-room – Harmer, who stood for half a dozen or so other businessmen with international interests; Tillotson, who stood for forward-minded, international-minded, middle of the road Trade Union leadership; a prominent zoologist or two from Italy or France or Spain; a Second Secretary from one of the European Embassies; occasionally, as this evening, a representative of the world of art, a literary critic of that older, more European-minded school who had now suddenly come once more to the fore: the cultivated, rich, cautious, go-ahead old men who had put an end to a wasteful war, substituted sense for sentiment, and were about to substitute prosperity for patriotism. All except the literary gentleman had matching wives; and he had been paired, following a stream of arch apology from Sophie, with another gentleman, unknown to us all – a Mr Hilary Blanchard-White. He was a man with an old-fashioned musician's mane of white hair, staring, liquid eyes, and over-regular, over-white false teeth with which he smiled at everything that was said. He spoke in an old-fashioned actor's dramatic tremolo and constantly rubbed his hands across his face as he talked.

'A funny sort of chap,' Englander told me before dinner, as we drank our sherry. 'I don't know whether you'll like him. He seems agreeable enough, smiles all the time. He's one of these Uni-European men. Not a man of substance at all. He's taught languages in Hamburg, Utrecht, Geneva, Toulouse, all over the place. But he organized a lot of the underground work and Harmer tells me the Government have got to give those chaps some sort of recognition. He's interested in zoos and museums. Though what he's got to say about them, I can't imagine, since he's not a scientist or a scholar. Of course, if this country had come to its senses sooner, and made peace sooner, events would never have brought such men to the fore. They're a product of violence. We'd never have heard of Uni-Europeans. But then if this country had had a little more sense, we shouldn't have to build up a Zoo from a collection of reptiles that an old man like me had the sense to evacuate in time.'

This was a favourite topic of Englander's. He was holding forth upon it even now to his dinner guests. It was his war story. In actual fact, he had spent the war itself very quietly at St Gallen; and his constant reiteration of the tale of the secret building of the reptile park was the one sign he gave of the garrulity of old age.

'If it hadn't been for me,' he was saying, 'there'd have been no Zoo. But I got in touch with our friend Harmer here and we built a full-scale reptile park up in the Hebrides, while you were fussing about losing animals down in Wales, Carter. Of course, Scotland Yard was pretty near on to us at one point, thought it was some sort of submarine base for the European fleet – and so it was, wasn't it, Harmer? But that had nothing to do with me. Then that chap Falcon tipped me off that the Yard were inquiring about me. I don't know why he told me, but there you are, he did. I'd have been home otherwise to take Sophie out before the big bang started.'

'And so you left me. And they put me in prison, Herr Kästner. And gave me a carbolic bath. Imagine an old woman like me scrubbed with carbolic soap!' She laughed until the tears ran down, 'And Mr Carter saved my life by sending me food. Yes, you did. Everybody else had forgotten the old woman. And this handsome young man who had never seen me, sent me food and books. You didn't know I was such an ugly old thing did you, Mr Carter? You thought Emile had a beautiful young wife. That's it I know.'

'We shan't forget what you did, Carter,' Dr Englander said. 'And as far as the Zoo *could* be kept going, Carter kept it going. They put a poor chap in charge who'd gone off his rocker – a chap called Beard. That's how Carter got stuck out in the back of beyond with this dysentery. This chap Beard panicked and rushed a lot of lemurs out into the country, Lord knows why! Just as the war collapsed. Nothing's ever been heard of him again, has there, Carter?'

I said, 'It's almost certain he was killed in the fighting that followed in that area. The farm where I left him and the family living there were blown up. I shouldn't have survived myself if it hadn't been that a country woman took me in, and fed me and nursed me.'

'And no doubt charged you for it afterwards. I know the ways of peasants. My grandfather came from peasant stock in the Engadine.'

Martha was indignant. 'They wouldn't take a penny, Dr Englander,' she cried. 'Not a penny! Neither she nor the boy. And they were so poor . . . and it was so awful.' Martha had been appalled at the conditions of English rural slums.

'They saved his life and she calls them awful. Oh, you're a naughty girl,' Mrs Englander cried.

The Director said, 'Beard had a lot of crippled relatives and other family encumbrances, didn't he? The Zoo will have to do something for *them*, Carter. After all it wasn't his fault they put him in charge. Anyway they never paid the chap a living wage. I tell you what, you go down and see what's happened to his family and, if they're in real need, I can fork out until we get the Committee working on salaries and pensions.'

I could hardly refrain from doing 'thumbs up' to Martha. I had scored heavily in my fight to establish the Englanders as decent people.

I said, 'I've been to see them. The spastic son's clever. He does some maths coaching, but, of course, it isn't easy to keep a sister and a grandmother on that. I don't know that he'll accept a pension – his relations with his father were very bad. Beard was very hard with them, or, rather, he became so. The boy seems to understand, but he can't forgive.'

As I spoke I could see the wretched fat neurotic daughter twisting her handkerchief round her fingers, and saying, 'You see, Dad never took any account of what happened to us, so we can't care what's happened to him.' The boy had squared his huge over-developed shoulders, 'That's not fair, Catherine. He did the essentials for us. But with such loathing. You couldn't help wanting him out of the way.' His handsome face turned to me. '*We* had years to form that view. It seems that you were quick to do so weren't you?' But he had spoken without bitterness.

Now Englander helped himself to a large piece of omelette surprise with raspberry ice and meringue from the dish the butler offered. He shovelled it down as he talked.

'Ah, well. All that sort of thing's not a subject to entertain guests with. Failure and illness! But we'll do something for them. The essence of getting a good collection together again is to have a competent well-paid staff and you won't get them if you neglect their widows and orphans.' He turned to Harmer. 'You say the scientists and technicians will come back as soon as things have settled down. But you industrialists have got to spend your money freely. We'll do your work for you at the Zoo, for example, but if you want that work well done you must pay better rates than we gave our staff before the war. I'm right, aren't I, Carter? You see why I want you back, to help me put the Zoo's case to these fellows.' He indicated Harmer and Tillotson. 'We're already losing some good men. Jackley, that's our ichthyologist, was interned by the Spanish at Funchal. Now he's elected to go to the States, not to come back here. He gives some clap-trap, political reason, but that's not it, of course. It's because of the poor wage he used to be paid.'

Sophie Englander now claimed my attention. She said, 'And so you say that many of these poor people are really in want. And you think we are selfish pigs with our saddles and our ice puddings, is that it, my dear?'

Martha replied, 'That's kind of what I meant to convey, yes, dear Mrs Englander.'

The old woman cried, 'Of course! And so we are! But we have to entertain, my dear. Emile's a big man now. But I'll tell you what, I'll come down to your relief centre and do some work. Maybe there are things that can be got for these people by bullying in the right quarters. And I'm very good at bullying, you know. I've always been spoilt and that makes you good at bullying. And in any case what's the use of Emile knowing all the large pots unless we can get something out of them?'

This time I really did make the thumbs up sign to Martha; and, catching a certain glance from her, we both began to giggle. Mrs Englander looked at us doubtfully for a second, then she too began to laugh.

'Well that is nice,' she said, 'to see people laugh at nothing like that. Do you know sometimes when I'm spraying in the orchid house or playing patience I begin to laugh until I can't stop, just thinking about the time Emile fell off a sleigh at Saint Moritz. But with your husband you're laughing all the time. Look at the way he mimics everybody. I'm sure he mimics old girl Englander behind her back.' She roared with laughter at the idea.

But now suddenly Mr Blanchard-White's elocutionary tones broke through our laughter. He leaned forward and compelled full silence by his gleaming smile.

'You ask me what we shall have to do. Well I haven't really formed an opinion yet. Not *really* you know. But if I may say so, this talk of recompensing or pensioning or what have you the dependants of traitors and the suggestion that we should out-bid the Americans for the services of other traitors sounds a little too like the old England, the illogical, sentimental England that has been moving for so many centuries farther and farther away from the main stream of civilization. If I may venture on a moment's autobiography, that's why I made my life on the continent – to escape from the lack of logic and the false sentiment here that left so little room for men of talent. You ask me,' he gleamed in turn at all of us around the table, like an expectant alligator, 'what I think people in England want. I take it that you mean the people who fought to save her from herself. Well – in so far as I can speak for the Uni-European Movement, I think I should say that we are hungry to see justice done. And what else?' He rubbed his hands over his face, stretching downwards the loose flesh of his cheeks and of his long chin. 'What else? Well, I suppose, to be rid of a little of the grey mist of puritanism. To have a little fun.' He smiled specially at the ladies. 'Yes. To see justice done and to have a little fun. I don't think they're such incompatible aims really. In fact quite the contrary, quite the contrary, particularly if, in throwing off the puritan legacy, we get closer to the rich vein of Mediterranean brutality on which our European legacy so much depends.'

No one spoke for a minute after he had done. Then Dr Englander addressed Piétaud, the curator of reptiles from Paris. 'What did you think of the paper on Loxocemus that that Mexican chap contributed to last quarter's "Herpetology"? The ecological data were new to me.'

'Yes. They were remarkably interesting. But these field workers should not go beyond their province. To question the classification at this stage is absurd, but absolutely absurd.'

'Yes,' said Dr Englander expansively, 'small nations!' and he caught his wife's eye.

In her turn, she caught the eye of Frau Kästner and with the rustling of silk and the glittering of jewels – mainly Sophie's – the ladies rose and were gone.

We finally settled the question of my returning to the Zoo when we got home that night.

I said, 'Well, at any rate, you can't help liking old Sophie. She's such an innocent old booby!'

Martha said, 'Yes. And I'm glad to see that you like her enough to treat her as grown up.'

'In what way?'

'Oh, only that you don't think she has to be spared the unpleasant side of life. Unlike those other poor old innocents Mrs Leacock and that boy's mother, I hated that, Simon, it was so insulting of you.'

I swallowed this and asked, 'But you accept the Englanders?'

Martha said, 'She *is* a darling and he's not half as awful as I thought at first, but I *don't* want to go there to dinner any more, Simon. It makes me feel wretched after dealing with near starvation all day.'

I thought it wise to concede this point. I said, 'Of course. We'll make my digestion the excuse.'

I think she had expected more opposition from me, for, after the squalors and dreariness of the last month, the absurd splendour of the Englanders' huge Highgate house fitted with my longing for relaxed frivolity. This set-up had been so unexpected to me and that alone made it a continual slightly ridiculous pleasure.

She said, 'Thank you, Simon.'

'Well?' I asked after a pause.

'Well?' She quoted it back at me. 'That might refer to two things – to the children or to you.'

'Let's take the children first.'

'Simon, while things are like they are here, I don't want to bring them back.'

'Then let *us* go to see *them*.'

'*You* do that this time. Oh, of course, I want to go more than anything, but *you* don't work on that relief committee, *you* don't see what I see. People – awful people, Simon, like that Stanley and his mother who saved your life! And they're lost and bewildered. Just keeping one's head and helping them to fill in forms seems worth while. Until I've done my bit of that, I can't leave England.'

'In that case, since the children are happy with Hester,' I said, 'I shall stay here with you. But do you still not want me to go back to the Zoo?'

'The doctors say . . .'

'The doctors say I can return in the New Year. Englander wants me. He's building up something useful there from scratch. The European zoos are being most generous. And what I like about it all is that Englander is approaching the thing modestly, by degrees. I want to go back, Martha. I've seen it through so far, I ought not to desert now.'

'And the British Reserve?'

'It won't get going again for some time. And then I think

my health . . .' The vile taste of roasted badger fat filled my mouth. I had to fight back memories. I said quickly, 'Well, I couldn't do field work again for the time being. I want to go back to the Zoo. Do you still object?'

'No, Simon, I suppose not, if you don't. Oh, it's so difficult for me – I'm not entirely British as you are and if you don't feel it . . . But, well, if I *were* wholly British I think I shouldn't like the present set-up . . .'

'My dear, the British people as a whole never objected to Federation with Europe. If they had, neither blockade nor threat of bacteriological warfare would have made them give in. No, the war came to an end because most people had never wanted it to begin. Why should we fight to keep the old crowd in power instead of Harmer and Tillotson? It's no good being highminded and opting out like Jackley and all the top men who've decided to emigrate. Englander may be a low-minded, materialistic old bugger, but he's putting sense before self-indulgent sentiment.'

'No, I know. In some way these people seem better to me. And yet . . . Well, look at that awful man tonight with the teeth. There is a lot of scum about.'

'There always has been. The war's churned it to the top for a while, that's all. As a matter of fact Englander referred to that Blanchard-White, when he spoke to me before dinner tonight. He asked me to help them keep those sort of people at bay. So you see.'

'I suppose so. Very well, darling, you do as you want. But watch out that we don't lose our way. Watch out that we don't lose touch with the sort of people we care about.'

Of course we did a little; we were bound to. Lord Oresby, for example, couldn't see his way to continuing as our President. This was undoubtedly the time, he said, for men to retire to their country seats, and he went down to Wiltshire; but then he was what one of my aunts would have called 'ultra correct'. Mr Harmer was elected in his place.

'Ultra correct', I suppose, was also Diana Price's position.

She wrote just before Christmas to ask me to visit her at her little Regency house in Lloyd Square – 'There are some things Matthew wanted you to have.' I went there on a very cold afternoon. She sat in a fur coat in their pretty drawing-room.

She said, 'I'm afraid it's freezingly cold, but it seems to me that any sort of firing is collaboration and that's that. How does Martha feel about it?'

I brought the conversation on to Matthew as soon as possible. 'He was so immensely original. He made me laugh so much,' I said.

'Did he? I don't think one can judge that if one's been brought up with somebody. He liked *you* very much. I should be very grateful if you would tell me exactly what happened that night.' When I hesitated, she said, 'I have a strong stomach.'

I told her as fully as I could. 'I still can't understand,' I said, 'what made him take that hopeless risk. I'd warned him, you know. And I thought he'd accepted my warning. I said it's not a time for suicide pilots and he agreed. You know how he joked about things, he said, "I'm not Japanese."'

'I don't think Matthew was joking. After all he *wasn't* Japanese, was he? But he *was* a man who always did his duty. If that person Beard muddled things up so that Matthew's parrots had not been evacuated, he would have felt it was his duty to protect them.'

'But it was risking certain death.'

She laughed, 'Matthew risked certain death many times in the war against Hitler.'

'Yes, I know. I'm afraid that I never knew much about that hero side of Matthew.'

'No? Of course, you were saying that he made you laugh so much.' She got up. 'However,' the word cut me sharply, 'however, he left you this parcel.' When I opened it later at home, it contained a first edition of *Fanny Hill*, a first edition of *Under the Hill*, and *The Cyprian's Guide to the London Bagnios for 1847*, also, rather incongruously, a large illustrated folio, *The Aviaries of our Great Houses* published in 1871.

Martha reported throughout that winter that Sophie Englander was working like a carthorse on the Relief Committee. 'She really *can* pull strings without their breaking and she's genuinely fine with the people, if only she would arrive a little less dripping in mink . . .'

I, too, sometimes wished when we were interviewing the many needy people who applied for uniformed keepers' posts, that Englander would exude a slightly less solid comfort; but otherwise he was a model of competence, good sense, and, above all, moderation. It had been agreed that the Zoo would reopen on 21 April, on what, now that the European Federation was finally established, was to be called European Day. I could not but think of Leacock's lost opening day and Bobby's Day of Wrath, but our new Director was determined that we should present a modest but solidly interesting collection.

'This is not a time for show,' he said, 'but it is a time to give an impression of the serious future of the Society's work and of the civilized, European essence of the Gardens as a show place for the public.'

The exhibition on opening day was to be divided into two sections, he decided. The first was to consist of a series of demonstrations showing the research work of the Society in terms comprehensible to the general public. Here our trouble was that, following the raids and the disastrous attempted evacuations by the Prosector, the material for research work had severely diminished. Only Englander's own work could be fully set out with living experiments as well as in diagrammatic or photographic form. His investigations into the undulating propulsion of snakes was to occupy pride of place. It would not, in fact, have been difficult with the willing assistance of European zoos, to have replaced the material for most of our other research workers. And, at first, these offers had been welcomed.

'This old chap Englander seems to be slightly more on the beam than all those duds we've suffered from recently,' Pattie told me on the phone, 'Nutting's frightfully bucked with the new grant he's getting and even Newton says the old boy almost understood what his work's about.'

But shortly afterwards they all three mysteriously and abruptly announced that they would not be contributing work to the opening exhibition. At first the Director was angry and distressed; but so many excellent zoologists from Europe had asked to show their work that he could afford to neglect this defection. In explanation Pattie would only say to me, 'It's simply no good questioning me because your name's not yet in the clear.'

In any case I was too busy with the other side of the ceremony which was to be, as the Director said, 'something to give you a chance, Carter, to show what you're good for'. It was – and this was Englander's sensible limiting idea – to consist of an exhibition of European fauna only, but of every kind, grouped geographically, with informatory films and lectures upon migration, breeding, general demography, adaptation to human environments, relation to human economy. It was also to contain a special palaeozoological section. Englander, in fact, hoped in this part of the exhibition to assert a claim to incorporate in the future Zoological Gardens many of the former functions of the Natural History Museum which had been totally destroyed in the raid.

I found my work taxing but extraordinarily interesting. Through Englander I made contact with every West European zoo and natural history museum. Donations came in not only from the great zoos at Hamburg and Copenhagen and Rome and Paris, but from all sorts of small collections in provincial towns. Europe was on her toes to reward capitulation. Through Harmer we received lavish grants from the federated West European industries; through Tillotson we drew upon the new pooled labour resources. The Italian architect chosen by Englander to rebuild the houses was a man of striking originality and great charm. It was a winter of slush, sleet, insufficient food and sudden power cuts, but nothing could chill the warmth I generated in my cocoon of busyness. Only, indeed, the voice of Sanderson unintentionally jarred me to the realization of a changing world outside. He had entered into the new régime with zeal – I did not tell him that the Director had said, 'We must hang on to that chap until we can get someone better to replace him' – and we spent a lot of time together devising exhibitions of pests and demonstrations of the interdependence of European insects and European flora. He was knowledgeable, helpful, but always naïve.

One day he said to me, 'Of course, I was very glad to see that war come to an end, Carter. I know some people thought differently. But then they probably weren't in touch with old people as I am. Mrs Blessington, of course, is an old devil. She'd have been for going on fighting, I think, but Miss Delaney felt the horror of it terribly. The blind have a sixth sense about these things. In any case this Government seems to be doing some fine things, especially since the changes of last week.'

Looking up from a pile of papers about potato blight, I asked, 'What changes?'

'Oh, they've taken in some of the Uni-European chaps. I think they're right. After all they did all the sabotage work. In any case they're all unknown men, people who've come up from nowhere. It's nice to see the little chaps taken notice of. And they'll think about the other little chaps, of course. This new law about putting the vagrant and the old and so on into special government homes is a magnificent idea really. There are so many lost people wandering about since the war and it only distresses everyone to see them. Old Mrs B.'s very fierce, of course; she says it should be voluntary. But I'm not sure the Government is not being kinder by taking the decision out of the old people's hands.'

It was typical of him that upon the very same morning, he told me with some admiration about the Jackley letter.

'It seems,' he said, 'that it's only one of many letters that these chaps from abroad are sending to the various places where they worked. Mind you, I don't know that I agree with their hostile attitude to our Government. In fact I think they ought to come back and pull their weight. All the same, there's something rather fine about this letter of Jackley's. I don't know how it got smuggled in, but it urges people not to co-operate now and sets out his plans for the future of the Zoo. It's had a tremendous effect on Miss Henderson, I think. She's been circulating duplicated copies. But you mustn't say anything to Englander, of course. He might get upset about it. I don't think it's to be taken seriously myself, but it cheers some people up. And I admire Jackley's simplicity of style. He begins. "*Dear Colleagues, as you know I have been for over a year in prison* . . ." I thought the simplicity of that was very moving . . .'

If the Uni-Europeans were going to take over, then I had no wish to hinder Pattie Henderson's resistance work; on the other hand, if Englander could continue his wise régime, I had no wish to help make way for Jackley. In such a dilemma, I found it best to bury myself in getting a really good show put on. Until ten days before the Opening Day I forgot all else; then suddenly it was announced that Mr Blanchard-White had been appointed to advise the Government on public exhibitions – museums, parks, art galleries, zoos and so on. Englander was most distressed. He taxed Harmer and Tillotson with not preventing such an absurdity. 'I can't think what men of your standing could be doing letting them appoint a chap like that, a man who's never had a proper position, a man without any scientific training. Heaven knows what cranky nonsense he may bother us with!'

Harmer said, 'It's a worrying time, Englander.'

Tillotson said, 'The only thing with incompetents is to give them enough rope to hang themselves.'

Mr Blanchard-White at his first Committee meeting was all smiles and few words.

'I just want to feel my way,' he said. But he did ask if he might participate on European Day. 'I know it's late,' he said, 'but if I could have a little corner just to try an idea of mine and then I think the Minister wants me to say a few words. After the important speeches of the day, of course. Just a post-scriptum or perhaps we should say *obiter dictum*.'

April 21 was warm; the daffodils waved their golden and

ivory and orange in a soft southerly breeze; the first lilacs had been tempted out and filled the air with their heavy, sensual perfume. Gates were opened at eleven in the morning. Dr Englander, old fashioned and solid in his view of entertainments, had procured the band of the Grenadier Guards to play selections and marches; the food which promised to be excellent was to come from Gunters. The first hundred or so visitors to arrive were the core of society that supported the Government – only different from those that would have come to Bobby Falcon's opening in its preponderance of foreign embassy staff and business magnates, and in the absence of country gentry. Many of the cosmopolitan set indeed were the very same stage stars and television personalities who had helped Bobby and Jane to put up the Victoriana. The end of the war had brought its usual reaction against utility – rich women's clothes that season trailed the ground in trains, nipped the ankles in hobbles, swayed in paniers, did everything in fact to make female movement a luxurious difficulty. Sophie Englander had not attempted such chic.

'Emile prefers to see me in something solid, my dear,' she told me and she indicated her emeralds and her furs, which were indeed uncomfortably hot for the day. 'But anyhow the pretty frocks look nicer on the pretty girls,' she added, taking Martha under her wing. 'You come with me, dear, and look pretty. And don't talk about hungry people and miseries because this is Emile's big day and we girls have got to look like a bouquet of flowers. That's what the old music master used to say at my convent school. "You girls are like a bouquet of flowers." We hated him! Poor old thing, I don't expect he was paid enough to keep body and soul together. Now you've got to be at Emile's right hand, Mr Carter, so off you go.'

The scientific demonstrations had been arranged in a series of temporary buildings between the Mappin Terrace and the Restaurant. The crowd here seemed to grow thicker as I made my way. The same types of chic women and of prosperous, important looking men – a good number of them foreign. Here and there I saw well-known zoologists, though there were many others I looked for in vain. Many members of the Zoological Society whom I recognized there – country colonels or parsons and their wives – were, I felt sure, quite out of sympathy with the times and showed it by the careful dowdiness of their dress. The largest crowd, as I had expected, had gathered round the booth where routine experiments with the conceptual vision of two chimpanzees were taking place. It was here that I came on Sanderson with an old lady on each arm. They proved, in fact, to be tough splendid old Mrs B. and the noble blind Miss D. In the fashionable throng they looked noticeably eccentric. Miss Delaney in a rather skimpy, short sleeved black silk dress, had a mane of uncovered yellowish white hair and a cigarette in the corner of her puckered tobacco-stained old mouth. She had also the senseless, very blue eyes that I had often seen in the blind. Mrs Blessington had more pretentions to be called dressy; her short-cut hair was frizzed and over-purple in the conventional style of very old ladies of today, and her make-up was as crazy but less orange than Sophie Englander's. She wore a battered ancient flowerpot hat. As soon as we were introduced, she said,

'Shockin' crowd, isn't it? Of course, I told Mr S. when he suggested comin', a big crowd like that always hums a bit. What with that and the stink of the animals. Anyway monkeys smell something chronic! Doin' their business everywhere! Nasty things!' Her voice was shaky and cracked. Her head quavered as she talked.

Sanderson beamed. 'Mrs B.'s in fighting form,' he said. 'Now Miss Delaney *loves* the animals, don't you?'

'She can't see 'em,' Mrs Blessington said angrily.

Miss Delaney whispered into the air, although I think she intended her speech as a confidence to me.

'I'm blind,' she said, 'but I *do* love animals. I had some guinea pigs when I was a girl. And our dog killed them. And when my father saw how upset I was, he told me that we are *all* God's creatures. It's in Genesis you know, "and every living thing that dwelleth upon the earth".'

Mrs B. turned on me, 'Are you a Bible readin' man?' she

asked savagely. But before I could answer, Strawson came up to us with a number of printed leaflets in his hand.

'Well, Sir,' he said, 'Jupiter Pluvius has withheld his inclement gaze from our festive day. I don't know whether I may persuade you to purchase a copy of this small poem I've written upon the occasion – hardly poetry, perhaps, but the traditional rhyme the day demands. The money will go to the staff fund for retiring messengers.'

'How very, very fine,' Sanderson said, and he read aloud, 'Upon European Day at the London Zoo, by Joseph Strawson, alias Elephant Joe –

> Peace shall come to this house
> When the hoopoe lies down with the grouse.

Yes, that's a very fine way of looking at it. You've done very well, Strawson.'

The two lines read in Sanderson's poetic voice caused me to guffaw into my handkerchief.

Mrs Blessington meanwhile had sternly demanded of Strawson, 'Are you a poet?' adding, 'you don't look like one. Poets look like *this*,' she sucked in her rouged old cheeks to represent hungry, Romantic fervour, '*you* look like *this*,' she blew out her cheeks in a passable imitation of Strawson's fat, floppy face.

Sanderson said, 'Mrs B.'s properly on the warpath today.'

Miss Delaney leaned forward, '*I* shall look forward to hearing your poem later. I'm blind, you see. But I'm very fond of poetry. I used to write little poems as a girl. My father . . .'

But we never knew what her father said, for suddenly with shouts and with singing a procession of people came through the main gates and, as the fashionable crowd parted to form a tightly packed bank on either side, it streamed down to the central gardens where the speeches of the opening ceremony were to be given. The newcomers marched in groups, each carrying the gay patchwork flag of Uni-Europe and the name of its district. Some, but only a few, were also gaily clothed in European peasant dresses made up in eclectic mixture of Bavarian, Piedmontese, Breton, Basque, Andalusian or any other combination that appealed to the wearer; otherwise they presented an extraordinary spectacle of defiantly sombre drabness. I knew at once instinctively who they all were – these sad-faced men and women of every age; they were the handicapped or handicap prone in all their many kinds, the ranks of those who had been our proles ever since the end of the Hitler war. Here they were – all the people who didn't quite qualify for grants or pensions; all the people who failed to get the professional qualifications or to pass the required psychological tests; all the women who couldn't get their alimony paid to them; all the men who'd mistakenly thought that luck was the easy road to affluence; all the people who'd emigrated and come back; all the people who'd immigrated and wanted to leave again; the ranks of those who were too obstinately individual to fit in, yet too weakly individual to make their mark. At their head, in feeble assertion of personality, strode their white-maned, sixth-rate leader, Mr Blanchard-White. The important people drawn up on either side looked amused, yet faintly apprehensive.

'They deserve their march,' said a woman near to me, 'they did invaluable work.'

But her friend said, 'I can't think where they've found them all from. I hope we shan't see them march about too often.'

And now it was announced over the loudspeaker that the speeches were to begin. I struggled to get through the crowds to the rostrum where Harmer and Englander and Tillotson, and even Sophie Englander had already taken their places, but the crowd was too tightly packed about me. The Uni-Europeans, too, had formed solid lines in front of the crowd in order to cheer Mr Blanchard-White as he took his seat; indeed they seemed to be acting as police for the occasion. Or rather as additional police, for the recently reconstituted police were also there in large numbers. Indeed this was the first time I got a distasteful impression of them, for despite all my assertions of my position as Secretary, I could not get them to let me through. I think I should have been able to see the comic side of this had they not pushed me so roughly that my shirt was torn. In any case if I was the most important, I was certainly not the only 'notable' kept from the centre of things that morning. A smart woman near to me kept protesting that she was a sister of Mr Harmer's.

'Mr Harmer's the President,' she cried; and a group of Dutch Embassy officials waved their invitations in vain.

The Uni-Europeans, in front, turned and hushed us, and one dreary woman dressed in an Arlesian cap and a Scots tartan waistcoat, called back,

'This isn't a *private* party. It's for the peoples of Europe.'

It was obvious that the policemen's sympathies were with them, for one near us ignored our demands entirely and another, turning on Miss Harmer, said,

'I can't help who you are, madam, we're here to see that the people have a chance to hear their leaders.'

I could see my chair empty and conspicuous among the celebrities on the rostrum; and could see Martha looking distressed. And now the band stopped playing its potpourri from some ancient musical and Dr Englander rose to his feet.

'Your Excellencies, my Lords, Ladies, and gentlemen, you will see here today the beginnings of a new London Zoo, a zoo that will not stand as an old landmark in a single capital city of a now vanished empire, but as one of a group of scientific institutions playing its part in the revival of *European* learning . . .'

I heard no more of his speech, for the word 'European' had brought deafening applause and here and there a dissenting cry of 'The London Zoo for ever!' Near me a jolly looking middle-aged woman in ear-rings cried in cockney,

'Don't you touch the London Zoo,' and a member of the Society, who was, I knew, a wealthy Norfolk landowner, cried,

'Quite right, Madam. A London Zoo and a free England.'

The fashionable guests began to call for order, but the Uni-European reaction to these mild interruptions was less helpful.

'Throw them out! Traitors! Throw them out!' they cried.

I was utterly disgusted by the sudden brutality of the police who literally dragged the ear-ringed woman along the ground in removing her and knocked the Norfolk gentleman down before they took him off. There were murmurs of disapproval, but these again were drowned by the Uni-Europeans shouting, or rather singing to some impromptu tune, Strawson's ridiculous lines, and in turn these same lines were taken up ironically here and there by 'patriot' groups. 'Till the hoopoe lies down with the grouse' resounded on every side. The Director now sat down in despair and Harmer took his place, but he was no more successful in imposing silence. Fights and scuffles broke out in various places among the crowd. Looking round, I saw that Sanderson and his old ladies had disappeared. My own aim now was to get to Martha and take her away in case there was real violence. It was thus that I never heard Blanchard-White's famous speech calling for the revival of the Roman Circus at the Zoo; although, as I walked round the Gardens in order to reach the rostrum from the other side, I heard the deafening cheers with which the Uni-Europeans greeted each suggestion that he made for realizing his ideal of justice combined with a little fun.

To get round to the back of the platform I had to pass by the former sea-lions' pool and through the magnificent glass hall that the Italian architect had built to house my exhibition of European fauna. As I came into the vast structure I expected my footsteps to echo in the emptiness as they had the day before, but instead I was greeted by a medley of voices, male and female, shouting – 'Don't shut up the animals, let England loose!' – and there chained to various railings were half a dozen or more energetic, fresh-faced young men and women. I knew how excellent my exhibition was, how much work and intelligence I had put into it, and I suddenly felt furious with these young 'patriots'. Surely they could see that by demonstrating against the Government they were simply making it easier for Blanchard-White and his gang to get full control. I have never hated the vanity of doctrinaire opinions so much as at that moment. My favourite lines of Pope echoed through my head – 'For forms of government let fools contest, What-e'er is best administered *is* best.' I walked through to the door at the other end with what I intended to be an expression of contempt – I doubt if I succeeded. But my expression immediately changed, for there, being frog-marched away by two policemen, was a familiar back view – grey short-cut hair above rolls of stubbly, red neck, a baggy Cambridge-blue rough tweed coat and skirt, heavy beige stockings and low-heeled golfing shoes. All around were scattered leaflets. I picked up one and read, 'Dear Colleagues, as you know I have been for over a year in prison . . .' I threw it down again angrily, but I ran after Pattie.

'You're making a terrible mistake,' I shouted to the police-men. 'Miss Henderson's a member of our staff.'

I think they would have arrested me but for my official Secretary's badge.

'We've orders to arrest anyone delivering these seditious leaflets, Sir,' the elder man said.

'I'm sure there's a mistake. Look, Pattie,' I cried, 'I'll be along and sort this out in two twos. Don't let them upset you.'

But her round face had grown redder than ever. 'That's all right, Simon, the more the swine lock up, the more will come flocking to us.' The policemen began to move her on, then she turned and shouted, 'Anyway, you mustn't mix up with me. You're the Vicar of Bray.'

And now another large woman descended upon me – poor Mrs Purrett in tears.

She said, 'Oh, Mr Carter, poor Miss Henderson! I think you don't know how I love this place. But it's not right to stay. They'll change it. They'll do something terrible with it.'

'For God's sake don't you start losing your head, Mrs Purrett, I need your services.'

'Don't try to persuade me, Mr Carter. I'm sure you know best for yourself. But I know what's right. Anyway you'll find some pretty girl to work for you instead of a fat old frump like me.'

I took her hand and she pressed mine, but dropped it

immediately and bustled away. I thought of James II and his deserting family. 'So big bum's gone too,' I said to myself. I was very near to maudlin tears.

I walked on to the booths set aside for Mr Blanchard-White's display, pondering what I could do for Pattie Henderson. He had asked for large circus tents and such we had provided; but I had no idea how he had used them. Near the entrance to a smaller tent I came on Sanderson's two old ladies wandering disconsolately on their own. Mrs Blessington's hat had been knocked sideways in the crowd: she looked tipsy.

'Oh, hullo,' she said, 'I shouldn't go in there if I were you.' She pointed her thumb towards the tent. 'There's an old bear there that smells to high heaven. Isn't the noise shockin' everywhere too? And what a nasty crowd! I lost Mr S. If you see him will you tell him that I've taken Miss D. back to Wimbledon by the underground? This is no place for her.'

Miss Delaney said, 'I'm blind, you see. So I can't manage crowds very well. When I was a girl my father took me to an exhibition that was being held at Earls Court, I think it was, and . . .'

But Mrs B. had taken her away before I heard the end of the story. I walked into the smaller tent. There in a pit dug seven or eight feet below the ground level was an old mangy brown Siberian bear. I don't know where Mr Blanchard-White had procured it, certainly not from the Society's collections. It was tethered by one foot to an iron stake and was disconsolately trying to shake away a cloud of flies. On the railings at the crown of the pit was a large notice which read: 'The Russian Bear in Difficulties'. High above was suspended a large bird cage in which a miserable looking American brown eagle was trying impossibly to spread its wings. The notice here read: 'The American Eagle taught a lesson'. The whole show was so pitiful, 'cheap', and ridiculous that elation soon overcame my disgust when I reflected that no movement that sank to such feeble idiocies could possibly last a week. I left the booth with the feeling that I must hang on, for things would soon come right. And there by the entrance to the huge water tank where a porpoise underwent behaviouristic tests of direction finding, stood Martha. She was flustered and hot, I could see, but I did not realize how angry.

'You've been in *there*?' she cried pointing at the bear and eagle booth. 'How could you? How could you put up with anything so disgusting and vile?'

I shook with anger that, on this day, when it seemed that people of every sort – 'patriots', Uni-Europeans, police – were behaving like barbaric children, Martha should allow so feeble and tasteless a jibe against the United States to upset her. I did not then, of course, know what she had heard in Blanchard-White's speech.

I said, 'Really, Martha, don't say you're going to join all this hysterical nonsense. I feel ashamed of English people. We try to show something of what can be done in the zoological field, experiments of fascinating importance, and a lot of hooligans choose to make a political demonstration!'

She stared at me. 'Are you going to leave this vile place now, Simon, or are you not?'

I shouted, 'No, I am not. What do you think I am, a weathercock? . . .'

But I was shouting at her back. As far as her hobble skirted green and white striped silk dress would allow her, Martha strode away.

I was stubbornly angry, but even so I would probably have run after her had I not been cut off from her by a procession of the notables coming towards the Blanchard-White tents no doubt to inspect them. Mr Blanchard-White himself was at the head chattering almost maniacally; Englander looked suddenly like an old, mummified Chinese; Harmer and Tillotson were flustered and red in the face; poor Sophie Englander, her furs thrown back on her shoulders, was panting to keep up with them and smiling in a strange fixed way which suggested that she was on the point of tears. My courage failed me; I dodged into the Porpoise House and out at the other end to avoid them. Most of the invited guests seemed to be going home, though some were visiting research houses with a desperate air of assumed normality; the Uni-Europeans, exhausted by their efforts no doubt, were picnicking all over the grounds. I decided to follow Martha home. Near the main entrance I met Sanderson. We walked together down through the Tunnel towards the North Entrance. He was deeply distressed.

He said, 'Of course, I've lived out of the world. But it seems terrible that people should take these views of theirs so seriously. I know I've been lucky in work that absorbed me here. But even if their work is dull, there's so much to do for others everywhere, at least that's what I've always found – the less fortunate, you know.'

My anger was still upon me. I said, 'Perhaps these people *are* the less fortunate.'

'There's always love to give out, you know.'

I remembered all the worn-out old cranks whose affairs he'd managed to lose interest in and to hand on to me.

I said, 'Even love needs charting with a little intelligence.'

'Yes. I suppose I've tended to lose sight of the shape of things to come.' He looked at me reflectively. 'Of course, one wouldn't think it, Carter. But we're two of a kind really there. Otherwise we shouldn't still be hanging around here.' He gave me a sad little encouraging smile. 'I'm too old to find my way now. But you'll have to do so, I expect. I hope you'll do it with loving kindness.'

We walked out into the Regent's Park Road. Two policemen were holding an old man up from the ground – his body sagged like a half-filled sack. Some Uni-European or 'patriot' straggler no doubt.

'I say,' Sanderson cried, 'that's old Paperbag Peter they've got there.'

He ran forward so fast that by the time I had reached the group, he was already protesting.

'I should advise you not to interfere,' one of the policemen was saying, 'this chap's got to go to the vagrants' camp. He's on the list. Watched for three days, he's been, and found habitually unoccupied.'

'I know him very well. We're old pals. Aren't we, Peter?'

The old man seemed too far gone to do more than mumble.

The policemen were getting angry, 'Will you kindly mind your own business?' one said.

I took Sanderson aside. 'There's nothing you can do. You said yourself only a few days ago that this new Government measure for putting homeless people into camps was a good one.'

'Yes, but I didn't know *them*. Good God, Carter, I've known old Peter for over thirty years. Poor old chap, he's always been a bit of a sponger. He won't change now.' He rushed back to the policemen and demanded, 'Constable, will you let that man go?'

'You'd better be careful or you'll get taken up yourself.'

And taken up Sanderson was, for his own answer was to hit the constable wildly on the chin. It seemed to me that I could best help by not getting arrested, so I called to him that I should go at once to the police authorities to get him released.

It was easier said than done. I telephoned to Sanderson's old women that he would be away for the night, then I spent three hours going from one police authority to another on behalf of Pattie and Sanderson, only to learn that, following the outbreak of riots that day of which the Zoo scenes were only a part, habeas corpus had been suspended and Sanderson would, in all probability, not even be brought to trial. I had some hope of helping Sanderson, but Pattie's crime, it seemed, put her outside all hope.

As one superintendent said to me, 'I'm afraid your friends have been arrested on an unfortunate day. These emergency imprisonments are likely to be rather lengthy and severe. As a measure of warning, if you take my meaning, Sir. Anyone in possession of treasonable leaflets is for it. But as to this Mr Sanderson, if he holds, as you say, an important position, you might well approach any influential friends of his...Of course, that's purely an unofficial suggestion.' He winked at me. Like too few of the policemen that day, his heart was in the right place.

In the end I set off for Highgate to ask Englander to use his influence. It was nine o'clock by the time I reached the large Regency house across the shrubbery of which gleamed the lights of London. Only these few rich men's houses on the heights of Highgate, I thought, were still padded and cushioned from the city, presenting so beautiful and distant a panorama, by acres of gardens and shrubbery and by miles of heathland. The butler showed me to the conservatory where the Director and his wife were taking their after-dinner liqueur. The heat was sub-tropical among the banana trees and poinsettias. Sophie Englander, almost the whole of her bony back naked above a black velvet evening gown, was festooned by the magenta and chocolate and almond green and white of the cypripedia, and cattleya and odontoglossa she was spraying. Among them her diamonds caught the light and gleamed like tiny reflections of the London lights below us. The Director in dinner jacket made no concession to the heat. He was bent over his snake pit; with one hand he held the forked instrument that forced open the jaws of a long snake, with the other he poised a minute glass scoop which he thrust once, then twice to take a sample of venom. The twists and coils of steel blue that on the underside turned now to ochre and now to orange seemed like some intricate straw plaiting.

'It's very beautiful,' I said.

Diadophis annabilis, Englander announced, as though that explained its beauty.

He siphoned the drops of venom into a glass tube.

'You call that old snake beautiful. Look at my orchids,' Sophie cried coyly.

It struck me that they were just an old couple like any other – he with his game of racing demon, she with her crochet work.

'Well,' he said, 'you weren't very helpful today, Carter.'

'No, you let poor Emile down. But he's come to apologize, Emile, I can see that.'

'I haven't, I'm afraid. Apology seems irrelevant to a ghastly occasion like that.'

The Director put down his apparatus. 'We don't want any post-mortems, Carter.'

'It's not a question of post-mortems, it's the future.'

'The future belongs to sanity, Carter. It *must* do. Too much is at stake. Men with vast fortunes all over Europe have invested in the new England, they're not going to let a bunch of maniacs run the show. No, no, the thing is simply to lie low for the moment. Besides most of it is talk.'

'That's much too easy an attitude.'

Sophie Englander broke in, 'You know Emile, this boy's right. When that horrible little man made that horrible speech, I thought he was joking. And then we saw that poor bear pulled down by those hounds, and the eagle torn to pieces. Emile, please, please don't go on there. You can say you are too old. My dear, we *are* too old.'

With his puffy white hand he patted her scrawny old sun-lamped shoulder. 'You said you would help me, Sophie. Please. This will be a battle for good sense. I hope you will stand by me, Carter, too. We have only to sit tight for a while, I am sure.'

But my mind was on Martha. 'Do you mean that those animals were tortured and that Blanchard-White announced it in his speech. No wonder Martha was so upset . . .'

'It was terrible,' Sophie cried, 'and he promises much worse things. We are too squeamish, he says.'

'Those people'll overreach themselves,' Dr Englander said, 'only we've got to sit tight. Are you with me, Carter?'

'I don't know. I think so. I'll have to see. But that's not what I came here about.'

I told them about Sanderson. 'You must do something for the poor man,' I said.

'Poor man! The chap's a born fool! Of course we can't do anything. Look, Carter, I talked to Harmer and Tillotson this evening. This Uni-European scum have put a Blanchard-White in every government department, institution, and local office in the country and at the moment their capers are what the mob wants. The tragedy is, of course, that if those damned fools like Godmanchester hadn't opposed European Federation these people would never have been heard of. However scum's only surface stuff, it always gets blown away. Whereas money and good sense are absolutes. But the one thing I promised Harmer was that we wouldn't on any account kick against the pricks at the moment. And we've got to stick to that. Sanderson'll have to cool his heels in jail until things are better.'

He was adamant; I appealed to her. '*You* know what prison is like,' I said.

She looked at her husband, then she said, 'Well, if he *does* have a bath in carbolic – No, please forgive me,' she cried, 'I shouldn't have said that. Poor man! But I can't say anything. I must help my old Emile. I can't say anything.'

When I saw it was no good, I turned and walked out of the hothouse, all my clothes clinging to me with sweat. Sophie Englander ran after me, tottering on her high heels.

'Give me the address of those old women. Those at least I can care for.'

I did so, and thanked her, but I could not return her smile. Later I heard that she brought Mrs B. and Miss D. to live at Highgate during all those ensuing weeks. They must have seemed a strange pair among the orchids and the pythons.

I returned home that night in a strangely mixed mood. I was ready to explain to Martha that I had not known all she did when I had responded so angrily, I was ready to apologize, to think seriously about my commitments to the future. But I was not prepared to grovel – I did not want her pity, I wanted her respect – for what I had been trying to do at the Zoo; and, for the rest, my attempts to help Pattie and Sanderson should speak for me. I was too late.

I found a note from her to say that she could not stay with me while I accepted working under such a régime. She had left the house and would join the children in California as soon as possible. She must have left in a reckless state of mind because she had taken no clothes with her. It seemed to me then as

though the rift that had separated us after Bobby's fall had only
been healed because of my collapse in the Essex cottage and
her consequent pity for me. I scrunched up her letter and threw
it angrily against the wall. 'You should extend your compassion
a little further,' I shouted to the empty bedroom. She had no
right to judge me so easily.

The next morning before I left for work, the doorbell rang
and I opened to find Jane Falcon on the doorstep with a large
suitcase. She had come, she said, to collect Martha's clothes;
Martha was staying with them until she could get a plane. I
tried to explain that I had not understood the cause of Martha's
hysteria when I saw her, that I knew now why she was so
upset.

'Are you going to leave Englander to stew in his own juice
then?'

I had thought about this all night. I answered 'I can't. No,
that I cannot do.'

'Well, I don't think you'll find Martha very ready to listen.
And I can't say I blame her. This régime's beginning to
stink.'

'Are the theatres closing?' I asked angrily.

'Well, that's a bit different. The show must go on, you
know. But even there Joan Plowright's refused to appear.
And I shouldn't be surprised if others follow suit. No, you've
lost Martha, Simon, and I'm not surprised.'

However, she never packed the bags, for I told her firmly
that I had no intention of staying in Martha's house; and
that Martha could return without fear of molestation from
me.

Before Jane left, I think that she felt sorry for me because
she said, 'My dear, it's a ghastly time, I know. And God knows
how long it's all going on. By the time all this is finished
there'll be a completely new sort of play in the market and
dozens of younger agents who will understand things better
than I shall. But, there you are, Bobby had his day of importance and I hated it; and then I had mine and he was miserable.
So perhaps if we're both out of the swim, we can happily take

a bookshop or something equally hopeless and go bust running it together and be reasonably happy.'

I tried after that to get in touch with Martha many times, but she refused to see me or to listen to me. I, on my side, became increasingly stubborn for, as she had predicted, while Englander had to compromise himself deeper with Blanchard-White, so my position became increasingly untenable.

8

DOWN AND UP AGAIN

I CAME to the Duke of Windsor every night now to get drunk; and I drank steadily there every lunch-time though I was seldom tight until the evening. But that morning I was very drunk already by one o'clock. The usual crowd was there, and I was telling them as usual why I found myself among them.

I said, 'You see when I saw what was wrong with my life, I had to do something about it.'

Mrs Molyneux-West, whose dress was covered in food stains, said, 'Of course, you did, darling.'

'I had to think what it was that was wrong. You see when a man's wife won't sleep with him and when he's doing all sorts of things at his work of which he's utterly ashamed. Because I *was* utterly ashamed, you know. Not, and I think I ought to make this point very clear, because surely the point of education is to avoid false generalizations and to make points very clear. Not that,' here I tried to illustrate to the Captain and to Mr Lawrence Heath all that I meant by manual gestures alone, but I was forced to return to speech, 'not that anything impermissible had occurred at the Zoo up to the time when I absented myself. I want to make that completely clear. Dr Emile Englander, the Director of the Zoo, is an eminent man and an eminent scientist and what's important a man whose boss I'm proud to be. I hope you can understand that.' I pointed my finger at Mrs Molyneux-West but it seemed to point at old Sheila.

She said, 'Happy days.'

I began to giggle. 'Am I being as pompous as I sound?' I asked.

Jasper Greenacre, the lugubrious journalist with the long dark hair, cotton trousers, and a stiff white collar, said, 'Not at all. You seek exactitude. Don't apologize for it. The educated classes have almost apologized themselves out of existence as it is.'

My anger at the length of his interruption made my head ache. I said, 'It seemed to me that what was wrong with my life was bothering about standards. Power corrupts and absolute power corrupts absolutely. I've never been an anarchist . . .'

Mr Lawrence Heath patted his hair. He said, 'Well that's one mercy, say we all.'

'But I realized that I'd got to go down to the depths.' I looked down and then shut my eyes because the depths seemed to be coming up at me. 'To purify myself from the stink of high places by association and . . . and that sort of thing with the rejected and despised, to redeem myself by rolling myself in ordure. You'll find it all in Dostoevsky . . .'

Mrs Molyneux-West was fumbling in her bag so she didn't hear my words, but she said, 'You're telling me, darling. I was the original one of that troupe.'

'I could have gone among the razor groups, the Swiss Cottage crowd. I could have got some big, strapping woman to beat me. I wasn't born yesterday. I know life. I've seen things.' I thought of Harriet and I began to cry.

The Captain said, 'My dear chap, you're a victim of your own temperament. Nobody holds it against you for a minute. Physical courage is simply a matter of chance . . .'

Old Mr Crowther, the retired chartered accountant, said, 'You've never said a truer word than that, old man. Time and time again I've had people come to me, people with big accounts, people who've risked fortunes, and there they were trembling like leaves because of some bloody tax inspector.'

I said, 'I could have done *vile* things. But I knew where it lay – the boue, the real boue, the mud that sticks and shall redeem thee.'

'Ah,' said Jasper Greenacre, 'I shouldn't be surprised if she claimed you yet, old boy, the Mother of Seven Hills.'

I said, 'So I took my room in Cromwell Road, near the flat of the man of God, and I came here among you.'

They all laughed now, as they always did at this point; it made me tremble with anger because it was true: I had chosen them out carefully – the saloon bar washouts, too sunk even to become Uni-Europeans – if *they* couldn't release me, who could? I felt large tears rolling down my cheeks.

I said, 'I wanted your help and you haven't been able to help me. It's all still there,' I said, and hit my chest, where indeed the drink had given me an indigestion pain like a lead weight.

Mrs Horniman, the manageress, spoke now; she said, 'Do you know what I'd advise you to do? I'd advise you to go right back to the Zoo and tell them what you think of them.'

Old Sheila remarked, 'I never liked the idea of it anyway. All those poor creatures shut up like that.'

The Captain said, 'Very good advice indeed, Mrs Horniman. You go back there. To the London Zoo. My godfather, Sir Alex Fitting, was a Fellow there and the old chap used to take me along as a kid. We used to go on Sunday mornings – Fellows only – and I used to be allowed to stroke the koala bear. If all that's gone down the drain, then we may as well pack up. And so you ought to tell this fellow Engledine. It's your duty.'

'And as to your wife,' Jasper Greenacre said, 'exercise the *droit de seigneur*. You're her lord and master. Good God, that's the foundation of the whole thing.'

Mr Lawrence Heath said, 'Well, I don't expect you believe in the psychic, but I'm rather gifted where human nature's concerned. As soon as you came into the bar for the first time, I said to myself, "Well, I know what *that* one's got to do. Take a pull on himself." And so you have. Hasn't he, dear?'

Mrs Molyneux-West said, 'I really couldn't care, darling, what he does. I've got to the point where I can't think of anything but number one.'

'What do you say, Sir?' the Captain asked a brown-hatted man who was a stranger to the bar. 'Do you agree with me in thinking that brains are more important than guts every time?'

The man said, 'Yes, I should think that's so.'

It seemed to me that they were all decided. I went outside. It was difficult to get a sanctioned taxi in those days. Two, coming down the Cromwell Road, refused to take me. However, in the end, my rather soiled Secretary's identity card did the trick. I was deposited at the Staff Entrance to the Zoo.

My legs seemed leaden and my head like an uncooked pudding, but I mustered up all the dignity I could find. I walked to the Administrative offices and up to my own room. I had not been there for seven weeks or more, but the staff, perhaps cowed by my sudden apparition, made no move to check me. I went to the Director's room. As I stood outside the door I could hear Blanchard-White's voice in full oratory.

'You don't seem to understand, Director, the degree to which these spectacles are needed to educate the public in European living. The Government demands them.'

Englander's voice came croaking a little, very troubled. 'We want to do all we can for the Government, you know that. But you've heard the most eminent zoologists from France and Germany on the vital importance of the research we're doing here. That *must* come first.'

'I'm not sure, Englander, if you realize the degree to which England has outpaced our good friends abroad in the quality and intensity of its Europeanism . . .'

I opened the door and stood as straight as I could manage. I opened my mouth but no words came.

Then I heard myself say thickly and not as clearly as I wished, 'Whatever people think, Englander, I know you're not a shit. So don't let yourself get caught up with shits.'

I think I was trying to find Matthew's moral voice. The surprise of my appearance had held them both still for a few moments; then Englander came over and took me by the arm.

'You shouldn't be here, Carter. You ought to be in bed. He's been very ill, White. I don't know what his doctors are doing letting him out.'

Blanchard-White cast a suspicious glance at me, but all he said was, 'Ah!'

Englander pulled me out into the corridor. 'You ought to be shot,' he said, 'and you would have been if I hadn't acted quickly. You don't think what harm you do.' He called to Rackham. 'Take Mr Carter and see that he goes out of the Gardens and give my orders that he's not to be allowed back.'

Rackham took my arm, but I struggled with him. Englander looked into another room and returned with Strawson.

'I've come about a little staff matter, Sir. *Pro bono publico*, as one might put it.'

'That can wait now, Strawson. You must help Rackham to throw Mr Carter out of the Gardens and don't let him come back.'

I struggled hard against the two men, but they used their force with long pent-up resentment and literally threw me on to the pavement outside the main entrance.

I pulled myself up, aching and dizzy, and set off to walk round the Inner Circle to the North Entrance. I knew that I was being followed – and, in great degree, I found relief in the knowledge. But I had things to do yet, so I hurried my pace. The hot July wind blew a cloud of dust into my face. I giggled. Should I try to get back to Englander or demand my rights of Martha? When, at last, having dragged, as it seemed, my legs through seas of treacle, I got to the Regent's Park Road, my hand, fumbling in my pocket, found my old latchkey. It seemed an omen. I crossed the road to our house, let myself in and discovered Martha bending over the kitchen sink. The curve of her back, the rounding of her hips, her long legs, all filled me with such lust and affection combined that I longed to take her in my arms and to soothe away her sadness – sadness that I knew must be great, for the Government would give her no pass to join the children, I guessed too that she was working for the underground movement. She turned her face towards me, it had crumbled with depression; and I loved her so that my body shook with care for her. Then her face hardened.

She said, 'You're drunk, Simon. It's bad enough that you should come here! But to come here drunk!'

I tried to fight down my anger. I said, 'I've broken with it. I've rebelled.'

She turned wearily back to the sink, '*Dutch* courage, I suppose,' she said.

I seized her by the hips and turned her round. 'You bitch! You self-righteous bitch!'

I smacked her face.

She said, 'All right, Simon. That's easy. You needn't do that. If you want me, you can have me. It's your right.'

She walked out of the kitchen. I followed up the stairs to the bedroom. She began to undress. I took off my shoes and my trousers. She turned to me, naked, and, as I came towards her, she said,

'You disgust me, Simon, absolutely. And yet I'm letting you do this. I suppose I still have some little pity for you, but that's all it is, remember. I'm doing this out of pity.'

I was terrified that I should burst into tears in front of her. I seized up my shoes and my trousers and ran downstairs. I was still barefooted and my trousers were not zipped up when the man in the brown hat and another policeman picked me up and bundled me into a van. I was taken to Enfield Camp and I was there until after Liberation Day.

The judge did not have the parchment white skin that I expected of judges. He was red faced, loose mouthed and had protruding eyes – all in all, he was as near a man could be to a jolly lobster. But it made little difference, for his voice in summing-up was of the thin, slow, dry kind that I associated with old parchment faces.

He said, 'Among other evidence you have heard was that of Mr Simon Carter at present acting as Director of the London Zoo. Mr Carter previously worked as Secretary and in the last month or so of his office he worked under the defendant. Now Mr Carter was at pains to make it clear that in his view the defendant never consented or intended to consent to the suggestions made by Blanchard-White for the pitting of political prisoners against wild beasts as a public spectacle. Mr

Carter asserted and asserted roundly that it was the defendant's intention merely to play for time, and, indeed that the defendant simply did not take these suggestions seriously. This, of course, supports the plea offered by the defendant himself that he had no intention of allowing these spectacles to take place, that he could not entirely believe that Blanchard-White intended them seriously, and that he would have resigned his post had there been any attempt to present such spectacles at the Zoo. But I draw your attention to the fact that Mr Carter evidently found something to make him so worried that he withdrew his services from the Zoological Society only a few weeks after the European Opening Day of which we have heard so much. What exactly caused him to do this remains obscure. He says that he resigned or rather absented himself because he was generally unhappy with the course of his life. "I felt I was on the wrong tack" were his words. But the suspicion must remain that he left the Zoo because he was horrified by some particular suggestion made by Blanchard-White and perhaps accepted by Englander. At any rate his evidence cannot be wholly accepted as an exoneration of the defendant's conduct even up to that time. Mr Carter may well wish not to incriminate the defendant more than his memory absolutely permits, and his memory after his term of imprisonment at the notorious Enfield Camp may well not be of the most efficient.'

So much for my attempts to help, I thought, as the judge's voice creaked on. I looked at Englander in the dock. He had closed his eyes. If only he could be told not to. It gave him the look of an obscene old parrot and must lead the jury to think that they were trying Tiberius. Sophie, sitting by Martha, seemed to have acquired a vacant, zombie look as she stared out of her messed up maquillage.

'The defendant,' the judge went on, 'has suggested that he regarded Blanchard-White's letters as a joke. But what sort of a joke is this to be made in official letters? – "*I shall select only the most splendid physical specimens of both sexes, the youngest and the strongest, those in fact most qualified to give the longest and most charming spectacles when pitted against the lithe grace of the leopard or the clumsy tenderness of the bear. This will be something truly Roman, truly European in its majesty."* I read only the least offensive extract from a correspondence that has already nauseated us too long. True, it is a one-sided correspondence. But can the defendant really have thought it a joke? A joke in shocking taste! It has been suggested elsewhere that these letters of Blanchard-White's were a sort of sexual fantasy put on to paper. Did the defendant receive them in that light and so disregard them? Well, I suppose that may be. But we have to consider that the building of an arena for these abominable purposes *was* commenced in the Zoological Gardens. The building went on very slowly, it is true. Building purposely delayed, says the defendant. Well . . .'

Dr Englander got two years. To most people, who thought him guilty, it seemed a light sentence. To me, who knew him to be innocent, it seemed monstrous. In any case he was an old man. Martha took charge of poor Sophie at the end of the trial.

I came away depressed and unhappy, or rather as depressed and unhappy as I could be at that time – and, to tell the truth, that was really less than it should have been for I was thoroughly enjoying acting as Director. There was a mass of work to do. Stability of a kind had come to us. The last three years had given me a wealth of ideas for the Zoo's future and a corresponding wealth of caution and moderation in my belief in their possible application. At last it seemed that I might have a chance to try for myself and I believed that I should enjoy doing so. The children were home. Martha and I were living together for their sake. And although I was cautious in my hopes of repairing the relations between us, it was a pleasanter life than I had known for some time. After Enfield, life on this bright, cold January day, with its clear blue sky and puffy white clouds above the busy London streets, seemed a demi-paradise. Even the prospect of luncheon with our new rather self-important Vice-President, Professor Hales of Brighton University, didn't damp my spirits. After all, old

Oresby was to be the host, and I delighted in the old boy. Together we could keep down any new man.

Through the long windows of the dining-room of Oresby's club I could still see the clouds, floating across the painted ceiling sky above Hales' head. It was a head, swollen enough heaven knew, for any rococo ceiling – like a hideous cherub's, all swollen cheeked, small-mouthed, vast-eyed, and with a fluffy babylike near baldness. He spoke rapidly, as though imitating machine gun fire, and brushed away other people's remarks with a similar staccato contemptuous laugh.

We had reached the Stilton before he said, 'Well, I hear Jackley's on his way back. Have you got everything ready to hand over to him, Carter?'

I hope that I did not betray my feelings, but I did not answer.

Oresby said, 'Oh come, Hales. You're rather putting your foot in it. The Directorship has to be decided by the Committee and there's – '

'Yes, yes, of course, but Jackley's the best man for the job.'

Lord Oresby smiled, 'There can always be two opinions about that. Some people would like to have our friend Carter here, if, that is, he were interested.'

Hales shot a sharp glance at me. 'Oh, sorry, Carter. Didn't think you were an ambitious chap. A fine administrator, of course, but I never think of you as a zoologist.'

'Well, I don't know that Leacock was outstanding as a zoologist.' Lord Oresby exaggerated the reflective note as he said it.

'Leacock!' Hales gave his little laugh. 'We don't want to go back to the murky past. Must have been an awful strain working with all those blighters. Your health hasn't been too good, has it, Carter?'

'I did have amoebal dysentery very badly at one time but strangely enough the rigours of camp life at Enfield seem to have improved my health.'

'Oh, you were at Enfield. Bad luck! How long were you there?'

'From last July.'

'Oh, I see, right at the end. Still you've worked your passage in the Resistance – just.'

This was too much for our host, he said, 'Carter's not being interviewed now, my dear fellow.'

Hales laughed again, 'No, no. I shall be more deadly than this on the day. By the way, Jackley's sent in some account of his present researches in San Francisco. He's working on carbon dioxide stimulation with bottle-nosed dolphins. Wants to create something on a large scale here for the same sort of work. Could be a big thing for the Society after a period of dud research.'

I said, 'My experience suggests to me that the Director mustn't be too tied to any one experiment –'

'Look here. I don't think we'd better discuss your views now, Carter, if you're going to be a candidate. Can I have a port, Oresby? I seem to remember this club having a very good port. Of course, I thought you'd probably want to get away from the Zoo back to your naturalist's work, Carter. I always think of you as a country man after those television talks of yours some years ago. Beautifully done they were for a popular audience.'

I decided to say nothing of my schemes for a Nature Reserve at that moment.

Lord Oresby said, 'Good heavens! Carter's no recluse. He's principally an administrator. The Treasury fought hard to keep him there.'

'Oh, yes, I was forgetting. I came across a chap from the Treasury – Ogilvie – he told me of some little tiffs he'd had with you. Admired you enormously as an administrator, but wasn't your greatest fan as far as personal relationships went. Poor chap, he died in Southampton.'

I wasn't going to be led into a discussion of my personal relationships at the Treasury.

Unthinkingly, I said, 'Died at *Southampton*?' I could have bitten my tongue off as soon as I had said it.

Hales said, 'I'm thoroughly enjoying this Stilton. Yes,

strangely enough, Southampton. Perhaps it escaped your notice that our major port towns were wiped out by enemy action. Some people think it was the reason we lost the war.'

Oresby was nettled this time, he said, 'Carter was practically running the Zoo at a desperate period. He had to remain detached.'

From deep inside me there arose a reply I couldn't hold back, '*Too* detached! I should hope if I were to become Director that I have now learned to be more engaged both with other people and with the animals.'

The tension in my voice alarmed me; it obviously embarrassed Oresby and Hales even more.

After a silence, Hales said, 'Well, you had the tough luck to be associated with a very bad period – Leacock, Beard, Falcon, and that old swine Englander – a shocking lot of old men. A very bad period in the Zoo's history.'

Oresby gave a modified assent by the nod of his head.

'I'm afraid,' I said, 'I can't see it as simply as that. You see, I knew them all.'

Hales laughed. '*Chacun à son goût*. What did that old scoundrel get by the way?'

Lord Oresby glanced at me nervously, 'I'm afraid he got two years,' he said.

'Afraid? In my opinion he should have got life. Well, anyway we have to thank the excesses of chaps like that for forcing world opinion to put things to rights. They managed to sicken even their friends, the French and the Germans in the end. And now we've got new men and a new order. How do you feel about the new world before us, Carter?'

'It excites me enormously,' I said, 'especially because I shall always be deeply involved in the old.'

After Hales had gone, I told Oresby that I should be definitely applying for the Directorship. He seemed pleased.

'I'll do all I can for you,' he said, 'but you mustn't forget that Jackley has the advantage of having been off the scene.'

'I don't,' I said, 'I hope the Committee may see the disadvantage of that, too, by the time I've made my case.'

As I returned to Regent's Park I felt very determined.

I played with the children that evening in continued happiness, but I knocked over Violet's brick castle.

She said, 'You'd better be careful. If you get to be a nuisance, Mummy will send you away.'

Reggie looked aside, blushing. He said to me quickly, "What's the strongest animal, Dad? I bet it's an elephant, or is it a hippo?'

Violet said, 'It's a giraffe.'

'Silly! A giraffe couldn't kill anyone. Could it, Dad? A rotten old giraffe!'

I answered, 'I hope not. I'm not sure yet.'